RHAPSODY IN BLOOD

ALSO BY JOHN MORGAN WILSON

THE BENJAMIN JUSTICE NOVELS

Simple Justice

Revision of Justice

Justice at Risk

The Limits of Justice

Blind Eye

Moth and Flame

WITH PETER DUCHIN

Blue Moon

Good Morning, Heartache

RHAPSODY IN BLOOD

JOHN MORGAN WILSON

ST. MARTIN'S MINOTAUR
NEW YORK

 For information, address St. Martin's Press, 175 Fifth Avenue, New York, N.Y. 10010.

www.minotaurbooks.com

Library of Congress Cataloging-in-Publication Data

Wilson, John Morgan, 1945–
Rhapsody in blood : a Benjamin Justice novel / by John Morgan Wilson.—1st ed.
p. cm.
ISBN 0-312-34147-4
EAN 978-0-312-34147-3
1. Justice, Benjamin (Fictitious character)—Fiction. 2. Women Journalists—Fiction. 3. California—Fiction. [1. Motion pictures—Production and direction—Fiction.] I. Title.

PS3573.I456974R485 2006
813.54—dc22 2005054193

First Edition: March 2006

10 9 8 7 6 5 4 3 2 1

In memory of Dennis Lynds

ACKNOWLEDGMENTS

So many people offer their support as we write our novels that it's sometimes difficult to know whom to thank and where to begin.

I'll start with Keith Kahla, my much-appreciated editor at St. Martin's Press, who works unbelievably hard and guides writers with such insight and skill, and the many others at SMP who helped this book reach its readers. I'll quickly add my long-time agent, Alice Martell, who has represented me on all seven Benjamin Justice novels, as well as other books. And I mustn't overlook Pietro Gamino, my close companion of many years, for everything he does that allows me to pursue my chosen trade.

I also must mention four loyal readers who made winning bids at various silent charity auctions for the right to have a character in one of my novels named after them: Martha Frech, Toni Pebbles, Kevin Tiemeyer, and Zeke Zeidler. Good sports all, they fully understood when they made their bids that they would have no control over which characters would bear their names. Suffice it to say that the characters named after them in *Rhapsody in Blood* are purely fictional and have no connection to anyone living or dead. The same must be said for nearly a dozen other characters in this novel who carry the names of valued people in my life: Lois Aswell, Scott Campbell, Karen Hori, Maggie Langley, Christopher Oakley, Dick Pearlman, Tony Valenzuela, Nan

Williams, and the Fox family—Beckee, Brent, and Brandy. They all granted me permission to borrow their names for characters quite unlike them, knowing I intended it as a tribute to them and to our friendship. (Some of us go back together nearly fifty years.)

I'm also grateful to Mystery Writers of America, Sisters in Crime, and International Thriller Writers, as well as the Lambda Literary Foundation and the board members who are working so hard to save it.

Last, I'd like to acknowledge three helpful research sources: the Southern Poverty Law Center, the Charles Chesnutt Digital Archive, and *The Rise and Fall of Popular Music,* by Donald Clarke.

RHAPSODY IN BLOOD

ONE

All I wanted when Alexandra Templeton invited me to join her for a brief getaway was a little rest and relaxation. Fresh air, a change of scenery, a few carefree days out of town, and the kind of sleep a writer doesn't get when he's on deadline with an important project.

At least not a writer like me, the type who takes his work to bed with him: tossing and turning night after night, rewriting gibberish in his troubled sleep, searching for words that don't exist, frantic to finish a story that makes no sense and has no ending. I'd just spent a couple of months like that as I'd worked feverishly to complete my autobiography and turn in my first draft on time. Now my friend Templeton was offering me a short road trip to decompress. We tended to get on each other's nerves if we spent too much time together—my fault more than hers—and the notion of several days in the same place seemed problematic. Still, I needed a diversion from West Hollywood and my life there, such as it was, and her invitation sounded tempting.

"We've never taken a trip together, Justice, not a real one," Templeton said as we shared a sidewalk lunch with my elderly landlord, Maurice, at La Conversation, our favorite West Hollywood café. "Just the two of us, on the road—think of how much fun we can have."

"I snore, you know."

"I'm not suggesting we share a room. I'm not a masochist."

Maurice slapped me lightly on the arm. "How many times have I told you to sleep on your side, Benjamin, and not on your back? I started rolling Fred over on his side thirty years ago. Trust me, it's one of the secrets to a long marriage."

"I'm not married, Maurice, like you and Fred. I've got nobody to roll me over in the middle of the night when I start snoring like an old bear."

"Only because I haven't found the right man for you, dear boy."

"Anyway," Templeton said, trying to reclaim the conversation, "we're taking separate rooms, remember?"

"I don't recall agreeing to go."

"Don't be silly, Benjamin," Maurice said. "Of course you're going. This trip is just what you need after all the hard work you put in on that wonderful manuscript of yours."

"You're jumping to conclusions, Maurice. I just mailed off the first draft two days ago. Who knows? They may reject it and refuse to pay me the rest of my advance."

"Nonsense! I don't have to read it to know that you did a fine job. You're long overdue to be published again. Those problems you had are years behind you."

"Those problems will never be behind me, Maurice."

He waved a bony finger at me, causing the bracelets on his narrow wrist to jingle. "Stop stalling and tell Alexandra that you'll be joining her on this fabulous trip!"

"You'll have another author to talk to," Templeton said, resuming her sales pitch as her brown eyes sparkled within the lovely confines of her darker face. "Richard Pearlman—he wrote *A Murder in Eternal Springs*, the book I told you about. He'll be there."

"Does that mean I have to read it? Maurice says it's heavy on Hollywood trivia and lore. Not something I'm terribly interested in."

Templeton sighed, exasperated. "Not if you don't want to."

"You'll drive?"

"Yes, and I'll even do all the talking. You can just nod from time to time and pretend to be listening, like you usually do."

"No alarm clocks?"

"For me," she said. "I'll be on assignment. But not for you."

A film production company was shooting a movie based on the book she'd mentioned, about the murder in 1956 of a movie actress named Rebecca Fox in the remote high desert town of Eternal Springs, and the lynching of a black man named Ed Jones that followed. Recent DNA analysis, not available fifty years ago, had concluded that Ed Jones may have been innocent of the crime. Templeton's editors at the *Los Angeles Times* had picked her to visit the film location and use the movie as a hook to write about the continuing impact of newly discovered DNA evidence on decades-old crimes and convictions, and the tragic lack of funding that left many police departments without access to current DNA or other modern crime lab technology. Maurice had read the book and filled me in on the highlights of the Rebecca Fox story, which included the suicide of her daughter, Brandy, twenty-five years after her mother's murder, in the same hotel room on the same date—March 15, the ides of March. I wasn't sure how they'd fashion a movie out of such a complicated story stretching over nearly five decades, but it certainly had the makings of a pungent script, if the writer could get a handle on it. Templeton was keen on the assignment, but not on driving alone to Eternal Springs, now known as Haunted Springs, where much of the film was being shot.

"You can sleep in every day until lunch if you want," Templeton promised me. "Take long walks in the afternoon. I'll pay for everything. What do you say, Justice?"

"Long naps sound better."

"Naps then, as many as you like."

"Do it, Benjamin!" Maurice clasped my wrist with his mottled hand. "You haven't had a genuine vacation in ever so long." He dropped his voice, looking sly. "Besides, Alexandra tells me that Christopher Oakley is among the cast members who'll be staying at the Haunted Springs Hotel. That alone should be worth the trip, if only for a fleeting glimpse of that gorgeous young man."

I didn't stay abreast of Hollywood business, had no idea who Maurice was talking about, and said so.

"Christopher Oakley is a gifted young actor on the brink of making it big," Templeton explained. "He has a key role in the picture."

Maurice lowered his voice yet again, ducking his head as if spies were situated at the nearby tables, instead of the usual mix of entertainment figures and neighborhood regulars. "Widely rumored to be one of us," he whispered, "though deep in the Hollywood closet." He winked. "Perhaps you can do some research, find out for sure."

I reminded Maurice that at some point almost every good-looking Hollywood actor had been rumored to be queer—in West Hollywood, it was a more important topic than politics or the weather—and that gossip like that failed to spark my interest.

Maurice sat up primly, looking hurt. "All right, forget about Christopher Oakley then, and whether he is or is not of the lavender persuasion. Still, I think this little excursion with Alexandra is a wonderful opportunity, and you'd be foolish not to go."

Maurice, who worried over me like a mother hen, appeared genuinely unhappy, and I felt a stab of guilt for not simply saying yes. I leaned back, pushed my hands through what was left of my thinning blond hair, and thought about it. I tend to find or foresee problems where many people don't; doing things the easy way has never been my first approach. I need to resist, at least long enough to cause a little friction and let others know that I won't be pushed around. Perhaps it comes from being raised by a whiskey-swilling father, an authoritarian homicide detective who used a strap with painful regularity when I didn't say or do as he wanted—and now and then his fist. But I didn't have that much fight in me anymore, not like in my younger days; my protests now were rote, largely for show.

I shrugged and said, "Why not? What could be more restful than a few days in a remote town that most of the world's forgotten?"

Nubia, our friendly and attentive waitress, brought the check. Templeton covered it with her gold card, since she was the one with the fat bank account.

When Nubia had gone inside to ring it up, we raised our iced teas to toast the impending trip: Maurice, a white-haired gay activist and retired dance teacher, who'd recently celebrated his fiftieth anniversary with Fred, the love of his life; Alexandra Templeton, thirty-five and single, an award-winning crime reporter at the *Los Angeles Times,* where I'd once worked; and me, a washed-up journalist in my late forties, ruined by a Pulitzer scandal, who'd just spent a year turning my troubled life into a memoir that promised financial solvency for a while, if nothing more.

Naturally, that sorry episode in my life—the Pulitzer business—had been the focal point of the manuscript, as my publisher had insisted. I'd tried to be as honest as I could, relating the circumstances leading up to it: the slow and horrifying death of my lover, Jacques, from AIDS, in the late 1980s, as I cared for him; the way I'd withdrawn emotionally as he died, to blunt the pain of my impending loss; and how, in the dreadful aftermath of his death, I'd changed our names and written up a rosier version of the truth, giving myself the courage to love him as I should have in real life, never thinking my fabrication would win the big prize and come under such intense scrutiny, causing a scandal and ending my career.

I'd dredged up other personal garbage as well, at the urging of my persistent editor. The writing had left me wrung out and exhausted, but also feeling lighter and clearheaded, as if I'd finally found a way to free myself of emotional baggage that had weighed me down for decades. My memoir was also the first real writing I'd done in the sixteen years since the scandal had ruined me, reigniting a flame inside me that I'd thought was long dead. After finishing the manuscript, and sensing that it wasn't half bad, I was left with a glimmer of hope that I might actually find my way back to writing full-time again. Though what I might write and who might publish me on a regular basis I wasn't sure, given the rancid reputation that clung to me like a bad smell.

"You might bring along a mystery novel or two," Templeton said, as she signed the credit card receipt and tore off her copy. "I don't imagine there's much going on in Haunted Springs, except for this movie they're shooting."

"I'll grab *Cinnamon Kiss* by Walter Mosley, and something by Pete Dexter. That should see me through. When do we leave?"

"Tomorrow, bright and early. I'd like to get there before noon."

The happiness on Maurice's wrinkled face suddenly changed to concern. "I didn't realize you planned to leave so soon, Alexandra."

"Is that a problem?"

"It's just that—well, tomorrow's March fourteenth, isn't it? That would be the day before the ides of March."

"That's the idea, Maurice. To get up there tomorrow, so I can start my interviews the next morning."

"Exactly fifty years after the murder of Rebecca Fox," Maurice pointed out, "and twenty-five years after the suicide of her daughter, Brandy. Not to mention that horrible hanging that followed the original crime." He shuddered. "How absolutely morbid."

"We'll be staying in the same hotel where the murder and suicide took place," Templeton said. "That should lend some atmosphere to my article."

Maurice put a pale hand to each cheek. "Oh, my goodness! Alexandra, you mustn't be up there on the ides of March. Any day but that."

She laughed, placing a comforting hand on his shoulder. "But that's just the dateline I want, Maurice—Haunted Springs on March fifteenth. It will help me set the mood for the reader, give my piece that extra edge."

Maurice smiled weakly, looking pliant but unconvinced. "Of course—you being there on the ides of March makes complete sense. You're thinking like a journalist, Alexandra, and I'm thinking like a superstitious old ninny."

"I'll be dealing with some serious issues, Maurice. I want my story to have real impact."

"Yes, yes, I know, dear." He perked up falsely and patted the back of my hand. "Finish your sandwich, Benjamin, so we can get you home and packed. You and Alexandra are going to go off and have the most wonderful time together in that nice old hotel. And then you'll both come back and tell me all about it."

TWO

To get to Haunted Springs, you leave the interstate about two hours northeast of Los Angeles, pick up a two-lane highway through Hungry Valley for roughly forty miles, then turn off onto narrow Coyote Canyon Road, which climbs slowly into the Lost Hills. Halfway up, there's an old, wooden bridge spanning Rattlesnake River that trembles as the tires bump their way across. Twenty minutes after that—fifteen, if Templeton's driving—you suddenly come around a sharp bend and find yourself looking down on Lake Enid.

"My goodness," Templeton said. "There it is."

I heard trepidation in her voice, or maybe it was awe, and thought I understood. For the ride up, she'd loaned me her copy of *A Murder in Eternal Springs*—the revised trade paperback edition, just published—and I'd read the foreword by the author, Richard Pearlman. It outlined the area's dark history, including that of Lake Enid.

FOREWORD

For nearly half a century, a town has lain buried beneath the deep waters of Lake Enid. Now the town is rising, as if trying to come back to life and help tell a story that remains unfinished.

Lake Enid sits in a deep pocket of Coyote Canyon not quite a thousand feet above Hungry Valley, among the rocky foothills of California's high desert, where the sun bakes the earth until it's parched and hard and crackling winds scour the landscape with relentless fury. Long before there was a Lake Enid, Kawaiisu Indians roamed, fished, and hunted here, until they were rounded up and packed off to government reservations in the latter half of the nineteenth century, or simply slaughtered by U.S. soldiers because it was sometimes easier that way.

After that came a little town called Eternal Springs. It sprouted toward the end of the nineteenth century, along the rock-strewn banks of Rattlesnake River. Above the town, nestled among the big boulders of the Lost Hills, rose the imposing Eternal Springs Hotel. Dating from 1925, it was a thriving resort, attracting the wealthy and celebrated to its natural mineral springs and its view of the winding river below. The hotel and springs were especially popular in the cooler months, when the winds felt cleansing and the sun was like a gentle balm. In the late 1940s, however, the springs inexplicably dried to a trickle. Visitors went elsewhere, the hotel suffered, and the town of Eternal Springs began to die.

Then, in 1956, the beautiful film star Rebecca Fox—you may remember her from January Heat, *her most famous movie—returned to the Eternal Springs Hotel. She and her husband, Brent, a dashing young soldier, had spent their honeymoon here in 1944, only weeks before he shipped out for Europe, where he died heroically among the Allied Forces storming the beaches of Normandy. Twelve years later, still grief-stricken, Rebecca Fox returned to Eternal Springs to film a movie inspired by their great love, playing herself, and staying in the same room where they'd shared their last, idyllic days together. But that film was never to be finished. On March 15—the ides of March, the day they'd met—Rebecca Fox was discovered dead in her room, her undergarments stained with semen and her throat slashed by a weapon that was never found. Ed Jones, a black handyman, was arrested for the crimes of sexual assault and murder. Hours later, an angry mob dragged him from his cell and hanged him from the jail's high rafters, the last recorded lynching in California.*

For a time, following the sensational murder and unfortunate hanging, business at the Eternal Springs Hotel picked up. Tourists trekked up the narrow road to stay in the same hotel where Rebecca Fox had died, or to take pictures of the jailhouse where hooded Ku Klux Klansmen had overcome the town sheriff and strung up Ed Jones. Jones had been a drifter and his body had gone unclaimed. So a local mortician had embalmed him, dressed him in a cheap black suit, and kept him on display behind the funeral home, where tourists could take snapshots if it suited them. Meanwhile, up at the hotel, business was brisk. Many visitors specifically requested the Rebecca Fox Room, as it was now called, which was said to be haunted by her restless ghost.

Again, prosperity was not to last. Times and attitudes changed, and the lynching of a black man kept more tourists away from the infamous town than it drew. Decency prevailed, and Ed Jones was given a proper burial in the cemetery up on the hill, with a modest headstone bearing his name. Toward the end of the 1970s, with the mineral springs completely dry and most of the town's buildings boarded up and abandoned, the state decided that the area could be more productive. It moved a dozen houses to higher ground, along with the historic Eternal Springs Public Library, which it placed between the hotel and the cemetery. After dynamiting the remaining structures, the state dammed the canyon to create a reservoir that served as a source of hydroelectric power. As the waters rose, fed by Rattlesnake River, Eternal Springs was buried deep beneath Lake Enid.

The man-made lake became popular with anglers, but they were not the kind to stay at a refined establishment like the Eternal Springs Hotel, which once again struggled to stay open. Then, on March 15, 1981, came another fateful occurrence. Brandy Fox, the daughter of Brent and Rebecca Fox and a failed actress, checked into the Eternal Springs Hotel. Taking the same room in which her mother had been murdered twenty-five years before, she slit her own throat in despair. Again, spurred by fresh headlines, business at the hotel picked up. Guests no longer looked down on the town where Klansmen had hanged a black man but on a peaceful body of water where small boats drifted or putted about as anglers trolled for bluegill and bass. The hotel's proprietors, who also owned what was left of Eternal Springs, changed the town's name to Haunted Springs, rechristened their hostelry the Haunted Springs Hotel, and got it listed in as many guidebooks as they could. Their efforts, and more recently those of their son, have been enough to keep the tourists coming and the old hotel solvent.

It's been a challenge—even the fishermen are gone now. Last year, in an attempt to rid the lake of predatory pike through controlled poisoning, the state inadvertently killed off all the preferred species as well. A costly restocking effort has proved a bureaucratic bungle. Today, Enid is literally a dead lake, with a dead town resting at its bottom. According to legend, the area is cursed because the hotel is built on ground that was sacred to the Kawaiisu, whose angry spirits sucked dry the natural springs in retaliation for their desecration. Others believe the curse began with the grisly murder in 1956 of Rebecca Fox and the hanging of Ed Jones that followed hours later. Still others claim that what happened to Eternal Springs is merely a symptom of man's arrogant destruction of the environment, a dire warning of things to come.

Whatever the truth, Haunted Springs is making headlines again, and the hotel has another lease on life. New evidence, based on DNA testing not available until recent years, suggests that Ed Jones may have been innocent after all. It is those findings that prompted me to write this book, bringing many new facts to light. Hollywood has acquired the film rights and A Murder in Eternal Springs *will soon become a movie. Some of the shooting, in fact, is taking place at the Haunted Springs Hotel, with scenes set in the very room where Rebecca Fox was murdered and her daughter, Brandy, took her own life twenty-five years later to the day, on the ides of March.*

Meanwhile, the drought that has plagued California off and on for decades has caused the waters of Lake Enid to seriously recede. Even heavy rains in recent years have restored only a few inches. On days when the water is clear, one can look down to see the foundations of the old buildings, including the front steps of the town jail where Ed Jones spent his final hours before dying in a hangman's noose.

Eternal Springs, thought to be forever dead, is rising from its watery grave.

As Lake Enid came into view, Alexandra Templeton steered her new Maserati onto a turnout and shut off the ignition. The Maserati was the stately Quattroporte model, worth about a hundred thousand without the extras, a gift from her wealthy father, who bought her a new ride every other year. With its combination of power, dignity, and problematic handling, it suited Templeton perfectly—her vehicular equivalent. She'd only had it a month and already she'd been pulled over twice for DWB—Driving While Black—by cops in white neighborhoods who'd assumed it was either stolen or she was up to no good. She kept her laminated *Los Angeles Times* photo ID next to her driver's license and made sure the cops saw it when she opened her wallet; that backed them off every time, usually with a polite apology.

We sat in silence for a moment, staring out at the lake before Templeton said, "I guess I didn't expect it to look so—"

"Desolate?" I asked, when she didn't finish.

"Gloomy."

The morning air was sharp with a high desert chill, and a mist hung over Lake Enid in ghostly drifts. Here and there, toward the center of the lake, the bare, black branches of dead but still-rooted trees broke the surface like bony fingers trying to claw their way to freedom. Templeton climbed out and stood at the edge of the turnout, studying the lake intently the way one becomes immersed in an atmospheric painting that has a lot to say if you give it enough time. I needed to stretch, so I got out and stood beside her. Templeton's willowy, only a couple of inches shorter than my six feet, and from the corner of my eye I could see the fine contours of her face in profile, and the steady line of her clear, unblinking eyes. A faraway chorus of small birds reached us but otherwise the hills were hushed, a harsh landscape of boulders and chaparral, and patches of withered cacti that had probably been there for centuries.

Templeton raised her right arm and pointed a long, painted nail toward the center of the lake, where the dead trees clustered most thickly. "That would be the town square," she said, knowledgeable from the research she'd been doing in preparation for her article. "The jail would have been on the east side."

"Where they hanged Ed Jones," I said.

"Yes." Her chin was high, her dark eyes solemn, her voice subdued. I realized it may not have been trepidation or awe that I'd heard earlier, but something deeper, more personal. "That's where they hanged Ed Jones."

Within ten minutes we were climbing the wide steps of the Haunted Springs Hotel, bags in hand. I had only one; Templeton had brought two, plus a laptop and a cosmetic case, not to mention a handbag large enough to contain her tape recorder and several reporter's notebooks, so I also toted one of hers.

The hotel, which stood four stories, was built of indigenous boulders, its design vaguely influenced by the Mission style, with a touch of Normandy castle; there were archways over the gates and entrance and turrets at the rooftop corners, giving it a slightly medieval look that had been popular in parts of California in the 1920s. It was the kind of solid-looking place you'd like to stumble on if you were lost in the wet and cold, but not necessarily during an earthquake, when those boulders might come tumbling down. A broad, covered veranda ran around much of the hotel's perimeter, set up with wicker chairs and settees equipped with comfortable-looking cushions. I'm not sure I'd ever spent time in a cushioned wicker chair on the veranda of a decent hotel; Motel 6 was more within my budget. But it looked like something I could get used to, at least for a few days and with a good book for company.

I remembered that Templeton was covering my expenses, which made it all the more inviting. The *Los Angeles Times* was paying for hers; it had a policy against its reporters accepting freebies connected to assignments, especially from studios and production companies, which were always looking for a way to buy the media off. All of the rooms had been booked months ago, nearly half of them by members of the Rebecca Fox Memorial Fan Club, the rest by the production company that was shooting portions of *A Murder in Eternal Springs* in various parts of the hotel and the surrounding grounds. Thanks to a couple of late cancelations, Templeton had managed to reserve our rooms the previous week, booking mine before I'd ever agreed to tag along.

We entered an expansive lobby of old oak, with rafters exposed overhead and sandstone-colored tiles below. Templeton had warned me that the hotel might not be as quiet as usual. Because the film was an independent production, she'd said, being shot on a modest budget, the cast and crew wouldn't be enjoying the kind of privacy and security usually accorded more costly studio projects. And the director had insisted on filming certain scenes during the same period of the year when Rebecca Fox had spent her last days here, including a crucial sequence to be shot in the Rebecca Fox Room. All of this meant that the cast and crew would be forced to mingle with the other guests, which probably explained the sense of energy and commotion we felt as we stepped inside.

"Over there," Templeton said. "It looks like they're getting ready to shoot."

Across the lobby, past glass-plated doors, was a dining room whose tables and chairs had been pushed far to one side. A movie crew clustered in the remaining open space; I could see sound booms above the heads of the assembled, and craftsmen scrambling about, adjusting lights that bathed that part of the room in their warm glow. The wall nearest where they were working was covered with a hand-painted mural that depicted a town along a river, and may have accounted for the shot being set up at that end, with the mural serving as a colorful backdrop. Hotel guests crowded close to the open doors, craning their necks for a peek or snapping photographs, while a young man with a clipboard and headset attempted to shoo them back and pull the doors closed.

Immediately to our left was an expansive lounge area, its boundaries defined by a thick carpet, where easy chairs and deep couches were arranged in various configurations; beyond the furniture, a massive stone fireplace occupied the corner, its blazing logs crackling and spitting. Colorful Natives-American tapestries were draped on either side of the broad stone chimney. Above the mantelpiece hung a large, dour portrait of a tall, sturdily built, hawk-eyed woman in a long, black dress; its vintage look fit the place, even if it wasn't nearly as warm and comforting.

"Enid Tiemeyer," Templeton said, when she caught me studying the portrait of the town's late matriarch. "She opened this hotel with her husband in 1925. Died in 1984. Her son owns everything now."

Near the edge of the carpeted lounge sat a polished black Steinway with a tall crystal vase filled with long-stemmed yellow roses; the piano was abandoned for the moment, with its keyboard cover closed. Immediately to our right, through a broad entrance without doors, was a club room with walls of darker wood. In it were booths, tables, and a dozen stools along the old but well-polished bar. Behind the bar, bottles gleamed faintly in the subdued light, like the sly wink of a prostitute with an eye out for a lonely mark. On the wall between the shelves of bottles, framed behind glass, was an oversize black-and-white glamour photo of a stunning brunette I recognized as the late Rebecca Fox; beneath the photo were more yellow roses. The way the whole thing was positioned and lighted suggested a shrine.

We were turning toward the front desk to check in when the actor Christopher Oakley appeared, trotting down the broad main staircase to the tiled lobby floor.

I didn't know it was Oakley just then—Templeton would identify him soon enough—but my eyes stayed on him just the same.

Like a lot of successful actors, he was on the short side, while giving the impression of being taller, or at least making it seem like his stature didn't matter much. I put his age at thirty, give or take a year; he had a classically handsome face, boyish yet masculine, with strong cheekbones and a good jaw that would probably help him age well. All around us, guests paused to stare at him; I noticed one woman stop in midstride, thunderstruck, putting a hand to her open mouth, as if he were a great political or religious leader instead of a talented young man who made his living in the entertainment industry. Lean, lanky, slim-hipped but broad-shouldered, he moved with the unaffected grace of a natural athlete or a born-in-the-saddle cowboy. There was an energy and confidence about him that no acting school could have taught, the kind that may be calculated but also comes only from within, to those who know exactly what they want and what they need to do to get it. I could see it in his easy movements, the firm set of his shoulders, his quick, observant eyes, and the pleasing smile that parted his shapely lips in a way that seemed both conscious and relaxed. He had what in Hollywood they refer to as presence, that indefinable quality that separates the gifted actor from the movie star.

As he reached the bottom step, he paused and glanced our way, just long enough to widen the smile and soften the disconcerting fact that he'd picked us out of the crowd and was making a quick study. I got the impression that he was scrutinizing me more closely than Templeton, but quickly chalked that up to foolish vanity, wishful thinking, and the loneliness of a man pushing fifty who hadn't hooked up with anyone for a while. A moment after that Oakley moved on, into the dining room, where a woman with spiked purple hair and rings through her lower lip hurried to him and began fussing over his face with a makeup brush. As Oakley stood there, passive and patient, allowing her to make him more perfect than he already was, he slid his eyes momentarily in our direction. They were brilliant blue, heavy-lidded, with the longest lashes I'd ever seen on a man outside a drag revue. Blonds don't turn my head that often, but exceptions come along now and then.

"Christopher Oakley," Templeton whispered. "The actor Maurice mentioned, who's on the brink of a major film career."

"Sorry, didn't notice him," I said, and turned to check in at the front desk.

Kevin Tiemeyer, the hotel's owner, greeted us with practiced aplomb. "Miss Templeton, Mr. Justice, it's my pleasure to welcome you to the Haunted Springs Hotel. I trust your stay will be as pleasant as it is productive."

"She's the productive one," I said. "I'm the sloth."

Tiemeyer smiled and took Templeton's hand in his. "Your fine reputation as a journalist precedes you," he told her. For a moment, as he dipped his head, I thought he might raise her hand and leave some lip balm on it. He was a slender man, at least a few years past sixty, with a long face that suited his tall frame, a sleek mustache, and streaks of gray in his dark hair, which was slicked back with pomade in the style of the old film stars. In one of the wide lapels of his gray jacket he wore a wine red carnation, and the subtle scent of good cologne bridged the air between us. His voice was deep and smooth, his manner elegant. If you'd looked up the definition of *debonair* in the dictionary, you might have found a picture of Kevin Tiemeyer next to it.

Templeton basked for a moment in his attention, which she tended to do with admiring men, particularly older males whose appreciation for women had some substance and seasoning to it. Then she produced her credit card while he personally checked us in. When the paperwork was done, he offered to see us to our third-floor rooms, and apologized because there was no bellhop available to assist us with our bags. "It's a challenge keeping good help these days," he said. "Haunted Springs isn't the most desirable location for young people. No disco or Cineplex, I'm afraid." We were on the third floor, he explained, because the entire fourth floor, with the exception of the Rebecca Fox Room, had been reserved nearly a year ago by members of the Rebecca Fox Memorial Fan Club; most of the remaining rooms were occupied by principals or crew members involved with the film production.

"And who has the Rebecca Fox Room?" Templeton asked.

"One of your colleagues," Tiemeyer said. "Due in later today. Paid a pretty penny, I imagine, to induce a fan club member to give it up."

We told him we'd find our way to our rooms on our own, thanked him, and headed toward the elevator. Before I could push the Up button, a slim young woman with long, dark hair and lovely Asian features emerged from one of the first-floor rooms, moving in our direction with the controlled intensity of a cruise missile. She was wearing fancy running shoes, snug-fitting designer jeans, and a sweatshirt that read **I Survived a Murder in Eternal Springs**. Tucked under one arm was a sheaf of papers, a bound script, and copies of the Hollywood trade papers, *Daily Variety* and the *Hollywood Reporter;* her other hand clutched an energy-boosting drink in a colorful plastic bottle. Breathlessly, she introduced herself as Karen Hori, speaking more to Templeton than to me. It was quickly apparent that she was the unit publicist assigned to the film, and that she and Templeton had spoken previously by phone.

Without being asked, Hori rattled off a litany of rules: no approaching the director or stars without prior clearance; no interviews without a publicist present; all copy subject to approval of the producer and publicist; and so on. As she continued on with her list of directions and restrictions, Templeton smiled placidly, biding her time. Hori's intensity was bewildering; as her words spilled out, trying to pick out a complete thought was like trying to pluck a small garment from a tumbling dryer.

Finally, Templeton raised a hand, causing Hori to pause in midsentence.

"First," Templeton said, "I promise to honor the privacy of the director and cast, within reason, as I would anyone going about their work. I'll also be happy to check facts, and quotes that are not recorded. However, I don't conduct interviews with publicists present. I find them distracting and obtrusive. And I certainly would never submit my copy for approval before filing a story. I can't imagine any self-respecting journalist who would."

"Then, then—then I believe we have a problem," Hori sputtered, trying hard to sound resolute but failing badly. "I—I'm not at all sure this is going to work out."

Templeton smiled benignly. "You're new at this, aren't you, Karen?"

"It's my first assignment as a unit publicist, yes."

"You'd be about twenty-four, twenty-five, not long out of college?"

Hori raised her chin indignantly and was about to speak when a grating female voice shred the air behind us. We turned to see the gawking guests step back from the dining room doors as a tough-looking, middle-aged woman emerged, pushing past them into the lobby; she was on the heavy side, wearing a loose-fitting pink sweat suit and green-thong rubber sandals, with frizzled, graying hair bound up messily and secured in a knotted lavender scarf. Completing the garish outfit was a set of earphones that rode atop her large head, clamped about her ears. As she screeched, she used an unlit cigarette to stab the air and punctuate her phrases. Hobbling beside her on a cane was a shorter bald man with bushy, white eyebrows and a small mustache, struggling to keep up. She stopped halfway between the stairway and the elevator, ripping off her headset and forcing him to pull up as she faced him in a fury.

"I can't shoot my picture under these conditions!" She threw out her hands in the direction of the hotel guests huddled near the dining room doors. "They're everywhere, like cockroaches. Except they have cameras and autograph books. They stop me in the hallways, for Christ sake, telling me how to rewrite my script and make my movie! They never stop with those damn cameras. Heather's beside herself! Can you blame her?"

"They're hotel guests," the man said, speaking softly. "Members of the Rebecca Fox Memorial Fan Club. We can't just order them from the premises, Lois."

"This is a motion picture, Zeke, not a student film!"

"It's something you'll have to live with. The hotel's booked. You knew that when we came up here. You're the one who insisted we shoot on and around the ides of March, during the peak season."

"Lois Aswell, the director," Hori whispered to us, looking chagrined. "And Zeke Zeidler, the producer." She glanced at Templeton. "None of what you're hearing is for publication."

"My editors and I decide what's for publication," Templeton said.

Zeidler glanced around nervously, saw us watching and listening, and suggested to Aswell that they take the conversation behind closed doors. He took her elbow, leading her past us toward one of the first-floor rooms behind the staircase. Halfway there, she shook free of his hand, facing him angrily again.

"Buy them out! Offer them double what they paid for their damn rooms, triple if you have to. But get me some privacy and security. We've got twelve more days of shooting here. It can't go on like this."

"I've added two security guards, Lois. That makes four, working two shifts."

"Hire more."

"That takes money."

"You're the producer. Find it!"

His voice took on an edge. "Maybe if you hadn't demanded period doorknobs and perfect knockers on every door, the budget wouldn't be so tight."

Behind them, a dwarf-size man with rugged, chiseled features poked his head out of a doorway. He was wearing a baseball cap emblazoned with the Hustler Hollywood logo on the front. "Did I hear someone say perfect knockers?" He winked lasciviously. "Where's she at? Just point me in her direction!"

The director glared at him until he disappeared back into the room, grinning.

"I'm serious, Zeke," she said. "I'm making an important picture here. Unless you've forgotten, I've won a DGA award and the Palme d'Or."

"A long time ago, Lois."

"Not that long ago."

"Your last two movies tanked."

"If I was a male director, I could tank at the box office four or five times before anyone held it against me. Tell me why I only get two."

"Because you're a woman, Lois, and because life isn't fair."

That seemed to take some of the starch out of her. She surveyed the lobby, trying to regain her spark, but it sounded false. "Where the hell is Deep Freeze? He was supposed to be here for shooting yesterday."

"I told you, Lois, we're trying to find him. We heard that he went to a pimp convention in Las Vegas, whatever that is. We've got calls out to his agent, manager, lawyer, and publicist. Everybody but his wife."

"Then call his wife. Or else replace him and get me someone else. There must be a hundred black actors with twice the chops who'd kill to get his role. And we could have them at a fraction of the salary."

Zeidler said quietly, "Are you finished, Lois?"

"Don't patronize me, Zeke."

He reached out, resting a hand on one of her shoulders, and looked her in the eye. "Listen to me, sweetheart. We need to bring this movie in on time and within budget. Or you'll be back directing commercials and I'll be turning my house over to the bank." The last of the fire went out of her eyes and the hardness from her face. "Why don't you go back in and finish shooting the scene," he said, "so we don't fall further behind schedule. While you're doing that, I'll see what I can do about crowd control. Fair enough?"

"And getting Deep Freeze up here," she said.

"Yes, we'll continue looking for the elusive Mr. Freeze."

Aswell was slipping her headset back on when she noticed us a few yards away, lapping up every word. "Who the fuck are they?"

"This is Alexandra Templeton," Hori said with false cheer, "from the *L.A. Times.*"

Aswell threw up her hands. "Great. Maybe you could bring in my three ex-husbands while you're at it, as long as everybody else is here."

She strode back across the lobby on her heavy legs while guests parted before her like the Red Sea before a whiskey-voiced, pink-clad Moses. As she stepped into the dining room, the young man with the clipboard pulled the doors closed behind her. The guests immediately surged forward toward the glass, slowly but relentlessly, in the manner of movie zombies. As they flashed their digital cameras, the young man began taping paper over the panes in the door. Zeidler turned the other way, into one of the lower rooms behind the staircase, which apparently served as production offices.

"It's been a tense shoot," Hori said, "for various reasons." Quickly, she added, "That's off the record." I pushed the Up button and a moment later heard the old elevator lurch into action, coming down. An awkward silence settled over us until Hori asked if she could help us with our bags.

"We'll manage, thanks," Templeton said, making it clear she wasn't looking for favors or deals.

"Maybe you can join us for dinner," Hori said, trying again. "Lois Aswell, Mr. Zeidler, the author, Richard Pearlman, and some of the cast. Things should be calmer by then. I'll see if I can arrange it." She glanced my way. "Your friend could probably join us, if he's not—I'd have to clear it beforehand."

Templeton introduced us, apologizing for not doing it sooner.

"Your name sounds familiar," Hori said to me. "Are you a writer too?"

I shrugged. "Trying to get back to it."

"Because I really can't accommodate you without prior clearance." She was winding herself up again; I wondered where she found the energy to get through the day in such a coiled state. "What's your affiliation? Because we're being very selective about who—"

"I'm strictly along for the ride," I said. "I promise to stay out of the way. If I'm not welcome at dinner, I'll do just fine by myself."

The elevator clanked and bumped to a stop and the doors parted. I picked up two of the bags and stepped in, as Hori held the doors open for Templeton.

"We'll be making a big announcement at dinner," Hori said. "Breaking news about two of our stars—on the personal side. It's going to be huge—the media's going to be pouring in over the next few days to cover it. You may want to call the *Times* and tip them to it after dinner, and I know you'll want to include it in your story."

Templeton faced her from inside. "For what it's worth, Karen, I won't be writing a conventional production story, and certainly no celebrity profiles."

Hori's almond-shaped eyes widened. "What *will* you be writing?"

"I'm more interested in the issues behind the movie than the shooting of the movie itself, or any of the celebrity business surrounding it. I don't normally work the Hollywood beat."

Hori looked taken aback, as if Templeton had just spoken blasphemy. "But our understanding was that you were coming here to observe production and interview the principals. That's why we're giving you so much access."

"And I plan to make good use of it," Templeton said. "How I write the story, however, will be strictly my call."

"Of course." Hori's smile was tight. "I wouldn't presume to tell you how to write your story."

Templeton mirrored the smile. "I'm glad we have an understanding."

Hori stepped back and the doors closed on her bewildered face. As the elevator lurched upward, Templeton glanced over, rolling her eyes.

"Publicists," she said, and let out a deep sigh.

THREE

After lunch in the hotel dining room, which had been converted back after the cast and crew had moved on, I unpacked my modest belongings and stretched out for a nap in Room 318. Templeton repaired to her room down the hall to scan the sections of *A Murder in Eternal Springs* she'd highlighted when she'd read the book through the first time. At half past two, as prearranged, she woke me by tapping on my door.

A few minutes later we were accompanying Kevin Tiemeyer as he gave us a tour of the Haunted Springs Hotel. Many of the guests had followed the production crew outside for exterior shooting, leaving the lobby nearly deserted and largely quiet, save for the pleasant crackle of burning logs in the corner fireplace.

Tiemeyer moved nimbly and carried his courtly manner comfortably, like a fine, well-tailored suit he'd worn for a long time. He started our tour in the lobby, pointing out the portrait of his mother, Enid, above the fireplace, and speaking of her in a tone that sounded respectful, if not quite reverential. He mentioned that Lake Enid was named for her, since she'd been such a driving force in the valley's history and development. In the bar, as he stood next to the photo of Rebecca Fox, his voice became wistful as he recalled briefly knowing her fifty years earlier. He recited her most famous film roles effortlessly, and filled us in on details of

The Ides of March, the movie she'd been making when she'd been murdered in 1956. I suspected he'd given this same speech countless times before over the decades; as he spoke, his eyes never left Rebecca Fox's face.

"As you can see," he said, "she was an extraordinarily beautiful woman." He used a cocktail napkin to polish away a smudge on the framed glass. "Despite her fame and success, she never treated me with anything but respect."

"It sounds like she made quite an impression," Templeton said.

Tiemeyer smiled. "I was seventeen," he said, as if that explained everything.

"I notice you're not wearing a wedding band. You never married?"

He shook his head. "Went off to music school, studied piano. Came back, helped run the hotel and our properties down in town, until the state bought them through eminent domain and dammed the canyon in 1979. Except for those few years away at music school, my life's been here, in Eternal Springs."

"Haunted Springs now," Templeton said.

"Yes, Haunted Springs."

"That's a long time to stay in a place so small, without companionship."

"It suits me." Quickly, he asked, "Shall we go upstairs?"

Templeton perked up. "To the Rebecca Fox Room?"

"Perhaps we'll encounter her ghost." Tiemeyer winked playfully. "If you're lucky, she might even grant you an interview."

"Here we are," Tiemeyer said, as he unlocked the door to Room 418 midway along the south corridor on the fourth floor. To preserve the hotel's character, he told us, he still used traditional keys, rather than electronic key cards. As he pushed the door open, his voice grew solemn. "This is the room where Rebecca Fox was murdered fifty years ago tomorrow, and where her daughter, Brandy, committed suicide twenty-five years later." He sighed deeply. "So much heartbreak in this room."

"It's just above mine," I said, taking note of the number.

"So it is, Mr. Justice."

As we followed him in, I saw that the room was identical to mine in size and shape—a hundred square feet by the look of it, maybe larger—with a similar, old-fashioned brass bed and a solid wood bureau that looked antique, or at least collectible. Nothing terribly fancy, but everything tasteful, if a bit on the worn side.

"And people actually request this room?" Templeton asked.

"Oh, yes," Tiemeyer said. "It's booked pretty much year round, long in advance. The film company held it through yesterday. They wanted to keep it longer, for more shooting, but I told them it had been reserved by the guest I told you about. I tried to get her to give it up, but she wouldn't budge."

"So the film company won't be shooting here?" Templeton asked.

"Not for a few days, until the guest leaves. It caused quite a dustup, I'm afraid."

"How so?"

"I'm not sure I should be speaking out of school, Miss Templeton."

"Off the record, then."

"An actor who goes by the name Deep Freeze was to have been here two days ago, to shoot scenes in this room with Margaret Loyd Langley, the actress playing Rebecca Fox."

"He's a rap star," Templeton told me, knowing I wouldn't have a clue.

"When Mr. Freeze failed to arrive as planned," Tiemeyer went on, "the film company had to rearrange its schedule. Miss Langley grew tired of waiting and left earlier this morning, angry about the delay. It's caused a bit of anxiety for the director and producer."

"We caught a whiff of that this morning," Templeton said, "just after we checked in. No wonder Lois Aswell was so upset."

Tiemeyer stepped to a window and drew back the heavy curtains. The window looked down on a massive, dome-shaped rock, as mine did from the room below. Beyond the rock, down a hillside strewn with smaller boulders and across a rocky shoreline, Lake Enid spread across the canyon floor to more foothills on the other side. The lake's small marina consisted of a few ramps for launching boats into the water, docks that were largely empty, and a bait shop that appeared to be closed up.

"We've had some problems with the fish," Tiemeyer explained. "The state tried a poisoning program that didn't work out too well. The town has suffered terribly because of it. The hotel and the marina are the primary sources of employment here."

"The big rock," Templeton said, looking down on the granite dome below the window. "That must be Whispering Rock, which I read about in Richard Pearlman's book."

Tiemeyer nodded. "Legend has it that on certain evenings, Rebecca's voice can be heard, whispering someone's name. Some say it's the name of her young husband, killed in the war. Others claim that she's whispering the name of the one who killed her."

"One of the legends," Templeton asked, "that's helped you stay in business all these years?"

Tiemeyer smiled amiably. "My parents made a conscious decision to exploit the tragedies that took place here, and I've followed their lead. I'm not sure the hotel would have survived otherwise."

I asked where the body of Rebecca Fox had been found the night she was murdered. Tiemeyer said matter-of-factly, "Right about where you're standing, Mr. Justice." I shuffled a step or two off a Persian-style throw rug. He knelt to lift back the rug, exposing the polished hardwood floor underneath. "She was right here, on her left side," he went on, "wearing a nightgown and undergarments—the same nightgown she'd worn on her wedding night. She'd saved it, and worn it when she re-created that night as a scene in *The Ides of March*."

"Couldn't have been easy for her," I said, "stirring up so much old pain like that."

"No," Tiemeyer said, frowning. "I don't imagine it was. Perhaps she felt that by making the movie, it might help her come to terms with her loss, and move on."

"Her throat was slashed," Templeton said, kneeling to inspect the floor. "There must have been a good deal of blood. But I don't see any sign of it."

"We couldn't get the stains out, I'm afraid. A few days after the murder, when the police were done investigating and taking their pictures, my parents pulled up all the floorboards and replaced them." Tiemeyer rose, staring somberly at the floor. "I wanted this room locked up after it happened, and never used again. I even urged my parents to sell the hotel. My mother wouldn't hear of it. She'd practically built this place herself—designed it, chose the materials, supervised the construction. I would have preferred to leave Eternal Springs, but she wouldn't let it go. This was her home, all she really had."

"You seem comfortable enough in this room now," I said.

"I've gotten used to it. Over time, I realized we had an opportunity to honor Rebecca's memory."

"While bringing in some badly needed business to the hotel," Templeton added, rising and studying Tiemeyer for a reaction.

He smiled painfully. "Life goes on, doesn't it?" He knelt again, carefully replacing the rug where it had been, and tugging it smooth. "I've made the best of an unfortunate situation, as my parents did."

We'd come full circle, back to the present. But Templeton took us jarringly back to the past again, in a manner that was almost combative.

"You were the one," she said to Tiemeyer, as he locked up Room 418 behind us, "who identified Ed Jones as the prime suspect in the murder of Rebecca Fox."

Her bluntness stopped the conversation cold. I'd only read the foreword to *A Murder in Eternal Springs,* and wasn't privy to many of the details, including this one. My eyes moved from Templeton to Tiemeyer, curious to see where this was going.

Tiemeyer paused a moment, his eyes thoughtful. When he spoke again, his words seemed measured, though not defensive. "I saw Mr. Jones coming out of this room that evening, an hour or so before her body was discovered. That was the extent of my input."

"It was your eyewitness account that put Mr. Jones under suspicion."

"He had no business being in this room, or even in the hotel. His work as a handyman was down in town, not here."

"Still, your account of what you saw triggered a series of events that culminated in a man's unlawful death." The intensity in Templeton's voice was rising. "DNA analysis didn't exist in 1956. All they had to go on was your word."

"I merely told them what I saw, Miss Templeton."

She set her jaw and squeezed out her next words. "But now we know that Ed Jones was innocent, don't we?"

"From what I've read," Tiemeyer said evenly, "the authorities apparently know that the semen found on the victim's panties wasn't his. That's all that remains for DNA testing. The murder weapon was never found, you know. I'm not sure anyone has actually concluded that Mr. Jones was innocent."

"Nor that he was guilty," Templeton said.

"No, of course not."

"He was innocent then, wasn't he? Innocent until proven guilty in a court of law?"

"Of course, if you look at it that way."

Templeton's voice was chilly. "How else would one look at it, Mr. Tiemeyer?" When he kept quiet, she said, "Ed Jones never got the opportunity to defend himself at trial, did he? Because a mob accepted your word that you saw him coming out of this room shortly before Rebecca Fox was found dead."

"That is what I saw, Miss Templeton. That's all I can tell you."

"You were certain it was Ed Jones, and not someone else?"

"Was, and still am."

"How can you be so sure? According to the book, you were down the hall, sixty feet away, and the lighting was dim."

"My mother always dimmed the lights late in the evening. She felt it added to the ambience. I continue to do the same today."

"Couldn't it have been another black man of similar build, with similar facial features?"

Tiemeyer dropped his eyes a moment. "Please don't be offended, Miss Templeton, when I tell you that in those days, African Americans were not exactly welcome in Eternal Springs. Ed Jones was the only black person here in the canyon, and there weren't many more down in the valley. Not back then."

"No hotel guests who were dark-skinned, as he was?"

Tiemeyer laughed uneasily. "It was 1956. There were hotels in Los Angeles and San Francisco at that time that didn't admit Negroes. We didn't have our first black guest until 1970, when I'd taken over managing the hotel from my mother. In fact, it was quite a sore point between us. For what it's worth, I insisted that we drop all forms of racial discrimination. It wasn't easy standing up to my mother, but I did."

Templeton's eyes flared. "Could it have been guilt driving you, Mr. Tiemeyer?"

"I'm not sure I understand."

"Guilt because a black man died—was murdered by a mob—because your identification had led to his arrest."

"I'll always bear that burden, Miss Templeton." His words sounded heartfelt, sincere. "I'll carry it with me to my grave. I don't doubt otherwise."

Templeton softened a little, but wasn't ready to quit. "You're aware that eyewitness accounts are notoriously unreliable, especially when witnesses are caught up in stressful situations. It must have been very upsetting for you that night, a murder here in the hotel when you were only seventeen."

"Of course, it was extremely troubling, for all of us."

"Faulty eyewitness testimony is by far the greatest cause of wrongful convictions. It's well documented. The same studies show conclusively that when race is involved, accuracy declines even further. Whites identifying African Americans as suspects pose a particular problem. Every reliable study shows that. Some of the wrongly accused have ended up on Death Row."

Tiemeyer grimaced. "Miss Templeton, I assure you—"

"But Ed Jones didn't even have the benefit of a trial, did he? The Eternal Springs Jail became his Death Row. At least for a few terrifying hours, until the local members of the KKK came for him with a length of rope."

Tiemeyer stared at his well-polished wingtips until Templeton was finished. Then he looked up with a sympathetic expression and said quietly, "I never accused him, Miss Templeton. I merely reported that I saw Ed Jones coming out of this room that night. Perhaps someone will open a new investigation and clear his name. If that should happen, I'd be more than willing to tell them whatever I know."

"I don't imagine anyone up this way is all that eager to reopen an investigation of a murder that occurred fifty years ago. Not with resources stretched as thin as they are these days. If they were, I think they would have done it by now."

"I really couldn't offer an opinion on that," Tiemeyer said.

"According to Richard Pearlman's book, your uncle was the deputy sheriff here in Eternal Springs when Rebecca Fox was murdered."

"Yes, that's correct. Jack Hightower, my uncle on my mother's side."

"His son, Jack Hightower Jr., is currently the sheriff for the entire county."

"That's right."

"What does your cousin Jack say about the possibility of reopening the investigation, since he heads the department up here?"

Tiemeyer met her eyes head-on, his voice betraying no emotion. "I suppose you should ask him that yourself, Miss Templeton."

"Believe me, I intend to."

As long as I'd known Alexandra Templeton, she'd been a passionate reporter; it had been one of her great strengths, along with her doggedness and intelligence. But her passion now was of a different quality than I'd ever seen, so heated, I thought, that it threatened to overwhelm her sense of fairness and neutrality. It was as if, with this assignment, she'd staked out a personal battleground, and intended to win at any cost.

Kevin Tiemeyer surely sensed it as we headed along the open hallway to its east end, where he turned into the stairwell to go down. Whereas he'd been chatty and informative before, now he seemed in a hurry to complete his business with us and get away.

I pulled up, pointing to a set of short steps leading up to a small door. "Where does this go?"

Tiemeyer came back, glancing up. "Just an attic, Mr. Justice."

"Not part of the tour?" Templeton asked.

Tiemeyer shrugged. "My mother used it for storage. I don't believe I've been up there since she died. Except for bats, I'm not sure there's much to see." He singled out a key from his chain and held it up. "I have things to do downstairs, but you're welcome to look around if you'd like."

Templeton wrinkled her nose. "Not if I have to contend with bats, thanks."

He withdrew the keys, smiling blandly. "Perhaps I'll have the pleasure of seeing you at dinner. We serve two sittings, at six and eight. Unless, of course, you plan on dining with the film company."

Templeton thanked him for the tour, and he resumed his trek down the stairs. She stepped to the railing, watching him emerge from the stairwell into the lobby, where he crossed to the front desk. Her eyes moved to the forbidding portrait of his mother that hung over the fireplace, then drifted back to him, as he greeted an arriving couple with his patented cordial smile.

I went over to stand beside her. "Maybe he really did see Ed Jones coming out of that room that night," I said. "Maybe he got it right."

"Maybe."

"Maybe you're getting a little too close to this story, letting your personal feelings interfere with your reporting."

"If I remember correctly, Justice, you were known to get rather close to your stories."

"Yes, and look where it got me."

She didn't say anything after that, just kept staring down, immersed in whatever it was she was thinking, and maybe lost in a past that meant something different to her than it did to me, and to a lot of us.

FOUR

I was exiting the stairwell on the third floor, pointed toward my room, when Templeton caught up with me, slipping her hand into mine.

"Let's take a walk," she said. "I need to get out of this hotel for a while."

"More history than you bargained for?"

"Something like that."

"Let me grab a jacket from my room."

We both slowed as we approached my door, and Templeton must have been as startled as I was. Just ahead, a little girl in a frilly yellow dress with a white sash at the waist was walking along the railing as one might a circus tightrope, her arms spread wide as she placed one toe carefully in front of the other. She was facing in our direction and when she saw us gaping with concern, an unpleasant grin split her pale face. Below, to her left, was a straight drop to the tiled lobby floor, where several guests had stopped to stare up, equally concerned. Behind them, Kevin Tiemeyer came from behind the front desk, looking alarmed as he raced for the stairs.

I was about to dash forward and reach for the child myself when a woman emerged from a door down the hall and came running awkwardly on stiletto heels. "Audrey! Audrey, get down from there!"

The girl's malevolent grin widened as the woman snatched her around the waist and plucked her from the railing, setting her firmly on the hallway carpet.

"Audrey, we can't have any more of this. You could have fallen. You could have killed yourself."

"I'm bored!" The girl stamped her feet like a petulant five-year-old, though she appeared to be at least twice that age. "I want to shoot my scene. I'm tired of waiting, waiting, waiting."

Her hair was auburn, done up in Shirley Temple curls, and her yellow dress with its lacy hem and puffed sleeves looked long out of style. Her face might have been cute once, with its pug nose, dimpled cheeks, and bright eyes. But now her features struck me as slightly sinister, those of a child approaching puberty who still craved attention like a grade-school brat. As we got closer, I saw that her face was fully made up, and figured the old-fashioned dress was for a movie wardrobe.

Her mother—Nan Williams, I later learned—turned her daughter around to look her over, fussing her clothes and hair back into place. Mrs. Williams was a heavily made-up forty-something, leaning toward fifty but fighting it with skin peels and tucks; her hair, worn in a modish shag, had been bleached nearly to the point of death and she'd stuffed her plump body into a too-tight pants suit of gold lamé that matched the glitter of the pointy heels. Her eyes were wide and dramatic, outlined with enough mascara for the farewell concert of an aging heavy-metal rocker. With the delicate caution of someone handling a live grenade, Mrs. Williams explained to Audrey that filming had fallen behind schedule and that she'd have to be more patient.

"I know we're behind schedule," Audrey said, spitting out the words as if her mother were stupid. "You think I don't know that? I know everything that goes on around here."

"Of course you do," her mother said. "You're very bright. Why don't we go back to your room, get you an energy bar, and go over our lines together?"

"They're my lines, not yours."

Her mother flinched like she'd been slapped in the face. "Of course, Audrey, they're your lines. Why don't we run through them one more time, so that you dazzle Lois when she's ready for you?"

"I'm sick of going over my lines! I want to see the producer, Zeke the Freak. I want to know how long I have to wait around in this stupid dress and hair."

"I thought you liked that dress, Audrey. Didn't you tell me you liked it? That you thought the color makes you stand out?"

Kevin Tiemeyer emerged from the nearest stairwell, laboring on his long, thin legs. He glanced at Audrey with exasperation, then at her mother. "Mrs. Williams, we really can't have this happen again. God forbid, if she were to fall—"

"Fuck off," Audrey said.

"Audrey! Apologize to Mr. Tiemeyer."

Instead, Audrey folded her arms across her chest and said, "I want to start doing my own stunts. I can do them as well as that little midget they hired as my stunt double. I might as well get some use out of those stupid gymnastics lessons you make me take."

"I'm so sorry," Mrs. Williams said to Tiemeyer. She included Templeton and me in an apologetic glance. "She's a handful, especially when her scenes get delayed and she hasn't eaten." She turned her head, covered one side of her mouth, and whispered dramatically, "Low blood sugar."

"Are you in the movie?" Audrey asked Templeton matter-of-factly.

"No," Templeton said.

"You should be. You're pretty."

Templeton smiled. "Thanks."

"Prettier than that bitch Heather Sparks. She gets all the good roles, because she looks like the girl next door. That's what they always say about her in reviews." Audrey scrunched her face up around her pug nose, while speaking in singsong fashion. " 'The girl next door.' 'As wholesome as apple pie.' What a bunch of bullshit."

Mrs. Williams grabbed her by the wrist. "Audrey, that's enough profanity for one day, thank you."

"I think Heather's doing it with Christopher Oakley," Audrey went on. "He's hot. He can do a lot better, if you ask me."

Templeton let a laugh escape and immediately put a hand to her mouth.

"That's it, young lady." Mrs. Williams dragged Audrey past us, while her daughter cursed and resisted with every step. "If you don't start behaving, no more room of your own. You can move back in with me."

"No!"

"Then start behaving."

We heard the girl start to cry as they stopped in front of a door and Mrs. Williams slipped a key in the lock. "You're going to ruin your makeup, Audrey. Lois won't be happy."

"I'm sorry for any disruption," Tiemeyer said to Templeton and me, while glancing down the hall with concern. He lowered his voice. "I won't make the mistake of allowing a film company to shoot inside the hotel again. I don't care how much revenue it brings in."

He turned back down the stairs, gripping the rail with his long, slender fingers. Down the hall, Mrs. Williams knelt outside her door, a hand on each of Audrey's shoulders, trying to find the girl's downcast eyes. "We want the same things, don't we, dear?" Her words and manner were as sweet and carefully spun as cotton candy. "To make you the best actress and get you the best parts we can? Don't we want the very same things?" She raised her daughter's chin, until their eyes met. "Remember our pact, sweetheart? All for one and one for all?"

"I'm tired," Audrey said, her voice small.

"We have something you can take for that."

"I don't want to take anything. I want to go home. I want to see Fluffy."

"Next time we'll bring Fluffy with us. I promise."

Audrey's face hardened, and her voice took on a nasty edge. "There won't be a next time. Because I'm not going to do another fucking movie. You can't make me."

Mrs. Williams reacted similarly, all the softness suddenly

gone, her voice chilly, her mouth set in a grim line. "Shall I go down and tell Mr. Zeidler that you can't continue, Audrey? That you're having an emotional breakdown and we're going home?" She stood, and took a step toward the stairs. "That they need to find another girl for your part, perhaps someone prettier. Is that what you want me to do, Audrey?"

Audrey looked up, her eyes troubled, her face puckered. "No."

"Are you sure? It's your decision."

Audrey's voice was barely audible. "I'm sure."

"Shall we have an energy bar and go over our lines now?" Audrey nodded weakly. Mrs. Williams brightened. "You see? We do want the same things. Remember, Audrey, it's the two of us together, working as a team." She glanced self-consciously in our direction, quickly unlocked the door and pushed it open. She stroked her daughter's head fondly as Audrey stepped in, then followed, shutting the door behind her. We could hear the security lock being turned from inside.

"Wow," Templeton said, staring after them.

"You still want to take that walk?"

Templeton nodded. "More than ever."

I grabbed my jacket while Templeton stopped by her room for a shawl. A minute later, we stepped out of the hotel to spring sunshine that hadn't quite taken the chill from the air.

Stone steps behind the hotel led to a grove of date palms and the site of the old mineral springs; we could see people and camera equipment up that way, apparently shooting footage for the movie. Beyond the palms, high above everything, was a large, proud-looking house, Victorian in style and well-maintained, that must have been the Tiemeyer place.

We heard someone in the production crew cry, "Action!" I asked Templeton if she wanted to take a look but she shook her head resolutely.

"I'd like to see the town," she said, "get my bearings."

The hotel was situated at the north end of the lake, a few

hundred feet above it. The town extended south from the hotel for three blocks along the lake's west side, above a two-lane street carved from the hillside. We climbed from the hotel parking lot to the paved street, strolling past a tiny park with benches facing the lake and, after that, three businesses: the Haunted Springs Museum and Souvenir Shop, the Haunted Springs Grocery and Liquor, which also sold gas, and the Haunted Springs Café, which was boarded up. The museum and souvenir shop occupied a small, one-story building made to seem larger and more imposing by its Regency Moderne design; the architecture featured broad front steps, a concave central bay, and a handsome curved relief panel above the double doors depicting the history of the valley—wildlife, Native Americans, ranchers, and townspeople shown in noble poses. It was closed for remodeling, but a bronze plaque informed us that the building had been constructed in 1936 to house the Eternal Springs Public Library, thanks to the tireless efforts of Enid Tiemeyer, and saved during the destruction of Eternal Springs in 1979 by the Hungry Valley Historical Preservation Society, of which Enid Tiemeyer had been the founder.

"This was the one building of distinction in the old town," Templeton said, "although the state moved a number of residences up here as well." We peeked through slatted blinds, saw some interesting photographs, and decided to come back later, if we could find someone to open it for us. "That would probably be Kevin Tiemeyer," Templeton said. "According to the book, he inherited what's left of the town when his parents died."

We continued into the second block, which consisted of faded single-story houses and cabins perched along or above the road, where the views must have been pleasant from the front porches. Smoke curled from a few chimneys and several residents were out, sitting in plastic chairs or working in their yards. Seeing Haunted Springs this way made it look like a good place to live, if you didn't need too much diversion or activity.

When we reached the cemetery Templeton turned in and I followed, past a gate that hung loose by one hinge; I imagine it's rare that a reporter, even a former one like me, passes an old cemetery in a small town without feeling at least a twinge of curiosity. Templeton kept the lead, glancing at names on grave markers as she moved past them. Before long we were standing in front of the headstone for Ed Jones. It was at the south end of the graveyard, not quite halfway up the hill, a simple but respectable marker of polished gray marble inscribed with his name, dates of birth and death, and the words: MAY HIS SOUL REST IN PEACE.

Templeton stayed at the grave site while I wandered the gentle slope, looking for nothing in particular. Many of the grave sites needed tending, suggesting that surviving family members had probably long ago moved on, and didn't come back to visit all that often, if ever. The markers told a lot of stories, at least the beginnings and the ends, with many of the endings bunched in years of plague, war, or natural disaster. Family plots were common, going back to the late 1800s, though obituary dates from recent years appeared scant. It struck me that the true community of Eternal Springs rested here, in these burial plots; Haunted Springs was just a figment of someone's imagination, the illusion of a town formed from a fragment of another, a fanciful name given to a forsaken place to gain attention in tourist guidebooks and help fill rooms in a struggling old hotel.

Templeton caught up, tapped me on the shoulder, and pointed up the hill, toward two sizable monuments that occupied a lofty section in the middle of the cemetery near the top, shaded by the only tree within its boundaries. They were larger and showier than all the other markers, with heavy marble bases of speckled pink supporting carved angels ascending on outstretched wings. We started up, winding through modest wooden crosses and concrete headstones, until we reached the lofty angels and could read the inscriptions carved below. They informed us that Roderick Tiemeyer had died in 1976 and his wife, Enid, had followed in 1984. In between the two big monuments was an empty plot, barren ground awaiting the arrival of another coffin and corpse.

"I suppose that's for Kevin," I said, "when his time comes."

Templeton turned away, to gaze across the cemetery and the road and down the hill to Lake Enid, where ripples drifted across the dark water. A wind had come up, and she pulled her shawl more snugly around her. Across the canyon, a solitary hawk glided and disappeared over the foothills to the east, its shadow skimming across the rugged landscape below.

"It must have been a lonely place," she said, "even when it was Eternal Springs, with a thriving town clustered along the river."

"He was always surrounded by people," I said, referring again to Kevin Tiemeyer. "Up here in the hotel, with his parents."

She gave me a funny look, not exactly reproachful but disappointed in some way. Then she said, "I was thinking of someone else," and let it go at that.

We stood in silence for another minute or two, while Templeton stared out pensively across the canyon, and I listened to the rising wind.

Somewhere behind us, I heard what sounded like a door banging shut, and turned to look. Up the hill, just beyond the cemetery's farthest corner, a few birds alighted from the drooping branches of a eucalyptus tree. To the left of the tree and partially camouflaged by its dusky bluish leaves stood a house that we'd missed in our fascination with the graveyard. Except for the big Tiemeyer home, this one was larger than the others we'd encountered along the way, a two-story stucco-and-wood with a broad front veranda and flower boxes at the windows; the veranda and the flower boxes sagged from disrepair, and the stucco needed patching and paint. Behind the house, for extra shade, rose two more eucalyptus trees; I could hear their leaves rustling like dry paper in the wind. I saw no movement about the house to account for a slamming door, no smoke curling from the chimney, nothing to indicate anyone was home. I figured the old place might be abandoned, not unusual for a little town like Haunted Springs, where so many people had left, particularly the young, looking for work or just a more interesting place to live. Still, there was that sound like a banging door, and birds rising.

"Shall we head back?" Templeton asked.

We started down through row after row of grave sites. As we hit the road and turned north toward the hotel, I stole a final glimpse back at the isolated house high on the rise.

This time I saw movement, at a window facing the lake. It might have been someone watching, I thought, but it could just as well have been a rogue draft passing through an empty old house, stirring tattered curtains left behind when the owner moved on, like so many others. The curtains settled and I thought nothing more about it.

FIVE

At half past six, Templeton and I entered a downstairs hotel banquet room with an invitation from Lois Aswell to view the latest "rushes"—raw footage from that day's shooting—which the director screened each evening for cast and crew.

A screen had been erected at one end of the Jack Hightower Room—so signified by a nameplate above the door—which the production company had reserved for the duration of its stay, before packing up to complete filming on a Canadian sound stage. Cast and crew were spread out at tables around the room, where the beer and wine were flowing, along with banter and laughter that contributed to a party atmosphere.

Karen Hori, the publicist, escorted us to a table near the back. She was surprisingly cordial, almost deferential; the wariness we'd experienced earlier in the day seemed to have evaporated. The rushes weren't due to begin for a few minutes, so Hori ran through the roster of principal cast members for our benefit, aligning them with their characters in the movie: Christopher Oakley, the promising young actor with the dark blond hair and bedroom eyes, had the key role of Kevin Tiemeyer, playing him from age seventeen until the present—according to Hori "a tour-de-force role sure to catapult him into the top rank among leading men"; Heather Sparks, already a big star, had been cast as Brandy Fox, the ill-fated daughter of Rebecca Fox, a smaller role that she'd taken because, in Hori's hyperbolic estimation, "it gives her a chance to stretch and show her great range as an actress"; Audrey Williams, the child actor, was portraying Martha Frech, the ten-year-old daughter of a hotel housekeeper, who'd discovered the body of Rebecca Fox in 1956. "Audrey has a cult following from the Demon Slasher movies," Hori said, "but this gives her a chance to work in a serious film with an acclaimed director. It's a small part, but she jumped at the opportunity to do something besides bloody horror flicks."

"Are you sure she wasn't pushed?" Templeton asked genially.

Hori quickly turned the conversation to Deep Freeze, the rapper-turned-actor who was to play Ed Jones, the accused murderer. He'd been "inadvertently delayed," Hori explained, and his scenes postponed, but he was due to arrive in the morning to begin shooting what Hori promised would be "a powerhouse performance—the critics are going to be very surprised." Margaret Loyd Langley, the Oscar-winning actress whose career had faded like so many other female stars after she'd hit her forties, had the central role of Rebecca Fox. She'd returned home temporarily, Hori said, to await word that Deep Freeze had arrived and was ready to work, since they shared a key scene yet to be shot. Meanwhile, a body double was being used for scenes in which Rebecca Fox lay dead on her hotel room floor.

"We were lucky to get an actress of Maggie's stature," Hori said, apparently referring to Margaret Loyd Langley by her nickname. "She doesn't come cheap."

"I imagine Heather Sparks is at the high end as well," Templeton said.

"Heather's working for scale, because her role is so rich. She says it's the best part she's ever been offered."

We looked up to see Christopher Oakley entering with Heather Sparks on one arm and Lois Aswell on the other. He hadn't shaved since early morning, by the look of him, and the stubble on his strong jaw and upper lip was a nice contrast to his boyish features; his hair was tousled into calculated disarray and his heavy-lidded blue eyes had a hint of mischief in them as he laughed at something Aswell was saying. For a moment, as his eyes scanned the room, they seemed to find our table. They settled after that on Heather Sparks, but without quite sticking, as if they'd rather come back in our direction, which they sometimes did, surreptitiously.

I'd never seen a Heather Sparks film but I recognized her from billboards and magazine covers; I also recalled reading an article once on movie star salaries that put hers at $20 million for big studio pictures, near the top for actresses. Her specialty was the light romantic comedy; from the few reviews I'd skimmed, she apparently excelled at them. She didn't have the head-turning looks that Hollywood leading ladies often do; she was attractive in a more ordinary way, with a trim but healthy figure, wide, lively eyes, and a pleasant, perky quality that reminded you of a buddy's friendly sister or your best friend back in college. She struck me as the kind of woman many straight men want to marry and be the mother of their children, and frequently do, only to lose interest in them romantically over time, returning to their hothouse fantasies of whores and bad girls and sex that's down and dirty, the kind they can't imagine engaging in with their polite and wholesome wives. Perhaps that's what accounted for Heather Sparks's audience appeal, I thought, particularly to more conventional young women who felt threatened by actresses who sizzled with sexual heat on screen. Sparks personified the loyal girlfriend, the earnest and well-adjusted wife, the pretty girl next door, who always got the guy and promised Happily Ever After, at least in the Hollywood version of life. Only now she was playing the doomed Brandy Fox in *A Murder in Eternal Springs*, apparently keen on showing another side of her talent.

"We're going to watch rushes of a romantic scene between Heather and Christopher," Hori whispered to us. "You're going to see some absolutely amazing chemistry between them. I expect the sparks to fly off the screen." She smiled and shrugged. "Sorry, no pun intended."

"I wasn't aware that Kevin Tiemeyer and Brandy Fox had been romantically involved," Templeton said. "That wasn't in the book, was it?"

"Lois added that," Hori said. "It's kind of a subplot. Otherwise, there'd be no romance. And it makes Brandy's death even more poignant, don't you think? On most things, Lois is a stickler for accuracy. But this is a movie, not a documentary. That's a direct quote from Lois. You can use it if you'd like."

"Thanks," Templeton said, "but I prefer to get my quotes firsthand."

"Anyway, Mr. Tiemeyer gave his blessing, so I guess it's okay." Hori lowered her voice even further. "From what I gather, he's quite the ladies' man. He got chummy with one of our makeup artists very quickly. So maybe he really did have a fling with Brandy Fox back then."

Zeke Zeidler, the balding producer with the small mustache, stood at the front of the room, waving his cane in the air to get some attention. When he had it, he thanked the crew for its hard work and patience with various production delays, citing several crew members by name. Each time he did, the impetuous dwarf we'd seen earlier jumped atop his table, hoisted his beer, and led a collective cheer amid cries of "Go, Scotty!"

"Scotty Campbell," Hori informed us. "Stunt double for Audrey Williams. Very outgoing fellow. I can introduce you to him, if you'd like."

"Maybe when he's calmed down," Templeton said.

The lights dimmed and the rushes started. I don't know about Templeton, but I didn't exactly get singed by sparks flying off the screen. The scene we saw, shot earlier that day at the site of the old mineral springs, should have been sexy—it called for Heather Sparks to pop open the buttons of Christopher Oakley's shirt, run her hands over his bare chest, then lock lips with him as he pulled her to him in a lover's embrace, while the palm fronds trembled above in the make-believe heat. But despite repeated takes, the two actors never seemed truly comfortable with each other. Heather Sparks, in particular, appeared to be working hard to create the illusion of real passion; there was a stiffness to her performance that belied the infectious personality for which she was famous. Maybe it wasn't her fault, I thought; maybe it was the director who'd failed her actors. Or maybe the role was simply a stretch beyond her grasp.

The other problem was Oakley. Even made up as a fortyish Kevin Tiemeyer, Oakley was the gorgeous one. There's no hard and fast rule in Hollywood that the leading lady has to be more attractive than the leading man. Still, the pairing felt somehow out of balance.

If Karen Hori found the footage less than scintillating, she never let on. She remained the loyal publicist, gushing about Oakley and Sparks as a "dream pairing," while reminding us that we'd just seen raw film, not the finished product. "So much can happen in the editing room," she pointed out, before quickly changing the subject to dinner. She invited us to sit at the director's table, where we'd be joined by the producer, the lead actors, and Richard Pearlman, the author, who'd just arrived to start several days of media interviews, starting with Templeton.

"I think you'll find Mr. Pearlman very interesting," Hori said to Templeton, as we crossed the room, while crew members scrambled to a well-fortified buffet table. "I've reserved a seat for you between him and Lois Aswell." Hori turned to me. "And you'll be sitting with Christopher Oakley, Mr. Justice."

"I beg your pardon?"

"He specifically asked that I seat you next to him." Templeton and I exchanged a curious glance. She raised her eyebrows with one of those looks that suggested romance might be in the air, which I quickly dismissed with a frown. "Chris told me that you were quite famous at one time," Hori went on. "I'm sorry, Mr. Justice. I had no idea."

I suddenly realized how young she was, young enough, at any rate, to have missed my fifteen minutes in the spotlight sixteen years ago when my misdeeds as a journalist put me briefly on the front pages of every major newspaper in the country and many of the evening newscasts. I'd suffered the media glare a few times since, related to sensational murder investigations I'd stumbled or pushed my way into, when the coverage was more favorable, but Hori had probably had her nose in the Hollywood trade papers when my name and mug had resurfaced on those occasions.

"Infamous would be more accurate," I told her.

"You've redeemed yourself many times over," Templeton said kindly.

"I appreciate the support, Alex."

"I'm afraid I don't understand," Hori said.

"Just as well," I said. "Not something one can put a positive spin on."

"Gather your wits, Benjamin," Templeton said. "Your big moment with Mr. Oakley is at hand."

We'd reached our destination and Christopher Oakley was rising to meet me, his smile warm enough to melt butter and his azure eyes direct enough to make mine falter. His hand wasn't big but the grip was firm and self-assured, and it lingered longer than it needed to, causing a pesky butterfly to flutter its wings somewhere deep in my belly. I tried to return his gaze but found it difficult, so I fell back on the old salesman's trick of peering *between* his eyes to create the illusion of directness. Meanwhile, I felt a bead of perspiration trickling down my temple, and worried that I might break out in a full sweat.

"Thanks for joining us on such short notice," Oakley said, a perfectly appropriate thing to say.

"The pleasure's all mine," I replied, a ridiculous phrase I don't believe I'd ever uttered, and hoped I never would again.

Good god, I thought, you're behaving like a prepubescent girl at a boy-band concert. During my lifetime, I'd been beaten, sliced, raped, and mutilated, lost my left eye in one violent confrontation, and nearly lost my life at least a couple of times. I'd faced some of the most violent, powerful, and scary individuals one could imagine, often with recklessness, even grinning bravado. The media had raked me over the coals for fabricating my prize-winning series for the *Los Angeles Times*, and I'd managed to survive. Yet here I was, crumbling to pieces at the prospect of chatting with a beautiful young man who happened to be a celebrity. So this is what being starstruck is like, I concluded. I felt completely out of control, in the grip of a benign madness. I didn't like it, not a bit. But the more I fought it, the more anxious I became.

"Hot in here, isn't it?" Oakley said, with a conspiratorial wink and in a comforting voice that carried the hint of a Tennessee drawl. He found an extra napkin and patted the side of my face, blotting away the embarrassing drip so casually and quickly it was almost like sleight of hand, with no one the wiser. I was completely in his debt at that point, not to mention in his thrall, and happy to have him take control. In a matter of seconds, he'd introduced me around the table, keeping the patter going so that I didn't have to, and giving me a chance to get my legs back under me and my queasy stomach settled.

At Oakley's suggestion, we were about to hit the buffet table when Nan Williams approached, teetering on her stiletto heels while vying for the attention of Lois Aswell, who was chatting with Templeton and reacted with thinly masked annoyance. Mrs. Williams had apparently freshened up for dinner and reeked of cologne heavy enough to make my eyes sting. She edged up to Aswell, wedging herself between Templeton and Richard Pearlman, and stood with a plaster smile on her face, impossible to ignore. Finally, Aswell excused herself and stepped away, listening with surface patience while Mrs. Williams whispered urgently, her eyes fixed on Templeton. Growing visibly irritated, Aswell silenced Mrs. Williams with an upraised hand and said curtly, "Okay, okay, fine, fine."

When our group returned from the buffet with our meals, little Audrey Williams was seated at the table, her feet barely touching the floor. Mrs. Williams brought her a plate, beaming as she introduced her daughter to Templeton, while promising to provide her with a list of Audrey's credits and a set of her most recent head shots, for use when Templeton wrote her article. As this went on, Karen Hori looked mortified but maintained her silence, using the time to eat quickly and efficiently in the manner of overworked employees who rarely have a moment to themselves. Not that there was a lot for her to put away. It was a meal typical of a young woman with Hollywood ambitions—heavy on the salad, light on the carbs and calories.

Oakley, meanwhile, had maneuvered me into the seat on his left, with Heather Sparks seated on his right. He informed her straightaway that he'd followed my escapades with great interest for years, reciting the high and low points of my life so fecklessly that it put me completely at ease. I apologized for not knowing nearly as much about him, and pried a few biographical details from him while nibbling broiled salmon and wild rice, and stealing glimpses at his heartbreaking face. In short order, I learned that he was raised by adoptive parents on a Tennessee horse farm, where he grew up riding, cleaning stables, and hefting bales of hay, which no doubt accounted for his lean but muscular frame. By the age of nineteen, he said, he'd moved to New York for several years of acting classes, auditions, and stage roles that eventually got him noticed by Hollywood. He related this to me in a charming and unself-conscious manner as he devoured his grilled chicken breast and mixed vegetables. I was eager to hear more, but he quickly turned the conversation back to me, making me seem like the most important person at the table.

Meanwhile, across from us, Templeton had settled into an animated discussion with Lois Aswell, Zeke Zeidler, and Richard Pearlman. But it didn't take long to see that it was Pearlman who had Templeton's close attention, to the point that she was ignoring her food. He looked fifty-something, with a solid build, wavy, graying hair, and a well-tailored, tweed-and-turtleneck look favored by self-important authors who often earn their primary income as academics but milk the writer role for all it's worth. I caught snatches of the conversation, which seemed to be about the limitations of the acclaimed director, Spike Lee, as a writer, for which Templeton had no shortage of opinions. The discussion, however, quickly became a battle between Aswell and Pearlman—strong-willed director versus pompous writer—to see who could get a viewpoint in edgewise.

Hori, sitting to the right of Heather Sparks, caught Oakley's eye at one point, and tapped the face of her wristwatch. Oakley reacted almost imperceptibly, leaned close to Heather Sparks, and slipped an arm around her shoulders while whispering into her ear. She nodded stiffly, propped up a smile, and folded her hands tightly in her lap. Oakley stood, tapping his beer bottle with his spoon to get the room's attention.

"I won't take too much time," he said, in his pleasant drawl, "because everyone's having too much fun. But Heather and I have an announcement to make."

Scotty Campbell, the dwarf, shouted from his table, "You're buying all of us drinks for the rest of the shoot, with all that damn money you make!"

Oakley grinned. "No, Scotty, that's not quite it." He reached down for Sparks and drew her up beside him, snaking an arm around her waist. "We wanted you all to be the first to know." He lifted her left hand, showing off a small diamond ring on her ring finger. "Heather and I are engaged to be married."

There was a collective gasp before the room erupted in cheers, whistles, and applause. I smiled gamely to cover my disappointment then chided myself for getting so worked up about Oakley in the first place. Yet my disappointment lingered; there was no ignoring it.

Oakley planted a kiss on Sparks's cheek and pulled her closer, while Karen Hori got to her feet to lead a standing ovation, and others rose around us, clapping fervently. I joined in, taking a step or two away but still feeling awkward standing next to a couple I barely knew, applauding their decision to spend the rest of their lives together, if that's where their engagement was really headed.

Wherever it led, I thought, it surely wouldn't be wasted. If nothing else, it was a surefire way to quell those nasty rumors regarding Christopher Oakley's sexuality.

Bottles of champagne were opened and a huge cake was rolled out, while I separated myself from the two lovebirds even further. Video and still photographers moved in, capturing Oakley and Sparks as they popped a cork, toasted each other, and kissed in a way that was arranged to show off the ring.

While that was going on, I ventured to the other side of the table where Templeton was chatting with Pearlman, or at least listening to him; she had an itch for good-looking older men with distinguished backgrounds, and appeared to be hanging on his every word. We got acquainted over coffee and cake, with Templeton between us, and it didn't take me long to dislike the guy. Pearlman talked about himself and his book as if no one had ever written a true crime story before, at least none as important as *A Murder in Eternal Springs.* On the ride up from West Hollywood, Templeton had given me her review of the book, pronouncing it heavy on film analysis and trivia, and a gushing tribute to Rebecca Fox, but not particularly deep or rich on the crime stuff. Pearlman was a professor of cinematic history and theory, she said, not a journalist, and his book had apparently suffered because of it.

When I finally broke in long enough to ask him if he'd reached any conclusions about who might have murdered Rebecca Fox, since Ed Jones seemed to be off the hook, Pearlman looked down the long bridge of his nose and said smugly, "I take it you haven't read my book."

"Only the foreword, I'm afraid. I glanced at Templeton's copy on the drive up, but I'm afraid I didn't get very far."

"Not interested in true crime, Justice?"

"I may finish your book, Richard, although I brought a couple of crime novels along that I may read first."

"Ah, yes—fiction." His smile couldn't have been more condescending. "That makes sense, I guess. It was fiction you were writing at the *L.A. Times* sixteen years ago that got you into so much trouble, wasn't it? Making things up, when you were supposed to be reporting facts."

Not too many years earlier, especially if I'd been drinking, I might have given him a taste of my right fist. Now, I just stared into his eyes without blinking until his nerve wilted and he looked away.

"Justice has just finished his autobiography," Templeton said quickly, playing the diplomat. "He's dealt frankly with all those old issues in his book. When it comes out, he's going to put all that behind him. Aren't you, Benjamin?"

Pearlman tilted his head and raised his eyebrows as if mildly impressed. "It's something of a publishing trend, isn't it? One does something reprehensible, then cashes in on his notoriety by airing his dirty laundry between the covers of a book. I imagine we'll be seeing you on *Larry King Live* when it comes out. He goes for the tawdry and sensational, doesn't he?" Pearlman laughed as if it was all said in jest, then gave the knife a twist. "I'm sure you've produced a fine book, Justice, and that we can trust every word you've written." His eyes finally settled on mine, holding this time like they were safely anchored in my shame.

"You still haven't told me if you have a theory about the murder," I said.

"I don't truck in theories or conjecture, Justice. I prefer to stick with hard evidence, of which my book contains a surfeit, based on years of rigorous research. You may find it interesting, if you ever get around to reading it."

"I'll make a point of it, Mr. Pearlman, and let you know what I think."

"Splendid. There are copies for sale in the lobby, you know. I'll be happy to sign one for you if you'd like."

"I'd have thought they'd all be gone by now, given your high opinion of the author."

"They were. I brought some with me to sell on my own."

"Carry a trunk full wherever you go, do you?"

Before it got any worse, Templeton jumped in to ask Pearlman some innocuous questions about the publishing business. Like a lot of writers, he had no end of answers and apparently no succinct ones. The other diners from our table drifted back with their cake and coffee, finding new chairs. Oakley and Sparks held hands while he nuzzled her slender neck and a still photographer snapped a few more pictures that were certain to be splashed all over the newsstands in the coming days and weeks.

Just as everyone was seated, Lois Aswell suddenly pushed her chair back and stood, staring agape out the banquet room doors and across the lobby to the front desk.

"Isn't that Toni Pebbles?"

The name ended the murmurs of conversation at the table as if a plug had been pulled. All eyes followed Aswell's across the lobby to a tall, hefty woman with large breasts and a surprisingly slim waist that didn't go with the rest of her, and gorgeous black hair that spilled onto her strong shoulders in a cascade of buoyant curls. She was dressed in a suit jacket with shoulders that looked padded but probably weren't, and a knee-length skirt tight enough to shrink-wrap a CD, with a split up one side of the skirt that showed off strong, shapely legs that tapered into stylish three-inch heels.

It was Toni Pebbles alright, making her usual indelible impression. I hadn't seen her for nearly twenty years, but there was no mistaking that carnivorous look in the glinting green eyes and that proudly voluptuous body, with her big breasts thrust up and out and her wide shoulders set squarely, as if she was commanding the world to look at her while daring anyone to get in her way. She'd always been striking, even in her forties when she'd started to put on weight, carrying herself in such a sexually brazen manner that even lusty straight men had been cowed; if anything, the extra pounds had added another element of intimidation to the package, allowing her to stride through life like a well-aimed bowling ball knocking down pins in a helpless clatter. I'd bumped into her a few times when I'd been a young reporter at the *L.A. Times* and she'd been freelancing for big money for the top national glossies that ran in-depth Hollywood features with a dark undercurrent and a sharp edge. I'd been a decent-looking guy back then, still trim and solid from my college wrestling days, and Toni had put the moves on me every time we'd found ourselves together, until she'd finally heard through the grapevine that I was more interested in men. Years had passed since I'd heard her name or seen her byline. But in her heyday, Toni Pebbles had been something of a media star, at least on the print side, both feared and reviled by the Hollywood establishment, with a reputation as a ruthless reporter who had no peer when it came to digging for dirt.

"What's she doing here?" Aswell asked. "She's not supposed to be here." Her fierce eyes fixed on Hori. "Did you clear Toni Pebbles to come up here, Karen?"

"I don't even know who she is," Hori said.

"Christ, you're so fucking young."

"Who is she?"

"A viper," Aswell said, "masquerading as a journalist."

"She must be here on her own," Hori said. "What do you think she wants?"

"Something no one else has," Zeke Zeidler said. "You can bet on that."

Scotty Campbell, the little stuntman, passed with a half-empty champagne bottle in one hand. "Hey, any publicity is good publicity, right?"

No one at our table seemed even mildly amused, Christopher Oakley and Heather Sparks least of all.

SIX

Toni Pebbles checked in and disappeared to an upper floor by way of the main staircase, without so much as a glance or a nod in anyone's direction. Karen Hori studied her keenly until she was gone, then joined Oakley, Sparks, Aswell, and Zeidler in a downstairs production office for a hastily arranged meeting.

Others with the movie headed here and there—upstairs for a decent night's sleep, to the lounge to relax by the fireplace, or across the lobby to the club room to continue drinking, led by the boisterous little stuntman, Scotty Campbell. As they drifted off to their various destinations, Kevin Tiemeyer sat at his Steinway, facing the lounge with his back to the main stairway, his long frame bent over the keyboard. He was putting his music school background to good use, playing a perfectly respectable version of George Gershwin's *Rhapsody in Blue,* the arrangement for solo piano Gershwin had written from his popular composition, whose unforgettable melodies had so enraptured America roughly eighty years ago. Tiemeyer's audience was small—most of the members of the Rebecca Fox Memorial Fan Club were older, and had turned in—but seemed appreciative.

Alexandra Templeton and Richard Pearlman decided to follow the drinkers into the bar for a nightcap. Templeton asked me to join them, if only for some sparkling water, since I'd been on the wagon for several years. It distressed me to see her wasting her time with someone as full of himself as Pearlman, but it wasn't the first time she'd gone down that particular path, and she was old enough at thirty-five to know what she was doing. I lacked the energy to wedge myself between them at any rate; so I turned down their offer and purchased a copy of *A Murder in Eternal Springs* at the front desk, intending to hit the mattress, crack open the book, and see if it was half as good as the author advertised.

A hotel guest, a middle-aged woman, saw me making my purchase and plucked at my sleeve. "A great read," she said. "Have you been a member of RFMFC for long? I don't remember ever seeing you before." I must have looked puzzled, because she added, "RFMFC—the Rebecca Fox Memorial Fan Club. You're not a member?"

"I'm afraid not."

"You're one of the movie people then?"

"Here with a friend, a reporter."

"Ah." She tapped the book knowingly. "Absolutely riveting. Mr. Pearlman did a marvelous job on the research. I had no idea that little girl, Martha Frech, had suffered such a terrible head injury after finding Rebecca's body. Or that Rebecca had fresh yellow roses delivered each day to her husband's crypt, because that had been their favorite flower. I tell you, I stayed up all night reading right to the last page."

"Please, don't tell me the ending."

"That's the interesting thing," she said. "There really isn't one. We really don't know who murdered Rebecca, do we?"

I found a crowd waiting for the elevator so I took a side stairwell to my third-floor room, climbing absentmindedly while I mulled over the sudden appearance of Toni Pebbles and the stir she'd created in the banquet room. As I emerged from the stairwell into a dimly lit corridor, I glanced at a room number and realized I'd climbed one level too many, to the fourth floor. I was about to turn back when I noticed a small figure crouched outside a door halfway down—the Rebecca Fox Room, I guessed—with an ear pressed to the wood.

As I approached, the eavesdropper straightened abruptly to face me. It was Audrey Williams in pajamas, a bathrobe, and furry slippers, her face covered by night cream.

"Who the fuck are you spying on?" she demanded.

"I might ask the same question of you, angel face. What is that stuff, anyway—acne cream?"

"Shut up! It's my beauty treatment. I don't have zits. I'm not going to get any, either. No chocolate, no grease, no zits. That's what my mom said."

"Did she say anything about anxiety?"

"I have a prescription for that."

I nodded toward the room behind the door. "So what's in there that's keeping you up past your bedtime?"

"Stop talking to me like I'm a little girl."

"Stop saying *fuck* all the time, and maybe I will."

"Fuck you. I know who you are. My mom told me. You were a newspaper reporter once. You really screwed up, like that black dude at the *New York Times.*"

"Worse, I'm afraid. I won a Pulitzer Prize for what I did."

"What's a Pullet Surprise?"

"A Pulitzer—it's an award for newspaper writing, kind of like an Oscar for what you do."

"I should have gotten an Oscar for *Demon Slasher: The Hair-Raising Return.* Best Supporting Actress. But they have a prejudice against horror flicks. The cheaper ones, anyway. That's what my mom says."

"Do you believe everything your mom tells you?"

"When I want to."

Movement could be heard from behind the door. Little Audrey's head swiveled in that direction faster than you can say *The Exorcist.*

"Must be Rebecca Fox's ghost," I said.

Audrey turned back, her face puckered with disdain. "Is not." But her voice didn't sound like she was entirely convinced.

"There was no one checked into this room when Mr. Tiemeyer gave my friend Alexandra and me a tour this afternoon. It was empty."

Audrey's eyes widened. "You went in there?"

I nodded. We heard another noise and Audrey glanced at the door again. "It's getting pretty close to midnight," I said. "Less than two hours away. You know what that means, don't you?"

"What?"

"It's almost the ides of March. I imagine the ghost of Rebecca Fox gets awfully restless when that date rolls around."

"You can't scare me, if that's what you're trying to do."

I lowered my eyes to the thin line of light at the bottom of the door. Audrey followed my lead. We saw a shadow moving, feet shuffling past on the other side.

"Probably just our imagination," I said. Audrey's eyes were two wide circles inside their mask of night cream. I shrugged aimlessly. "I wouldn't worry about it."

"Why not?" She was whispering now.

"Because if she comes after you, with your face looking like that, you'll probably scare her to death."

I smiled and she wrinkled her face in anger. "You'd better shut up. I can have you thrown out of here, you know. All I have to do is talk to Zeke the Freak."

"From what I hear, on the ides of March, if you happen to encounter the ghost of Rebecca Fox, you can see the blood dripping from her neck."

"What a stupid story. Anybody knows ghosts don't bleed. They don't have blood."

"So who's in there, Audrey, if it's not Rebecca Fox?"

She fixed her eyes again on the door, then on me. "If I don't sleep tonight, it's going to be your fault. I've got scenes tomorrow. I have to get up at six for makeup."

"Break a leg, sweetheart. I'll be sleeping in myself. No alarm clock for me."

She turned away and shuffled down the hall in her furry slippers, showing me her upraised middle finger as she went.

In my room, I called Maurice in West Hollywood, knowing he was usually up through the ten o'clock news.

"Sorry, Maurice," I said. "I should have called earlier, to let you know we got in okay."

He demanded to hear "all the juicy details," which meant whether I'd gotten the chance to meet Christopher Oakley and what might have come of it. I mentioned that Oakley and I had eaten dinner together, which nearly sent Maurice into apoplexy. Then I let him down quickly with the news that Oakley was engaged to marry Heather Sparks.

"There goes another one," Maurice moaned, "over to the other side. What a waste, such a beautiful lad. Well, I suppose we can't claim them all, can we?"

"I wish them all the happiness in the world," I said, stifling a yawn.

"But you say he asked you to dine with him? What was that all about, Benjamin?"

"Truly, Maurice, I haven't a clue. Maybe he just wanted me to feel at ease during my visit. He seems like a very decent guy."

Maurice asked me to keep my ear out for "recyclable gossip," reminded me to eat well, and to take my HIV meds on schedule. I asked him to give my best to Fred, and we bid each other good night.

I kicked off my shoes, plumped my pillows against the headboard, and stretched out to read *A Murder in Eternal Springs*. I'd finished the intriguing foreword on the drive up, so I skipped to the first chapter, which related the discovery a few years ago in a DNA lab that a mob might have hanged an innocent man for the murder of Rebecca Fox in 1956. I also learned that the author, Richard Pearlman, had paid for the DNA tests himself, because of his deep curiosity about the half-century-old murder; he'd had to overcome resistance within the sheriff's department that served Hungry Valley, which had jurisdiction over the case and felt its meager resources could be put to better use, in the investigation of more current crimes. Pearlman's determination to get to the truth cast him in a more altruistic light, I thought, and may have explained Templeton's interest in him. On the other hand, the startling DNA results gave him a fresh hook for his book and had surely been the centerpiece of its publisher's promotional campaign.

In the second chapter the narrative returned to 1956 to start the story over from its beginning—at least the beginning as Richard Pearlman saw it: Rebecca Fox at home in Beverly Hills, packing her bags for a trip to Eternal Springs to shoot *The Ides of March,* which she considered the most important movie of her career. From the outset, Pearlman seemed as fascinated with Rebecca Fox and her iconic status in Hollywood as he did with the crime elements in his story. I found his writing serviceable if a bit dry, but reasonably compelling; it kept me turning the pages, even if it was heavier on Hollywood history and film data than I would have cared for. As I reached the fourth chapter, however, a yawn escaped me, and I got up to open a window to clear the stuffy air.

That was when I saw the lady in white, three stories below, standing next to Whispering Rock.

The old woman was caught in the light from the hotel's first-floor windows, which also illuminated the lower section of the big rock, while leaving the rest in shadow. She was rail thin and deathly pale in a long, white dress, her ashen hair hanging like strands of worn thread past her shoulders, staring up with pallid, pink-rimmed eyes as if transfixed. A gentle wind teased the flimsy dress and brittle hair, causing them to float lightly on the night air, but the woman never moved. I thought at first that her sickly eyes were fixed on me, until I realized they were drawn to the window above—Room 418, the Rebecca Fox Room.

The wind picked up, rustling down through the hills to stir the curtains as I opened my window. Then I heard it pass with a soft hiss across the rock, just as Kevin Tiemeyer had suggested it might. The whispering wind caused the old woman to prick up her hearing like a wild animal attuned to the threatening sounds of the night. Then she covered her ears with her hands, her face contorted like someone being driven mad by voices only she could hear, before turning and running barefoot into the darkness.

I stood at the window for a minute or two, listening for what might have rattled the old lady so badly, but all I heard was the whisk of a canyon wind across a big boulder buried solidly in the earth. I left the window open and returned to *A Murder in Eternal Springs*. As hard as I tried to stay with the story, I found my concentration divided, as the wind persisted outside my window, like someone urgently whispering close to your ear but maddeningly just out of range.

SEVEN

I woke the next morning to the disorienting sound of helicopters overhead and imagined for a moment that I was back in the city. Then the blur of sleep cleared and I remembered that I was actually on a brief vacation in Haunted Springs.

I drew back the curtains and spotted three choppers circling above the town and the lake, though it sounded like there might be more. The ones I could see were emblazoned with TV network or syndication logos, apparently here to shoot aerials of the now-hallowed ground where Heather Sparks and Christopher Oakley had gotten engaged. I could almost hear the blare of banal headlines on the evening entertainment news shows, trumpeting the arrival of Hollywood's Latest Royal Couple. There would be endless photos and video of the lovebirds shot by paparazzi, speculation on how much Oakley had paid for the ring, and a gallery of other celebrity couples whose engagements or marriages had grabbed attention before going bust—the usual junk that had come to glut the airwaves, which the public seemed to gobble up insatiably like bloated lemmings being led not to the sea but to the cultural garbage dump for feeding. Throughout all the overheated coverage, of course, would be prominent plugs for *A Murder in Eternal Springs,* the movie the golden couple was currently shooting.

Karen Hori works fast, I thought.

After gulping my morning meds and taking a shower, I headed out for some badly needed caffeine. At the end of the corridor, taped to one of the elevator doors, was a handwritten sign:

Temporarily out of service during this morning's filming—please use side stairwells (quietly). Thank you.

As I emerged from the southwest stairwell to the first floor, a production assistant stopped me with a finger to her lips before I could cross the lobby. She kept me at bay with several other guests while Lois Aswell and her cinematographer set up a shot on the main staircase for another take. Scotty Campbell, the diminutive stuntman, stood on the first landing, decked out in a curly auburn wig and small girl's yellow dress like the one Audrey Williams had been wearing yesterday. Campbell had forsaken his usual clown act for a more sober and professional demeanor as he trotted up and down the steps to measure their distance, pausing between trips to perform a series of stretching and limbering exercises. The production assistant explained that Campbell was about to recreate a real-life scene from 1956 in which Martha Frech, the hotel housekeeper's daughter, flees from the fourth floor after finding Rebecca Fox dead, before tumbling down the final flight of stairs to the lobby floor and suffering a serious head injury.

"We've already shot the close-ups with Audrey," the production assistant explained. "Now Scotty steps in for the risky stuff. Audrey can dub in the screams later in her own voice. From what I'm told, she's a great screamer."

Aswell signaled Campbell and he climbed the next flight of stairs on his stubby legs, then pulled down the sleeves of his dress to cover his hairy forearms while the assistant director called for quiet. On Aswell's hollered cue, the camera rolled and Campbell came running down the stairs, flailing his arms as a frightened child might, his mouth open wide in a silent scream. Tracks for a dolly shot had been laid across the lobby behind the cinematographer, and he backed smoothly away with his camera, keeping the stuntman in frame and in focus but also at a distance, to obscure his features. Campbell pretended to trip as he reached the final set of steps, tumbling violently to the tiled floor at the bottom, where he lay motionless until he heard the director's shrill voice.

"Cut! That's a take! Thank you, everyone. Great work, Scotty. Let's move on."

Campbell climbed to his feet and worked a kink or two out of his neck and shoulders, but otherwise seemed unfazed. The production assistant thanked us and allowed us to proceed on our way. I crossed to the dining room, where I found Templeton at a far corner table finishing up an interview with the producer, Zeke Zeidler. When he was gone, and I had my coffee and a muffin, Templeton suggested we find wicker chairs on the wide veranda and enjoy the vistas, before a media horde descended on Haunted Springs by ground, as it was already doing by air.

"I take it Karen Hori put the word out," I said.

"She's been on the phone since early morning. *Entertainment Tonight* is sending a crew with one of their top reporters, with the copycat shows sure to follow. Karen would probably be doing cartwheels, if she wasn't so busy setting up interviews."

"Let's find those wicker chairs," I said. "It might be my last chance for a little peace and quiet."

My peace and quiet didn't last even that long.

As we stepped out the double doors at the hotel's entrance we were bombarded by a stream of profanities, of which *motherfucker* was the most prominent. They came gruffly from a black guy behind stylish Ray-Bans, dressed in a burgundy cape and a fedora of green felt festooned with a golden feather, which would have looked fine on him if he'd been Oscar Wilde. As I was about to learn, and Templeton was already aware, he was the rap star Deep Freeze, arriving in Haunted Springs two days late to shoot scenes as the ill-fated drifter and handyman, Ed Jones.

I've never claimed to be a fashion expert and certainly wouldn't want to crimp anyone's style. But to my eye, Deep Freeze looked fairly ridiculous in his flamboyant getup, which included a pin-striped suit beneath the flowing cape, shiny black boots with sharply pointed toes, and enough rings and other flashy jewelry to qualify as bling, or even bling-bling. Deep Freeze might have pulled it off if he'd been taller and slimmer, allowing the outfit to hang dramatically the way runway models do, but he couldn't have been more than five-seven and he was on the chubby side, with a generally soft look that contradicted the pimp stereotype he'd embraced, and belied the exaggerated glower on his round face. The whole thing struck me as the calculated act of a man trying hard to appear to be something he wasn't.

His companion, however, looked genuinely scary. He was hustling toward us from a Cadillac Escalade, gripping Gucci luggage in his beefy hands, chasing after Deep Freeze, whose smaller hands were empty. We'd learn later that the second man was Sweet Doctor Silk, a failed rapper who served as Deep Freeze's bodyguard, chauffeur, and all-around errand boy. Silk was a shade lighter than Deep Freeze and looked younger by a decade, which put him somewhere just shy of thirty; unlike Deep Freeze, Silk's glower and snarl didn't look theatrical. A jagged scar across one cheek and heavy scar tissue over both eyes suggested a history of combat, maybe in the street or the ring, or possibly behind bars. He wasn't that much taller than Deep Freeze but his wide frame looked solid, not soft, even camouflaged as it was beneath baggy pants and a loose tank top emblazoned with a Detroit Pistons logo; his massive biceps alone were enough to tell you he worked hard to keep himself in shape. The only bling I could see was a heavy gold chain draped around his thick neck and nestled against his furry chest. Completing the hip-hop uniform was a pair of basketball shoes, one of the cool, must-have brands that make pro athletes wealthy from endorsement deals and that poor kids sometimes kill for.

Sweet Doctor Silk stopped at the top of the steps to stare at Templeton, an appreciative smile parting his lips, one tooth glinting with gold to match his jewelry.

"Fine-looking bitch, ain't she?" Deep Freeze said, raising his Ray-Bans and eyeballing Templeton up and down like he was thinking of placing an order and having her shipped COD.

Silk said nothing, just stared and grinned. Templeton raised herself up and allowed the fury to inflame her brown eyes, looking down at Deep Freeze from her full height, an advantage of several inches with her pumps. He kept his hungry eyes on her, nervously kneading his heavily ringed fingers, maybe to hide the wedding band I'd glimpsed a moment earlier.

"You're Deep Freeze, aren't you?" she asked.

"That's right, baby."

"You're even smaller than you appear in your videos." She glanced at his busy fingers. "Why, your hands are almost dainty."

Deep Freeze did a slow burn, kneading his fingers more furiously. Before anything more could be said, the hotel doors burst open behind us. Zeke Zeidler came through them faster than you'd expect from an older man moving with a cane.

"Where the hell have you been?" Zeidler asked.

"I got caught up in stuff. You know how it goes."

Zeidler reined in his anger. "Now that you're here, Mr. Freeze, perhaps we can get you checked in quickly and start trying to recover some lost time."

"Sure, we can do that." Deep Freeze winked at us, like it was all a big joke. He reached into an inside jacket pocket in a leisurely manner and produced a thin brown cigar, his eyes drifting back to Templeton. Silk set the bags down, located a lighter, and sparked the flame while Deep Freeze lit up, slowly drawing in the smoke. Zeidler sputtered something about time being money. Deep Freeze said, "Don't worry, old man. I know my lines. We had two weeks of rehearsal down in L.A., remember? Anyway, I'm a pro."

"Are you aware that for the past two days we've had to completely rearrange our schedule to shoot around you? That Miss Langley has gone back to Malibu?"

Deep Freeze glanced at Zeidler again like he was barely there. "I had some promotion to do. My new CD, it's just out. Silk, give the people a sample."

Sweet Doctor Silk scrambled to hand each of us a shrink-wrapped CD with a photo of Deep Freeze on the cover, posed in an ice house wearing his pimp garb and a pretty young woman on each arm, with a cute title: *Freeze Rapped.* "It's the real deal," Deep Freeze said, "an injection of truth, if you can handle it." He eyeballed Templeton one more time, ran his tongue slowly across his lips, then turned and sauntered toward the doors.

"You can't smoke in there," Zeidler called after him.

"I can until same fool stops me," Deep Freeze said, and waltzed in as a young couple came out, holding the doors for him almost timorously. Silk grabbed the bags and scurried in after him.

Zeidler closed his eyes a moment, taking a deep breath. When he opened them, he glanced from me to Templeton. "He lobbies for this role for more than a year," Zeidler said, shaking his head and sounding truly perplexed. "Puts his manager and agent on it like attack dogs. Calls in every favor and connection he can. Even invests some of his own money to get the picture made. Then he shows up two days late, as if he's deliberately rubbing our noses in shit. If I could, I'd fire the sonofabitch."

Templeton had her notebook out. "Is that on the record, Mr. Zeidler?"

He stared at her a long moment, a weary smile forming below his small mustache. "Sure, why not?" He laughed sadly. "What the hell do I care anymore?"

EIGHT

While I finished my coffee and muffin on the hotel veranda, watching TV satellite trucks pull into the parking lot, Templeton was in a quiet corner of the club room with Richard Pearlman, conducting a formal interview.

"My main complaint with his book," she said later, settling into a wicker chair beside me, "is the short shrift he gives to Ed Jones. It's as if the key figures are Rebecca Fox and Brandy Fox, while Ed Jones is little more than an afterthought."

"Women drive the book market," I said. "Maybe the emphasis on the others was a commercial consideration."

"In case you've forgotten, Justice, Ed Jones was lynched by the Ku Klux Klan. He deserves to be a flesh-and-blood character as much as any of the others."

I shrugged. "Then rectify it. Do the work that Pearlman didn't."

She smiled slyly, tapping her laptop. "I'm way ahead of you. I started my research on Ed Jones two weeks ago, when I got this assignment."

"Turn up anything interesting?"

"When I do, you'll be the first to know."

"Aren't you afraid you'll make smarty-pants look bad?"

"Pearlman?" I nodded. "I know you don't like him, Benjamin, but he's actually a pretty decent guy."

"He's arrogant, combative, and full of himself."

Templeton smiled knowingly. "Actually, he kind of reminds me of you."

"That's what I just said."

We had some spare minutes before lunch, so we spent them at Whispering Rock, observing the assistant director blocking a scene with Heather Sparks and Christopher Oakley, to be shot later when they were in period dress and makeup.

Templeton had read the script the previous night, and filled me in. The scene called for Oakley and Sparks to stroll around the big rock hand in hand with Lake Enid in the background, before pausing in the shadow of the rock for a stolen kiss, just as a cloud passed across the sun as an ominous sign of the trouble that would follow. Local townspeople had been hired for the afternoon to take boats out on the lake, to simulate its look in 1981, when the waters had thrived with fish and angling had been popular; we could see them gathering down at the marina. Later, in an editing room, special effects would be used to create the darkening sky, if the weather failed to cooperate.

Karen Hori had turned the blocking into a prime photo op. She'd herded over several TV crews, which shot video of Sparks and Oakley as if they were a pair of exotic creatures newly arrived at a local zoo. Once, at Hori's urging, Sparks held up her hand to show off the ring, although her forced smile suggested she wasn't enjoying being on display so much, at least not in the new role of blissful fiancée.

Sparks suddenly stepped away from Oakley, looking alarmed as she pointed up toward the hotel's fourth floor. "It's her!"

All eyes turned toward a top-floor window, where Toni Pebbles stood framed, peering down in all her glory. I counted windows from the left and calculated that she was in the Rebecca Fox

Room, which explained the activity Audrey Williams and I had observed from outside the door the night before.

"I can't work this way," Sparks shouted in a shaky voice. "I can't do this knowing that she's watching me!"

Oakley reached to comfort her but she pushed him away and took off for the hotel, while the cameras swiveled to capture her flight. Oakley quickly followed, calling after her to no avail, while the frustrated assistant director muttered an epithet under his breath.

"Heather's head-over-heels in love," Hori told the assembled TV producers. She glanced irritably up at the window, where Toni Pebbles continued looking down, a faint smile forming on her red lips. "As you might imagine, Heather doesn't want any uninvited intruders to spoil this special moment in her life."

Hori suggested they all go inside for lunch, then prepare for their face-to-face interviews after that, when Heather had calmed down. As they packed up their gear and turned away, Hori told them they'd each be allotted eight minutes with the couple to get their sound bites, instead of the five they'd originally been promised, as they conducted their round-robin interviews in a room that would be set up and ready to go, with lighting in place. "But no more than eight," Hori said, "and we'll need you to sign agreements putting certain areas of questioning off-limits, which will be strictly enforced."

When they were gone, Templeton studied Toni Pebbles. "She's obviously here for a reason. I wonder what she's after."

"I know." The voice was young and precocious. We turned to see Audrey Williams standing nearby, a smug look on her freckled face, sans makeup. "Everybody's talking about it."

"Talking about what?" Templeton asked.

"What that whore Toni Pebbles is doing here."

"So what are people saying," I asked, "that makes you think you know so much?"

"I don't have to tell you if I don't want to."

"You don't know," I said. "You're just making it up to get attention."

"Am not!"

"Prove it, Freckles."

"Don't call me that!"

"I think your freckles are cute."

"I hate them. My mom says they limit the kinds of roles I can get. That's why I have to be extra good, so I can keep working."

"So tell us what people are saying about Toni Pebbles," Templeton said. "That is, if you really know anything."

Audrey folded her arms across her chest and her manner got prissy. "They're saying she's here to 'out' somebody. So there."

"Out someone," Templeton said.

"You know, somebody who's homo and in the closet. They say she knows stuff, and she wants them to spill their guts to her, so she can write up a big, exclusive story and sell it for a bunch of money." Audrey uncrossed her arms and plucked self-consciously at a sleeve, pulling it down, but not before I glimpsed several neat, parallel scars inside the wrist that looked like old cuts. "You want to see me climb up on Whispering Rock? All the way to the top? Because I can you know."

"It sounds dangerous," Templeton said.

"I'm not afraid. So do you want to see me do it?"

"Not really."

"Okay," Audrey said blithely, and ran off toward the hotel, no doubt in search of another audience.

I glanced up at the window from which Toni Pebbles had caused such a commotion moments earlier. She was still there, holding my gaze and smiling mischievously like someone who knows where all the secrets are buried.

I was headed for the southwest stairwell, intending to wash up in my room, when a sharp voice in one of the production offices off the lobby caught my attention. It was clearly Lois Aswell, and she wasn't happy.

"I want that room for filming, Zeke. Get me the goddamn room."

"I've spoken to her, Lois. She won't give it up."

"How could you let this happen?"

"I reserved the room through yesterday. If Mr. Freeze had shown up when he was supposed to, we could have shot his scenes with Margaret there, as scheduled, and we wouldn't be having this conversation."

"Don't tell me what I already know! Tell me what you can do to solve the problem."

"We can shoot the scene in another room. The rooms on the third and fourth floors all have the same configuration. We'll dress the other room the same as the Rebecca Fox Room for continuity. Problem solved."

"There's history in that room, Zeke. Two women died horribly in that room. There's an ambience, a dark energy. I want that for my actors. I want it for my picture."

"Toni Pebbles has the room, Lois. She's not budging, and Kevin refuses to get in the middle and help us out. He says that our shooting here has already caused enough problems."

"The man's spineless."

"He's been very cooperative. You should be grateful."

"I don't understand why Pebbles is so adamant about keeping that room. It's not like she's one of those fanatics who belong to the RFMFC."

"There's speculation that she'll attempt to use the room for leverage."

Aswell's voice became wary. "What are you talking about?"

Zeidler sounded distressed. "That she might offer the room in trade—in exchange for an interview with a member of the cast."

"No one in our cast wants to talk to that vulture."

"That's the point, Lois. Like I said, it gives her leverage."

"Christ, what a mess."

"Are you sure shooting in that room is worth it? If it helps Toni Pebbles get what she wants?"

There was silence. I could almost imagine Aswell locked in a stare with Zeke Zeidler as his words took hold.

Finally, more quietly, she said, "Maybe not." There was frustration and resignation in her voice now, with an undercurrent of anger. "See what you can do about getting another room. I guess I'll have to concede this one."

"You still got your period doorknobs and knockers," he said.

She didn't laugh. "Just get me a goddamn room, Zeke, so we can put at least one scene with Deep Freeze in the can this afternoon." She sighed heavily. "And see if you can do something to head off that Pebbles woman, before she does some serious damage. I'm afraid Karen's over her head on this one."

I heard footsteps and tried to duck away, but Aswell moved fast. As she came out the door she caught me, but kept going with only a sharp glance. Zeidler was a few steps behind on his cane. He stopped in the doorway, sagging wearily. He didn't seem to be bothered that I was there, or by what I might have heard.

"You know why I'm a producer?" he asked.

"Not really, but you can tell me if you'd like."

"Because I love making movies more than anything else in the world. I shouldn't say this, but I probably love it more than I love my wife and kids, and my grandkids, and they mean a lot to me. Only I'm not really good at anything. Tried directing, never got the hang of it. Can't write worth shit. Acting? Never had a shred of talent. But I know a good script when I read it, and I can raise money, and figure a budget. I can organize and orchestrate. I know how to help the people with real talent, the artists, do what they do best. I can pull the whole thing together. That's what a good producer does."

"Sounds like a lot of work."

"Yeah, a lot of work. Two years of my life I got in this film, and it's not over yet." His countenance changed as he glanced over, his weariness giving way to something darker. "Then this broad Pebbles brings her *mishegoss* up here and threatens to destroy an entire movie, maybe even somebody's career. For what?

To write up some trash that's nobody's business anyway. I should never say this, a Jew who lives with the shadow of history. But they should have extermination laws for vermin like Toni Pebbles, may God forgive my terrible thoughts."

He studied me a moment, then asked if I might be willing to loan out my third-floor room for a day or two. "It wouldn't be all day. A few hours this afternoon, maybe the same in the morning. I'll get you tickets to the premiere when the movie comes out. Get you into the party afterward. I'll even cover your room while you're here, up to three days. It's the best I can offer."

"Templeton's already paid for my room," I said, "so don't worry about that. But I'll take the tickets and the party invitation. Templeton likes that kind of thing."

His face registered surprise. "You're saying yes? So easy?"

"Sure, I could loan you my room for a few hours."

"You're a good boy." He stepped over and patted my cheek. "You just made an old producer's day a lot easier. Now I just got to figure out how to deal with that Pebbles person."

NINE

I grabbed a quick nap after lunch, then cleared out as a set designer and prop master moved in to transform my room into a near facsimile of the one above. The fact that I tend to travel light made stashing my belongings a lot easier.

While that was happening, Kevin Tiemeyer escorted Templeton and me to the Haunted Springs Museum and Souvenir Shop, which was getting a makeover. Remodeling was nearly done, he said, with the workers due back in a few days to finish up; meanwhile, we had the place to ourselves.

"This is my mother, Enid, as a young woman," he said, taking us directly to a photographic history of the Tiemeyer family. It was displayed in a lighted alcove in the first of three rooms that comprised the seventy-year-old building. A caption below the photo stated that it was taken in 1923, the year Enid and her husband Roderick arrived in Eternal Springs, and two years before they opened the hotel. "She would have been in her early twenties then, fresh from Macon, Georgia. Married not quite two years. My father was several years older, on the frail side from a bout of childhood tuberculosis. Fairly well set up, from family money. Unfortunately, most of that was wiped out by the Depression a few years later, but at least they had the hotel."

"Your mother was attractive," Templeton said, digging in her handbag for her notebook and pen. "She had a strong look about her—resolute."

"Yes," Tiemeyer said, "my mother was nothing if not resolute."

If I looked hard enough, I could find the fierce visage of the corseted older Enid Tiemeyer from the portrait over the hotel fireplace in the face of the prettier young woman before me now, but it took some effort. The obvious similarity was in the directness of the gaze and the erect posture, which suggested no shortage of single-mindedness and self-possession, in direct contrast to her less impressive husband. From the first photograph to the last, Roderick Tiemeyer looked unchanged except for age: a slender, mild-looking man, bespectacled and slightly shorter than his imposing wife, with passive eyes that revealed little, except perhaps a detached acceptance of fate.

"Was it her idea to come to Eternal Springs," Templeton asked, "or your father's?"

"Mother was the strong personality in the family." Tiemeyer smiled mildly. "Dad followed her lead on most things, as I did."

It had been his mother's dream as a young woman, Tiemeyer said, to find an unspoiled place in a dry climate where she might build a profitable business and leave her own personal stamp, while creating an atmosphere for her husband and child conducive to a healthy and virtuous life. She'd been a devout Methodist with a strict religious upbringing, he explained, whose values never wavered. Her only concession to more liberal ideas had been the hotel bar; she'd disapproved of liquor but had realized after Prohibition had been repealed that the hotel would have to offer alcoholic beverages if it was to remain popular and survive financially. She'd reluctantly given in, permitting the bar to open while warning guests that drunkenness or other ungentlemanly or unladylike behavior would not be tolerated.

"When my mother spoke," Tiemeyer said, "you knew she meant business. People came here to rest and enjoy the mineral springs, not for revelry and debauchery. There was a good deal of socializing, though. Mother liked to organize wholesome events."

It was clear from the photographs that Kevin Tiemeyer had

been an only child; he was in many of them with his parents, growing from a chubby toddler to a slim, good-looking teenager to a handsome young man with a fine-looking mustache and dark, somber eyes, the kind of bachelor who probably broke a heart or two along the way. In none of the pictures did I see Enid or Roderick Tiemeyer with a smile that looked genuinely joyful; they apparently had been a hardworking but fairly dour pair. The only photograph in which Roderick Tiemeyer looked even slightly relaxed was a shot of him at his office desk, as editor and publisher of the *Hungry Valley Weekly.*

"Mother became even more conservative in her ways as she got older," Tiemeyer said, as if reading my mind. I was studying a photograph of Enid from the early 1950s, when she would have been middle-aged. In the picture, she stood tall and straight, the eyes keen and sharp—judging eyes, I thought—in a long, dark dress that hung nearly to her ankles and looked more appropriate for an older woman in an earlier time. "She felt the world was going to hell." Tiemeyer smiled painfully. "That was the decade the word *teenager* became part of the national vocabulary, when middle-class kids began to have their own spending money, their own cars, and a lot more freedom."

"Rebel Without a Cause," I said. *"The Blackboard Jungle. The Wild Ones."*

Tiemeyer laughed. "Those movies never played at the little theater in Eternal Springs. My mother made sure of it. And in our house, rock and roll was forbidden."

"Is that when you discovered Gershwin?" I asked, thinking of the *Rhapsody in Blue* I'd heard him performing solo on the piano.

"Around that time."

He led us to a gallery of photographs taken of the hotel, from its opening in 1925 to its first renovation and refurbishing in 1957, followed by another overhaul in 1982. Interspersed were photos of Eternal Springs as it developed along the banks of Rattlesnake River until its removal and demolition in 1977 to make way for the dam that would create Lake Enid. Another wall was devoted to the tragic Fox family—Rebecca Fox and her husband, Brent, and their daughter, Brandy—three fine-looking people whose lives all ended in different ways but prematurely: Brent, killed nobly in battle during World War II; Rebecca, murdered mysteriously in 1956; and Brandy, a despairing suicide in 1981. As Templeton peppered Tiemeyer with questions about the murder, jotting in her notebook, I was fixed on the photograph of Brent Fox, struck by the general resemblance he shared with Kevin Tiemeyer. I would have commented on it but Templeton was persistent with her questions and I didn't want to interrupt.

"Where are the others, the vigilantes who executed Ed Jones?" She'd wandered over to a display that focused on the night of the murder, stopping to study a grim, grainy, black-and-white photograph credited to the *Hungry Valley Weekly*. It showed a single Ku Klux Klan member in white hood and long, white robe, standing next to Ed Jones's limp body, which hung by the neck from a rope strung to a jail rafter. Jones had been a wiry man of medium height, not quite forty, with pronounced Negroid facial features and skin that looked as dark as coal, even beneath the pallor of death. His eyes were open wide in shock, or maybe stunned disbelief that the mob wasn't simply trying to frighten him, but really meant to take his life; the camera had recorded a wet spot on the front of his wrinkled trousers, his final degradation.

"Father was forced to take that picture." Tiemeyer stood at Templeton's shoulder, speaking softly. "They came up here to the hotel not long after midnight, dressed in white hoods and robes. Ordered my father to get his camera, took him away at gunpoint down to the jail. Forced him to shoot that photo. They threatened to hurt mother and me if he didn't do what they asked. He didn't have much choice."

"You were lucky," Templeton said.

"How's that, Miss Templeton?"

"Lynch mobs sometimes hanged people simply for being opposed to lynching, or for trying to protect the targets, particularly blacks. It accounts for a sizable percentage of whites who were lynched in the South during the nineteenth century." She glanced over at Tiemeyer. "You were there when they took your father away?"

"I was up at the house, in my upstairs bedroom. After giving my statement to my Uncle Jack about what I'd seen—"

"Jack Hightower, the local sheriff," I said.

Tiemeyer nodded. "After I spoke to Uncle Jack, mother saw how upset I was and ordered me to bed. But I saw them from my window as they took my father away. I wanted to get his gun and go after them to stop them, but mother wouldn't let me. She said it was better to let things take their course. 'God will take care of it'—that's what she said."

"How many were there?" Templeton asked. "Richard Pearlman's book was vague."

"Several men came up to the house for my father but most of the others were gone by the time they reached the jail." Tiemeyer pointed to the photo of the hanging. "Only this one wanted his picture taken. The others were afraid there would be an investigation and they might somehow be identified."

"I thought the KKK was more brazen than that," I said.

"This was 1956," Templeton said, apparently citing from her research. "And it wasn't the Deep South, where the Klan had once had such widespread influence. If anything, the KKK in Eternal Springs was a weak remnant left over from the 1920s, when the Klan had genuine political power out west."

Tiemeyer glanced at her sympathetically. "I'm sorry you had to see this, Miss Templeton."

Her eyes swung toward his. "Why? Because I'm black?"

He shrugged awkwardly. "Well—"

"It should be troubling to anyone, Mr. Tiemeyer." Her voice became more conciliatory as she studied the photo again. "I'm glad you have it up. I admire you for including it in the history of the town. One sees a lot of these historic photos—black men hanging from nooses, usually from trees. But one rarely sees their names in the captions. I suppose most people don't really want to know who they were." Templeton smiled, though not pleasantly. "It's easier to forget them that way, isn't it?"

The three of us studied the remaining photos in silence. The most disturbing to me was a crime scene photo of Rebecca Fox sprawled on the floor of her hotel room, a pool of blood beneath her slashed throat. Even in death she looked good for the camera, her face unmarked, her hair and makeup in place. It might have been a movie still from an old *noir* flick, I thought, snapped moments before she got to her feet and went home for a relaxing highball and bubble bath. Nearby was a photo of her daughter, Brandy, taken on the set of a B movie in 1972 as she signed an autograph book for a fan, a stylish Mont Blanc pen poised in her left hand. Next to it was a photo that apparently had been cropped and blown up from a larger crime scene photo; it showed only her left hand and forearm as she clutched the knife she'd used to kill herself, the edge of the blade turned outward, slick with blood. A caption noted that Brandy had cut her own throat on the same side—the left—on which her mother had suffered a similar wound from her assailant twenty-five years earlier.

"Not very pleasant, I'm afraid," Tiemeyer said. "These aren't the most grisly photos, however. Even Dad wouldn't publish those, though it might have sold more newspapers."

Templeton glanced at her watch. "You told me we could sit down for a formal interview, Mr. Tiemeyer. Would this be a good time?"

"Yes, now would be fine. We can go to my office if you'd like." Tiemeyer turned to me. "Coming along, Mr. Justice? Or would you like to stay a bit longer and see more?" He mentioned exhibits in the other rooms on local geology, wildlife, and Native-American history. "There's a stuffed bobcat that might interest you, and a desert fox, and a couple of other creatures that we don't see much of around here anymore."

"I'll stay awhile," I said, "if it's not a problem."

He removed a key from a set, handed it to me, and asked me to lock up on my way out. I watched them go, then returned to the gallery of photos focusing on the doomed Fox family. The people, not the animals.

TEN

The archival image that drew me back was of Rebecca Fox with Kevin Tiemeyer, taken the day before she died, when he was seventeen.

They were huddled in the hotel bar—he must have sneaked in when his mother was out—while the actress autographed a cocktail napkin. The actual napkin was displayed next to the photo, framed with its graceful inscription: *To My Good Friend Kevin, With Love Forever, Rebecca.* And the date: *March 14, 1956.*

I glanced again at the photograph of Brent Fox, taken while he was in his U.S. Army uniform twelve years earlier, at the age of twenty-seven. Again, his general resemblance to Kevin Tiemeyer caught my eye—the slender build, the narrow, handsome face, the attractive dark mustache that Tiemeyer would also cultivate when he was older. The similarity between the two men was especially evident in the photo from the hotel bar, as the seventeen-year-old Tiemeyer secretly studied Rebecca Fox, looking captivated.

"Beautiful, wasn't she?"

I turned to find Toni Pebbles sidling up beside me on my right, her emerald eyes sparkling seductively as they had in the old days, when she'd pegged me wrongly for a possible bedmate. In her heels, she topped my six feet by an inch or so, and carried all of it with a heft and sensuality that seemed part and parcel of the whole package. She had to be pushing sixty, I thought, but she'd taken care of herself, and used makeup skillfully. I felt her left breast press against my arm, a technique she'd favored back then, when she'd found certain men drinking at the bar after L.A. Press Club meetings, using her body to cut through the small talk and make her intentions crystal clear.

"Hello, Toni. Long time, no see."

"From what I hear, Justice, you don't see too well these days."

"Reasonably well, but only with one eye now."

"I guess you've been kicked around and carved up pretty good in recent years, letting that hero complex of yours get you into some nasty scrapes."

"I've had a few misadventures, but I'm still in one piece."

She looked me up and down appreciatively. "Not a bad-looking piece, either, from my perspective. I'd take a roll with you, if you were in the mood." A playful look crept into her eyes, but it was more mean than mischievous. "Oh, that's right, you prefer boys, don't you?"

"Men, actually." I glanced at her left hand but didn't see a ring. "Aren't you spoken for, Toni? The last I heard, you were married to a short, fat, bald man with a lot of money, about two decades older than you. Isn't that why your byline disappeared? I heard you found that sugar daddy you were always looking for and finally settled down."

"Irving died," she said, matter-of-factly, "but he wasn't fixed as well as he'd led me to believe. I got what there was, but I put too much of it in the dot-com boom."

"Back to freelancing, are you?"

"A girl's got to pay the bills."

"Not always easy getting reestablished, I guess. The old celebrities get cold, the connections dry up, the editors move on or retire. And the younger bottom-feeders move in to replace the dinosaurs like you, who haven't broken a good story since Hugh Grant got caught getting a blow job from a hooker. Meanwhile, the world of gossip is all TV and sound bites and split-second graphics. Which doesn't leave too many high-paying print assignments for an old warhorse like you, does it?"

She brushed her brunette curls off one shoulder with a show of indignance. "There are still a few publications out there paying several bucks a word for the right story."

"Written by thirtysomethings for readers even younger."

Her eyes grew steely, her voice tough. "The name Toni Pebbles still means something in the business."

"If the right people remember it," I said.

"If they don't, I'll remind them."

"Is that why you're here in Haunted Springs, Toni? Looking to score an exclusive off a Hollywood closet case, and get your byline noticed again?"

"Why not? If it works out." She ran the backs of her fingers up my face, stroking my three o'clock shadow. "Maybe I'll even get laid while I'm here. You man enough, Justice? Or do real women still scare you away?"

"What's on your mind, Toni? Besides busting any balls that might be handy."

I felt her hand drop away, sensed the gears shifting behind her calculating eyes. "I was wondering if you'd do a favor for an old friend."

"You and I were never friends, not even close."

"We had a few laughs, didn't we?"

"Only when I'd had too much to drink, which doesn't happen anymore."

"I'd make it worth your while, Justice. I'd see what I could do for you down the road, when I'm back on top again. And I do plan to get back on top."

"I couldn't picture you in any other position, Toni."

She smirked at that. "You curious about the favor I want, or not?"

"Let me take a wild guess. You've seen me chumming around with some of the principals in the movie they're shooting here. You want to use me to get to someone, maybe convince them to sit down with you and open a vein while you have your tape recorder running. Come out of the closet on their own so they don't look so pathetic being exposed against their will. Stop me if I'm getting cold, Toni."

"You've always been good at staying one step ahead, haven't you?"

"Don't give me too much credit. You're not that difficult to figure out."

"So," she said, "will you help me out, or not?"

"I'll pass, if it's all the same. I've never had much stomach for your kind of reporting, if that's what it is."

"Awfully high and mighty, aren't we, for someone with your history? Benjamin Justice, the reporter who had to FedEx his trophy back to the Pulitzer people."

"Actually, I delivered it in person. Unfortunately, I was roaring drunk at the time. Puked all over myself as they threw me out."

"Charming anecdote. I'll remember it if I ever write a story about you."

"Definitely a low point on my résumé. Still, I never stooped to dragging queers from the closet for a buck. At least I've got that."

"Since when did you start defending closet queens, Justice? Aren't you supposed to be the great champion of the truth? You and your buddy Templeton?"

"I've got an idea, Toni. Why don't you write about your own truth?"

She stiffened, and her voice didn't sound so sure of itself. "Why would I want to do that?"

"I don't know—therapy, maybe? You could put down all your dirty little secrets on paper, reveal yourself, warts and all. The insecurity and envy that drives you, the resentment you have for anyone who's more successful than you, or who gets more attention. The kick you get hurting and humiliating people. How it makes you feel powerful, at least for a little while, before you start to feel small and unworthy again, and need another power fix by airing someone else's dirty laundry, while making sure your own is safely stashed away."

"No one's interested in me, Justice. I'm just a boring feature writer, a sad little wallflower at the orgy."

"On the contrary, Toni, I think you're fascinating, like a lot of people who end up reporting on Hollywood. You started out wanting to be in the business yourself. Maybe you wanted to be a screenwriter or a producer, maybe even a director or an actress. Only you didn't have the talent or the discipline. So you ended up writing about people who succeeded in a business where you failed. Some writers who end up that way fawn all over the people they write about. Some find professional balance and use their passion for the industry to write about it thoughtfully and perceptively. And some end up like you, unable to get past their envy and bitterness, and spend their lives writing hatchet jobs to get even. Now that's a Hollywood story I'd read, Toni, if someone were willing to write it honestly. Why not you, since nobody's closer to it than you are?"

She'd glared at me through my entire diatribe, letting me spew. Now a small, self-satisfied smile transformed her features, and she closed the trap she'd set for me. "Because nailing a Hollywood big shot is so much more fun."

Her eyes were confident and steady again, as if she knew where one of *my* secrets was buried, or at least one of my weaknesses. I swallowed uneasily, trying to hide it. "So who do you have your sights set on this time, Toni? Whose career are you intent on ruining by revealing their homosexuality to all the losers out there who lap up the drivel you write? No offense intended, of course."

"You don't really think your insults bother me, do you, Justice?"

"No, but they make me feel better. So who is it that you've got in your crosshairs?"

"I'm not telling unless you agree to work with me."

"I take it you have concrete evidence—photographs, a diary, personal letters, an affidavit from a lover, something like that."

"You know I wouldn't waste my time if I didn't."

"If you have what you say you do, why not just use that? Why do you need me?"

"You came up here with Alexandra Templeton. You're on the inside, and I'm not. God knows why, but some of the people involved with this film seem to trust you."

"You want me to grease the wheels for you, help you get your interview."

"I want the confession, Justice. Otherwise, an exposé just looks cheap and petty, the kind of secondhand crap the tabloids print. I offer my subject the chance to come out voluntarily, to do it with class. And it makes my article worth a lot more money, the kind of piece that grabs some attention from the mainstream press. Nobody pays attention to the tabloids anymore, even when they get it right. Nobody who matters, anyway."

"Either way, the actor's career takes a hit."

"They might survive. You never know."

"I always knew you had a soft spot in you, Toni."

"So which is it, Justice? Yes or no?"

"I'm afraid you'll have to find someone else to go gutter-crawling with you. I don't handle the stench as well as you do."

"If you change your mind, you know where to find me."

"Room 418?"

She nodded, then squeezed one of my biceps, letting her hand linger. "Shall I keep the sheets warm? In case you get lonely and change your mind about that too?"

"I'll never be that lonely, Toni. Besides, I never sleep with anyone over fifty."

She showed me a sour smile but was apparently tired of the battle, because a moment later, without another word, she was headed out the door. I followed, locking up behind me, wondering who her target was and what kind of ammunition she had, and surprised that it mattered to me as much as it did.

ELEVEN

I hadn't given much thought to the issue of "outing" for years, but it weighed heavily on my mind as I strolled back to the Haunted Springs Hotel after my unpleasant encounter with Toni Pebbles. Suddenly, I was awash with questions and feelings that had once torn at me, both as a journalist and a gay man, just as the more troubling subject of lynching must have emerged from the past to shake up Alexandra Templeton as she covered the filming of *A Murder in Eternal Springs*.

Outing—publicly exposing closeted celebrities and public figures—got its start in the United States in early 1989, when a militant New York gay weekly called *OutWeek* coined the term and hatched it as a potent new political weapon in the struggle for gay rights. I'd been a reporter in my early thirties then, working at the *Los Angeles Times*, as outing first struck terror in the hearts of the country's most prominent closet cases, especially those in Hollywood, where so many had managed to keep their private lives under the radar for so long, abetted by a cooperative press. At the time, as an openly gay man, I felt little sympathy for those who cowered in the closet, validating the shame, especially when AIDS was killing gay men by the thousands and we needed all the visibility and political clout we could muster. I was disheartened by closet queens who took advantage of the progress others had forged, often at great personal risk, but who were unwilling themselves to stand up and be counted, whatever their excuses about the potential harm to their fabulous careers and incomes. Yet I also believed in an individual's right to privacy and to come out in their own time and in their own way, if they chose to. It was a personal choice that even many hard-core gay militants supported, since most of them had once been closeted themselves and knew how painful publicly declaring one's homosexuality could be at the outset.

To this I made two exceptions: First, if a closet case was directly harming queers by actively supporting antigay causes and positions, especially in the political arena, I felt they'd surrendered their immunity and deserved to be exposed for the liars and hypocrites they were; second, if a closeted celebrity deliberately tried to mislead the public, particularly by using the media to distort the truth, to my mind he or she was fair game. Anyone, I figured, could offer a "no comment" to invasive questions about their private life, as some closeted stars had, with no apparent backlash to their popularity. But no one had the right to deceive and use a reporter to help propagate a lie, no matter what lengths they went to attempting to justify it.

However one felt about outing, there was no denying its impact, in concert with other forces within the gay movement. As famous gay figures were forced from their closets, outing affected the way mainstream media treated gay issues, made it easier for others to come out on their own, and helped transform the public's perception of homosexuality in general. A quiet revolution was taking place in families, newsrooms, corporate boardrooms, the halls of Congress, even churches. Editors and reporters no longer handled gay subject matter with tweezers and latex gloves, as if it was inherently filthy. Gay entertainment executives could openly support gay-themed projects without the fear of being suspected and ostracized. Miserable gay kids who might have been contemplating suicide finally had role models to look up to—prominent and successful queers living their lives openly and without apology. Prior to outing in 1989, it was difficult to name a celebrity of much stature who was openly gay; today, you could count dozens in the fields of music, stage, movies, and TV, and countless others who work behind the scenes.

No major stars though.

That was the last bastion of homosexual shame and secrecy in Hollywood—those leading men and women who made their fortunes in romantic or action roles on the big screen and feared the gay label. Plenty of character and comedic actors had come out over the years with little or no damage to their careers, but not a single bankable star whose career was still thriving. Conventional wisdom had it that to survive as action heroes and romantic leads, they depended on their appeal to heterosexual fantasies and their ability to keep the cinema's fragile illusion intact. At a time when the public's appetite for scandal seemed insatiable, many believed that the lucrative career of a closeted star could be engulfed and destroyed if their sexual orientation suddenly became public knowledge. Star careers in Hollywood were like small business empires; they supported and made a lot of people rich. Agents, managers, lawyers, and publicists went to great lengths to protect closeted clients from exposure, operating in a near constant state of vigilance and fear.

That's why a vicious gossipmonger like Toni Pebbles seemed so dangerous to certain people that day as she nosed around Haunted Springs, sniffing for a big story on the ides of March.

Pebbles entered the hotel a few strides ahead of me, disappearing across the lobby and into a stairwell toward the upper floors. Not half a minute later I saw the stuntman, Scotty Campbell, reach up to push the elevator button on the ground floor and step in, heading in the same direction.

The last of the TV crews were heading home with the sound bites and images that would flood the airwaves for days and weeks to come, as the networks milked every drop they could get from the love match between Heather Sparks and Christopher Oakley.

If there'd been vacancies at the hotel, I imagine some of the field producers would have hung around for another day or two to see what else they could scrounge up. But the rooms were all taken, so they climbed into their big vans and gas-guzzling SUVs and headed down twisting Coyote Canyon Road before dusk settled over the Lost Hills.

I stopped briefly at the edge of the lounge to listen to Richard Pearlman, who was giving a talk about the Rebecca Fox murder while hawking copies of *A Murder in Eternal Springs*. They were stacked high on a table beside him; nearby, a large poster was propped up on an easel, duplicating the book's cover and flaunting several favorable blurbs from critics. Pearlman had reached the final minutes of his program and was winding down. For his last illustration, he displayed a grisly autopsy photo that caused a number of people in the audience to groan and look away. It showed a ragged gash, not all that deep, on the left side of the victim's neck, a badly managed butcher job that had left her lovely alabaster skin torn and shredded. Unlike the photo of a dead Rebecca Fox in Kevin Tiemeyer's little museum, this one was a close-up, and more revealing.

"I realize how ugly this image is," Pearlman said, in his high-mannered way. "But this is what murder looks like, ladies and gentlemen, in all its horrifying dimensions."

Next, he capably summarized the DNA analysis done on the victim's panties nearly five decades after the crime, which had proved that the semen found on it could not have belonged to Ed Jones. This didn't prove Jones innocent of murder, Pearlman pointed out, but it did suggest that someone else might have done it, which left the crime unsolved. He saved his last two minutes for a final tribute to the talent and beauty of Rebecca Fox, speaking of her the way religious zealots go on rapturously about their chosen gods and icons. After that came innocuous questions from the audience, followed by the obligatory applause and, finally, the author happily autographing copies of his book for a long line of eager readers.

I turned away, that image from Rebecca Fox's autopsy stuck in my mind like a wad of gum on a new leather sole, aggravating and impossible to ignore.

By late afternoon, Templeton and I were on the third floor, huddled behind Lois Aswell and her cinematographer as the director prepared to shoot the last scene of the day, using my room to double for the one above that was unavailable. Zeke Zeidler, who'd invited us to observe the shooting, stood with us. Richard Pearlman and the publicist, Karen Hori, were also close by.

The shot involved Christopher Oakley and Deep Freeze playing their respective characters at that point in the script—Kevin Tiemeyer at seventeen and Ed Jones as he neared forty, exactly fifty years ago. Since the scene was set at night, any visible windows had been covered and the curtains tightly drawn, while the lighting crew had taken pains to keep the illumination low. People and objects would be essentially visible yet slightly obscured, Zeidler told us, which would not only create the illusion of night, coinciding with the actual events, but also help Oakley pass for a teenager.

True to her meticulous nature, Aswell had done some period research and dimmed the antiquated lighting along the hallway even further, to replicate the lower wattage of earlier decades. The script called for the Tiemeyer character to approach Rebecca Fox's room with an order of hot tea before pulling up when he sees Ed Jones emerge, closely following Tiemeyer's own account of what he'd observed that night. Aswell had asked Tiemeyer to stand a few feet behind Oakley, out of camera range but with a vantage point that would allow him to watch the scene unfold from Oakley's POV, again for purposes of accuracy. To record the scene from different perspectives, a camera had been placed inside the room and at each end of the hall. There would be no spoken words; everything had to be expressed in the posture and movements of the two actors, since their facial features would be obscured in the modest light.

The assistant director called for quiet, Aswell called for action, and the cameras rolled.

Oakley moved expectantly down the hallway from the far end, carrying a tray with a teapot and cup, on his way to deliver his order. Just ahead, a figure appeared, coming out the door of Room 418—actually my room, with the first digit of the room number temporarily changed from three to four. The figure was recognizable as a black man of modest height in knit cap and workingman's garb, but not much more than that. Staying in character, Oakley pulled up, startled by the sight of a Negro in a whites-only hotel. The dark-skinned man paused in the doorway, staring back into the room. He put his hands to his head as if in torment, looked around with the wide whites of his eyes indicating fright, pulled the door closed with a gloved hand, then turned and fled past the camera nearest us, and into the corner stairwell, racing down. Oakley approached the room curiously, knocking on the door and calling, "Miss Fox? Miss Fox, I have your tea."

At that point, Aswell hollered for a cut in the action, telling the crew to get ready for another take, while offering a couple of notes about what might be done differently. Tiemeyer approached from down the hall, looking pleased. The director asked him if she'd blocked and shot the scene properly, according to what he'd seen that night fifty years ago.

"It was very well done, Miss Aswell. Really, I have no complaints."

"And you're happy with the performances? Deep Freeze seems right as Ed Jones?"

"Very much so. Both actors did an admirable job. It was just as I remember it."

"And you were watching closely?"

"Oh, yes. You've truly recaptured that moment, I must say."

"That's interesting," Aswell said. "Because Deep Freeze wasn't in the shot."

"I beg your pardon?"

She turned to the stairwell, where the figure dressed as Ed Jones stepped from the shadows. As he approached, and we got a closer look, we realized it was Sweet Doctor Silk, Deep Freeze's tough-looking buddy. A few steps behind was Deep Freeze himself, grinning like the cat that ate the canary.

"We used a stand-in," Aswell explained. "A little experiment I wanted to put to the test."

Tiemeyer looked bewildered. "Whatever on earth for?"

"I wanted to duplicate the real-life scene as closely as possible, to test the accuracy of what you claimed to see that night." Tiemeyer looked dismayed, but said nothing. "I've been tinkering with the script," Aswell went on. "I've decided to tell the story from different perspectives, in the style of *Rashomon*. Do you know it—the film by Kurosawa?" Tiemeyer nodded weakly, staying quiet. "I'm sure you *thought* you saw Ed Jones that night fifty years ago, Mr. Tiemeyer. But now it seems at least possible that you were mistaken. Wouldn't you agree?"

"Because you honkies think all niggers look alike," Deep Freeze said. The edge in his voice was softened by an underlying playfulness and a twinkle in his eyes that suggested he was enjoying himself to no end. "It's just like I been saying all along in my songs. If you don't fight for yourself and your people, the white man will crush you like a miserable worm every chance he gets."

"That's awfully harsh," Karen Hori said.

"Yeah?" Deep Freeze turned on her, all the playfulness gone. "Maybe you should ask Ed Jones if it's harsh."

Tiemeyer stared at the rapper a moment, then at Aswell. "I—I thought we had an understanding. About how the story would be told."

"Film is a fluid medium, Kevin. To some extent, a script is always in flux, until the final take. Then comes editing. One makes discoveries along the way."

His troubled eyes seemed to lose their focus and his narrow shoulders sagged. He dropped his head, turned, and ambled away on his long legs, down the hallway to the far stairwell and out of sight.

Aswell clapped her hands twice. "Let's set up for another take!"

The crew scrambled about its work, making the ordered adjustments. I stepped to the railing and saw Kevin Tiemeyer emerge three stories down. He appeared even more stooped than before, almost broken. He crossed the lobby toward the club room without looking up, lengthening his stride, making a beeline straight for the bar.

TWELVE

Following Lois Aswell's experiment involving the Ed Jones character, a new sense of purpose seemed to settle over the production. For the most part, the wisecracks and horsing around were gone, as if cast and crew had suddenly been reminded of the film's gravity during its remaining days in Coyote Canyon, where Ed Jones had died so horribly, struggling for breath at the end of a hangman's rope.

Templeton was intrigued by the turn of events, and excited that she'd been there to witness it. It played perfectly into the piece she'd be writing, helping her to focus on the issues she considered most important. It wouldn't have surprised me if she were to use the incident with the stand-in as the lead for her article—an attention-grabbing anecdote captured in the heat of production that etched the racial angle in sharp relief.

For the remainder of the day, Kevin Tiemeyer all but disappeared. We spotted him once or twice skulking around with a drink in hand, but no longer saw him behind the front desk, attending to guests with his characteristic hospitality; he left that to a much younger underling, one of the local residents he was able to lure to work in his understaffed hotel. Tiemeyer had planned a special dinner presentation for the Rebecca Fox Memorial Fan Club that night in which he was to recall his memories of Rebecca

Fox and her daughter, Brandy, and the events surrounding their deaths; Templeton and I dropped in to listen, but Tiemeyer canceled without explanation. The club's president, a heavily powdered older woman draped in a gown she'd purchased decades ago from the Rebecca Fox estate, filled in as best she could. She made much of the fact that the actress had worn the gown in her most famous picture, *January Heat,* while confessing that she'd had to let it out more than once. After dinner, a screening of *January Heat* went on as scheduled, but Tiemeyer didn't attend, as had been anticipated. Late that night, around a quarter to eleven, as a number of us relaxed in the lounge, he finally appeared with a tumbler of bourbon, looking drunk and morose.

Without a word to anyone, he slid onto the bench at his piano, where he began playing *Rhapsody in Blue* while staring vacantly at the flickering logs in the fireplace.

A minute or two later, Christopher Oakley and Heather Sparks passed through on their way upstairs, coming from a stroll in the crisp night air. They were holding hands and nuzzling in a way that struck me as too obvious, but perhaps they were just flaunting their heterosexuality the way so many straight people do. As they bid us good night, Oakley slid a discreet glance in my direction like a clever thief eying something he wanted, but biding his time. I didn't chalk it up to my vanity or imagination and dismiss it as I had before; fleeting as it was, his look was too direct and deliberate for that.

Aswell excused herself soon after, reminding everyone that it was after eleven and an early crew call was scheduled in the morning. On her way out, she stuck her head into the dining room, where Zeke Zeidler and Karen Hori were huddled in earnest discussion. Nan Williams, who'd been boasting about her daughter's acting talents to anyone who would listen, sent Audrey upstairs to bed and found a chair closer to the piano; she took her glass of white wine with her—her third since dinner, when she'd had at least two—and perched herself on one arm of the chair to steal glances at Kevin Tiemeyer as his long fingers moved with fluid skill across the keyboard.

Scotty Campbell, sitting on a couch, jumped down and drained his mug of ale. "I guess we made it through the ides of March without another corpse showing up," he said, clearly looking to stir people awake. "Maybe the curse ends this year at two."

"I think you mean three, don't you?" The gruff voice was that of Deep Freeze, sitting alone near a window not far from the fireplace, dressed for show in his burgundy cape and green felt fedora. "A black man lost his life, remember? Or do only the two white bitches count?"

"Actually," Templeton said, "Ed Jones died after midnight, technically on March sixteenth. Maybe that's why Scotty excluded him."

The rapper cast a surly glance at her, but it didn't look like it had much genuine feeling behind it. "I'd expect that from a token who works for the *L.A. Times.*" Deep Freeze seemed to be playing his usual game, trying to keep everyone on edge and off-balance. He suggested that a better name for the movie was *A Hanging in Eternal Springs,* and that it should be rewritten from the point of view of Ed Jones, with Deep Freeze as its leading man. That generated some good-natured laughter and ribbing, causing him to grumble, "You can laugh, but how often do you see a black man starring in a movie that ain't a comedy or action picture?"

"Count your blessings," Scotty Campbell said good-naturedly. "At least you're not black *and* vertically challenged."

That drew laughter, but Deep Freeze shrugged it off without a reply, turning to stare petulantly out the window. Campbell led a procession to the bar, and Pearlman invited Templeton to join them, as he had the night before. She glanced my way but I shook my head and covered a yawn with one hand. While she and Pearlman adjourned to their nightcaps, I rose and headed for the stairs, glancing at a clock behind the front desk that put the time at a few minutes past eleven.

Behind me, the lobby and lounge were nearly deserted. Deep Freeze was still hunched in solitary silence by the window, staring out. Zeidler and Hori could be seen in the dining room, their heads together as they continued hashing out whatever it was that was so important to them. Nan Williams remained poised on the arm of her chair, gazing with moony eyes at Kevin Tiemeyer like the last woman in a straight bar at closing time sending a message of desperation to the last man. Otherwise, the lobby and lounge were empty. Even the front desk was unattended.

The logs in the fireplace collapsed into embers as Tiemeyer continued his uninterrupted cycle of *Rhapsody in Blue*, playing it over and over as if he was lost in the music, or maybe lost somewhere in time.

In my room, I brushed my teeth, cracked the window for some air, and knocked off another two chapters of Pearlman's book before another yawn told me it was time to get some shut-eye.

As I went to draw the curtains, I looked out to see the moon shimmering off Lake Enid and casting its pale light across the distant hills. That's when I noticed the lady in white again, just below my window, standing in the shadow of Whispering Rock—the same flimsy white dress, the same tangle of long, white hair, the same pale, stricken eyes staring up past my room to the one above. One of the locals, I figured, sadly in need of therapy and medication.

I drew the curtains, killed the light, crawled into bed, and drifted into an uneasy sleep.

I've always been a light sleeper, so it wasn't surprising when I woke to the sound of thumping overhead.

I pricked up my ears in the dark and heard the commotion grow briefly louder and more frenzied before the sound of hurried footsteps, followed by silence. After that, for the better part of a minute, I heard nothing more out of the ordinary and told myself it was none of my business, anyway. I rolled over and closed my eyes, but only long enough—a minute or two—to know that I wouldn't go back to sleep unless I checked upstairs. In my gut, I knew what I'd heard didn't sound right. Some people have no problem ignoring odd sounds in the night and falling back to sleep. Unfortunately, I'm not one of them.

I switched on the light and pulled on my pants, shirt, and shoes. A minute after that I was in the southeast stairwell, climbing to the fourth floor. As I emerged, the hallway leading to the Rebecca Fox room was empty. Down below in the dimly lit lobby, Kevin Tiemeyer had abandoned the piano. Nan Williams was also gone. Deep Freeze, it appeared, had commandeered the Steinway. Pouring forth was an old blues number, pounded out with surprising feeling, while the rapper's fedora and golden feather bobbed to the music and his cape trailed out beneath him on the floor.

Just before knocking, I realized Toni Pebbles might mistake my concern for an overture of another kind, and I experienced a change of heart. I decided to return and call her from my room, keeping some distance between us. At least I'd know she was alright and I could settle back down for a decent night's sleep. But as I turned away and approached the stairwell, a small figure stepped suddenly out, giving me a bad start.

It was Scotty Campbell, with a bottle of wine and two glasses in his hands.

"Sorry," I said. "I thought I was alone up here."

"You were, until I came up."

"I heard a noise coming from the room above mine. Thought I'd come up and check."

"Room 418?" I nodded. "What kind of noise?"

"I'm not sure. I was going to knock, make sure the occupant was okay."

"So why didn't you?"

He stepped past me on his stubby legs and waddled down the hall. I started after him but he had his knuckles on the door before I got there. While I stood above him, the top of his head roughly at my waist, he rapped on the wood a couple of times. There was no answer and he was about to knock again when he realized the door was ajar. We exchanged glances and he pushed it open.

A small lamp was on at a writing desk, the only light in the room. But it was enough for us to see Toni Pebbles sprawled face-up over her writing desk, her throat slashed cleanly and deeply and her eyes open wide in death.

Somewhere in the hotel a clock struck midnight, chiming once to signal the end of the ides of March.

THIRTEEN

I heard the distant chime of the clock as I kept my eyes on the motionless form of Toni Pebbles, staring wide-eyed and unblinking at the ceiling of Room 418.

"Stay outside." I raised a hand toward Scotty Campbell, who looked as uneasy as I felt. "No need for both of us to be in this room. It's a crime scene now."

Campbell took a compliant step back, looking suspicious, while I took a few careful steps in. I placed two fingers on the side of Pebbles's throat that was intact, then pinched one of her wrists between my thumb and forefinger.

"No pulse," I said.

Campbell stood at the threshold of the door, peering in. "You got experience with this kind of thing?"

"Some."

I glanced around the room, then checked the closet to make sure we were alone. I asked Campbell if he was carrying a cell phone to call 911. He wasn't, so I suggested he alert Kevin Tiemeyer and have him make the call, on the double.

"Why don't you use the phone right there?" Campbell said, nodding toward a phone on a nightstand. "Save some time."

"Fingerprints. It's a crime scene, remember?"

"Maybe you should go make the call, and I'll stay, keep an eye on things until the cops get here."

"I'm already inside, Scotty. No point in another person or pair of shoes disturbing the surfaces."

He studied me skeptically for a moment. Then he glanced at Toni Pebbles's body again, his high forehead creased in a deep frown, and headed off, still carrying his bottle of wine and two glasses.

I surveyed the room quickly, taking mental notes.

Toni Pebbles was fully dressed in a heavy red sweater, tight black skirt, and pearl gray pumps. By the look of it, the slash on her neck was deep enough to sever a carotid artery and cause death. Still, the pool of blood below her neck on the desktop was modest, not the copious amount, for example, that I'd seen in the crime scene photo from the Rebecca Fox murder. There was no sign of a knife or other sharp weapon left behind, no muddy footprints, nothing obvious like that.

Logic dictated only two ways in and out: the door and the window. The window was half open, just enough to allow passage for a very small person. As I stepped over for a closer look, I glanced down to see if the strange woman in the white dress might still be there, staring up. She was gone. Outside, just below the window, was an ornamental ledge about a foot wide that a small person might traverse, if he or she had excellent balance and nerves of steel. I recalled seeing vertical drain spouts at the corners of the hotel connected to the rooftop rain gutters, a possible means of escape for someone willing to risk their neck clambering up or down. There were also fire escapes near each corner stairwell.

Inside the room the bed was made up, but the bedspread was rumpled in a way that suggested Pebbles might have recently stretched out for a nap. A chair was pushed in at the writing desk, which appeared tidy, if you discounted the corpse and the blood that had drained from the neck wound. On a corner of the desk a small tape recorder had been set out and plugged in. A hotel notepad lay on the floor near the nightstand. I kneeled for a closer look. In the lamplight I could just make out the indented outline of a phone number on the top slip of paper, apparently left when someone had torn away the previous slip. I glanced in the waste can and saw a couple of tissues blotted with lipstick but no crumpled piece of notepad paper, which suggested someone might have taken it with them. I studied the outlined numbers again, scrawled the number on another notepad from the writing desk, tore off the top several slips of paper and shoved them all into my pocket to avoid leaving a trace of my own handwriting behind. The number came with a Los Angeles area code—213—and a prefix that suggested Hollywood, if my memory was any good.

I was taking a last look around when I spotted an open valise in a corner. It was on the floor next to a chair; a woman's jacket was draped over the arm of the chair, partially hiding the valise from view; it wasn't something someone in a hurry would have noticed. I knelt, pinching the edge of the coat and lifting it just enough to see the contents: roughly a dozen file folders, some of which bore handwritten headings that duplicated a number of familiar names from the film in production: Lois Aswell, Margaret Loyd Langley, Christopher Oakley, Heather Sparks, Audrey Williams, Nan Williams, Zeke Zeidler. Margaret Loyd Langley, the actress cast as Rebecca Fox, was the only one among them I hadn't met. There was also a file slugged with a name I didn't recognize: Percy Childs. The folders were thick with papers and arranged alphabetically, reminding me that however much Toni Pebbles had been reviled as a feature writer who specialized in hatchet jobs, she'd been a pro.

The Christopher Oakley file nagged at me like a bad habit. I knew I had no business fretting over what might be inside—no justification to even be in this room, really—but the folder drew me closer just the same. The instinct to snoop had been bred into me since my earliest years—my old man had been a homicide detective, after all—and my later years as an investigative reporter had transformed me into a human bloodhound. But my curiosity about the Oakley file felt different, and just a bit dangerous. I was in the grip of something I couldn't quite define, yet I knew it had to do with loneliness and longing, and the pressures those confusing emotions can exert, encouraging a weak person to take chances he shouldn't. I'd already taken a small risk by copying down the phone number I'd discovered indented on the notepad, which fell somewhere between innocent meddling and tampering with a police investigation. Removing a bulky file folder from a crime scene was another kind of gamble altogether. Yet I was acutely aware of what Toni Pebbles had been capable of as a journalist, that she'd been as heartless at her work as she was good at it. I figured that if these files were ever entered into evidence at a murder trial, they'd become public record, open to every prying eye out there. I also realized that the only file that concerned me was the one with Christopher Oakley's name on it.

I glanced cautiously toward the doorway, felt the anxiety rising in me like a fast tide, and reached for the folder. Just as my fingertips touched the edge of the file, I heard a clamor and commotion in the hallway, coming in my direction. I withdrew my empty hand, let the coat fall back over the valise, rose, and stepped to the door, knowing I'd waited a second too long and unsure whether to feel angry with myself, or relieved.

I saw Templeton and Pearlman first, leading the charge from the stairwell. They were followed closely by Kevin Tiemeyer, with Scotty Campbell lumbering along, trying to keep up on his little legs. From the lobby, distantly, I heard a few more blues notes from the piano trail off into silence. Deep Freeze appeared a minute later, as I was filling the others in about what I'd observed, at least the details I wanted to share, which included the news that Toni Pebbles was most surely dead and beyond saving. The usually fastidious Tiemeyer was so distraught he seemed ignorant or unconcerned about the smudge of pink lipstick on his white shirt collar. He was intent on entering the room to see the body for himself, but I stood my ground, keeping everyone out.

"Believe me," I said, "it's not a pleasant sight. No reason to look if you don't need to."

Deep Freeze craned his neck for a gander anyway and said matter-of-factly, "I seen plenty of dead people, growing up in the 'hood. This ain't nothing special, man." Yet the look on his face as he viewed the mutilated corpse suggested at least a touch of queasiness. "Man, somebody really did a job on the bitch."

Heather Sparks and Christopher Oakley were the next to arrive. Against my advice, they glanced in at the body and the blood, and sparks erupted into screams loud enough to wake any hotel guests who might still be asleep. Oakley took her aside, wrapping his arms around her, while she sobbed on his shoulder. As word spread through the hotel, guests started crowding the landings or climbing the stairs for a closer look. At my suggestion, Tiemeyer stationed himself at one end of the hallway and asked the president of the Rebecca Fox Memorial Fan Club to stand at the other, stopping anyone else from coming up, while assuring them that the police had been notified.

Lois Aswell pushed her way through, anyway, followed in short order by Zeke Zeidler and Karen Hori. Nan Williams appeared a minute after that, buttoning her sweater, her pink lipstick a mess.

Oakley mentioned pointedly that he and Heather Sparks had been together in her bedroom for the past hour, which struck me as odd, because no one had asked him. That triggered a flurry of defensive statements. Nan Williams blurted out that she'd been in her room with Kevin Tiemeyer, discussing Martha Frech, the little girl Audrey Williams was playing in the movie; Mrs. Williams explained, rather too earnestly, that she often did "personal research" to help her daughter with her roles. Pearlman announced that he and Templeton had been together in the bar, among numerous witnesses. Zeidler waved his cane for a turn, declaring that he and Hori had been in the dining room, discussing "a serious publicity matter, should our whereabouts ever become an issue." Deep Freeze backed them up, saying he could see them from where he sat at the piano, as he ran through a few old blues numbers to kill some time.

"Nothing better to do up here," he grumbled, "until my wife arrives this weekend to take care of my needs." He cupped a hand over his crotch and looked straight at Templeton, who laughed aloud and rolled her eyes. "You know you'd like some of this," he said, and kissed the air. "Don't pretend you don't, baby."

I asked Deep Freeze about the whereabouts of his buddy, Sweet Doctor Silk.

"Ask him yourself," he snarled. "I ain't his keeper. Anyway, where were you when the bitch got cut? I don't see nobody backing you up."

"He's right," Campbell said. "I saw you coming from this room when I got up here. You seemed pretty nervous when we bumped into each other down the hall."

"Because you startled me, coming out of the stairwell." I glanced at the others, dumping my alibi on the heap. "I was asleep. I heard something up here that didn't sound right. I waited a minute or two, then came up to see what it was about."

"If you were concerned, then why didn't you come up right away?"

"Same reason I hesitated to knock on her door, I suppose. Toni's not one of my favorite people. I wasn't looking forward to seeing her in the middle of the night."

"Sounds like you knew her," Pearlman said, suggestively.

"We were acquainted."

"On good terms?"

"We had our differences."

"So you don't have an alibi," Campbell said, looking up at me. "Not one that anybody can vouch for."

"Do you, Scotty?"

"You saw me coming up the stairs. I was on my way to see her."

"With a bottle of wine and two glasses?"

He hesitated, fidgeting. "She told me to drop by around midnight. We had a date. So what?"

The image of Toni Pebbles and Scotty Campbell entwined romantically was a striking one. I noticed a few of the others stifling laughter.

"So I like big women," Campbell said, the blood rising in his thick neck. "Is there some law against that?"

"Sounds kinda kinky to me," Deep Freeze said, keeping a straight face. "What if you fell in and nobody could find you?"

Campbell stepped over to him, his little fists clenched and the muscles bulging in his stumpy, powerful arms. "Zip it, pal. I may be small, but I don't take crap from you or anybody else."

"You've got quite a temper," I said.

He whirled on me, his fists still coiled. "So would you, if you had to take the kind of crap I've put up with my whole life."

"Maybe you were angry at Toni Pebbles for some reason," Pearlman suggested. "Maybe she'd spurned you earlier, because of your size."

"Believe me, buster, I've got plenty of size where it counts."

"Still," Deep Freeze said, smirking, "it doesn't look too good for you, does it?"

Campbell pointed his finger at me. "*He* was the one coming from her room, not me. This guy right here, Benjamin Justice."

"Her window was half open," I said. "Enough for a small person to crawl through and surprise her. There's a ledge outside, just wide enough for a trained stuntman your size to make an escape. You ditch the weapon, slip back into the hotel, grab a bottle of wine and two glasses, then hurry up here with an improbable story about a hot date."

"You can all go to hell if you think I had something to do with this." Campbell swiveled, taking us all in, his eyes furious. "Every one of you, straight to hell."

He stomped off down the hall, punching the button on the fourth-floor elevator so hard I was afraid he'd break a finger. A moment later, as he stepped in and the doors closed, Audrey Williams pushed into the semicircle, dressed in pajamas and a robe and rubbing sleep from her eyes.

"What's going on up here?"

Her mother kneeled and explained that there'd been "a terrible accident," and suggested Audrey go back to bed. Instead, before anyone could stop her, she stepped over to the doorway and stuck her head into the room.

"Doesn't look like an accident to me," she said, facing us again. "It looks like somebody gave her the bloody smile." Audrey giggled. "The bloody smile—that's what we called all those cut throats in *Demon Slasher: Terror on Sorority Row*. That was the one where the Slasher sliced up a bunch of college girls. I thought it was pretty funny, but it didn't do that well at the box office, not like the others. That's what they get for opening on a Friday against a Tom Cruise action movie." She glanced back in at the corpse. "So why isn't there more blood?" I thought I knew the answer but before I could offer it, Audrey was entertaining us again. "You know how they make blood in most of my movies? Chocolate syrup and red food coloring. You want Hershey's for thickness and texture. That's the secret—it's all in the chocolate syrup."

"Audrey," Mrs. Williams said, "I don't think anyone wants to hear about that right now."

"What's so troubling to me," Templeton cut in, "is why there's been another murder on March fifteenth in this room, exactly fifty years after the first, with a suicide midway between, on the same date. What's the connection?"

"I guess that's the million-dollar question," Karen Hori said.

"No," I said. "I believe the million-dollar question is who among us did it."

"Jesus." Oakley looked genuinely troubled. "I hadn't even thought of that."

"I suppose it makes sense." Zeke Zeidler leaned on his cane, glancing uneasily from face to face. "Still, I wouldn't want to think that anyone here was capable of such a thing." He shook his head resolutely. "I'm sorry, I just can't make that leap."

"Anybody's capable of snuffing somebody," Deep Freeze snarled. "You learn that real quick on the streets. You learn you can't trust nobody."

"There are more than two hundred guests in this hotel," Nan Williams said, sounding indignant. "It could have been anyone, anyone at all."

"Even someone who came in from the outside," Templeton suggested, "and is gone by now, back into town or down the road, out of the canyon."

"Several minutes passed from the time I heard the noises until I got up here," I said. "Time enough for someone to get out of the hotel unseen, if they knew the layout and the right exits to use." I shrugged. "Or maybe they stayed, and they're still here."

Sparks got teary again, staining her pretty face. "When are the police coming? Why is it taking them so long? I'm frightened."

Lois Aswell stroked Sparks's hair. "Take it easy, Heather. I can't imagine that someone who's still in this hotel was responsible."

"Maybe it was the ghost of Rebecca Fox who did it," Audrey said, grinning again. "Maybe she was pissed off about the room service."

"Please don't say things like that," Sparks said, clinging to Oakley.

"I'm so sorry." Mrs. Williams scanned the group plaintively with her eyes. "Audrey, I think you should apologize. Then I want you back in bed. You can sleep in my room tonight. You'll be safe there."

She reached for her daughter, but Audrey pulled away, returning to the doorway for another look at the stiffening corpse.

"I didn't like her." Audrey's voice was flat, devoid of feeling, the voice of a pint-size girl who hadn't been a child for a long time. "I'm glad she's dead."

Nan Williams grabbed her daughter roughly by the arm. "That's a terrible thing to say, Audrey. Terrible!"

"Maybe," I said, studying the faces around me and thinking of one or two that weren't there. Inevitably, my conflicted eyes lingered on Christopher Oakley. "But I doubt that Audrey's the only one who feels that way."

FOURTEEN

A few minutes past one, I saw a pair of headlights snake up Coyote Canyon Road and turn off into Haunted Springs toward the hotel.

I was standing at the window in my room, worn out but unable to get back to sleep. It wasn't just the murder in the room above me that had me so unsettled. It was how close I'd come to snatching that file folder marked with Christopher Oakley's name, the problems it might have caused me, and what it told me about myself. I obviously cared about the guy, yet there was no good reason, except that he was so charming and so damned good-looking. I didn't really know him, yet I'd come close to making a reckless move to protect him. It was a foolish risk I'd taken too many times in my life, sticking my neck out for a dangerous man I'd fancied, and one I didn't want to repeat.

So I'd taken myself out of temptation's way, pressuring Kevin Tiemeyer to take charge of the situation until the authorities arrived, and vowing to keep my distance from Oakley and whatever game he was playing with me. At my urging, while I stayed out, Tiemeyer entered Room 418 to shut and lock the window and then lock the door from the outside as he made his exit, while a few of us looked on as witnesses for his own protection, able to verify that he'd done no tampering. He'd reluctantly agreed, entering the room hastily, stepping well around the desk where the body was draped face-up, averting his eyes and getting out of there in under a minute. On his own, he'd posted a security guard on duty to sit watch outside the room, with strict instructions not to allow anyone in or out until the cops got there.

I watched the arriving car pass the Haunted Springs Museum and Souvenir Shop and keep coming, straight into the hotel parking lot. At first, I'd taken the vehicle for a county sheriff's patrol car until I saw there were no lights on the roof and no sheriff's department logo on the side. Now I could see that it was an unmarked detective's car, pale green, with a spotlight next to the driver's side mirror. Police departments typically send a patrol unit first on a call like this, to take a preliminary look and report back to dispatch before calling for additional assistance, should it be needed. But we were in the high desert, far from a sheriff's substation of much size, and I figured maybe they did things differently out here.

Templeton was in her room, on the horn to the *Los Angeles Times,* alerting the overnight editor to the news of Toni Pebbles's murder. Templeton knew it was too late for the *LAT* to remake any pages in the first edition, which would hit the streets in a few hours, so her public account of things would have to wait until tomorrow. Templeton wasn't all that bothered by the delay; with the extra time, she'd be able to collect more facts, get some perspective, and write up the article herself, without a rewrite guy taking loose dictation over the phone and putting the piece together in his own way. She'd lose her exclusive, her front-page scoop, but she was still the reporter on the spot, in the middle of a developing story with plenty of juice to it. Part of me envied her that experience, which had once been such a driving force in my life. With each succeeding year that gnaw of envy diminished a little more, but I figured it would never quite go away. I accepted it as a small part of my penance, living with it the way one lives with the nagging pain of an old injury that never fully heals. You're always aware that it's there, reminding you of what you've done, and what you can never undo. All you can do is live the rest of your life trying to make up for it, trying to make it right, if you're lucky enough to get the chance.

I rinsed my face and went downstairs to meet the unmarked car and whoever might be in it.

Out front, a middle-aged Hispanic man in a western-style sport coat, hat, and boots climbed from behind the wheel. He had a ruddy brown complexion, a thick, dark mustache and bushy side-burns going gray, and a paunch that hung far enough over his turquoise-and-silver belt buckle to tell you he liked to eat but not so much that he needed to be ashamed of it.

He had trouble getting out, and that's when I realized he was wearing only one of the boots. He hopped on the booted foot before bending back into the car to grab a pair of aluminum crutches from the backseat. After that, he removed his hat and tossed it on the front seat. As he hobbled toward me on the crutches I saw that his other foot was in a cast, with five brown toes sticking out like a litter of piglets.

He introduced himself as Sergeant Tony Valenzuela and showed me a detective's gold shield. I told him my name and what I knew about the death of Toni Pebbles in twenty-five words or less, including the fact that I—along with a stuntman named Scotty Campbell—had discovered the body. I held the hotel door open for him and followed him inside, where he took half a minute to survey the expansive lobby, commenting that he'd never been in the Haunted Springs Hotel, even though he'd grown up in the valley and been with the Sheriff's Department twenty-six years. Tiemeyer had called all the hotel employees he could reach at home and asked them to come in, promising overtime. One of them was behind the front desk, and went to find Tiemeyer. Meanwhile, Valenzuela climbed into the elevator for the trip upstairs, asking me to go with him.

As the old lift lurched into motion, he informed me that he'd worked alone since the retirement of his partner several years ago. That wasn't uncommon these days, he said, since budget restrictions had rendered two-person detective teams a remnant of the past, at least in some agencies. He told me he'd busted his ankle showing his eight-year-old grandson how to run interference on the football field and was supposed to be home with his bad foot elevated. But all the other detectives were out on a dangerous bust of a methamphetamine lab, so when the homicide call had come in he'd agreed to drive up and take a look. If the call checked out, he figured, a detective would have to handle it eventually, anyway, so it might as well be him. Then he brought the subject back around to football, asking me if I'd played when I was younger, as he had. I told him no, but that I'd wrestled in high school and college. He looked me over and said it showed, adding that he'd tried wrestling himself but didn't have the stamina without the substitutions, halftimes, and huddles. Besides, he added, patting his ample stomach, there'd been that problem of making weight every week, and he never had.

Before the elevator reached the fourth floor, I'd learned a lot about Sergeant Tony Valenzuela. He was a talker, which isn't always true of detectives; a lot of them play it closer to the vest. But I also realized that by the time the elevator came to a stop on the fourth floor I was pretty much at ease with the man, even trusting. He'd developed a confidant in me, and I don't think it was even remotely an accident.

In short order, Valenzuela confirmed that Toni Pebbles was dead, secured the crime scene, called for crime lab personnel, and asked headquarters to send any officers who could be spared for temporary assistance. He left the hotel security guard posted outside the door and huddled with Kevin Tiemeyer in his office, learning who among the staff had recent contact with Pebbles and who might be recruited to help verify registration information and valid identifications of all hotel guests. He also gathered all four of the security guards who had come in to work extra shifts, split them into two teams, and assigned them to begin searching the hotel room by room, looking for a weapon or bloody clothing, even though it was unlikely that evidence that incriminating would still be around. Zeke Zeidler volunteered to take a head count of the movie's entire cast and crew; the president of the Rebecca Fox Memorial Fan Club did the same for the remaining guests, which accounted for everyone.

When the roll call was completed, only one guest was missing: Sweet Doctor Silk, who hadn't been seen since late the previous night, at least an hour before midnight.

I learned all this from Valenzuela when he called me in to be interviewed in a hotel office, which he'd turned into a temporary command center. He'd taken off his jacket, rolled up his sleeves, and propped his broken leg up on a chair. After filling me in on his investigation—the harmless stuff, anyway—he asked me to start with what had drawn me up to Toni Pebbles's room a few minutes before midnight and proceed from there. I started a bit earlier than that, recalling the woman in the white dress I'd seen outside the hotel before I'd turned in, which seemed to interest him. As I talked, he jotted in a spiral notebook, looking up when it suited him. I took him through my confrontation with Scotty Campbell upstairs and our mutual discovery of the body, but I didn't mention what I'd done in the couple of minutes when Scotty had left me alone.

He quickly keyed on the victim, which is ground zero for murder investigations that lack an obvious suspect. I filled him in on her background as a journalist but he seemed just as interested in her personal habits, relationships, and personality, even what kind of money she had or made. I offered what I could, but told him I didn't know exactly why she was in Haunted Springs, which was the truth, in a manner of speaking.

"When was the last time you spoke to her?"

"Midafternoon, in the museum."

"You two had a date to meet?"

"I'd been browsing with my friend Alexandra. She'd left with Kevin Tiemeyer, I stayed behind. Toni dropped by, caught me by surprise."

"Were you and Miss Pebbles fond of each other?"

"Not really."

"She made a point of seeking you out, though, at the museum."

"She wanted to get me into bed, Sergeant. Or at least screw with my head."

"Why don't you extrapolate on that?"

"Years ago, when I was in my twenties, Toni wanted to sleep with me. I'm gay. Certain women don't let you forget that. They like to use it as leverage, a way to keep you off balance, make you feel small. Poke at you, trying to find a nerve."

"Why would they do that?"

"Gives them an edge, I suppose, the upper hand. Not all women, or even a lot of women. Just women like Toni, insecure types who need their power fix every once in a while and find gay men a convenient source. The way some blowhard men like to needle women who aren't interested in them."

"Must have pissed you off, when she did that."

I shrugged. "You get used to it, like a lot of things."

Valenzuela leaned back with his pudgy hands behind his head. "My partner was homosexual—the one that retired."

"You don't say."

"He never said a word about it. Kept it to himself all those years. But I knew. I could tell."

"Must have been difficult for him, living a double life."

"I think it probably was. Apparently, you don't—live a double life, that is."

"I gave up living my life to please other people a long time ago."

"So tell me more about this meeting between you and Miss Pebbles. You must have talked about something besides your disinclination to hop in the sack with her."

"This and that. Nothing very important."

He smiled mildly. "Let's start with this, and move on to that later."

"Mostly, we talked about why she was in Haunted Springs."

"I thought you said you didn't know."

"I said I didn't know exactly."

"Generally then."

I hesitated, wished I hadn't, but knew it was too late to hide it. "I got the impression that she was up here in search of a story she might sell."

"Why else would she be up here?"

"Vacation, like me."

His hands came down from his head and he leaned forward. "What kind of story are we talking about?"

"Connected to the movie, I guess."

"An interview with the stars, something like that?"

I nodded. "She didn't mention any names."

Valenzuela shifted his big behind and adjusted his upraised leg, wincing a little. "Did Miss Pebbles have any enemies you were aware of? Up here with this movie or anywhere else?"

"Toni made a name for herself by prying the lids off people's secrets, Sergeant. No one in the public eye was immune, not if they were big enough to make a loud noise when they fell."

"That sounds like a yes."

"She knew a lot of people, sources and connections, but I don't think too many of them liked her very much."

"If they didn't like her, why would they help her out, give her information?"

"Ax to grind, score to settle against someone she was after. An opportunity to damage a big shot, be part of a story, if only anonymously. Those are the usual reasons."

"So she came up here to pry off another lid?"

Again, I hesitated. "It seemed that way."

"But she didn't indicate who." I shook my head. "You care to venture a guess?"

"Not really."

"Why's that?"

"I've never cared much for gossip, Sergeant. Not the kind Toni traded in, anyway."

"What kind was that?"

"The kind that hurts people for no good reason when it gets into print. I think that was part of the kick for her, along with the paycheck."

"It made her as big as them, at least for a little while, is that what you're saying?"

"That's a good way of putting it, yes."

He chuckled. "I thought all the secrets were out by now, that all the taboos had fallen. My wife keeps telling me she's seen it all or heard it all and barely believes half the garbage that's out there, anyway."

"Half might be generous."

"Some of it must be true, though." I didn't say anything; his smile went away and his eyes grew keener. "So it must be a pretty good secret somebody's keeping to bring Miss Pebbles all the way up here, chasing after that exclusive story you mentioned."

I don't think he blinked once for the next half minute, while he waited me out.

Finally, I said, "I honestly can't tell you what she had, Sergeant, or who she was after. She kept that part to herself."

"All the way to the grave, apparently. Unless I find something in her files that suggests otherwise."

I kept my mouth shut, and he thanked me for coming in.

After interviewing some other essential witnesses, who included the principals in the film, Valenzuela assembled the hotel guests in the dining room, where Tiemeyer had set up coffee, juice, and rolls. Sweet Doctor Silk was still AWOL. Where and how he spent his nights was his own business, of course, but it was all the buzz around the hotel, given what had happened while he was off the radar screen.

Valenzuela thanked everyone for their cooperation and patience and provided a succinct update on his investigation, which included the fact that he had yet to apprehend a suspect. At that point, a lawyer whose wife was a member of the Rebecca Fox Memorial Fan Club interrupted, pointing out that under the law potential witnesses cannot be held against their will. Citing safety concerns, he announced that he and his wife would be checking out immediately. Despite Valenzuela's protests, that triggered a stampede from the room and a rush to grab or pack suitcases. Some guests were standing at the front desk to check out still dressed in their robes and slippers. As sunrise approached, the only remaining guests were Templeton, me, and the cast and crew of *A Murder in Eternal Springs*.

"Thank God," Lois Aswell said, standing on the front steps with a cigarette while we watched a stream of cars pull out of the parking lot and form a slow procession heading south through town. She'd exchanged her pink sweat suit for a yellow one, but her frizzy gray hair was bound up in the same lavender scarf, and her feet were still clad in rubber, open-toed sandals, despite the cold. At the request of Sergeant Valenzuela, Aswell had reluctantly suspended shooting for the day, putting the film even further behind schedule. "I haven't had such a rough shoot," she said, pulling hard on the burning tobacco, "since my third husband filed for divorce in the middle of my last movie. I warned him before we got married that I was both ambitious and a control freak. In a marriage, there's only room for one of those. You married, Justice?"

"I'm afraid not."

"At least now we won't have interfering guests to worry about when we resume shooting tomorrow." She tossed the smoking butt to the veranda floor and ground it under a toe. "Maybe we can make up some of the time we've lost."

"I guess having Toni Pebbles out of the way has its advantages," I said. "She won't be writing any nasty articles, either, will she?"

Aswell didn't reply to that, she just cut me with a sharp glance as she turned inside, looking hell-bent on finishing her movie without anyone else getting in her way.

Twenty minutes later, after watching the sun come up over Lake Enid, I was headed for the stairs and some sleep when I saw Templeton pressed against a wall outside the banquet room. She was trying hard to look like she was there innocently minding her own business, but not doing a very good job of it.

Inside, Zeke Zeidler and Lois Aswell had assembled the cast and crew for a breakfast meeting. Someone had pulled the banquet room doors closed without latching them and one had drifted open an inch, allowing Templeton to eavesdrop by standing out of sight just beyond the doorway. As I sauntered over, she grabbed me and pulled me next to her against the wall.

"What's going on?" I said.

She put her finger to her lips. "Just listen."

As we did, the central issue quickly became clear: whether to continue shooting the movie in the wake of Toni Pebbles's death, or suspend production indefinitely until things got sorted out and everyone felt less on edge. Aswell reminded the group that only ten days of shooting remained in Haunted Springs, mostly interiors and exteriors at the hotel and around town; every day was crucial, she said, because of the complex structure of the script, along with the new scenes that she'd written *Rashomon*-style.

"The budget's already stretched to the breaking point," Aswell said, her voice both pleading and tough. "This may be an independent film, but we're looking at twenty million dollars. We simply can't afford to stop and lose more days. We're all pros here. I say we keep going, finish the picture on schedule."

"I'm with Lois," Deep Freeze said. "I wrote a big check to get this movie made. I got a significant investment to protect."

"I wish you'd thought of that when you were off at your pimp convention," Zeidler said, "while the rest of us were up here waiting for you."

"So I'm here now. So let's just move forward, and get the motherfucker finished."

Heather Sparks and Christopher Oakley favored suspension. "Heather's a wreck," Oakley said. "She's never been through anything like this. Hell, *I've* never been through anything like this. A woman was murdered and whoever did it is running around loose. We're not safe here."

"He could be right in this room." It was Scotty Campbell, back to his old tricks. "I hope this isn't another *Ten Little Indians*, with another body turning up every night."

"Make him stop!" Heather cried.

"Shut up, Scotty," Aswell said. "You're on thin ice as it is."

"Another word," Oakley warned, "and I'll shut you up myself." I peeked around the doorway to see Oakley pointing a finger at Campbell, before turning back to Sparks, who looked haggard and wrung out. He ran a hand through her hair, she appeared to be fighting tears. "You see how she is? She's a mess. She shouldn't have to work under these conditions. None of us should."

"Believe me," Aswell said, "I understand what Heather's going through. She knows that. But we're filmmakers. We don't work by the same rules or standards as other people. We create. We take risks. We spend a lot of money. And we do what we have to do to get the movie made."

"I've already called my agent," Sparks said, her voice small. "He wants me to come home."

Aswell turned on her, fury replacing sympathy. "When? You didn't tell me this."

"A few minutes ago." Sparks cast her eyes down. "He wants me back in L.A. where it's safe."

"What neighborhood do you live in?" Scotty Campbell asked.

"*We* live behind big gates," Audrey Williams said. "Mom says it's to keep out the riff-raff and the homeless people."

"This is great," Aswell said, throwing up her arms in disgust. "This is just wonderful. You're all going to start jumping ship like a bunch of scared rats."

"I'm sorry!" Sparks burst into tears. "But I'm frightened!"

"Heather's right," Nan Williams said. It sounded like Mrs. Williams had weighed who was the more important, Aswell or Sparks, and Sparks had won. "I don't want Audrey up here another minute until our safety can be assured."

"You people make me sick," Aswell said. "Why don't you all just put your tails between your legs, crawl back to Hollywood, and find work in the soaps?"

"She's a child," Mrs. Williams said. "She shouldn't be exposed to this."

"No disrespect meant, Nan," Zeidler said. "But you've had

Audrey working in the Demon Slasher movies since she was five. What's the average decapitation count in one of those? Half a dozen?"

"It's not the same," Mrs. Williams said. "This is real. She knows the difference."

"I want to stay," Audrey piped in. "This is better than *COPS*. Maybe that fat detective will catch the killer and pump a few rounds into him. Now that would be really cool."

Mrs. Williams put on a stern face. "We're going home, Audrey, and that's final."

"We'll be right behind you," Oakley said.

"You can't go," Karen Hori said. "I need you and Heather here for the media I've got coming in for the remainder of the shoot. With what's happened, the interest will be even greater than before. If word gets out, we may even see a horde of reporters today. This could break on the network news."

"What about Audrey?" Mrs. Williams said. "Don't you plan to schedule any interviews for her?"

"I thought you were leaving," Zeidler said.

"Well—if there's press coming in, I suppose we have an obligation to be here." Mrs. Williams turned to Hori. "Can you get us on *Access Hollywood?* Audrey's always wanted to be on that show."

"We're talking about publicity opportunities," Oakley said, sounding disgusted, "while there's a woman lying dead upstairs."

"Actually," Campbell said, "they carted the body out a couple of hours ago. Stiff as yesterday's mackerel."

"Don't talk like that!" Heather Sparks shrieked. She sat down, covering her ears, tears spilling over. "I won't listen to this anymore. I won't!"

"Do you think I'm pleased there's been a murder?" Hori asked, facing Oakley.

He pinned her with his intense eyes. "I don't know, Karen, are you?"

Hori seethed silently for a moment. Then, very calmly, she said, "I worked extremely hard for the wonderful coverage you and Heather got the past twenty-four hours. It breaks my heart to see it overshadowed by what happened last night. But there *has* been a murder—on the ides of March, no less. As long as it's happened, we might as well make the most of it."

"Lemons into lemonade," Campbell said, but no one seemed to be paying attention to him anymore.

Zeidler rose to stand next to Aswell, looking solemn. "Suspending production for any length of time will be a disaster. I'm not even sure we're indemnified for something like this."

"Maybe you should call your insurance guy," Oakley said.

"I have. We've been playing phone tag."

"Sounds like me and my agent," Deep Freeze said. "That's what I get for signing with CAA."

"At least wait until we know that we're covered," Aswell pleaded. "Don't threaten the film's completion by making a hasty decision. By tomorrow morning, you may feel differently. Get some rest first. Then decide."

Oakley sat next to Sparks, slipping an arm around her shoulders. "What about it, honey? Can you hold out a little longer, until Zeke straightens out the insurance business?"

Sparks looked up, brushing away tears. "How much longer?"

Oakley fixed his eyes on Aswell and Zeidler. "You've got until the end of the day. Then I'm driving her down the hill and back home. We won't spend another night in this place if we don't have to."

"If we do suspend production," Deep Freeze said to Aswell, "I think you should use the time to rewrite the part of Ed Jones. I don't think you're paying proper respect to the man. I see him as a martyr—a modern black Christ figure, crucified by the KKK."

"I'll get right on it," Aswell said, rolling her eyes in apparent disbelief.

"Are we done here?" Audrey asked. "Because I need to do my Pilates."

"Yes, Audrey," Aswell said, "by all means go do your Pilates."

Just then, my attention was drawn to a muscular figure

advancing at a leisurely pace across the lobby toward the banquet room. Sweet Doctor Silk stopped just inside the doorway, freezing everyone where they were. He was wearing a dark, pin-striped suit, a lavender silk shirt open at the collar, and a different gold chain—heavier, fancier—than the one I'd seen him wearing yesterday. It had been a while since he'd shaved; his dark stubble was heavy. The dining room had grown quiet as a tomb; every eye was on him. When he spoke, however, he directed his words only to Deep Freeze.

"What's up, homes?"

A moment later, another figure appeared in the lobby—Sergeant Valenzuela, swinging himself across the tiled floor on his crutches with as much speed as he could muster. He pulled up a few feet behind Sweet Doctor Silk. I noticed that he'd unfastened the guard on his belt holster, giving him easier access to his gun.

"Excuse me," he said. "Would you be the gentleman known as Sweet Doctor Silk?"

Silk swiveled, looking Valenzuela over with no visible expression. "Yeah, that's me. Who wants to know?"

"We need to have a chat," Valenzuela said.

FIFTEEN

A few minutes after the reappearance of Sweet Doctor Silk, I was up in my room with the curtains closed, my head on a pillow and a sock over my eyes. Gradually, I sank into sleep. Sometime after that the dream started.

I was underwater, swimming down toward strange shapes in shadowy light and a world of translucent green. As I descended, I saw that the shapes were buildings from early in the last century; lettering and signage on the walls told me I was in the old town of Eternal Springs.

A male figure appeared ahead of me, pulling his body through the murky water with broad, graceful breaststrokes. Without thinking I gave chase. As I followed in his wake, I caught glimpses of bare flesh—pale buttocks, a tightly muscled back, a pair of white feet kicking rhythmically as he parted the water with his cupped hands, propelling himself forward. I hurried my pursuit but he was younger and stronger, undulating effortlessly like a mermaid as he kept some distance between us. We wound our way around the library, down to a fountain and statue in the town square, and up past a church steeple before descending again. Each time I seemed about to catch him he'd dart away, just beyond my reach.

Finally, he plunged deeper, down to where the water was

darkest and icy cold. He slowed, looking over his shoulder teasingly, allowing me to glimpse his face. It was Christopher Oakley. I reached for him but he dove again, through the open doorway of an unadorned brick building, kicking hard as he disappeared inside. Again I followed, drawn by a force I didn't understand. I found myself in a small room where almost no light reached. Ahead, barely visible, a male figure faced me, no more substantial to my eye than a shadow. I thrust myself forward, desperate for the elusive embrace. He waited, passive and still. Just as I reached him, touching his dark face, peering into his dead eyes, I realized I was clutching the cold, stiff body of Ed Jones, as he hung by a noose from a jailhouse rafter.

I woke abruptly, staring at the ceiling, finding my breath.

Some people think dreams and nightmares have no meaning, no significance at all. I take the opposite view.

If dreams are merely random and accidental, arising from nowhere and nothing, with no link to who we are or how we feel beneath the surface, then those of us whose minds produce such fantastic visions must be insane; our minds must be broken, cracked open like so many cans of paint pouring their colors into a pool of wild and ever-changing images that only we can see. If these surreal movies inside our heads have no connection to who we are and what we're experiencing at some subconscious level, then we're seeing things that don't exist, which means we must be crazy.

I lay still for a minute, thinking of what the dream revealed about how lost and confused I was, and where that might be taking me. I still didn't see everything clearly, any more than Kevin Tiemeyer had seen the character of Ed Jones clearly two days ago, when Lois Aswell had filmed a scene inside this room, duplicating the room above me. I doubt that anyone was quite sure exactly what they'd learned during that unannounced experiment of hers, except perhaps how malleable and illusory memory can be, how time and emotion can alter it the way an editor can manipulate images and change a story line in an editing bay. Yet as confusing as it had been for many of us, something profound had been revealed, for Kevin Tiemeyer most of all. I was certain of it. I'd seen it in his agitated eyes. He hadn't been the same man since.

As I stared at the ceiling in the quiet of my room, I focused on the one above: what Room 418 had looked like last night when I'd been alone there for a minute or two, with Toni Pebbles's corpse. What the room had felt like, smelled like, sounded like. What I'd done there. How I'd almost made a stupid choice, driven by my desire for a man I hardly knew, drawing back from the brink in the nick of time. Then I remembered another choice I'd made, not quite so risky: copying a phone number and shoving it into a pocket, something I'd forgotten in the hubbub of activity that had followed.

I rolled off the bed, dug into my pants pocket, and found the slip of note paper. After I dialed the number, it rang once before I heard a recorded message: *You have reached Club Ebony, a private club for discriminating gentlemen of color. We are open seven evenings a week, from ten P.M. until four A.M. to members only. If you wish more information about Club Ebony, please leave your name and number at the tone, and someone will get back to you. All calls will be handled in strict confidence.*

I hung up and called Maurice in West Hollywood.

"Benjamin! How absolutely delightful to hear your voice. Fred and I were speaking of you, only just this minute."

"Kindly, I hope."

"We were wondering how you were getting on with that gorgeous lad, Christopher Oakley. Well, actually, I was the one who was wondering. Fred tells me I should leave it alone, especially now that Mr. Oakley's up and gotten himself engaged to Heather Sparks, the All-American Girl. I'm sorry, but I just don't see that one working out. She seems like a nice girl, but she's much too bland and squeaky clean for a hot little number like Oakley, don't you think?"

"She's a celebrity, Maurice. We never really know them like

we think we do. Maybe she's a tigress behind that beauty pageant smile."

"Let an old queen have a bit of fantasy and fun, will you? I've always been enthralled with Hollywood, you know that. Hollywood and gossip go together like premieres and red carpets. I know it's silly, but I just can't help myself."

"Listen, Maurice, something's happened—I need a favor."

"What is it, Benjamin? You're alright, I hope? And Alexandra?"

"Yes, we're fine. We had a murder up here last night. Fortunately, neither of us was the victim."

"A murder!"

"I'm afraid so."

"You see, I knew the ides of March was a bad date. Don't say I didn't warn you, Benjamin. So tell me, who got dispatched? Anyone famous?"

"Toni Pebbles, a freelance writer."

"I'm afraid I don't know the name."

"She's been out of circulation awhile. Permanently now."

"This happened in the hotel?"

"In the Rebecca Fox Room—the same room where the previous two deaths occurred. Her throat was cut, just like the others."

"Oh my Lord! Why haven't I heard anything on the news?"

"Give it more time. I'm sure you will."

"I trust that you and Alexandra are coming right home. Since there's a homicidal maniac running around loose in that haunted old hotel."

"It's a very nice hotel, actually. A lovely place for murder."

"Don't joke about this, Benjamin. You know the kind of trouble you've gotten into before, being so cavalier."

"I expect we'll drive home tomorrow, Maurice. In the meantime, I need you to do something for me, if you're willing."

"Connected to this killing?"

"I'm not sure. But it needs checking out."

"Of course, Benjamin, whatever I can do."

I gave him what little information I had on Club Ebony, and asked him to see what he could find out about the place. "If I'm right, the prefix puts it in Hollywood, toward the east end, not far from Thai Town."

I heard the excitement rising in his voice. "You're doing some amateur sleuthing, aren't you, Benjamin?"

"I'm curious about a couple of things, that's all."

"This is so exciting! You obviously need a partner, a fellow gumshoe, down here in L.A., to pound the streets and squeeze some information from some reluctant sources."

"Before you slap anybody around, Maurice, just make a few discreet inquiries, will you? See if you can get an address on the club, maybe check it out, let me know what it's all about. It may come to nothing, but I'd like to follow it up."

"I'll get right on it, Benjamin. If it appears at all dangerous, I'll take Fred with me. He's a very well-built fellow, as you know. I don't think anyone will mess with Fred."

"In all due respect, Maurice, he's eighty-three."

"Just the same, we'll go together and see what we can find out—dig up the facts, as you private eyes like to say."

"I'm not a private eye, Maurice, I'm just—"

"In the meantime," he went on, "I want you to look your best for Mr. Oakley. There's no telling if this engagement of his is the real thing or not, and I don't want such a fine opportunity to slip away from you. He might just be attracted to intelligent butch types, which means you're just his cup of tea." Maurice rattled off a list of grooming tips like a gay drill sergeant. "Leave at least a day's stubble—it's one of your sexier attributes. A little product in your hair, but not too much. A gentle facial scrub, followed by an oil-free lotion. A blue shirt to bring out your eyes. And most important, be yourself!"

"I don't really expect to be spending too much time with Christopher Oakley, Maurice."

"It doesn't hurt to think positively, Benjamin. He wouldn't be the first Hollywood closet case to seek cover in a marriage. Perhaps you'll be the one to lead him out of the darkness and into the light."

"Call me here at the hotel if you learn anything about Club Ebony, will you?"

"I'll ring up as soon as I rattle a few skeletons, as you amateur detectives are fond of saying. And do be careful, Benjamin. You know how you can be sometimes, when you catch the scent of blood."

I showered and shaved, ignoring Maurice's advice about stubble but following the rest. As I slipped into a navy polo shirt, I had to smile, thinking about his fanciful matchmaking as he paired me in his mind with the likes of Christopher Oakley, who would soon be out of my life, if he wasn't already. But I wasn't smiling long.

As I hit the lobby, looking for a cup of coffee, Oakley drew me aside and asked me if I'd care to go rowing out on Lake Enid.

I cocked my head curiously. "What about Heather? Don't you think you should stay with her, given the state she's in?"

"Nice of you to think of her, Justice. The fact is, she's down with a sedative. Karen Hori will look in on her for me. I've got to get out of this damned hotel, get some fresh air and exercise." He stretched—a sinewy arm in either direction—and the light from an upper window caught the hair on his forearms, turning it to spun gold. I tried not to stare too obviously.

"You sure there's not somebody else you'd rather go rowing with?"

"If there was," he said, "I wouldn't have asked you."

The marina was closed, but a few members of the crew had gone out on Lake Enid in small rowboats reserved for hotel guests. We could see them moving slowly through the water as we ambled down the trail to the lake's rocky edge. As we got closer, the odor of dead fish struck our nostrils, sharp and pungent, reminding me that Lake Enid was poisoned and lifeless.

"There goes your chance for fresh air," I said.

Oakley clapped me on the shoulder and blessed me with his winning smile. "I'll settle for some exercise and good companionship."

We struck out in a fiberglass two-seater equipped with one pair of oars. Oakley offered to do the rowing, facing me from the bow with his back to the lake, and I was fine with that. He was wearing a tank top that revealed baseball biceps and a sprinkling of golden hair at his breastbone, shorts that showed off his muscular legs, and running shoes without socks, revealing slender ankles. There was nothing about him that I didn't enjoy looking at, especially his upper body when he stroked deeply with the oars and all the muscles strained in perfect anatomical harmony. I attempted to turn the conversation to the wedding he'd eventually be planning with Heather Sparks, about how big it would be and who might attend, hoping to probe a bit about his closest male friends and what roles they might take in it. But he seemed more interested in me and what I was up to, and by the time we were in the middle of the lake, I was telling him more about the memoir I'd just written than I really wanted to.

"Sounds like it might have been therapeutic," he said. "Good for the soul."

"I did it for the money more than anything else," I said. "Writing it wasn't easy, to be perfectly honest."

"Nothing good ever is, is it? If it's worth having, you've got to work for it."

"Does that apply to your relationship with Heather?"

He pushed quickly past that. "You've got quite a story to tell, Ben. The problems with your father, the Pulitzer business, the adventures you've had since. I imagine your book will be a damned good read."

"It's not all pretty, and I didn't leave much out."

"We all have some history we're not proud of."

"Even you, Christopher?"

His gaze was steady again, but his smile cryptic. "The nice thing about mistakes is the opportunities we sometimes get to correct them."

Clouds had moved in and a pesky wind rippled the slate gray water, making the rowing a challenge. Oakley let up on the oars and we drifted for a minute, among the upper branches of the dead trees Templeton and I had viewed from the road on our way in. Slick, green algae clung to the dark branches like bilious saliva, entangled in a mess of old fishing lines and lures. From one of the rusting hooks hung a fish skeleton, its flesh picked clean by birds and its bones bleached white by the merciless high desert sun.

"You seem to know a lot about me," I said. "About some of the problems I've had, some of the scrapes I've gotten myself into."

"Like I told you before, Ben, I've read about you from time to time."

"Then you must know I'm queer."

"I recall that part being mentioned."

"That's not a problem for you?"

"Would we be out here together if it were?" He reached over, touched my knee. "Relax, Ben. We're just out for a row, enjoying the lake."

"Are you sure that's all we're doing, Christopher?"

Our eyes locked. I tried to see behind his, to figure out what was going on in that mystifying brain of his. But I couldn't get past his smooth answers and constantly shifting surface. All I knew for sure was that he was the kind of man a lot of women and men fall in love with as easily as walking off a cliff blindfolded.

Above us, a cloud opened, and for a moment the sun broke through. Oakley pointed toward the water. "Take a look."

Directly below us was Eternal Springs—the foundations of the old town, anyway. The eerie remnants of the community were roughly twenty-five feet down, just close enough to make out through the opaque water. Oakley grabbed the oars and started pulling us along again, taking us on a tour. I glanced around, getting my bearings from the way the trees were grouped, remembering Templeton's description two days earlier up on the road, and a map I'd seen in Richard Pearlman's book.

"This would be the town square," I said. We could just make it out below, an old stone fountain at its center and concrete benches along the walkways that had escaped the planted dynamite, probably because whoever had been in charge of damming this valley had never expected the water level to drop so low. I pointed east, maybe fifty yards. "If I'm right, the jail would be just over there." Oakley rowed in that direction, until we were floating over a square foundation that included three steps leading down to the street. "I'm sure this is it—the place where Ed Jones died, fifty years ago today."

As we sat in silence, staring down, the wind picked up, causing the ripples to rise again and gently rock the boat. Oakley glanced up at the darkening sky.

"We'd better head back." He pulled hard on one oar, bringing us around until we were pointed back toward the hotel.

"I apologize for being such a slacker," I said. "We came all this way, and I let you do all the work."

He used both arms to pull in unison again, the muscles of his chest and shoulders bunching up each time he took a bite from the water. I'd stopped trying to keep my eyes off him and he didn't seem to mind.

"Next time," he said, "I'll let you take the oars, and decide how far we go."

SIXTEEN

As we reached the top of the trail a bulky figure became visible, standing on a first-floor hotel balcony off the dining room, his eyes turned in our direction. As we got closer, I recognized the thick mustache and bushy gray sideburns, then saw a crutch tucked under each arm. Sergeant Valenzuela was smoking a cigarette that was almost down to the nub, which meant he'd probably been out there observing us awhile. As we passed beneath him toward the hotel entrance he reached over to stub his smoke but kept his eyes on us.

Christopher Oakley departed to get something from his Porsche and I went inside alone. I was mounting the stairs when I heard Valenzuela call out my last name. When I turned, he said, "Got a minute? Something I'd like to run by you."

A minute later he was setting his crutches against a desk in the office he'd commandeered while we both found chairs. Dark circles were forming under his eyes and I realized that he'd probably gotten less sleep than I had, if any at all.

"You need some help up here, Sergeant. You must have done something pretty terrible for the brass to hang you out to dry like this."

"I busted somebody's nephew for pot. He's had it in for me ever since. This isn't the first time he's squeezed my balls." Valenzuela changed the subject quickly, asking me what I was hearing around the hotel, what the general mood was. I told him people were curious about Sweet Doctor Silk and his alibi for the previous night, since he was the biggest question mark among the guests and didn't look like he'd won any Mr. Congeniality contests.

"I can understand if you don't want to talk about him," I said. I glanced toward the door. "I'm just letting you know what the buzz is out there."

Valenzuela smiled wearily. "Mr. Silk claimed he drove down to the valley last night, a couple of hours after dinner, looking for pootie tang."

"Come again?"

"That's what the man said—pootie tang. Sounds like a kid's breakfast drink, doesn't it?"

"I have a feeling it's not."

"You know you're getting old," Valenzuela said, "when you have to ask a fellow what he means by pootie tang."

"Did he get any?"

"He says he met a lady in one of the bars at the nearest casino, spent the night with her. I plan to follow up on it. My guess is it'll check out."

"Why do you say that?"

"Because he's smart enough to know I'll follow up. He's not an educated man but he's not stupid, either."

"An alibi like that can account for a lot of time, without getting too precise."

Valenzuela nodded in agreement. "Time down, time back, time wandering around the casino, maybe getting a meal or a drink in a place so crowded nobody would be expected to remember. Lots of wiggle room, like you said."

"On the other hand," I added, "casinos probably have more security cameras than the Pentagon. You might get some help there."

"You weren't a cop once, were you, Justice?"

"No, but my father was a homicide detective. Why?"

"Every so often, you sound like one. You did right off, when I first met you."

"Is that why you wanted to gain my confidence at the outset, on the ride up in the elevator?"

He reached over to the desk for a file folder. "The one with blood on his hands doesn't typically walk up to the first cop on the scene and introduce himself. That's not how it usually works."

"Maybe that's why I did it, to throw you off."

"I considered that."

"If I was a good suspect for you, I guess you wouldn't be spilling inside information to me like this."

"I ran a background check on you, caught up on your history. You have a way of getting involved in homicide investigations, even when you're not invited. I guess I should have recognized your name when I first heard it." His brown eyes narrowed; his voice took on a darker shade. "I also get the impression you're holding something back. Not hard evidence necessarily, but close enough. Something more personal, that you don't want to give up too easily. I think you're conflicted about it."

"Is that why you're sharing this business on Sweet Doctor Silk? Hoping to reel me in even closer, get me to open up?"

"You mind looking at some photographs for me?"

"What kind of photographs?"

"Pictures of one of the cast members."

"I imagine there are a lot of those. Actors are always having their portfolios updated. New publicity photos, that kind of thing."

"These are more private. Not the kind you'd want published or handed around."

I got an uneasy feeling in my gut. "I don't see why you want me to—"

"I'd like to get your feedback," he said. "The whole thing needs to stay between us, at least for now. It might be useful to me, as an investigator."

The file folder in his hands looked familiar, which didn't settle my queasy stomach. "Sure, I guess I can take a look. If you feel it's important."

He opened it and extracted a set of photographs—five by sevens, color, sharp quality. He showed me the first one: Christopher Oakley and another man sunning on a rock by a river, probably shot with a hidden telephoto lens, given how unself-conscious both men appeared. And considering they were both naked. The other man appeared to be older than Oakley, with more meat on him, attractive in a rugged, beefy way. Oakley was Oakley, lean and youthful but every inch a man; seeing him naked, stretched out in the sun, caused the saliva to sluice in my mouth.

One by one, Valenzuela showed me the rest of the set, which were all variations on a theme: Oakley and his friend horsing around on the rock, diving into the water, splashing and wrestling, grins and water drops lighting up their sun-baked faces. There was real beauty in the pictures—not just the natural setting and the well-muscled bodies, but the camaraderie and spontaneity between the two men, the open and unabashed affection they obviously shared. The images were radiant, celebratory; we should all have moments like that, I thought, outbursts of unfettered joy that most of us forbid ourselves out of prudishness and propriety. It disturbed me to think that in the wrong hands something so healthy and positive could be turned into a weapon of ridicule and humiliation—even destruction—by nothing more than their public distribution and a bunch of tightassed media wags making an issue of it.

"Do these surprise you?" Valenzuela asked.

"To see Christopher Oakley having a good time? Not really. He seems like a well-adjusted guy, the type who isn't afraid to let his hair down once in a while."

"I don't know a whole lot about Hollywood," Valenzuela said, "except what I pick up through my wife and kids, and catch on the news from time to time, which isn't much. And I don't claim to know that much about the gay life, except the seedier side that I come across when criminality gets into the mix. But I'm going to take a wild guess here and suggest that maybe a movie actor in Mr. Oakley's position wouldn't want these photographs printed up in the tabloids or put out over the Internet. That maybe being a good-looking guy like him, the masculine type, pictures like these and the stories they'd generate wouldn't be the best thing for his career. You have an opinion on that, Justice?"

"I suppose they could be misconstrued."

Valenzuela reached over to pour himself a cup of coffee from a pot; he offered me a cup but I shook my head. "When I was growing up," he said, "you never knew who was and who wasn't. My grandmother watched Liberace play his piano every week on TV and thought he was the sweetest young man on earth, and wondered why he'd never met the right woman. My mother used to say that Rock Hudson had been created by God, without a flaw that you could see, and his wife had been crazy to let him get away. Nobody knew for sure who was and who wasn't because it wasn't really talked about back then, except in whispers by people who cared about such things. As long as it wasn't talked about, as long as appearances were maintained, I guess it didn't matter all that much."

"It mattered to the people keeping up the appearances, Sergeant. Living in deception that way has to take its toll on a person's psyche and soul."

Valenzuela looked down for a moment like he was studying the floor. "I guess what I'm asking is, where does homosexuality fit in on the Hollywood scandal scale these days? You hear about the Ellens and the Rosies and others who don't seem to care who knows." He held up the photos. "Does something like this even matter anymore?"

"They're not having sex, Sergeant. They're engaging in some horseplay in a river, for God sake."

"Without their clothes on."

"Skinny-dipping. Ever done it yourself?"

"You know what I mean, Justice."

"I guess it depends on what type of entertainer you are, what direction your career's headed."

"From what I hear, Mr. Oakley appears headed for what they call stardom."

"It would seem so, yes."

"You and Mr. Oakley pretty close?"

"We had dinner the other night, went rowing today. That's about it."

"You aren't strangers, though. And the fact that Toni Pebbles had these pictures, and I have them now, doesn't sit easily with you. Does it?" When I said nothing, he finally got to the point. "It was Oakley you didn't want to speculate about, wasn't it, when I was trying to get a bead on who Toni Pebbles was after up here?"

A sadness settled over me so heavily I almost felt ill. Not just sadness for Oakley and what all this might mean to him personally, but a deep dispiritedness about a world in which images like these could be so valuable, providing more titillation for the small minds and empty souls that drove the tawdry market that made them worth so much.

I spoke quietly. "Do these photographs have to become public, Sergeant?"

"Is that important to you?"

"I'm not a big fan of closet cases. I see them as part of the problem, rather than part of the solution. Still, a person has a right to live how he or she wants. If we value privacy for ourselves, we can't arbitrarily deny it for others."

"I could do my best to keep these pictures under seal. That's about all I can promise. It depends to some extent on how this investigation develops."

"That would be decent of you."

"You want to answer my question now?"

"I think there are a number of people who could be damaged in different ways if these pictures become public. Especially if Toni Pebbles had something more to go with them. Lurid details she could back up. Factual documentation."

"You think Oakley's vulnerable then."

"Every celebrity of any stature is vulnerable in some way, Sergeant, because they're all human and they're always under the microscope. And because there are always buzzards like Toni Pebbles out there looking to pick them clean."

"But Oakley seems especially vulnerable, wouldn't you say?"

"He was with Heather Sparks when Toni Pebbles was murdered," I said. "He has an alibi. She backed him up."

"Miss Sparks could be protecting him. I understand they got engaged the other night. The timing seems interesting, don't you think?"

"In what way, Sergeant?"

"Coinciding with the appearance of Miss Pebbles as it did. Maybe they knew she was working up a file on him. Their engagement could take the punch out of the story she was planning, couldn't it? Maybe even kill it before it gets into print."

"Maybe that's all it is—a coincidence. What about the other files?" I nodded at the set of photos in his hands. "Did you find anything in them as strong as this?"

"How do you know there are other files, Ben?"

He'd nailed me; I smiled, while he sipped his coffee and kept his eyes on me over the rim of his cup.

"Last night," I said, "when Scotty Campbell left me alone, I poked around in the room."

"You didn't tell me that when we talked early this morning."

"You didn't ask."

"I'm asking now."

"I didn't touch anything, Sergeant. Nothing got moved or disappeared. So, did you? Find anything else like this?"

"No photos. Mostly notes and computer printouts. I haven't had time to go through it all."

I studied the top picture again, of a lean and lanky Christopher Oakley stretched out naked next to his buddy, his sun-bleached hair like a halo against the rock. I didn't want someone that beautiful to be guilty of murder; I wanted someone else to have done it, someone who didn't make me salivate when I saw photos of him unclothed. It was foolish to think that way, primitive and irrational. But how often are lust and infatuation driven by reason?

Valenzuela gathered up the photos, tapping them together like a deck of cards. "To answer your question, when I skimmed the files, these caught my eye."

"I imagine they would," I said.

SEVENTEEN

I left Valenzuela with his photographs and headed for the stairs again, intending to go straight up to Templeton's room and ask her if we could please go home.

She and Maurice had talked me into coming to Haunted Springs as a vacation but after two days I felt immeasurably tired. With HIV and the toxic meds involved, one sometimes feels mysteriously fatigued, so I was used to that. But this exhaustion felt more emotional than physical. I wanted to be away from this place and forget that I'd ever met Christopher Oakley, or basked in his enigmatic Hollywood charm. Get home, draw the shades, crawl into bed with a good book and get lost in it. Templeton would have filed her news piece on last night's murder by now, for publication in tomorrow's *L.A. Times*. She certainly had enough material to write her longer feature, or could pick up what she needed from Los Angeles, by e-mail and phone. There was no good reason to hang around that I could see.

As I hit the stairs, Richard Pearlman was coming down. He was surprisingly cordial, and even invited me to lunch with him.

"Wouldn't you rather eat with Templeton?" I asked, trying to keep it neutral.

"Just came from her room. She's buried in research—Lexis, Nexis, Google, all kinds of database sources. Apparently she's been at it every spare minute. Won't tell me what she's after. Anyway, she's tied up, so how about you and me breaking bread together, Justice? My treat."

I was hungry and tired of doing battle with him, so I accepted. "I never turn down a free meal. Old reporter's habit, I guess."

We ate on the dining room balcony, watching the clouds gather and darken over the lake and buttoning up against a chill wind that was rising fast. After briefly touching on the Toni Pebbles murder—Pearlman seemed to have no connection to her whatsoever, or so he claimed—the conversation turned to the surprise Lois Aswell had pulled during filming, when she'd used Sweet Doctor Silk as an unannounced stand-in for Deep Freeze, fooling Kevin Tiemeyer and everyone else. Pearlman mentioned that he'd alluded to the issue of eyewitness fallibility in his book—the point of Aswell's surprise experiment—but admitted that he probably should have delved more deeply into it, particularly the racial angle.

"Alexandra's opened my eyes to some things I missed," he conceded. "Frankly, my publisher was more interested in the Hollywood elements."

"You could have stood your ground," I said. "Every author has that right."

"They might not have published it."

"Then you take it elsewhere."

He shrugged haplessly, out of excuses. "To be honest, the DNA analysis that I financed was fortunate serendipity. It was always the Hollywood angle that drew me to the story. I'm a professor of film history and cinematic theory, not a crime reporter." He said it like he was waiting for me to absolve him. When I said nothing, he added sheepishly, "It was my first book. Next time, I hope to be more diligent, to do a better job."

"Perhaps you'll write a sequel," I suggested, "incorporating the Toni Pebbles murder. Who knows? Someone may have solved the Rebecca Fox murder by then."

He brightened. "Actually, I've suggested to Alexandra that we might work on a book like that together."

"There you go," I said. "A chance to do some things you didn't the first time around. And the opportunity to spend some quality time with Templeton. Not a bad deal, all around."

The conversation grew strained at that point, with meaningless small talk taking us through the main course, until Pearlman suddenly cleared his throat and blurted out an apology for treating me rudely the first night we'd met. With great self-consciousness, he told me he'd admired my work as a reporter before things had fallen apart for me and said he hoped my memoirs would be a big success. I couldn't be sure if he was sincere, if Templeton had put him up to it, or he was trying to get into my good graces to enhance his chances with her, but it didn't matter much at any rate. I was weary of jousting with Templeton over her choices in men and my own petty jealousy in that regard. If she genuinely liked Pearlman, I thought, I could certainly learn to get along with him. He was intelligent, gainfully employed, and clearly smitten with her, so why not?

I accepted his apology, we shook hands, and fell into a discussion about the craft of writing, the kind of self-important talk writers often slip into that masks an undercurrent of competition and one-upmanship, a form of bragging camouflaged as shop talk. As we finished our meals and he called for the check, he asked me what I thought of his book. It seemed like the kind of gaffe a neophyte author would make and one that I hoped to avoid when my turn came, since it puts the other writer uncomfortably on the spot. I told him diplomatically that I hadn't finished *A Murder in Eternal Springs* but that it had me turning the pages, which was true enough, and assured him I'd finish it shortly, probably back in West Hollywood.

That got his attention. "You're leaving soon for home?"

"I hope so."

"And Alexandra?"

I shrugged. "We came together. She's my ride."

"Of course." He looked crestfallen but smiled anyway. "What a shame. And I was so enjoying her company."

"There's always e-mail," I said helpfully.

I thanked him for the lunch and excused myself, resuming my trek upstairs with the hope of departing as soon as possible.

"Justice! You're just in time." Templeton stood in her open doorway, holding up her promotional copy of *Freeze Rapped,* the new Deep Freeze CD. "I'm about to slip it into my Walkman and have a listen. Come on in."

"Rap gives me a headache."

"So do I, but you still listen to me. Sort of."

"Rap's a blight on black culture. Isn't that what you always tell me?"

"Not all of it, just most. Still, I think we should hear what Deep Freeze has recorded."

"Why?"

"Because he's central to the feature I'm writing. He's playing Ed Jones, after all. And he's always haranguing Lois Aswell to expand his role in the movie."

"Seems reasonable," I said. "He wants more lines, more screen time. The guy clearly likes attention. What performer doesn't?"

She smiled coyly. "Maybe there's more to it than that."

I glanced past her to a laptop and a pile of printed data beside it. "You've come across something?"

"I'll tell you all about it." She grabbed my hand, tried to pull me inside. "After we listen to a few of these cuts."

I planted my feet, resisting. "Let's listen in your car, on the way home. Kill two birds with one stone."

She regarded me curiously. "There was a murder last night, Benjamin. Why would we go home now?"

"Because there was a murder last night."

"Since when has an unsolved homicide left you disinterested?"

"Can't we just go? I'm sure we can find another murder in L.A. for you to write about, every bit as interesting as this one."

"Not likely." Her eyes narrowed. "What's happened? What's bothering you?"

"I want to get out of here, that's all. This place creeps me out."

"It involves Christopher Oakley, doesn't it?"

"Why would you say that?"

"Because you've been drooling over him ever since you first laid eyes on him. And because he's such an obvious suspect in Toni Pebbles's murder, given all the rumors about his private life."

"He's got an alibi, remember? He was with Heather Sparks at the time of the murder."

"She could be covering for him. She's engaged to him, isn't she? Whether or not the engagement is genuine or bogus, they must be close, or she wouldn't be involved with him the way she is."

"It's really none of our business, is it?"

She studied me closely, pushing in on my eyes. "What is it? What have you found out that you're not telling me?"

I looked away, swallowed uncomfortably. "It's confidential. I gave my word to Sergeant Valenzuela."

"He's uncovered something. He's zeroing in on a suspect."

"Stop talking like a reporter."

"I am a reporter."

"I just told you I can't talk about it."

She tugged on my hand more forcefully, pulling me in and shutting the door behind us. "Then the least you can do is listen to this CD with me, and we can talk about that."

"And after that, we'll talk about going home?"

She removed a Diana Krall CD from her Walkman and slipped in *Freeze Rapped.* "One thing at a time, Benjamin."

I liked listening to rap about as much I enjoyed hearing a jackhammer pound concrete. But in recent years I'd stopped to pay attention from time to time, because rap was such a powerful cultural force and because I found some of the lyrics so compelling. Not compelling because they uplifted my spirit or dazzled me with their artistry and brilliance, although some rap may have achieved that. What so engrossed me was the unabashed hatred for women, gays, Jews, and cops that I heard in certain cuts. Gangsta rap, they call it. That was the rap that always caught my ear, not the gentler, more thoughtful stuff. Gangsta rap was too ugly and pervasive to ignore.

As a white guy pushing fifty, I was hardly an expert on the subject, but I'd read enough to know rap's basic history. It originated in the 1970s as street poetry, improvised by young urban black men with nimble tongues who knew how to rhyme and liked performing. Eventually, it worked its way into the mainstream, embraced by middle-class kids and profitably co-opted by the recording industry. Its critics denounced hardcore rap as primal and obscene, a cultural cancer that bred hatred and violence. Others labeled it a viable new vernacular tradition that reflected the anger and frustration of America's inner cities, a new means of expression for the disenfranchised and voiceless. I figured there was some truth to both arguments; when someone screams, it's usually because that person's in pain, and can't endure it in silence anymore.

There was one thing I knew for sure, however: rap was part of the tragic and continuing erosion in the great musical legacy of Duke Ellington, Louis Armstrong, and other jazz pioneers that had once been the cultural heart and soul of the black community. The generation that had followed—jazz icons like Charlie Parker and Dizzy Gillespie—had thrived because even the poorest black kid in urban America had access in public school to musical instruments and training. But that kind of education no longer existed for most inner-city kids, who were lucky to get restroom toilet paper when they needed it. The result was musical starvation, and today rap filled the vacuum. A new generation of kids who'd probably never heard of Ellington grew up listening to lyrics like "Suck my dick, bitch, and make it puke" by 2 Live Crew and "Life ain't nothing but bitches and money" by NWA—Niggers with Attitude.

Deep Freeze fit that general mold. That's what Templeton and I discovered as we listened to *Freeze Rapped* sitting side by side on her hotel bed, while the wind played with the curtains at her open window and sent a blast of cool air through the room. The first refrain offered the rapper's heartfelt feelings about "punks"—homosexuals in black street and prison vernacular—delivered at the rapid-fire pace that gave rap its aggressive syncopation.

Don't need no gun
Don't need no knife
I'll strangle the punk
Looks at me twice
Use my own damn hands
To end the motherfucker's life.
And when I'm done
I'll go jump my wife.

As the number ended, Templeton glanced over at me, looking disheartened, even distressed.

"Not exactly Cole Porter," I said.

She attempted a smile. "Nice beat, though—danceable."

More cuts followed—cops and Jews blasted as the evil enemy, in equally profane language—before Deep Freeze launched into several tunes aimed at what seemed to be his favorite target for debasement: women. One refrain went like this:

Spread your legs, bitch
The main course has arrived.
Deep Freeze and his meat
Sizzling and super-sized.

By the end of the album, Templeton and I weren't making light of it anymore. She sat straight up, staring ahead, her hands folded in her lap, with a look on her face that suggested equal parts anger and disgust.

"He obviously hates women," she said tightly.

"You knew that yesterday, the first time you met him."

"He's not too fond of gay men, either."

"So what's new?"

She shuddered audibly. "It disturbs me to think that kids are listening to this garbage the way their parents listened to Marvin Gaye or Bruce Springsteen."

"Sorry you listened to it?"

She shook her head resolutely. "I'm more determined than

ever to figure this guy out—especially after what I discovered this morning." She glanced my way, smiling slyly. "But you don't want to know about that, do you? You just want to go home, get away from this place."

"You really found something interesting on the guy?"

She smiled slyly. "Interesting would be putting it mildly."

I tried to save face with a shrug. "I guess I could hang around a little longer."

Her smile widened. She got to her feet and I followed her to a writing desk, where she'd stacked a number of files. As she riffled through them, I stepped over to close the window and shut out the cold. As I reached up, I heard a keening outside, the eerie sound I'd heard once before as the wind passed across Whispering Rock.

As I looked out, I saw the pale, white-haired woman in the threadbare white dress. She stood where I'd seen her last night, barefoot on the hard ground, her eyes fixed again in the direction of the Rebecca Fox Room. As the wind teased her flimsy dress and dirty hair, she flattened both hands over her ears as if it was screaming at her in a language only she understood. The sky had grown dark, but I could still see the old lady's eyes—the stark desperation, or maybe the dementia.

"Your file on Deep Freeze will have to wait," I said, and started from the room.

Templeton stepped after me, to the doorway. "Where are you going?"

"I have to talk to someone."

"Who?"

"Out your window. Take a look."

Templeton frowned and turned back into her room. I sprinted to the stairs and started down, taking two at a time.

EIGHTEEN

Outside the hotel, the wind was stirring dust devils and the massing storm clouds had turned the afternoon as dark as dusk.

When I reached Whispering Rock the old lady was gone. The wind continued hard, hissing off the granite like the strangled voice of someone pleading to be heard. I hugged myself against the cold, scanning the main street that ran through town, but she wasn't there. She wasn't in the hotel parking lot, either, when I searched, or along the trail behind the hotel that led to the site of the old mineral springs, or the steps above that leading to the big Tiemeyer house. I rounded the front of the hotel again, about to return and apologize to Templeton for my rude departure, when I glimpsed a figure—white hair, white dress—disappearing around a turn in the trail down to the lake.

I ran in that direction, calling for the old woman to stop, but my voice was lost against the wind. By the time I reached the trailhead she was halfway down, moving with surprising speed and agility on her thin legs, her bare feet skimming hard rock as if it was well-tended lawn. I raced after her, putting on the brakes for the switchbacks and steepest stretches, sprinting ahead as the trail neared the lake and gradually leveled out. She flew toward the water as if she were weightless, propelled more from the power of her mind than was possible from her rail-thin body. As she neared the beach I hollered as loudly as I could and she pulled up to look back.

"Wait! Talk to me, please!"

She turned and dashed on. Out on the lake, the wind was driving whitecaps across the water that broke in small waves along the rocky shore. She ran straight across it and dove into the water without another glance back. I kept my eye on her as she swam; her strokes were remarkably strong, like someone who had been swimming in Lake Enid for years, maybe decades. As I ran, transfixed by her progress, I struck a rut in the trail and took a violent tumble—off the trail and down a hard dirt slope, coming to a painful stop as the ground flattened out. By the time I got to my feet, checked for damage, and regained the trail, the old woman was a couple of hundred yards out. Her strokes had slowed but they were steady, taking her relentlessly toward the circle of treetops visible in the middle of the lake, where Christopher Oakley and I had stopped earlier in the day to study the remnants of the ghost town resting at the bottom.

Her destination seemed clear. She was swimming directly into the heart of old Eternal Springs.

I started down again, limping, which slowed my progress. As I reached the shoreline I could barely see the swimmer. Every few seconds a thin arm rose up, then the other, coming down to chop the water with a small splash. There was no one else to be seen, on shore or out on the lake; the weather had driven everyone back to the hotel. I glanced at a posted sign: UNDERWATER HAZARDS—BOAT AND SWIM AT YOUR OWN RISK. Then back at the old woman, as she neared the ring of trees bunched around the center of the old town.

I grabbed the same rowboat Christopher Oakley and I had taken that morning, pushed it from the sand into the water and jumped in, pointing the bow in the same direction that I'd last seen the old lady. I took the deepest bites from the water that I could, pulled as hard as I was able, using every old muscle available. Panic born of guilt rose up inside me; I did my best to channel it into the rowing, but it consumed me just the same. I'd driven the old lady to the water the way wolves sometimes chase fleeing deer into mountain lakes, where they swim too far out in their terror and drown when they lack the strength to return. If the old woman didn't come back, if her body was found floating in the hours or days ahead, I'd have to live with that, and somehow try to explain it. The truth was I'd had no business chasing after a frightened old woman, whatever my curiosity about who she might be, or what it was about the Rebecca Fox Room that had her transfixed, or the message she thought the wind carried as it caromed off Whispering Rock. It was one thing for my overweening curiosity to get *me* into trouble, as it had so many times; it was quite another to put the life of a disturbed individual at risk, because of my personal obsession to know things others didn't.

Several hundred yards out, I eased up on the oars and looked around, letting my burning muscles get an infusion of blood and oxygen. I'd gained significantly on the old woman; her strokes had grown weak, infrequent. She was among the thickest trees now, using a crawl stroke to penetrate the circle they formed where the center of Eternal Springs had once risen up. A moment later, her movement abruptly stopped. For a second, relief washed over me: I would row out to her, get her into the boat, transport her back to shore, make sure she got proper medical attention at the hotel. It seemed simple enough. She'd be safe, and I'd be off the hook—even something of a hero, for having rescued her.

That was when I saw her dive and disappear. I waited ten, maybe fifteen seconds. She didn't come back up.

I was pulling on the oars again, deeper and harder than I'd imagined myself capable, ignoring the pain that spread like fire through my upper body. As the bow of the boat nosed through the ring of trees into the center, I could hear thunderclaps in the distance. I knew where I was—my sense of direction was just sharp enough—but the water was too dark for me to make out the foundations of the old town below. As I kicked off my shoes, the old woman surfaced. I called out to her, begging her to wait for me.

By the time I'd stripped off my shirt, she'd gone under again, and a new wave of fear and adrenaline engulfed me.

I went over the side into the shock of frigid water, which helped clear my head. I swam over and dove in the general area where I'd last seen the woman go down. As I swam down I kicked frantically; seconds later I neared the bottom, where the visibility was no more than a few feet. There was just enough to reveal the benches and the fountain of the old town square that Oakley and I had observed from above that morning, when the light had been stronger. But the old woman was nowhere in sight. My lungs felt close to bursting. I hadn't been under a minute when I popped back up for air.

This time I waited, treading water. When the woman appeared again, she was less than a hundred feet from me to the east. Again I hollered, again she dove. I swam to the spot where she'd gone under, took a deep breath, and plunged after her.

As I went down, the outlines of the foundation below gradually emerged in the murky water. I sensed movement on the side of the building's foundation where the street would have been. As I continued down, her white dress showed itself first, so thin it looked like tissue wafting in the underwater current, about to dissolve. Then I saw her face, and those confused and desperate eyes.

She was at the steps of the town jail, swimming through watery space where a doorway once would have been, looking frantically around as if the building might reappear around her if she conjured it with sufficient willpower. I swam down again, straight for her. She turned toward me just as I was about to reach her, looking utterly perplexed, as if amazed and disturbed to find the old jail gone. She stared straight into my eyes, as if for answers, and it struck me that she hadn't fled so much as led me here to be a witness.

She turned away to search the emptiness within the missing walls while tiny air bubbles escaped her mouth and nostrils with increasing volume. I darted toward her with two or three strong kicks and grabbed her around her narrow waist with my left arm. She fought to free herself as I dragged her up, kicking and flailing, but her stamina seemed dissipated. For a moment, as I swallowed water, I almost let her go to save myself. I hung on, kept crawling toward the surface. The twenty feet of water above us seemed like a hundred fathoms. Nearing the top, she stopped fighting and I felt her go limp in my arms. It made our ascent easier but filled me with dread at the same time.

I popped into the bracing air, coughing up water, gasping for breath. I got her head above the lake's surface. She wasn't moving.

Thunder rumbled across the storm-darkened sky. A moment later, at the south end of the lake, a tendril of lightning appeared, touching the water and crackling the air with its lethal voltage.

I looked around. The boat was gone. Then I saw it forty or fifty yards off, moving away from us, driven by the wind and the whitecaps toward the distant shore. Well beyond my strength to reach.

I was clinging to the upper branches of a dead tree with one arm and the old woman with the other, trying to revive her with my mouth on hers, when I heard the putting of a small outboard engine.

A minute later, Scotty Campbell was there with Kevin Tiemeyer in an aluminum boat from the marina, steering through the trees in our direction. The old lady was unconscious but still had a pulse. I told them that as they maneuvered closer and lifted her into the boat. Campbell went to work on her and seemed to know what he was doing. He turned her face down and got some water out of her, then flipped her over and began resuscitating her in earnest, using his short, powerful arms to do the chest compressions before alternating with mouth-to-mouth, his small body clearly advantageous. Tiemeyer looked on, more troubled than ever, opening up the little engine to its top speed, which wasn't much. Behind us, another bolt of lightning found one of the taller treetops in the lake, electrifying its branches and trunk and causing the water around it to crackle and spark. As he steered, Tiemeyer used his cell phone to call the hotel, asking someone there to phone down to the valley for a medical helicopter to transport the victim to the nearest emergency room.

I must have been shivering from the cold, but I didn't notice. The only things I could think about were the old lady, how I'd been complicit in all this, and how I'd square that with myself or her survivors if she didn't make it.

As Campbell worked on her, her right arm flopped to her side, near my feet. I noticed an odd-looking bracelet on her bony wrist—plastic, with an inscription of some kind. As I looked closer, I saw that it was a medical alert bracelet, inscribed with a name, birth date, contact information, and medical condition, which included chronic paranoia and delusion. The name on the bracelet was Martha Frech.

NINETEEN

Before we reached shore, Martha Frech began to cough and spit up water. She opened her eyes as we lifted her from the boat to a pile of blankets on the beach.

Templeton was waiting for us, along with a small crowd that included Lois Aswell, Deep Freeze, Christopher Oakley, and two security guards from the hotel. Sergeant Valenzuela, I soon learned, had spotted the old lady in the white dress from a hotel window as she ran down the trail; remembering my account of seeing her the previous night, he'd watched through binoculars as I'd chased her to the lake, and what had transpired from there. Since he couldn't go himself on his busted foot and crutches, he'd sent Kevin Tiemeyer and Scott Campbell down to rescue us—Tiemeyer because he had the keys and access to a motorboat, Campbell because he was certified in CPR. The others had come down out of simple concern; it heartened me to see Deep Freeze drop his tough guy act long enough to help a stranger in distress.

Tiemeyer asked us to help him clear stones and driftwood from the beach so the helicopter could set down safely there and we got busy doing it. Templeton and Aswell took Martha Frech aside and, using a blanket as a shield, got her out of her wet dress, and wrapped her in two heavy blankets, while the old woman mumbled incoherently and shivered against the hypothermia she'd begun to suffer.

Tiemeyer suggested I go up to the hotel for a hot bath and dry clothes. Instead, I wrapped myself in a blanket and joined him as he cleared debris from the sand, peppering him with questions that he answered dutifully if uneasily. The woman was indeed Martha Frech, he confirmed; she lived alone at the south end of town, in the old, two-story house above the cemetery that was in a state of disrepair. The daughter of an unmarried housekeeper, she'd been ten when she'd discovered the lifeless body of Rebecca Fox late on the evening of March 15, 1956. I asked him how an unwed hotel housekeeper could afford such a fine house, as it must have once been, compared to the smaller houses in town, excluding the grand Tiemeyer place, of course.

"Maybe my mother bought it for them, I don't know," he said tersely.

"When would that have been?"

"I'm not really sure of the date. Late fifties, sometime around there. Get that big stone, will you? It's a bit much for a man my age."

I lugged the rock down to the lake, dumping it into the water before rejoining him. "An extravagant gift for a menial employee," I said. My teeth had begun to chatter but I kept talking, ignoring the cold. "Considering the financial straits the hotel was in for so many years. At least from what I've been reading in Richard Pearlman's book."

Tiemeyer paused in his work, facing me. "Mother was very good to Miss Frech. She took her on at the hotel, even though Miss Frech had borne a child out of wedlock. Martha was a sweet child. A bit timid, but everyone cared heaps for her. We wanted to help her family if we could. Mother introduced Miss Frech to our church, helped get her life back on track. Miss Frech always told us she'd been blessed, coming to Eternal Springs and meeting my mother."

I glanced at Martha, huddled in her blankets between

Aswell and Templeton, mumbling and pointing a bony finger in my direction.

"I guess her daughter wasn't so lucky," I said.

"She suffered a terrible accident, Mr. Justice." Tiemeyer bent to his work again. "Life isn't always kind, is it?"

"Why would such a timid little girl be running so recklessly down a staircase the way she did? You'd think she'd know better."

"Are such arcane details really so important?"

"The devil's always in the details, Kevin."

His eyes flickered and his jaw tightened for a moment. As he turned away to gather up driftwood, he explained that fifty years ago, after finding Rebecca Fox dead, Martha ran down the main staircase in fright; she'd fallen and tumbled, suffering a serious head injury as she struck her head on the tiled lobby floor. Through the years, she'd grown mentally unstable, he said, often spouting gibberish no one could make sense of.

"She lives off her disability checks," he added. "I try to help her when I can, and keep an eye on her. It's not easy, as you can imagine."

"You two are close then?"

"As close as one can be, I suppose, to someone who lives in her own world." He regarded me carefully. "The tragedy of that night brought us all together in unexpected ways, Mr. Justice."

"Did she see a murder weapon that night, Kevin?"

"Apparently not."

I mentioned that it was my understanding no murder weapon had ever been found; that Ed Jones's fishing knife, which he'd been unable to produce, had allegedly been used to cut the victim's throat. "That was according to the sheriff, Jack Hightower, your uncle. He said he found Jones washing blood from his hands. Could that have been blood from gutting fish, Mr. Tiemeyer?"

"I really couldn't say, Mr. Justice. Perhaps you should finish reading Mr. Pearlman's book. I've told him everything I know about that night. It's all there, quite ably reported."

"But if it wasn't Ed Jones you saw coming out of that room that night, then another knife must have been used in the murder."

Tiemeyer straightened, facing me again, but not quite looking at me. "As you might imagine, Mr. Justice, it's not something I enjoy discussing, given how unpleasant it was for everyone involved."

"Especially for Rebecca Fox," I said.

Anger flared briefly in his usually mild eyes. He carted off his armload of driftwood and avoided me thereafter.

Minutes later, I heard the chop of rotary blades from the south end of Lake Enid and turned to see a red-and-white helicopter rising into view above the dam, coming up the canyon. Tiemeyer set about scattering us to safe distances as the agile chopper approached and landed on the small beach.

Two air medics jumped out and unloaded a stretcher, dropping its wheels down. They wrapped Martha Frech in a thermal blanket while letting the hotel blankets drop at her feet. She resisted, pointing at me and becoming increasingly agitated. They managed to get her onto the stretcher; one of the medics checked her pulse while the other secured a Velcro strap around her ankles and waist. Suddenly, she sat straight up, crying out and motioning to me frantically with a gnarled hand. Against Tiemeyer's protests—he expressed concern for her fragile state of mind—they allowed me to come close, hoping it might calm her. The rotating blades pounded us with their downdraft and the noise was nearly deafening. She reached up with her insistent fingers and pulled my head down until my ear was close to her mouth.

"I need to go back," she whispered. "I must go back."

"Back where, Martha?"

"Back, I must go back."

"To the jail?"

She nodded desperately. "Back!"

"To the past?"

She nodded eagerly, as if I was finally getting it. "I need to tell them the truth. I need to go back and tell them what I really saw."

She pointed up the hill, toward Whispering Rock. "I can hear her whispering to me, whispering my name, begging me to go back and tell the truth."

"Rebecca Fox whispers to you?"

Again she nodded; her rheumy eyes glistened with tears. "My lie cursed this place. My lie keeps causing people to die."

A medic nudged me aside as he put a stethoscope to her upper chest. I moved to the other side of the stretcher, leaning close again. "What lie, Martha?"

"About the knife. You know, don't you? That's why you went with me down below. You want them to hear the truth."

"You saw Ed Jones's knife that night?"

"No! The pretty knife she brought with her from Hollywood. The knife that was in her hand." She covered her eyes, shrieking. "All that blood. So much blood!"

I was stunned by what she'd related and wanted to hear more, but the medics separated us and finished strapping her down. As they loaded the stretcher into the chopper, she opened her eyes wide, looking straight at me, and cried out, "Why did they make us lie? Why did they make us lie about what we saw?"

I had no end of questions for her, but a medic pulled the door shut from inside. I heard it being locked and stepped safely away to stand between Tiemeyer and Templeton, my mind going back to the flurry of words I'd just heard.

"I warned you that her mind was fragile," Tiemeyer said. "She hasn't been in touch with reality for years. I'm sure you mean well, Mr. Justice. But you do her no good by listening to her nonsense or pressing her with questions."

"Did Richard Pearlman press her with questions before writing his book, Kevin? Or did you make sure he left her alone and undisturbed?"

He bristled, but tried to hide it. "I'm not sure he was aware she still lived here."

"And you didn't tell him, did you?"

Templeton was listening now, and Tiemeyer noticed.

"You almost got her killed," he said, "chasing her down here the way you did. Haven't you done enough to the poor woman? Can't you just let her be?"

"You're right, Tiemeyer. I have no right to hound her. I won't bother her again."

His demeanor softened, along with his voice. "That would be decent of you, Justice." He glanced at Templeton. "Both of you. She doesn't need anyone asking her questions, reminding her of a chapter in her life that obviously distresses her."

"What will happen to her?" Templeton asked.

"They'll keep her for a day or two, get her back on her medication. I'll see to it that she gets excellent care. I always have, as my mother did when she was alive. We try to take care of our own, here in Haunted Springs."

The wind came in violent gusts now and thunder continued to growl in the turbulent sky. The helicopter revved and lifted off in a rumble that became a roar. We watched it speed in a smooth trajectory down the length of the lake, gently rising as it approached the dam, before banking west into a muted sunset of gold and gray, as the sun fought a losing battle with the building storm. Raindrops began to pelt us; we gathered up the damp blankets, shook off the sand, and headed up the trail for the hotel.

Out on Lake Enid, the storm was churning the water, causing its surface to darken and wrinkle, like the scowling face of a furious old woman.

TWENTY

As darkness fell and the skies opened in a downpour, I shut the window in my room, locked it tight, and settled into a warm bath with a cup of hot tea and my new copy of *A Murder in Eternal Springs*.

I found myself skimming, looking for salient names, dates, incidents, details. As I roved the pages, jumping from line to line, certain facts caught my eye: I learned that no one had ever been charged for the lynching of Ed Jones in 1956; so secretive and tight was the local Ku Klux Klan—a long-dormant "klavern" from the Klan's heyday in the 1920s—that not a single member was ever identified. At his death, Jones, the son of sharecroppers and grandson of a couple born into slavery, was unmarried but had left behind a young daughter in Gulfport, Mississippi, where he sent the mother money when he could. Not much more was known about him or his family—not that Richard Pearlman had included in his book, anyway—other than a couple of minor scrapes Jones had with the law before drifting into Haunted Springs looking for work and refuge. After the lynching, Jack Hightower, who had followed his sister from Macon, had stayed on as the local sheriff. The fact that he'd been overcome by a mob and allowed his prisoner to be hanged apparently had not been held against him; eventually, he was elected sheriff of the entire county. Jack Hightower Jr., his son and Enid's nephew, had followed his father into the Sheriff's Department, where he served as the chief investigator in the Brandy Fox suicide in 1981, under his father's supervision, before going on to replace him as sheriff in a later countywide election.

As an author, Pearlman had a habit of dropping in sidebars of encapsulated information that might otherwise slow down his narrative. One sidebar offered a thumbnail history of the Klan, putting into historical context the tiny band of diehard Klansmen in Eternal Springs who'd strung up Ed Jones.

> *The Ku Klux Klan got its start at the end of the Civil War as a fraternal organization of Confederate Army officers dedicated to socializing and prankishness. But in 1867, as Reconstruction governments came into power in the South, the KKK became committed to destroying or driving out the Reconstructionists, both black and white, whom it saw as hostile and oppressive. Because Klansmen considered blacks innately inferior, the Klan was violently opposed to former slaves or anyone of color exercising their newly acquired political power, including voting or holding political office. White supremacy and the inviolability of white womanhood were at the heart of the Klan doctrine; its members relied on kidnapping, flogging, mutilation, arson, and murder to carry out their mission of keeping blacks in their proper place.*
>
> *Their campaign of terror, waged in white robes and hoods, was largely effective. Even though its escalating violence forced the Klan to officially disband in 1869, and federal laws and proclamations that followed drove the organization into deep secrecy and weakened its power, the Klan was able to subjugate blacks socially and politically throughout much of the South.*
>
> *In 1915, the Klan was resurrected in Georgia, open to males sixteen and older who were white, native-born, and Protestant. This new version of the Klan specifically*

excluded blacks, Jews, and Roman Catholics, who became their primary targets for persecution. Following World War I, during a period of economic instability and social unrest, the Klan expanded its reach to many states outside the South and its range of targets to include anyone whom it felt threatened traditional American values. Despite its violent tactics, few Klansmen were prosecuted for their crimes and many had the tacit approval of local officials in the South and elsewhere.

The Klan peaked in the early 1920s, when one estimate put its membership in 1924 at roughly three million. As far west as Los Angeles, the KKK was able to wield considerable influence in local politics and legislation, including efforts to keep blacks segregated in ghettoized communities to contain their voting power and political reach. But public opinion and political opposition, along with inept leadership and internal conflict, badly damaged the Klan, which had been reduced to a few thousand members by 1929.

By 1940 the Klan was loosely affiliated with Nazi Germany, another blow to its reputation. Following the entry of the U.S. into World War II, and the Klan's failure to pay back taxes owed to the federal government, the KKK formally disbanded, although Klansmen would continue to agitate and commit random violence, including bombings and murders that escalated during the civil rights struggle of the 1950s and early 1960s. With passage of the U.S. Civil Rights Act of 1964, guaranteeing blacks the right to vote, Klan membership jumped once more, to about forty thousand in 1965, but the KKK would never again know the power and glory of its peak years decades earlier.

I didn't learn much from the sidebar that I didn't already know, but I did make mental notes on a couple of details before moving on to leaf through the extensive gallery of photographs in the middle of the book. One that intrigued me captured Rebecca Fox leaning appreciatively on a grand piano, while the famous pianist Errol Garner played *Rhapsody in Blue,* her favorite composition; the caption mentioned that a version of *Rhapsody* was still spinning on the record player in her room the night she was found slain. There was also a publicity still of Rebecca Fox taken on the set of *The Ides of March,* the film she'd nearly completed at the time of her death; this caption mentioned that it was the most expensive picture of her career at nearly three million dollars, a notable budget for a movie at that time, even for a major star like Fox. Brandy Fox, quite pretty but not the classic beauty her mother had been, also had her share of illustrations. The one that drew my attention was a bloody crime scene photo taken the night she committed suicide; she could be seen crumpled on the floor, still clutching in her right hand the knife she'd used to end her life with a deep, clean slice across the left side of her neck, from which a serious amount of blood had gushed before her heart had stopped pumping and the blood had ceased to flow.

I'd read and seen enough about the tragic Fox family for one evening and put the book aside to finish later. The water in the tub was growing cool so I soaped down, used some shampoo, rinsed off under the shower, and let the water out. I was stepping from the bathroom naked when there was a knock at the door. Given recent events, I used the peephole first for security and saw Christopher Oakley standing outside. I wrapped a damp towel around my waist and pulled the door open.

"You caught me just getting out of the shower," I said.

"I can see that." His eyes took me in, top to bottom. He apologized for coming at a bad time, but asked if he could come in anyway.

I told him he could.

In my prime, I'd had a couple of affairs with attractive young actors, and if I'd learned anything about them it was that they almost never make the first move. The other person is supposed to be the one who's interested, not the actor; you must go to him, making him the center of attention and the object of affection, and, above all, reassuring him of his desirability. The pretty actors with whom I'd been involved had always been tentative, holding back enough to feel safe against potential rejection, while allowing the flame of fantasy to flicker without quite going out. It was the age-old dance of intimacy—one step forward, one step back—with a strong dose of narcissism and insecurity in the mix, the kind that seems to keep so many good-looking performers forever at war with themselves, caught between their desperate need to be loved and their equally deep fear of getting truly close and exposing who they really are. I assumed the same would be true of Oakley, but I was wrong.

He stepped directly to the center of my room, facing me with his usual confidence, earnest but relaxed, never averting his eyes for a moment. His boldness threw me off; I found it as disconcerting as I did exciting. Except for the occasional flash of lightning beyond the window, the only light in the room came from a small table lamp. I reached to switch on another one.

"Leave it off," Oakley said. "It's nice this way, don't you think?"

"Sure, if you like it."

"I came to see how you're doing, after your ordeal down at the lake. It looked like you had a pretty rough time out there."

"I'll probably be sore tomorrow. Otherwise, none the worse for wear."

His eyes dropped to the towel around my waist. "You were about to dress for dinner?" I nodded. "Don't let me hold you up. We can talk while you get ready."

"You don't mind?"

He laughed easily. "It wouldn't be the first time I've seen a man naked."

I reached for a fresh pair of briefs off the bed, turned my back to him, and dropped the towel. I was about to step into my shorts when he came up behind me, so close I felt his breath on my neck. A moment later I experienced a shock of pleasure as I felt his hands on my shoulders.

"Maybe what you need is a good massage." He began kneading the tender meat of my shoulders, gently at first, then deeper, digging in. "Preventive body work," he explained, "to ward off some of that stiffness you're expecting tomorrow."

"It may not take that long." He grinned at that; I saw it as he peered over my shoulder into a full-length mirror that revealed the inches I'd acquired since he'd put his hands on me. I let go of the briefs, closed my eyes, gave in to the waves of pleasure sweeping through me. "You've got a nice touch, Christopher. Strong but sensitive."

"I studied massage when I first went to New York. Supported myself that way while I took acting classes and made the audition rounds."

"I'll bet you had a loyal clientele."

"Business was pretty good."

"Men or women?"

"Both."

"What am I going to owe you for this one?"

He turned me around to face him. "This one's on the house, Benjamin. Strictly between friends."

He placed one hand behind my neck for support and used the other to work on my tender pectorals, threading his fingers through the dark blond hair on my chest, as comfortable handling me as if we'd been lovers for years.

"You baffle me, Christopher."

Lightning flashed, illuminating sections of his face. "I guess I'm more complicated than I look."

We were so close now I could have counted the lovely lashes on his baby blues. He was looking directly into my eyes, not the slightest hesitation. The only sound in the room was the distant thunder, the drumbeat of raindrops on the windowpane, and our breathing; his calm, mine quickening. It struck me that there was nothing left to do but kiss him.

I was about to do just that when we heard a scream. It was close enough that it had to be on the third floor. Oakley's eyes left mine, in the direction of the door.

"Heather."

That was all he said before he dashed from the room. The screaming became hysterical, while a gathering of footsteps pounded down the hall.

TWENTY-ONE

When I reached a knot of people in the hallway, I saw what all the commotion was about: Someone had stuck a bloody knife in Heather Sparks's door.

The blood, which lay along the edge of the eight-inch blade, was reddish brown, dry, and sticky-looking. The knife protruded dead center roughly halfway down, between the room number and the doorknob, which put it somewhere between three and four feet from the floor.

By the time I got there, tucking my shirt into my pants, Christopher Oakley had his arms around a sobbing Heather Sparks. He pressed his lips to her hair, murmuring to her, and avoided my eyes as I approached. A dozen or so others had already gathered: Kevin Tiemeyer, Alexandra Templeton, Lois Aswell, Deep Freeze, Karen Hori, Nan Williams, three security guards, and a few crew members whose names I didn't know. Others stood in the lobby below, talking among themselves or staring up. Still more emerged from their rooms, standing at the railings on the various floors like curious drivers passing a bad wreck, knowing it was wrong to gawk but unable to look away.

"It looks like one of our kitchen knives," Tiemeyer said. "We don't lock the kitchen overnight. Anyone might have taken it."

I asked if Sergeant Valenzuela had been notified.

"I'm right here, Justice." Valenzuela came lumbering down the hallway, a crutch under each arm, swinging his heavy foot and carrying a small tote bag. "Sorry it took me so long. That elevator could use some oil."

"I assure you, I have it inspected regularly," Tiemeyer said. "It's old, but quite safe."

"Just a joke, Mr. Tiemeyer." Valenzuela's face darkened as he stopped to study the door. "Has anyone touched this knife?"

"I guess whoever stuck it there touched it," Deep Freeze said, chuckling at his little joke.

Valenzuela ignored him, instead turning to Tiemeyer. "Mr. Tiemeyer?"

"It may have come from our kitchen, although I doubt I've handled it. I don't get into the kitchen much."

The rest of us assured him we hadn't put our hands on it. Heather Sparks stopped bawling long enough to relate how she'd discovered it. About half an hour earlier, she said, she'd gone to Lois Aswell's room for a meeting about the future of the movie. She'd returned a minute ago to find the knife stuck where it was; it hadn't been there when she'd left, she said, and she hadn't seen anyone in the hallway as she came back.

"Why aren't there more police here?" Aswell demanded. "We're obviously in jeopardy. Why are you here alone?"

Valenzuela reached into his tote bag, found a fresh pair of latex gloves and began slipping them on. "Because somebody high up in the department has it in for me, and he's turning the screws. For what it's worth, I've been promised two uniformed officers no later than tomorrow morning. I have a feeling that after headquarters hears about this, we'll see the uniforms a lot sooner."

"I intend to write a letter to your superiors about this," Nan Williams said.

"Please do, Mrs. Williams. I'll give you the names myself."

He pinched the knife at the lower end of the handle and gently worked it back and forth until it popped free. "Whoever did this didn't stick it in too deep."

"Perhaps they were in a hurry," Mrs. Williams said.

"Or not that strong," Valenzuela said. He examined the bloody blade closely, squinting and holding it up to the nearest light. I stepped close behind him, and saw a long, dark hair matted in the dried blood, and thought immediately of Toni Pebbles. Valenzuela backed me off with a sharp glance and placed the knife in a plastic evidence bag, which he sealed up. He found a piece of white chalk in his coat pocket and returned to the door, where he circled the spot where the blade had left its mark.

"Not very high up, either," he said.

"That doesn't necessarily mean a small person did it," Mrs. Williams said, so defensively it drew a prolonged look from the detective.

His eyes left her and scanned the rest of the group. "Anyone seen Scotty Campbell in the past half hour?"

"Did I hear my name?" Scotty Campbell came waddling down the hall to stand just outside the gathered circle, looking up at Valenzuela. "You have an APB out for me, Chief?"

"Just wondering where you've been for the last thirty minutes, Mr. Campbell."

"Downstairs, with Zeke Zeidler, getting fired." His jaunty manner changed, becoming sterner, as he cast his eyes toward Aswell. "Lois didn't have the nerve to can me herself, so she had Zeke do it."

"You crossed the line, Scotty," Aswell said. "That mouth of yours got you into trouble once too often." She reached over, stroking Heather's hair. "Heather was justifiably upset last night, and you just had to make it worse, didn't you?"

"Half an hour's a long time to be getting fired," Valenzuela said.

Campbell folded his stumpy arms across his well-developed chest. "You can check with Mr. Zeidler if you want, Sergeant."

"I will."

"If you must know, I was venting," Campbell went on. "Letting Mr. Zeidler know how hard it is for little people to make it in the world, and how Hollywood makes it harder by only using us as freaks or as the butt of jokes."

"Or as stuntmen for child actors," Valenzuela said. "That seems to keep you gainfully employed."

"Not at the moment," Campbell said, shooting a glance at Aswell.

Valenzuela turned to Nan Williams. "Speaking of child actors, where's Audrey?"

Mrs. Williams placed a hand against her upper chest, fingers splayed, looking affronted. "Why would you ask about Audrey?"

"I have a few questions for her, Mrs. Williams."

"What kind of questions?"

"I'd like to know where she's been and what she's been doing for the past thirty minutes."

"You can't think Audrey had anything to do with this."

"I won't have an idea about that until I look into it, will I?"

Mrs. Williams drew herself up farther, her voice brittle. "I'm not exactly sure where Audrey is. She's eleven years old, and I don't keep track of her every move."

"Perhaps you should start."

"I don't like the tone of your voice, Sergeant, or your attitude in general. I find it offensive."

"Duly noted," Valenzuela said. "With all due respect, Mrs. Williams, I'll suggest that you find sweet little Audrey and ask her if I might have a few words with her, if it's not too inconvenient for either of you."

"I suppose I can do that."

"What was Audrey wearing when you saw her last?"

"That yellow dress she likes so much. The one with the puffed sleeves and the white ribbon at the waist."

"She had some scenes in that dress," Aswell explained. "It was just like the dress Martha Frech was wearing the night she found Rebecca Fox's body. Audrey's grown attached to it. I told her she could keep it."

"I wore one just like it," Campbell said, "when I doubled for Audrey, falling down the stairs. Although I'm not as fond of it as she is." He ran a hand down his rump and raised his nose in the air, playing fey. "I think it makes me look fat."

Valenzuela glanced at his watch, then at Nan Williams. "May I expect to see you and Audrey in the next fifteen minutes, Mrs. Williams? Does that sound reasonable?"

"I see no problem with that. Audrey certainly has no reason not to speak with you."

"As for the rest of you," Valenzuela said, "I'd appreciate it if you'd all gather in the lounge after dinner. Let's make it nine sharp."

"I'm afraid Heather and I won't be there," Oakley said.

"Why is that, Mr. Oakley?"

"We're leaving, as soon we pack our bags."

"Because of this incident involving the knife."

"And other things. We've told you everything we know."

Valenzuela glanced from Oakley to Sparks and back again. "Have you, Mr. Oakley?"

Oakley tensed. "You know where to find us if you need anything more."

He started to turn away with Sparks. Valenzuela raised one of his crutches, catching Oakley lightly on the arm. "There are still a few questions I need to clear up, Mr. Oakley. I need to run a few things past the entire group. Before I do that, I'd like to talk to you again one on one."

"I've answered all your questions, Sergeant."

"Some things have come up that need clarification." Valenzuela's eyes were on a steady line with Oakley's. The set of Oakley's mouth was grim. "If you could give me just a few hours more," the detective said, his polite tone softening the threat, "I'd consider it a sign of your cooperation."

Oakley swallowed uncomfortably, and his eyes shifted uneasily. I didn't like seeing him like that, human and vulnerable, with chinks in his armor; I wanted him shining, perfect, the way the objects of our fantasies are meant to be.

"I suppose we can wait another couple of hours," he said. "If you feel it will help you in your investigation. We certainly wouldn't want to be perceived as uncooperative. We want all this cleared up as much as anyone else." He turned to Sparks, who looked small and miserable under his protective arm. "It'll give us time to pack properly, honey, and to say our good-byes."

"Christopher, please," Aswell said. "Don't go. Don't destroy my movie."

"I'm sure Zeke will straighten things out with the insurance people," Oakley said. "When Heather's pulled herself together and you're ready to start shooting again, we'll be back, just as committed as we were before."

"And if we can't afford a shutdown like this? What if we have to fold up the tent?"

"I'm sorry, Lois. We're not staying here another night. It's not fair to Heather, especially after what's just happened." He led Sparks away, in the direction of his room, rubbing her back with one of his fine-boned hands.

Scotty Campbell looked up at Valenzuela. "I won't be hanging around, Sergeant. If I don't work for this outfit, there's no reason for me to be here."

"Even for the sake of the investigation?"

"Am I under arrest?"

"Of course not."

"Then you can't keep me here." He raised a hand and offered Valenzuela a little wave. "Bye-bye."

We watched him shuffle back down the hall and out of sight.

"Sometimes," Aswell said, "I could wring that little midget's neck. Even if he did help rescue Martha Frech."

Valenzuela arranged a crutch under each arm and faced Nan Williams. "Fifteen minutes, Mrs. Williams. Then we take over, looking for Audrey ourselves."

Karen Hori turned to face Nan Williams, offering to assist. "I'm sure Audrey had nothing to do with this, Nan. She's probably playing some kind of game. You know how she can be."

"That's very kind of you, Karen." Mrs. Williams's voice was chilly. "But I'm quite capable of finding Audrey myself."

As Valenzuela turned to go, the elevator doors slid open and the hotel's evening chef burst forth. He was a short, rotund man in a white chef's outfit, complete with tall hat; a small, black mustache twitched on his upper lip and his round face was pebbled with perspiration as he ran down the hall toward us.

"Mr. Tiemeyer!" Tiemeyer stepped forward to meet him, with Valenzuela at his side. "The kitchen knives," the chef said, mopping his face with a small towel. "There are several missing. Some of the bigger ones."

"You're sure of this?" Valenzuela said.

"I keep a count of the better knives. They're expensive, and tend to disappear."

"But not in a bunch, like this, I don't imagine," Valenzuela said.

"No, we've never had a theft like this."

Valenzuela addressed the rest of us. "Keep your rooms locked and stay inside until dinner. I suggest you come down and return to your rooms in groups, with people you feel you can trust." He assigned an armed security guard to help Mrs. Williams search for Audrey, and another to stay near Heather Sparks. "If anyone sees the girl, notify me immediately." Then he asked Mrs. Williams if Audrey had ever run away.

"I wouldn't say run away exactly," Mrs. Williams said. "From time to time, Audrey has taken brief breaks from routine when I haven't been aware of her precise whereabouts."

"How long have these 'brief breaks from routine' lasted?"

"Anywhere from a few hours to a few days. Once, she was gone for a week. But she had her credit cards with her."

"That sounds like running away to me."

"She's a very independent child, Sergeant. She's quite mature for her age, with a remarkable IQ, and no shortage of talents."

"Does one of them happen to be knife juggling, Mrs. Williams?"

Twenty minutes later, when Mrs. Williams had failed to find Audrey within the allotted time, Valenzuela gathered the remaining security guards and ordered a search of the hotel, room by room. By then, Kevin Tiemeyer had reported an extra set of his keys missing that included both the master for all guest rooms and individual keys to all other rooms; that meant that Audrey could be hiding in just about any of more than a hundred locked spaces, if indeed she was hiding at all—there was always the possibility that she'd fled the hotel into the stormy night, or even been abducted or met with foul play. While the guards started on the first floor, opening doors one by one to thoroughly search each room, the storm outside grew in ferocity, buffeting the hotel with wind and rain, and adding to the general feeling of unease.

As we sat down for dinner at half past seven, Audrey Williams still hadn't been located. Neither had the missing knives or keys. Sweet Doctor Silk showed up, putting down his fork and flicking a lighter when Deep Freeze held a thin cigar aloft, against Tiemeyer's protests about smoking in the hotel; when the lighter failed to ignite, sputtering out of fuel, Deep Freeze castigated Sweet Doctor Silk in front of the rest of us, ensuring his humiliation. Silk asked around for matches but no one would loan him any, and Deep Freeze flicked his unlit cigar to the floor, as petulant as ever.

"You never did tell me what it was you uncovered about Mr. Freeze," I said to Templeton.

"Not now," she said, keeping her voice low. "Later, when we're alone. I have several things to show you. You and Richard Pearlman."

"Your new writing partner," I said.

She smiled archly. "Possibly. You have a problem with that?"

"Of course not. I wish the two of you nothing but success."

Scotty Campbell was also there, enjoying a last meal at the film's expense before packing his bags and heading home; he cracked wise as he ate, making tasteless jokes about who among the cast or crew might be the next to turn up with "a bloody smile," until Zeke Zeidler banged his cane on a table and ordered Scotty out. The dwarf bid everyone a fond adieu and scampered off to pack his bags, leaving a room choked by tension and silence.

From time to time the lights flickered as the storm threatened a blackout, causing a few gasps each time and nervous laughter afterward. I noticed more alcohol being consumed than usual.

TWENTY-TWO

As dinner ended and the search for Audrey Williams continued, Sergeant Valenzuela postponed his general meeting until ten and suggested everyone lock themselves in their rooms until then. He was trying hard to sound cautious without inducing panic and a stampede to the parking lot, but there was no doubt that he wished he had more officers to assist him and to offer protection to those of us still in the hotel.

Templeton and I met in her room, joined soon thereafter by Richard Pearlman, at her request. She seemed genuinely excited about the possibility of writing a book with Pearlman that would pick up where *A Murder in Eternal Springs* left off, updating the Rebecca Fox case and including the recent Toni Pebbles murder, even though there appeared to be no connection between them except the shared date and location of the crimes.

Templeton and Pearlman already had their title—*A Murder in Haunted Springs*—and were eagerly discussing the book as if it were a done deal, the way less experienced collaborators tend to do before one reality or another sets in and the project crashes or gets abandoned. Still, Pearlman had one successful book under his belt and Templeton was one of the more respected crime reporters in the country, and their material had all the elements for a first-rate true-crime saga. *A Murder in Haunted Springs* struck me as just the kind of book Templeton and I should have been writing together if my utter lack of credibility as a journalist hadn't made such a prospect unfeasible. So I was out and Pearlman was in as Templeton's writing partner. I'm not proud to admit that their cozy alliance had me wallowing like a hog in the shameful slop of envy and self-pity. My earlier vow to stop meddling and get out of Templeton's way had gone by the wayside.

"If you do go ahead with this book," I said to Pearlman, as I stretched out on Templeton's bed with my hands folded behind my head, "it'll be a great opportunity to correct some of the glaring lapses of the first one."

Pearlman peered at me quizzically. "Glaring lapses?"

"Some of the shortcomings we spoke of at lunch today." Templeton was shooting daggers at me, her dark eyes fierce, so I kept mine on Pearlman. "You know, fill in some of the holes and correct some of the misstatements of fact. The kind of errors and omissions authors rarely get to address in a substantial way."

Pearlman squirmed uncomfortably in his chair. "We'd discussed my approach, but I don't recall anything about gaping holes or errors of fact."

I smiled benignly. "That's not what we're here to talk about now, is it?" I turned to Templeton, who was still glaring. "I believe Alex wants to show us some of the material she's dug up on Deep Freeze."

"What factual errors exactly?" Pearlman persisted.

I ignored him, staying on Templeton. "Isn't that why you asked us in, Alex?"

"Deep Freeze, and a few other people," she said, her voice frosty.

"It's as if you've already got a head start on your book with Richard," I said. "The two of you will probably have it written in no time at all. You can give it another Hollywood spin, like the first one, since Pebbles got snuffed during the shooting of a movie. The Oakley-Sparks romance alone should get you featured in *People*."

Still seething, Templeton retrieved some files from a desk,

then propped her shapely posterior on the edge, looking down at the two of us, but directing her next words at me. "Do you want to hear what I've got? Or are you more interested in taking potshots at our book project?"

I smiled sweetly. "Please, I'm all ears."

"Deep Freeze isn't at all what he pretends to be," Templeton said crisply, as if delivering a lecture. "He didn't grow up in the ghetto, didn't run with a gang, and never did jail time as he claims, not that I've been able to confirm."

"He wouldn't be the first rapper who exaggerated his street credentials," I said.

"His father was a career army man," Templeton went on, breezing right past me. "Rose to the rank of lieutenant colonel, with a distinguished service record. Mother ran a profitable company, supplying military bases with personal hygiene products. Deep Freeze—real name, Percy Childs—was raised on or near army bases in Europe."

I perked up. "Did you say Percy Childs?"

"Does the name mean something to you?"

"It might." I settled back against the pillows. "Go on, Templeton. This is fascinating."

She studied me curiously for a second before continuing. "Percy Childs attended art school in Paris. He wanted to be a sculptor but gave it up because of early onset arthritis in his hands that made dexterity difficult."

"That would explain why he's always massaging his hands and rubbing his knuckles," I said. I glanced at Pearlman, folding my hands behind my head again. "Would you agree, Richard?"

He brightened. "Oh, yes, definitely. I'd noticed the same thing."

"Sixteen years ago," Templeton went on, sounding irritated by the interruption, "when hip-hop was engulfing pop culture, Percy Childs came to this country and worked his way into the rap scene. He had some money from a modest inheritance and used it discreetly to buy friends and associates in the right places. He adopted the name Deep Freeze, made up a past as a gangbanger and outlaw, practiced the swagger and rough language, got the whole act down pat."

"To develop some 'street cred,'" Pearlman put in awkwardly, overenunciating the last two words as if they came from a foreign language he'd never spoken.

"Exactly," Templeton said, all but patting him on the head. "He started rapping and writing, landed a very shrewd manager, and emerged as Deep Freeze, spewing out all those angry lyrics while conveniently hiding his comfortable middle-class background."

"Just because he's middle class doesn't mean he can't be angry," I said. "You come from a privileged background, and you harbor a fair amount of anger on certain issues."

"It's different with Deep Freeze," Templeton said. "He's built a lucrative career on his bad-boy image. If someone were to expose him—"

"Someone like Toni Pebbles, you mean?"

"It occurred to me."

"But I thought Toni Pebbles came here to 'out' someone," Pearlman said. "Isn't that what we were all hearing when she first arrived?"

"The term's taken on a broader meaning since it was first coined by gay activists," Templeton explained. "You hear it used now to describe efforts to expose corruption in high places, athletes who use performance-enhancing drugs, all manner of closeted activity. Outing isn't limited to just secretive gay people any longer."

"Of course," Pearlman said. "I hadn't considered that."

"And you think Toni Pebbles might have been here to get Deep Freeze," I said, "to let the world know that he's really an army brat named Percy Childs."

"I think it's worth our attention, don't you?"

"What's important is what Richard thinks." I glanced over at him. "He's your research and writing partner now. What do you think, Richard?"

"Oh, definitely, definitely."

"Well, I guess Deep Freeze is our man then. He must have

done it. Case closed." I sat up and swung my legs over the edge of the bed, keying on Pearlman again. "There's just one little problem, isn't there?"

"Something I've overlooked?" Pearlman asked.

"Deep Freeze has an alibi."

Pearlman looked stumped. "That's true. We'd have to consider that."

I clucked my tongue. "Those alibis can be downright annoying, can't they?" He smiled awkwardly, but had nothing to say. I shifted to Templeton. "What else have you got, Alex? Anyone without a solid alibi?"

I could almost see the steam coming out her ears as our eyes met. I briefly regretted behaving so childishly, letting my competitive streak get the best of me. But I was already down that road again, and it seemed too late to turn back, even if I'd feel bad about it later, which I surely would.

Templeton put her file on Percy Childs aside and picked up another one. "Last year, Toni Pebbles wrote a nasty article for *Hollywood Now* on child actors."

I winced. "*Hollywood Now*? Isn't that rag a few cuts below the high-paying slicks she used to write for? I thought only lightweights fed at that trough, the kind of hacks who are good at scrounging up gossip but need their copy heavily rewritten. That doesn't sound like Toni. If nothing else, she could write."

"I imagine it offered easy entry back into the trade, as she tried to get reestablished as a freelancer. She needed fresh clips, and *Hollywood Now* was probably happy to work with someone with her credits."

"And she dished on Audrey Williams?"

Templeton glanced at an article she'd marked with highlights. "Pebbles reported that Audrey is bulimic, a self-mutilator, and given to deep bouts of depression. She characterized Mrs. Williams as a neurotic stage mother who's living out her own frustrated ambitions through her more talented daughter. Pebbles suggested that Mrs. Williams risked her child's mental health by putting her into a succession of gory horror films at an impressionable age."

"No wonder Audrey was happy to see her dead," I said.

"I don't imagine Nan Williams was a member of the Toni Pebbles Fan Club, either," Templeton added.

Pearlman raised a finger, looking primed. "You're forgetting that Mrs. Williams has an alibi. She and Kevin Tiemeyer were together. He vouched for her, and I saw lipstick on his collar that matched hers. So she couldn't have done it."

"That's very good, Richard," I said. "Excellent observation and deduction."

Pearlman beamed. "Thank you, Justice. I remembered what you said earlier about the importance of alibis."

"Unless they're both lying," I said, "covering up for each other. He's got the hots for Mrs. Williams, so he agrees to provide an alibi for her. It wouldn't be the first time an older man fell for a younger woman who then led him into trouble. That old notion of the femme fatale working her charms on a vulnerable chump."

Pearlman immediately deflated. "I hadn't thought of that."

I shook my head, clucking again. "There are so many possibilities, aren't there, Richard? False leads, shaky alibis, missing evidence, modus operandi, opportunity, motivation, all manner of deception. It can be a real challenge sorting through this stuff, let alone organizing it all and writing a readable book that makes sense."

His smile was pained. "I'm beginning to see that."

Templeton was glaring at me again, her jaw clenched. She opened another file folder and stuck her pretty nose in it. "I also found this here in the fax machine. It's a press release that Karen Hori must have left behind by mistake."

She handed each of us a copy. It was comprised of two stapled pages, bearing today's date and Hori's name as a contact person. Templeton waited patiently while we read through it.

FOR IMMEDIATE RELEASE

Haunted Springs, CA—Continuing tension surrounding the murder of freelance journalist Toni Pebbles on March 15 during the filming of *A*

Murder in Eternal Springs is threatening to derail the storybook romance of the film's stars, Heather Sparks and Christopher Oakley, according to well-placed sources.

The two stars became engaged on March 14, while staying at the legendary Haunted Springs Hotel, where much of the filming is taking place, and appeared headed for a long and happy life together.

The next night, however, Toni Pebbles was found with her throat cut while staying in the same room of the hotel where legendary film star Rebecca Fox was discovered murdered fifty years ago, also on the ides of March. The film's story line revolves around that unsolved, real-life murder and the tragic events it triggered, including the suicide of Brandy Fox, the actress's daughter, twenty-five years later in the same room. Heather Sparks has the role of Brandy Fox.

Late this afternoon, Miss Sparks discovered a bloody knife thrust into the door of her room. It is unclear if the incident, which is under investigation, was a prank or possibly the work of the same person who murdered Toni Pebbles the previous night.

Knowledgeable sources report that the escalating terror has left Miss Sparks an emotional wreck and Mr. Oakley struggling to comfort her and keep their relationship intact.

"This should be the happiest time in the lives of these two fine young people," confided a source close to the couple. "Instead, it's turned their moment of bliss into a nightmare that seems to have no end."

According to sources, Miss Sparks is reconsidering her decision to make a matrimonial commitment during a period of such personal stress. Mr. Oakley is said to be heartbroken at the prospect of losing the woman he considers the love of his life.

"He's absolutely shattered," a source said. "He's told friends that if he can't marry Heather, he may never marry at all."

With fewer than two weeks of shooting left, filming has been temporarily suspended, pending the outcome of the investigation into Toni Pebbles's death.

A Murder in Eternal Springs is being directed by Lois Aswell and produced by Zeke Zeidler, based on the best-selling book by Richard Pearlman. Margaret Loyd Langley, Deep Freeze, and Audrey Williams also have prominent roles.

"I didn't know your book had made the national best-seller lists," I said to Pearlman, when I'd finished reading the press release.

"Perhaps Miss Hori was using the term a bit loosely. My book was on the *Boston Globe* best-seller list, and I believe one or two other regional lists."

"Boston's your hometown, isn't it?"

"That's right."

"Got some extra promotion did you, through the university where you're employed?" He nodded uncomfortably. "I guess that would explain it then."

"Justice, do you mind?" Templeton's scolding voice intruded. "Could we discuss this press release, which I discovered less than an hour ago?"

"Karen Hori doesn't waste much time, does she? Not one to bypass an opportunity to plant another item about her movie."

"Maybe she was the one who stuck that knife in the door," Pearlman suggested.

Templeton ignored him, peering down at me from her perch on the desk. "You don't see any other possible ulterior motives here, Justice?"

I did, but I didn't want to go there, and she surely knew it. The tables had clearly been turned. "Richard seems to be on to something," I said falsely. "An ambitious young publicist, assigned to her first picture, creating her own opportunities for media attention. There may be some merit to that."

"Possibly in concert with the producer, Zeke Zeidler," Pearlman said, rising to the bait. "Maybe they hatched it together, to squeeze another press release out of it." He stood suddenly, gesturing with excitement. "My God! What if they had a hand in Toni Pebbles's death? She was here, threatening one of their stars, putting their film in jeopardy. Isn't it possible that the two of them—"

"Think, Richard," I said. "What was it we talked about before?"

He sat, getting control of himself, wrinkling his brow and looking cerebral, like the professor he was. Finally, he looked up and said bleakly, "Alibis?"

"Those pesky alibis," I said.

"Deep Freeze vouched for them," he said, picking up the thread. "He could see them in the dining room as he played the piano. I remember that quite distinctly."

"Which leaves us with the question Justice conveniently avoided," Templeton said. "The possible ulterior motive in this press release, beyond the obvious publicity it generates for the movie."

I smiled tightly, preparing myself for the coup de grace. "And what would that be, Templeton?"

"You don't know, Benjamin?"

"You tell us. I wouldn't want to spoil your fun."

She lost her smile, but continued the game just the same. "It provides your friend, Christopher Oakley, with an easy out. He established his heterosexuality by becoming engaged to Heather Sparks two nights ago. Last night, the woman who may have come here to out him and destroy his career was eliminated." Templeton held up the press release. "Now this lays the groundwork for his exit from the relationship. Not quite as solid as a marriage of convenience that later ends just as conveniently in divorce, the way so many others handle it. But close enough."

The room was silent until Richard Pearlman said quietly, "I hadn't thought of that, either. I'm not much of a reporter, am I?"

"Don't worry," I told him, as Templeton and I continued to lock eyes. "You'll get the hang of it. All you have to do is think the worst of people."

TWENTY-THREE

I returned to my room feeling crappy about what had just gone down between Templeton and me—the unpleasant jealousy and one-upmanship that had plagued our relationship for years. I was still thinking about it, and what I might do to make amends, when the phone rang. It was Tony Valenzuela, asking me to come down to his office.

"I never caught up with you about Martha Frech," Valenzuela said, as I entered. He was stretched out on a couch, carrying heavy luggage under each eye; his western-style boot was planted on the floor, while his plaster cast was propped up on pillows at the other end. "Too damn much going on, and I'm not at my best."

"It's curious, Sergeant—you having to work this thing on your own. I can understand a beef with a superior, the brass pulling rank, leaving you stranded for a few hours. Petty, but I know that kind of crap goes on, even in law enforcement agencies."

He laughed dryly. "More than you might think. You'd be surprised how vindictive some cops can get."

"But it's gone on pretty long, hasn't it? Considering you're up here with a homicide, and a bloody knife stuck in someone's door for show."

"Like I told everyone earlier, I'm working on it. Since then, headquarters promised me at least two officers by midnight. Better late than never."

"No sign of Audrey Williams?"

He shook his head, yawning. "The two security guys I have on it are finishing up on the third floor now. Heading for the fourth floor shortly."

"You figure the girl for a good suspect?"

"I'm still undecided on that one."

"What about Sweet Doctor Silk? Anything new there?"

He cocked his head, got a better angle on me. "You're full of questions all of a sudden, Justice. What's up?"

I smiled with chagrin. "I need a peace offering for my friend Templeton. I've been behaving badly, I'm afraid. I think she'd appreciate a few choice tidbits, if there's something you could throw her way."

"She'd have to confirm it with me before she could use it."

"She'll know that. She's a crack reporter, Sergeant, one of the best."

"So I've heard."

"So are you going to cough up something on Silk, or are we finished here?"

"And then you'll fill me on Martha Frech?" I nodded. Valenzuela yawned again, covering it with his meaty fist. "Sweet Doctor Silk—I believe I already told you about his alibi, the trip he claims to have made down to the casino in the valley. So far, it checks out. Otherwise, all I can give you is what I pulled off the national criminal database, and a phone call I made to a prosecutor who put Silk away on a couple of felony counts a few years back."

"Templeton would certainly be interested in that."

The detective grinned. "How about you, Justice? Does it maybe interest you a smidgen?"

"Maybe a smidgen."

"Sweet Doctor Silk, whose real name is Kennedy Mayhew, was convicted of a string of felonies going back twelve years ago to when he was seventeen. Grand theft auto, strong-arm robbery, and the one that got him his longest stretch—voluntary manslaughter."

"So he's got a taste for violence."

"Claims it's all behind him. Hasn't been in trouble for at least two years, not that we know of."

"What's the story on the manslaughter?"

"Killed the owner of a tavern where he'd been tinkling the ivories when he got out of the joint. That's where he'd learned to play, from some old-timer who'd toured with Howling Jimmy Hawkins decades back. You familiar with Howling Jimmy Hawkins?" I shook my head. "I had a college buddy who listened to him," he continued. "The point is the tavern owner hired Sweet Doctor Silk as a piano man and then decided not to pay him because all he knew how to play was old Delta blues tunes. A fight ensued, the other guy threatened Silk with a knife, Silk knocked him down and kicked him a few times too many. That's how he tells it, anyway. After he did his time, he tried to make it as a rapper but it didn't work out."

"Maybe he knew too much about music."

Valenzuela smiled. "Yeah, maybe that was it. So he ended up being a lackey for Deep Freeze. Bodyguard, errand boy, stand-in, whatever."

"He's got to be pretty high on your list of suspects."

"I've got nothing solid that ties him to the Pebbles deal. Maybe the crime lab guys will find something under their microscopes. But for now, I've got nothing I can book him or hold him on." He yawned yet again, shook it off, and adjusted his foot on the pillows. "Your turn, Justice. I understand you had a conversation with this Martha Frech woman before the medics flew her out of here."

"What do you know about the Rebecca Fox murder, Sergeant?"

He offered me a small shrug. "I'm generally familiar with it. It's the most famous crime that ever went down in Hungry Valley. I was a toddler when it went down. My mother drove up here with me one time when I was in grade school to show me where it happened."

"I thought you'd never been in the hotel before yesterday."

"We didn't come in. She stopped the car a block away, kept her distance. Kissed her crucifix and crossed herself to be on the safe side. Told me the place was damned, that the devil lived here."

I told him that Martha Frech had been ten in 1956 when she'd discovered Rebecca Fox dead in Room 418. His eyes changed as I talked; the weariness seemed to go out of them and he kept quiet and listened. I related what Martha Frech had whispered to me down by the lake, and told him that she lived in an old house above the cemetery that her mother had purchased not long after the murder.

"You have any interest in the Rebecca Fox case," I asked, "now that it's no longer considered solved?"

"It was never considered solved. We got active cases, inactive cases, and closed cases. A man was lynched for the Rebecca Fox murder without benefit of trial or any conclusive evidence being presented, so it was never officially closed. It was deemed inactive."

"Which means it's officially open," I said, "but nobody really gives a damn about it anymore."

"That about sums it up."

"Does that include you, Sergeant?"

"I'm interested in any unsolved violent crime within my jurisdiction, which includes Haunted Springs. That said, I'm carrying a heavy caseload of more recent homicides that need my attention."

"Have you ever considered reactivating the Rebecca Fox case?"

"It's crossed my mind, given the DNA evidence that turned up a couple of years ago."

"Have you read Richard Pearlman's book?"

"Skimmed it. Not much there, really, from a law enforcement angle. Other than the DNA findings, he hasn't come up with a whole lot more except question marks."

"Did you ever go back to the old reports and evidence from 1956?"

"Tried. Never got that far."

"What stopped you?"

"Jack Hightower Jr."

"Enid Tiemeyer's nephew, the current county sheriff."

Valenzuela nodded. "Expected to run for higher office at some point, probably state senate. Might get elected too. He's a big name in the valley. Wields a lot of clout."

"You're a sergeant, homicide, more than twenty-five years on the force. That has to count for something."

"My parents were migrant workers, *illegales*. Neither of them had a green card until they'd been here almost thirty years and caught a break with asylum. He's Jack Hightower Jr. That's all you need to know on that score."

"He's your boss then?"

"I don't report directly to the man but he signs my checks."

"By the edge in your voice, it doesn't sound like you like him much."

"No comment."

"Is he the one who's got you on his shit list? For busting his nephew on a marijuana possession charge? The one who's stranded you up here without any uniforms for backup?"

He was quiet for a few seconds, looking thoughtful. Then he said, "I need to go off the record here. It stays between us, at least for now."

"I can work with that."

"First of all, it wasn't possession, it was sales."

"Even more serious then."

"The case got taken away from me early on. I'm talking right at the scene, where it all went down. Certain people were contacted by phone. My captain stepped in, took over. The kid never got written up. The evidence is long gone. Basically, it didn't happen. That's how these things work sometimes. I'm not saying it's an everyday thing, but it goes on."

"You decided to keep quiet, go along with it?"

"It was a long time ago, Justice. I was a few years from pension and had two kids in college. You learn to pick your battles. That one wasn't worth it. If something more serious than marijuana had been involved, I'd have to stick my neck out. But it was marijuana. Marijuana isn't at the top of my list, to be perfectly frank."

"Still, it must rankle. Especially now, when the old man puts his boot up your ass, just to remind you who's in charge."

"Jack Hightower Jr. is fully certified by the American Prick Academy. That's really all I want to say on that."

"About the Rebecca Fox case then."

"What about it?"

"Would it make a difference if new evidence cropped up that sorted out what happened the night she died? Could you get the case reactivated?"

"It would have to be damn strong evidence, and serve some purpose. It takes a lot of manpower and costs money to go after an old case like that."

"What if it cleared Ed Jones, once and for all?"

"There'd be merit in that, certainly."

"What if it had a connection to the Brandy Fox suicide in 1981?"

He hesitated, and his eyes came alive again. "I guess that would make it more interesting, wouldn't it?"

"What if it implicated Jack Hightower in the Rebecca Fox investigation in a negative way, and his son, Jack Junior, similarly in the Brandy Fox incident?"

He leveled his eyes on mine, took a deep breath, let it out slowly. "I'd have to be very sure of myself before I went ahead on anything like that. I'd have to proceed carefully, because I'd be pretty much on my own."

"But you wouldn't be opposed to it?"

"I would never oppose the facts coming out in an unsolved homicide, even one that's considered as cold as a witch's tit."

"No matter who got hurt and how powerful they might be?"

"I hit twenty-five/fifty a couple of years ago, Justice. Fifty years old, twenty-five years in. My pension's assured, and my kids are out of college."

"Would it make it easier if you had Alexandra Templeton behind you?"

"You mean in terms of her breaking the news about these mysterious matters you've been alluding to?" I nodded. He finally smiled a little. "The *Los Angeles Times* is a mighty big newspaper. Difficult to ignore."

I stood. "I'll keep you posted, Sergeant."

"Nothing you want to tell me now?"

"I have some loose ends to tie up first. With my credibility problem, I have to have all the cards I need before I show my hand."

"That can't be fun, carrying around that monkey."

"Makes me work harder, truth be told."

"You probably would have made a good detective, Justice, like your old man."

"If I can help it," I said, "I don't ever want to be like my old man."

"That's funny—I feel just the opposite. I've always wanted to be like him. Except for picking beans and berries in the fields. That part never appealed to me."

"You look tired, Sergeant. A nap's probably in order. You're no good to anyone if your brain isn't working."

"I might do that." His eyelids started to droop. "For a few minutes, anyway."

"The security guards will let you know if anything turns up." I switched off the light on my way out. "I'll check back in when the time's right."

"Be careful out there," he said from the dark, as I closed the door.

TWENTY-FOUR

I stepped into the lobby to the crackle of burning logs. Otherwise the place was as quiet as a graveyard.

I could see a couple of dozen crew members in the club room, but they were talking low, beyond earshot. The chairs and sofas in the lounge were empty; so were the dining and banquet rooms. Behind the front desk, Kevin Tiemeyer dozed with his head on his arms, an empty Manhattan glass near an elbow. Following the murder and the incident involving the bloody knife, most of his staff had quit, leaving him to take over all manner of tasks, from watching the front desk to helping out in the kitchen; room service had been suspended, along with routine housekeeping. Up on the fourth floor, security guards moved quietly from empty room to empty room on the west side, working their way east, using their master key to enter, looking for Audrey Williams. Behind the central staircase, the door to the movie's production office was open; light came from inside, and I suspected Zeke Zeidler and Lois Aswell were at work, on the insurance matter or one of the myriad other problems threatening to wreck their picture.

I crossed to the fireplace and warmed myself at the hearth for several minutes as I studied the portrait of Enid Tiemeyer, trying to imagine what it must have been like to grow up under her rule in an isolated little town like Eternal Springs, where she'd presided like a queen. Feeling roasted by the flames, I moved on to the Tiemeyer family portraits hanging along the walls outside the dining room: Jack Hightower, Enid's brother—a big, genial-looking man in a deputy's uniform whose smile seemed comfortably self-satisfied, resting his hand easily on the stock of his holstered gun; his son, Jack Hightower Jr., not quite as big as his father but better-groomed to the point of looking slick, in a two-piece suit rather than a uniform; Roderick Tiemeyer, Enid's husband, his mild eyes peering out passively from wire-rimmed spectacles and a narrow, pale face that revealed so little; and their handsome son, Kevin, when he must have been in his thirties, sometime between the deaths of Rebecca Fox and Brandy Fox, sporting the dark mustache that added to his resemblance to Brent Fox, the ill-fated love of Rebecca's life.

As I studied each photo, connecting the faces to dates and events in my head, I got the feeling I wasn't alone. I dismissed it as a case of nerves, which was going around, and moved on to more photos from the Tiemeyer and Hightower clans. Then my eye sensed movement just above me, in the vicinity of the second-floor railing on my side of the central stairs. I glanced up to see a pair of eyes peering back at me through the slats. After that came a flash of yellow and the patter of small feet running.

I dashed to the main stairs and started up, just in time to glimpse the yellow dress disappear in the direction of the hotel's southeast corner.

Some people give in to a moment of recklessness and later say they don't know what came over them or what caused them to act so impulsively. But I knew exactly why I gave chase that night to the fleeing figure in the frilly yellow dress.

I wanted to know the truth—about the death of Toni Pebbles, the knife stuck in Heather Sparks's door, the missing knives from the kitchen, so many things I figured Audrey Williams might be able to tell me. But most of all I wanted to know how Christopher Oakley fit into all this, and I thought that Audrey might shed some light on that as well. Once, out by Whispering Rock, she'd told Templeton and me that she knew everything that went on around the hotel; I was beginning to believe her.

As I took the stairs two at a time, I shouted at the security guards three floors up. One of them heard me and turned, but the other had already entered the room. I motioned to the remaining guard, pointing in the direction of the stairwell. He nodded and went into the room after his partner. Behind me and below, the commotion had awakened Kevin Tiemeyer; he raised his head off the front desk, looking bleary with drink and sleep, but seemed vaguely responsive. As I turned back up the stairs, he was at the door of Valenzuela's office, pounding hard.

As I reached the southwest stairwell on the second floor, I heard footsteps inside, going up, and started up myself. As I climbed, gaining ground with my longer legs, I glimpsed the yellow dress above me, rounding a banister at the third-floor landing and continuing on. When I got there, I caught another glimpse of yellow, disappearing out the door on to the fourth floor. The missing knives were on my mind as I continued up, and the blood on the edge of the knife in the door, and the crescent-shaped slice that had opened Toni Pebbles's throat nearly from ear to ear. Someone was playing a game, but it was deadly dangerous, and I had no great desire to end up like Toni Pebbles. I pulled up and proceeded with more caution as I emerged from the stairwell at the top, half-expecting Audrey to jump out, brandishing one of the knives and giggling demonically about the bloody smile.

It didn't happen. As I stepped out to the open hallway, I caught sight of the yellow dress again, beneath a mop of auburn hair. The small figure who'd fled in such haste was up on the railing that ran around the fourth floor, walking away from me with arms stretched wide for balance, placing one foot carefully in front of the other, the way Audrey had the day Templeton and I had first encountered her, showing off her acrobatic skills. I froze, keeping silent, not wanting to startle anyone, and unsure exactly what I should do. By then, the two security guards had come around from the west side; we faced each other from each end of the hallway, with the pint-size show-off between us, walking the railing like a circus tightrope, with no safety net and only a long drop to the lobby floor below. Neither the guards nor I moved; we stood where we were, paralyzed.

Moments after that, the elevator doors opened and Kevin Tiemeyer stepped out. He held them open, allowing Sergeant Valenzuela to follow on his crutches. They came around the corner of the railing to join the security guards, pulling up when they saw what was going on. The detective spoke quietly to Tiemeyer, apparently urging him to step closer and coax Audrey to come down.

"Audrey," Tiemeyer said in a tremulous voice that was barely audible from where I stood. "Audrey, come down from there, dear. We've seen how clever you are. Please, dear, jump down now. Audrey?"

Suddenly, the little acrobat tottered, arms waving as all balance was lost. One small foot left the railing and lifted—the inside foot—while the arms flailed desperately, drawing wild circles in the air.

"Dear Jesus, she's going to fall." Zeke Zeidler, drawn by the commotion downstairs, had come up and stepped out beside me. "Audrey!"

I raced in that direction, arms outstretched, as Tiemeyer and the two security guards came from the other end. Before we reached the middle, the little person we'd thought was Audrey suddenly regained his balance, pulled off the auburn wig he was wearing, and stood perfectly straight and still. Scotty Campbell turned to face outward toward the lobby as if taking a curtain call; he bowed once at the waist and tossed the wig out, watching it float four stories to the floor below.

He made a one-hundred-eighty degree turn, jumped back down to the hallway floor, and straightened his dress like he was getting ready for the prom. Zeidler, who'd caught up to me, muttered something in Yiddish that I didn't understand and turned back into the stairwell. Valenzuela approached on his crutches, breathing fire.

"Damn you, Campbell. If I thought it was worth the trouble, I'd arrest you for interfering with an investigation."

Campbell's grin was wide. "It was just a little joke, Sergeant, an attempt to lighten things up around here."

"How would you like to lighten things up down at the county jail for a couple of days, while we decide whether or not to charge you?"

"What's the alternative, Chief?"

"You're out of this hotel and driving down the hill within ten minutes, without a peep to anyone between now and then."

"How about five? I'm all packed."

"Five would be better."

When Campbell was gone, I told Valenzuela that he didn't look all that rested from his brief nap. He said it didn't matter; it was almost ten and nearly time for the general meeting he'd called, so he had to be up and awake, anyway. He asked the guards to return to the west side and continue systematically searching rooms, and followed them in that direction toward the elevator. Tiemeyer lingered, using his handkerchief to polish the wooden railing where Scotty Campbell's shoes had left scuff marks.

I turned back toward the stairwell, intending to stop by Templeton's room to tell her what I'd learned about Sweet Doctor Silk. Before I got there, my eye fell on the short set of steps leading up to the attic door I'd spotted two days earlier, the one Tiemeyer told me his mother had used for storage and that he hadn't entered for years. It struck me as just the kind of place a mischievous kid like Audrey Williams might hide, especially if the missing set of hotel keys was in her possession, which seemed possible.

"Kevin?" Tiemeyer looked up from inspecting the railing, slipping his hankie into a rear pants pocket. I asked him if he was carrying his set of master keys. He indicated that he was. I pointed up the steps toward the attic door. "I'd like to poke around up there."

"Shouldn't we have the security guards do that?"

"Why don't you leave the keys with me and go get the guards. I'll watch the door, to make sure no one enters or leaves."

"You really think Audrey might be in there?"

"Worth a look, I'd think."

He separated a key from the rest and handed that one to me. "I'll just be a minute or two," he said, and ambled off in the other direction.

I was up the steps in seconds, working the lock. If the sound of it turning hadn't been enough to warn anyone inside that I was coming in, the creaking of the door on its old hinges certainly was. I stuck my head in to the musty aroma of an attic that had obviously been shut up for years. The light coming from behind me was scant, but I was able to see small footsteps in the dust just inside the threshold.

"Audrey?" I reached around, patting the walls just inside the door for a switch, but couldn't find one. "Audrey? It's Benjamin Justice. I'm coming in."

Not a sound. I stepped farther in, stumbling on something. I kneeled down, found an old chest that was opened, saw clothes strewn about.

"Audrey? Are you in here? It's time to end the games."

Silence. I stepped farther in and stopped, letting my one good eye adjust to the near darkness. "Audrey? Don't you think this has gone far enough?"

Gradually, objects began to take shape in the feeble light—old furniture, an antique lamp with a frayed cord, boxes stacked one atop the other. Then, as I turned to my left—my blind side—a figure suddenly loomed up, almost next to me. I cried out and leaped back, nearly falling. A moment after that I was laughing, embarrassed and thankful I was alone. It was an old female mannequin, the full-figured kind that a more matronly woman might use when taking in or letting out a gown. I glanced around, squinting into the attic's deeper recesses. Except for a sliver of light, all I could see back there was darkness.

I moved cautiously in that direction until I saw that it was *reflected* light—the faint light from the doorway behind me caught by the glass of a full-length mirror. All around the mirror, more old clothes were strewn about—women's dresses, hats, and shoes. Audrey had apparently been playing dress-up to entertain herself.

I peered into the darkest corners. "Audrey? Why don't you come out and talk to me?"

As I glanced around, I noticed another piece of clothing—two pieces, actually—different from the rest. They were draped over an old chair, pure white cotton, familiar yet frightening, as they were intended to be. I picked up the white robe first; it was stiff with age, probably decades past its last laundering. Then the pointed white hood, with its two holes for the eyes, which felt much the same. I stood before the mirror, holding the robe in front of me; it reached my shins, which suggested that it had been tailored for someone shorter. It was an exciting discovery. Yet holding a robe of the Ku Klux Klan in my hands, perhaps a robe that had been worn the night Ed Jones was hanged, left me feeling more on edge than I already was. I draped the garments over the chair, wondering what was keeping Tiemeyer and the two security guards.

"Audrey? I'd really like to hear your story about the last two days, what you've been up to. Why don't you come out and talk to me?"

I backed up a few steps, craning my head to look beyond the door for Tiemeyer and his guards. As I did, my foot made contact with something, creating a clatter. I looked down to see half a dozen kitchen knives scattered at my feet. After that, I didn't call out again; I just wanted out of there. I started making my way to the door, looking for a light. When I was nearly there, something touched my face. I reached up, found a dangling piece of heavy string. I pulled it, heard a chain catch. A bare lightbulb came on, faintly illuminating the attic almost to its corners, though not quite.

In the same moment, something came at me in a rush. I threw up my hands as a flurry of fluttering wings and black, rodent-like bodies swarmed around and above me, coming down from the rafters en masse. In seconds, the bats were drawing together and moving away from me—away from the light—pointed toward what looked like a small window set in the attic's south wall. Then they were gone, out the window and into the storm, where a bolt of lightning briefly illuminated the night, the slanting rain, and the dark, winged creatures. For a moment, the attic was silent. With the light, I saw more small footprints in the dust, leading toward the open window. I heard footsteps behind me, coming closer. Tiemeyer appeared in the doorway.

"You sure took your time," I said.

"I decided to get Sergeant Valenzuela." Tiemeyer turned to assist Valenzuela as he labored up the steps on his crutches. "I thought it best."

I told them I'd found the missing knives, but not Audrey, though I had an idea where she might be. I pointed toward the open window and crossed to it. It was octagonal in shape, barely big enough for a child to squeeze through. The footprints ended at a wooden box that apparently had been placed under the window for a step. I stretched up and poked my head out into the weather.

Outside, on a parapet, Audrey Williams stood in her bedraggled yellow dress, soaking wet and shivering. Her back was against the parapet and her feet were on a narrow ledge as she stared out, clutching a large kitchen knife in one hand. Below, four stories down, was an outcropping of small boulders. Thunder growled somewhere behind the heavy clouds.

"Audrey, it's me, Benjamin Justice. Come in now. It's okay."

"I don't want to come in." She kept looking out as she spoke; her voice was different, grown-up and self-assured, and eerily calm.

I leaned back in and told Tiemeyer he needed to find Nan Williams and bring her up here, on the double. He took off faster than I'd ever seen him move. Valenzuela crowded up beside me, craning to see out. I stuck my head out again.

"Audrey, please come in. You can tell me all about what you've been up to."

"I don't want to tell any more stories."

"You can tell me about the roles you want to play then, about the movies you're going to make."

"I don't want to make any more movies." She looked over briefly, with vacant eyes. "I'm tired." She looked out again, shivering violently from the cold but not as if it mattered much. Lightning flashed distantly, briefly illuminating her pale, rigid face.

I'd had some experience with would-be suicides. Not quite twenty years earlier I'd worked the regional AIDS hot line in Los Angeles as a volunteer. Most of the questions we'd fielded were medical in nature—symptoms, testing and treatment options, organizations for referral—but we also got the occasional suicide call. It was the eighties then, years before the medicinal AIDS cocktail would come along to save or prolong so many lives; in those days, a diagnosis was considered a death sentence, the afflicted were dying horrifying deaths, and suicides among the diagnosed were not all that uncommon. The calls typically came in late at night or in the early morning hours. Our training on how to handle them had been very specific. We were taught not to coddle the callers or try to talk them out of ending their lives, which was rarely effective and could actually exacerbate the situation. Instead, we tried to get the caller to think very concretely about what they were planning or threatening to do, by presenting them with certain questions: What method had they chosen? What would it do to their bodies as it killed them? How long might it take them to die and what would that feel like? What would they look like when their bodies were found hours or days later? Who did they expect to find them or identify them at the morgue? What was their relationship to that person? And so on.

We were trained to ask these questions in a matter-of-fact and nonjudgmental way; ultimately, we were taught, what happened after the call ended was the sole responsibility of the caller; we were to remain as emotionally detached as possible. If the caller seemed particularly desperate and determined, we notified the proper authorities so they could intervene, while we kept the caller on the line. Sometimes these calls went on for hours; if a listener was unable to go the distance, another volunteer would take over. Our final goal was to get a promise from the caller to contact a specific person or agency for help. When they hung up, we rarely knew how things turned out, since any further contact with the caller was strictly forbidden, for our own emotional well-being. I'd lasted a little over a year working the AIDS hot line; I'd quit after losing a caller to a gunshot that had boomed in my ear over the phone, while in the background the cops pounded on the door of his apartment, trying to save him from himself.

Audrey Williams struck me as desperate and determined. Yet she hadn't mentioned suicide, and I wasn't about to bring it up. My mind was racing, trying to stay ahead of her, in case she did. I would ask her if she planned to slit her wrists with the knife. I would ask her if she planned to jump, and what she would do if her jump proved less than fatal, and left her alive but paralyzed and disfigured. I would ask her what the impact would do to her body, as it struck the hard rock. I would try to get her to visualize what her mother would see when she found her. It seemed so cold, so pathetically inept; yet it was all I could think of, the only thing I knew how to do.

"I slit her throat," Audrey said, in her new, adult voice that sounded so distant and detached.

"Let's not talk about that now, Audrey. Tell me what you're doing, out here in the weather like this, so high up."

"I put the knife to her neck and gave her a bloody smile. Only there wasn't that much blood. That part surprised me."

I wanted to help her; at the same time, I wanted her to spill her guts, to end all the questions about how Toni Pebbles had died, if she really could. For a wrenching moment, I realized I wasn't sure which one I wanted more—those answers, or for Audrey to survive.

She turned to look down at me. "You probably want to know why I cut her throat, don't you?" She smiled strangely, looking neither happy nor sad. "To see what it felt like, that's why. To see how different it was from the Demon Slasher movies."

"I'd like to talk more about it with you, Audrey."

She seemed to perk up at that, to come back a little from wherever her mind had been. "Really?"

I nodded eagerly. "I want to hear all about it. Come inside, and you can tell me."

"You really want to know?" The pitch of her voice rose, sounding more childlike. "Because there wasn't much blood and I'd like to know why."

"I know why."

"You do?"

Again, I nodded. "Come in and I'll tell you. I promise."

"You really know why?"

"I swear. The reason's kind of cool, actually. A doctor explained it to me once. Dr. Lyle. He wrote a book called *Forensics for Dummies.*"

"And you'll tell me?"

"On my honor."

Her smile changed; it wasn't pretty but it had some mischief in it. I thought I saw the Audrey I knew coming back, the Audrey who needed an audience, who craved attention like a drug. "That was her blood on the knife I stuck in the door," she said. "The knife I stuck there to scare that bitch Heather Sparks, who thinks she's so pretty, who thinks she's such hot shit, being a big star and getting all kinds of publicity because she's fucking Christopher Oakley." Her laugh was downright sinister; Audrey was back. "If that's what they're really doing."

"I'd like to hear about that," I said. "I bet you know some really neat stuff you could tell me."

"I know everything that goes on around here. I can tell you lots of things."

"Great. Come in then, and tell me everything."

"My mom's going to be really pissed."

"Let me handle your mother."

"You mean like Mr. Tiemeyer handled her last night, when they got naked and did the nasty?"

I grinned. "You're ruthless, Audrey. You know that?"

She mimicked my grin and turned toward the window, stepping in my direction. As she came, she raised the knife to make a cutting motion through the rain. "I'll tell you what it's like to give somebody the bloody smile."

"Watch your step. Be careful."

"This is nothing, walking out here like this. I can do lots more dangerous stuff than this. You want me to show you how I do it with my eyes closed?"

"No, Audrey. Just—just come in. Please."

She grinned again, and there was actually some sweetness in it—to let me know she'd just been joking. Thunder rumbled, louder and closer than before.

"Drop the knife, Audrey. You don't need it now."

"No way, José."

"You've got lots more inside. Please, lose the knife."

"Uh-uh." She shook her head defiantly, and kept coming. A second later, when she was only a step or two from the window, reaching for my outstretched hand, a finger of lightning reached down and touched the tip of the steel blade. I saw the spark, heard the sizzle as the voltage shot through the knife and scorched a path through her small body. She gasped and her eyes opened wide with pain and surprise, while her skinny legs buckled.

Then she was gone, away into space, down toward the rocks, her dress billowing out around her like a big yellow flower falling from a punishing sky.

TWENTY-FIVE

I clamped my eyes shut for a few seconds, wanting to keep them closed forever.

When I opened them, Sergeant Valenzuela was slumped beside me against the attic wall with an exhaustion that I suspected went far beyond the physical. He stared into the attic but I don't think he saw anything there. If he was like me, he saw Audrey falling. Falling, and falling, and falling as if in slow motion, a descent that took only a second or two before it ended with a horrifying thud we imagined but couldn't hear.

I felt like I might throw up, and fought the rising tide of nausea. Valenzuela gathered himself up, made a quick exit from the attic on his crutches, called his security guards together, and began dispensing orders.

The guards were sent racing down to the girl. One of them was a volunteer with the local search and rescue team, with advanced emergency first-aid training, although he had no use for it that night. Audrey was lifeless when they reached her, probably dead on impact, if not before; all they could do was cover her with a tarp to protect her burned and broken body from the elements, before moving her inside.

Kevin Tiemeyer had located Nan Williams at the bar, washing down a Valium with a martini. Valenzuela met them in the lobby and delivered the news to Mrs. Williams himself. Not surprisingly, she reacted badly, in a way that might be described as semi-hysterical, even with the tranquilizer and booze for sedation. By then, word of the accident had circulated through the hotel and guests were emerging from their rooms and from the club room in various states of shock and distress. Privately, Valenzuela asked Tiemeyer to see Mrs. Williams to her room and to stay with her, but he refused.

"I've had enough," he said. "Someone else will have to take care of it." As he spoke, he didn't seem so much cold and cruel as he did a man receding into some deeply private place, as a coping mechanism for the horror show that continued to play out at his old hotel, seemingly beyond his or anyone's control.

When it was clear that Tiemeyer was no longer of use to anyone, Valenzuela asked Karen Hori and me to accompany Mrs. Williams upstairs and to be sure someone was with her until she calmed down. That seemed to be happening as we rode up in the elevator to the third floor and got her into her room, where she told us she wanted to be alone. We stayed, anyway, sitting quietly side by side on the bed. Mrs. Williams stood silently at the window, staring down as a blue tarp was thrown over her daughter's body, hugging herself as she rocked back and forth.

Finally, she said, "I warned her not to go out on that ledge, you know. I told her it was absolutely forbidden. I did everything I could to stop her. I can't be blamed for this." I suspected that Mrs. Williams had lived long enough with the truth of what she'd done to her daughter in the service of her own needs that this ending to their script wasn't all that great a shock, merely the final, numbing moment in a last act authored by a parent whose neuroses and narcissism seemed to have no limits. I wanted to feel sympathy for her, and I suppose I did, but mostly I felt sorry for little Audrey.

After that, Mrs. Williams insisted on seeing her daughter's body, so we got umbrellas, slickers, and flashlights and escorted her out into the storm. Despite his crutches, Valenzuela went with us, out of a sense of official duty. One of the security guards pulled back the tarp, Mrs. Williams cried out with a hand to her mouth, and we bundled her back into the hotel and upstairs to her room, where she took another Valium. Hori stayed with her and later, as I passed her door on the way to visit Templeton, I heard Mrs. Williams sobbing. I'd suddenly gained a new respect for publicists and the thankless tasks they execute so selflessly; a lot of listening and hand-holding goes along with their work, and I was thankful Hori was inside that room instead of me.

As cast and crew gathered in the lobby, shock and grief gradually gave way to a measured relief. It was hard to blame them, I thought, since Audrey was no longer a threat, running around with a set of sharp cutlery, and, before her death, had confessed to the violent act she'd committed against Toni Pebbles. Some of the guests mingled in the club room, others in the lounge, huddled together in small knots. Even Deep Freeze and his buddy Sweet Doctor Silk were there, not saying much but managing demeanors that were somber and respectful. Valenzuela postponed his meeting until half past ten and no one grumbled about the delay, not even Christopher Oakley and Heather Sparks.

Tiemeyer also resurfaced, with another cocktail in hand. I saw him from the railing outside my door, crossing from the club room to the piano without speaking to anyone. He set the drink on a coaster, lifted back the keyboard cover, pulled back the bench, arranged his long legs under the piano, and began playing *Rhapsody in Blue,* his fingers teasing out every possible bit of melancholy one could from a song known more for its rhapsodic melodies than its soulfulness. As he played, it was without the usual warmth and cheer from the big fireplace nearby. The regular delivery of firewood had never arrived that day, probably because of the weather; the logs had turned to ash, deepening the gloom that now permeated every inch of the Haunted Springs Hotel.

As I approached Templeton's door, my intention was to apologize straightaway for my bad behavior earlier that day—for the way

I'd toyed with Richard Pearlman as a way of sparring with her. But the moment she opened the door I realized that making up wasn't necessary. In light of what had happened to Audrey Williams, our personal contests and squabbles suddenly seemed petty and ridiculously immature; everything we needed to say we said with our eyes and with the embrace that followed, as Templeton reached out to hug me as a loving sister might. After that, she broached a few questions about the incident involving Audrey Williams that she had to ask as a reporter, before turning the conversation to me.

"How are you holding up, Benjamin? It must have been horrible, being there when it happened."

"You know me. I'll get over it." I changed the subject, relating what I'd learned about Sweet Doctor Silk's criminal background from Sergeant Valenzuela earlier that day. Templeton thanked me but suggested it probably didn't mean a whole lot now, since Audrey had confessed her role in the Toni Pebbles matter.

"I suppose that's the one positive in this whole sorry mess, isn't it?"

"What's that, Alex?"

"That we know it was Audrey who killed Toni Pebbles." She rubbed my arm sympathetically. "You can stop worrying about your friend Oakley now, about the possibility that he might have been involved."

"Are you sure about that?"

Her hand fell away and her eyes grew keen. "What, Benjamin? What am I not seeing?"

"Think, Templeton. What do you remember about the crime scene? What was it that so intrigued Audrey Williams that night?"

She thought a moment before her eyes widened with realization. "Oh, my God. How could I have missed it?"

"There's been a lot going on. You've had a lot of responsibilities, running around playing reporter." I glanced at my watch. "We should get downstairs to that meeting, hear what Valenzuela has to say. I imagine he'll explain it to the others, if he has a mind to."

"I'll bring my tape recorder along."

"I would think you should."

We reached the lobby and lounge to find everyone gathered, except for Nan Williams, who'd finally sent Karen Hori away, asking to be alone. Hori had shown the presence of mind to confiscate Mrs. Williams's various prescription drugs, at least the ones that are dangerous to someone who's despondent and prone to drama. Hori brought them down with her in a plastic bag and asked Kevin Tiemeyer to keep them in a safe place until Mrs. Williams was more stable. He failed to respond, just kept playing his piano and staring off toward the photo of Rebecca Fox hanging in a halo of light behind the club room bar, so Hori locked them in a drawer in the production office.

Valenzuela was also missing; he'd sent word that he'd be on the phone for a few minutes more, attending to matters involving Audrey Williams and her death. While we waited for him to make an appearance, Zeke Zeidler huddled away from the rest of us with Lois Aswell, Christopher Oakley, and Heather Sparks. When the group broke up, Sparks's deep agitation was still apparent, but in a different way now. Her vulnerability had been replaced by something harder, tougher; I could see it in the stiff set of her jaw and her troubled eyes, which looked less frightened now and more angry. She still struck me as someone teetering close to the edge, but if something pushed her over this time, I expected curses rather than more tears and helplessness. She reconvened with Oakley and Aswell at the window next to the cold fireplace, talking low and staring out at the downpour. Beyond the glass another round of lightning illuminated the driving rain. A moment later, the hotel lights flickered and dimmed for a few seconds, followed by a wave of gasps and shrieks and the predictable nervous laughter afterward.

"Hell of a thing, isn't it?" I turned to find Zeke Zeidler standing next to me, leaning on his cane. "I'm sorry you had to get mixed up in this, Justice. You came up here for some R and R, as I recall."

"Trouble seems to find me. Or maybe it's the other way around."

He raised his bushy brows in a way that suggested he knew about the darker episodes from my past. I asked him what was going to happen to his movie, now that there'd been another untimely death, this time closer to the family.

"Fortunately, our indemnity policy covers us for any lost time and money caused by most crimes, including murder. So whatever disruption we've experienced from the Toni Pebbles business won't be an issue. My broker assured me of that."

"And the loss of Audrey?"

"More problematic. Audrey still had two scenes left to shoot. Both were exteriors. We may be able shoot them from a distance and hire someone with a similar voice to loop the dialogue later. Being a perfectionist, Lois is opposed to that. She wants to hire a new actress and reshoot all of Audrey's scenes. Between you and me, she wasn't terribly happy with Audrey's performance, anyway. Lois is rarely satisfied, which may be why she's such a good director. Pain in the butt to work with though."

"I imagine the cost of reshooting Audrey's scenes would be prohibitive."

"Under certain circumstances." He shifted his eyes and swiped a hand over his bald pate. "Had Audrey jumped from the hotel roof, instead of being electrocuted and falling, we would have been in a real fix. The policy came with a suicide exclusion covering the cast."

"Is that customary?"

"No, but it's not unheard of. Audrey's had some serious emotional problems. Hospitalized twice for suicide attempts."

"Then why cast her at all?"

"She was talented beyond her years, and she could play younger than she was, which was useful to us. And I thought her cult following from the Demon Slasher films might help us get a younger crowd into the theaters, sell enough extra tickets to get us into the black." He shrugged. "We took a chance. It didn't work out."

"Not for Audrey, either."

He dropped his eyes. "No, not for poor Audrey." When they came back up, they carefully sought mine. "Fortunately, you were there and saw what actually happened. It was a bolt of lightning—an act of God—that killed Audrey. She didn't die by her own hand. So the production's indemnified, should we suffer any financial loss because of her untimely death." His pause was telling. "That is what you saw, isn't it?"

"As I told the sergeant, she seemed intent on coming back in." I smiled unhappily. "Or maybe that's what I want to believe, for my own peace of mind."

"If that's what you told Valenzuela, I imagine that will be the official version."

"Which means you'll collect your money."

"Believe me, Justice, none of us wanted this."

"Still, it looks like you're out of the woods, doesn't it? Either way, whether you reshoot Audrey's scenes or not, you should be able to finish your film."

"Maybe." Zeidler studied the trio at the window. "It pretty much depends on Heather at this point. She still has another week of shooting left, all scenes that are vital to the movie. But she's in no condition to continue at the moment."

"She does seem awfully upset," I said. "Considering."

"Considering what?"

"I would have expected her to feel more secure, now that we know who butchered Toni Pebbles and stuck that bloody knife in Heather's door. Heather seems as agitated as ever, maybe worse."

Zeidler's voice grew sharp. "One of her fellow cast members just fell to her death, electrocuted. How do you expect her to behave?"

"Of course, that must be it," I said, and looked over to see Sergeant Valenzuela hobbling on his crutches in our general direction.

Valenzuela faced us from the edge of the lounge, next to the piano, which was now silent. He delivered his words bluntly.

"In two nights, two people have died at this hotel. Some of you are not telling me everything you know or suspect. By midnight, I expect anyone with something relevant to my investigation to bring it to me. I'm talking evidence, motivation, something you may have seen or heard, anything that might be helpful. If you don't, and I learn later that you've been evasive or untruthful with me, I'll hit you with obstruction of justice charges and do everything I can to make them stick."

Christopher Oakley spoke up first. "Are these threats really necessary, Sergeant?"

"Do you think I'd be making them if they weren't, Mr. Oakley?"

"It's our understanding that Audrey confessed to killing Toni Pebbles. I don't see why you have to browbeat us like this. Unless maybe you enjoy it."

"I can assure you, Mr. Oakley, that I haven't enjoyed one minute since arriving in this place. I've shipped out one body, and I'll be sending out another, a child, before I'm finished here." He raised a finger and aimed it at the actor. "Don't make the mistake of saying something like that to me again. I'm damn near the end of my patience with you, and everyone else."

"All I'm suggesting," Oakley said, "is that you've solved your case. Why do you need anything further from us? What could we possibly tell you that would help you now?"

Valenzuela surveyed us with his intense brown eyes, while his voice lost its emotion and became more businesslike. "Audrey Williams may not have murdered Toni Pebbles. In fact, I strongly suspect she didn't."

That generated a chorus of curiosity and consternation. Oakley looked at Valenzuela like he was crazy. "What?"

"Audrey confessed to cutting the victim's throat," Valenzuela said. "I couldn't see Audrey from where I stood, but I could hear every word. I believe that she may very well have mutilated the body. But Toni Pebbles was almost certainly dead before Audrey got to her. There was very little blood involved—enough to stain the edge of the knife that cut her throat but not much more. That's because Toni Pebbles died from a puncture wound to the heart. The coroner's people found a small but deep stab wound just below her left breast, more likely made with a small stiletto than a large kitchen knife. The red sweater she was wearing absorbed the blood and covered the wound. When the heart stops, it ceases to pump blood. That accounts for the modest amount of blood when Pebbles's throat was cut. You folks like lots of blood in your movies, but it doesn't always happen like that in real life."

"What you're saying," Heather Sparks said, "is that you still don't know who killed the Pebbles woman."

"I believe Audrey scampered along the ledge outside Room 418 with a knife, intending to frighten Toni Pebbles, perhaps to get even for an unpleasant article Pebbles had written about Audrey and her mother. I think she found Pebbles already dead. She may even have seen the murder take place. She entered through the window, cut the dead victim's throat out of vengefulness or morbid curiosity, then left the same way she'd come. She returned to her room, washed up, changed into her pajamas and slippers, then joined a small group of people outside Room 418, pretending that she'd been asleep the whole time. That's my take on this, at least for now."

Lois Aswell stepped forward. "And what's your theory about who might have killed the Pebbles woman?"

"My gut tells me that it's someone who's still in this hotel. Obviously, security is paramount. If you choose to leave, I won't attempt to stop you. But I do expect you to speak with me before you go, if you've got something pertinent to tell me."

"Someone here did it? You still think that?" Sparks glanced around with uncomprehending eyes; her fists were clenched so tightly the knuckles looked like bleached bone. "Then I won't stay in this place another night. I won't."

Oakley slipped an arm around her, but she seemed oblivious to it. "I'll go with you, baby," he said. "We'll leave immediately."

All around the lounge and lobby, others concurred; it seemed like just about everyone had finally had enough. Before anyone departed, however, thunder rolled across the sky with such fury we could feel the building tremble. The lights flickered and dimmed again, came back on, then seconds later went out for good, leaving us in total darkness. Several people shrieked and there was a general clamor.

"We have a generator." It was Tiemeyer's slurred speech, coming from the general direction of the piano. "There's no need to panic. I'll take care of it."

We heard the piano bench scraping tile in the dark and his footsteps crossing the lobby. There were candles on every table—with the hotel staff so depleted, none had been lit—so I asked around in the dark for matches.

"I got some." It was the deep voice of Sweet Doctor Silk, near my right elbow. I put out my hand, he found it with the matchbook, and I lit a candle and starting looking for others. By the time I'd put matches to half a dozen the generator kicked in, and the hotel lights came on again. I was about to hand the matchbook back to Sweet Doctor Silk when I noticed two words embossed in gold against black on the cover: CLUB EBONY. He'd turned away by then, to confer in hushed tones with Deep Freeze. I slipped the matchbook into my pocket and didn't mention it again.

"Come on, Heather." Oakley took her hand, and they started toward the stairs. "There's no reason for us to be here any longer. We're going home."

"I don't think so, Mr. Oakley." The annoying voice was familiar, but unexpected. We turned to see Scotty Campbell standing just inside the hotel entrance, dripping wet.

"I thought we had an agreement," Valenzuela said tightly. "That you were to be out of this hotel for good."

"Exactly my wishes, Chief, but I'm afraid there's been a change of plans. The river's taken the bridge out, and part of the road too."

"What are you saying?" Oakley demanded.

"Nobody's going anyplace, at least not tonight," Campbell said brightly. "There's no way out of Coyote Canyon."

"That explains why we didn't get our firewood delivery this afternoon," Tiemeyer said, dutifully but drunkenly, as he rejoined the group.

"And why we never saw a media invasion," Karen Hori said.

Heather Sparks was muttering to herself. "This can't be happening." Her voice was spare and strained; she sounded like a woman on the verge, trying to hold everything in but about to tear apart at the seams. "I wish I'd never come up here. I wish I'd never taken this role. My agent warned me. Why didn't I listen?"

"Take it easy," Oakley said. He reached for her but she pushed him off, stepping away to pace alone in circles, her arms folded tenaciously across her chest. I noticed Lois Aswell, Zeke Zeidler, and Karen Hori exchange uneasy glances.

Sparks suddenly faced the three of them with accusatory eyes. "This whole thing is a nightmare." Her chin trembled and her eyes were wild. "And it never stops."

Scotty Campbell raised his stumpy arms, palms up, looking like he was having a grand time. "As long we're all stuck in this creep show another night, we might as well make the most of it." He grinned devilishly. "So—who wants to buy me a drink?"

TWENTY-SIX

Following Scotty Campbell's announcement that the bridge was out, Kevin Tiemeyer returned to the bar to replenish his Manhattan glass. Campbell soon followed, merrily leading a procession of drinkers who seemed less jolly.

Templeton and I discussed the situation briefly before she headed back upstairs to phone the *L.A. Times* and then continue the secretive research she'd been involved in for a couple of days. As she climbed, Richard Pearlman studied her shapely legs and backside from the bottom step, looking more like a lovesick teenager than a tenured professor at a respected Boston university. Sergeant Valenzuela organized the five security guards he'd been working with into a new detail; they'd come armed with their own weapons, and he posted a guard in the lobby and the others on each of the four floors, knowing the officer assistance he'd expected by midnight wouldn't be arriving after all, because of the impasse at the river washout.

Valenzuela was hobbling past me toward his office when I stopped him and asked if he was carrying an evidence bag. He produced one from a pocket. I asked him to open it, he did, and I dropped in the matchbook from Club Ebony I'd been handed by Sweet Doctor Silk during the blackout.

"What's it mean?" Valenzuela asked.

"I'm still working on that part. Hang on to it for me, will you?"

"You've got until midnight to brief me on what you know, same as the others. I can't have you holding anything back longer than that. Not after what's happened."

"Duly noted, Sergeant."

He tucked the plastic bag into a coat pocket and hobbled off. As I turned toward the stairs, Pearlman was waiting for me. He offered to buy me a drink. I told him I'd been on the wagon for a few years, but thanked him just the same. I was about to start up when he spoke again, obviously needing to talk.

"I never had that problem with alcohol, thank God. A lot of writers do, from what I hear." He shrugged dejectedly. "Although I'm not really a writer, am I? Only one book and not a very important one at that. Who am I kidding?"

I glanced at my watch, wanting to get away. "What's on your mind, Richard?"

He held up his pipe. "This is my only vice. This, and movies." He attempted nonchalance. "I wouldn't mind a smoke just now, out on the veranda. Care to join me?"

I didn't, but there was a pleading quality to his hangdog manner and I'd begun to actually like the guy. Besides, I wanted to keep the peace with Templeton. "Sure, I'll get some air with you. If you promise to stop the tiptoe routine, and tell me what's got you so bothered."

Outside, the rain was coming down so hard and the thunder and lightning was so spectacular it looked like one of those cinematic storms where the production designer has the actors soaked to the skin seconds after they step into frame.

Pearlman and I watched it standing deep under the eaves of the veranda, while he flicked his lighter over the bowl of his fine-looking pipe and puffed several times until the tobacco had a nice glow and gave him the smoke he wanted. From the side, in his turtleneck and with his precisely shaped beard, he looked good with a pipe; it suited him, or at least suited the image he'd obviously cultivated with considerable care.

"My first wife left me because she found me so stuffy," he said, without a word of prompting from me. I hadn't known he'd been married and wasn't all that interested, but I let him talk. "My second wife left me because she said she couldn't spend the rest of her life with a man who had no passion and never engaged in a single activity that wasn't safe or predictable." He glanced over. "I suppose they amount to the same thing, don't they?"

"Is that why you wrote your book, Richard? To try something different, something you'd always dreamed of doing?"

He nodded, and puffed on the pipe again; the nicotine seemed to help him relax. "I got my tenure by publishing articles in academic journals and contributing essays or chapters to a few texts on film history and cinematic theory. They were strong on research and analysis—lots of intellectualizing—but they didn't have a shred of feeling in them. Nothing that came close to getting at the essence of life, or expressing who I really am." He smiled sadly. "They kept me employed, but they didn't feed my soul. That sounds terribly pretentious, doesn't it?"

"You don't need my validation, Richard. You've got a mind of your own. A rather good one, from what I can tell."

"A good mind." His laugh was small, self-loathing. "A few years ago, I woke up to find myself alone, middle-aged, childless, and altogether miserable. A lot of good my mind has done me."

"Has anything changed, now that you've got a book out there?"

"The publication of *A Murder in Eternal Springs* changed nothing, except my bank account."

"I'll keep that in mind if and when my own book comes out."

"You're probably wondering where I got the idea to write it."

I wasn't, but I lied. "It's been on my mind since I started reading it."

"I knew my ex-wives were right. I was a stick-in-the-mud—a pompous, self-important professor who knew an awful lot, except how to seize the moment, how to squeeze the juice from life. It wasn't always that way. When I was a teenager, leading a rather sheltered life, I discovered Rebecca Fox on the Late Show. I fell in love with her, at least to the extent that an inexperienced, hormonal teenager can be in love with an image on the screen. When I learned that she was dead, and how she'd died, I became obsessed with her. For a boy like me, from a family where feelings had no place, where joy simply wasn't embraced, that kind of passion was exhilarating. As a middle-aged man who felt like he was slowly drying up, I wanted to recapture that feeling."

"So you wrote a book about Rebecca Fox, hoping to rekindle the flame."

He faced me squarely, looking tormented. "I wanted it to be a great book, Justice. I really did."

"I suppose every serious author wants that, at least their first time out."

"I wanted to peel back the layers, to get inside the hearts and minds of the people I was writing about, to explore the social and cultural issues connected to her death, to see the larger picture. A book that might have made a difference."

"That's a lot to bite off with one book."

"Other writers have done it. It's not impossible."

"For what it's worth, I thought your foreword to the revised edition was well-written and intriguing."

"Yes, colleagues have told me that. But the rest of the book doesn't measure up to that foreword, does it? It promises something I was never able to deliver." He turned to face the weather again. His pipe had gone out and he tried to relight it in the wind. He grew frustrated, stared at the pipe and lighter a moment as if they represented something in his life he loathed, then hurled them almost violently out into the storm. "I should have written a great true crime book, one with historic sweep and penetrating social insight." He shook his head miserably. "Instead, I wrote a puerile homage to a beautiful movie star, and gave the more important elements of the story short shrift. I failed utterly and pathetically."

"Don't be too hard on yourself, Richard. You got it published, it sold reasonably well, and it's being turned into a movie."

"If you and Templeton had written it, it would have been the genuine article. I can see that, just watching the two of you together, seeing how your minds work, how you challenge each other and don't let go until you've gotten what you're after. You would have done something special with it, something profound."

"Don't give us too much credit. Maybe we're just nosier than you, and find it entertaining."

He looked over again, pleading with his eyes. "It's like you said earlier, Justice—this murder of Toni Pebbles gives me a second chance, an opportunity to write a sequel, to get it right." He dropped his eyes uncomfortably. "An opportunity to fill in those holes and correct some stupid mistakes, as you pointed out so perceptively. Maybe even accomplish more than that, by writing a book that's worth a damn."

For a fleeting moment, I wondered if it was possible that he'd eliminated Toni Pebbles himself, to provide the hook he needed to write another book. Then I remembered that he'd been having a drink with Templeton during the minutes she'd been snuffed, and let my suspicions go.

The frigid air was getting to me; I hugged myself, shivering. "Where are you going with all this, Richard? Maybe you should get to the point, before we freeze to death out here."

His eyes reconnected with mine. "I want to learn from you, Justice. I want to learn from you and Alexandra. If you'll allow me, I'd like to be your friend. All my life, I've taken the safe path, lived with my head in movies and books, while people like you and Alexandra took chances. That woman has more brio in her little finger than I have in all my silly fantasies and dreams."

I placed a sympathetic hand on his shoulder. "This sudden desire to change doesn't have anything to do with your feelings toward Templeton, does it? The fact that you can't keep your eyes off her and that you think about her night and day?"

He swallowed with difficulty. "Certainly, I'm fond of her."

"Besotted might be a better word."

"She's an incredible woman, Justice. I—I've never had the honor of spending time with a woman of such—"

"I know, she's drop-dead gorgeous. Flawless face, sensational body. Magnetic personality, first-rate mind. The whole package."

"She's everything I ever wanted in a woman." He said it like a man in pain, admitting the unbearable truth.

"You're convinced you've found the woman who can transform you into something you've always wanted to be, who can fill that emptiness in your life that you haven't been able to fill on your own."

"Yes!" It was like a last flame of hope in the raging storm, sputtering foolishly against the odds. Immediately, he sagged. "You probably think I'm a fool, giving voice to these feelings."

"Actually," I said, "I've been going through something similar myself recently. Loneliness tends to make us lose perspective, Richard."

"My feelings toward Alexandra are overwhelming. It's as if they've taken control of me."

"Probably because you've kept them in check for so long."

His smile was rueful, but wiser. "You're not being very encouraging, are you?"

"If it's any consolation, Richard, she has this effect on a lot of men." He winced as if I'd stabbed him in the gut. "She doesn't do it intentionally. Not always, anyway."

"You're telling me I don't have a chance with her."

"That's between you and Templeton, although I suspect you already know the answer."

A moment passed as he absorbed it. I felt for the guy, but there wasn't much I could do. Finally, he said, "Even if it isn't what I want it to be—my relationship with Alexandra—I'd still like to know you both better, to count you as compatriots. Perhaps even work together on something. Maybe that book I spoke about—my next one."

"You don't want my name associated with any book you write, Richard. It can only hurt."

"I understand. But I'd so much like to learn from you, Justice. How to look at things differently, how you see more than I'm capable of seeing, how you figure things out."

"There's some brainpower involved, but a lot of it's intuitive, gut instinct."

"Just what I need to develop! Please, Justice, let me get involved, even in some small way."

I thought about my conversation earlier with Zeke Zeidler. "There might be something," I said. "A piece of research related to filmmaking. Let's think of it as your first assignment. See how it works out."

His voice rose with excitement. "I'd be honored, Justice. Just tell me what you need."

"See if you can find out what kind of indemnity coverage was in place in 1956 during the filming of *The Ides of March*. You never mentioned that in your book, at least not that I've come across yet."

"One more thing I overlooked, I suppose. But what could that possibly—?"

"I'd like to know if there were any special exclusions in the policy, particularly regarding suicide among the cast members."

He cocked his head curiously. "But I don't see what—"

"All I'm suggesting, Richard, is that you look into it and let me know what you find. Can you do that?"

"Yes, of course. I had that material scanned into my database archive as I was doing my research. I can probably access it from here. When do you need it?"

"An hour ago."

"I'll get right on it." He grabbed my hand, shook it enthusiastically. "I can't tell you what it means to me, getting an opportunity like this. I'm very excited."

"That's good, Richard. Hold on to that excitement."

He turned away, hurrying back into the hotel. I was about to go in myself when Templeton came through the door, looking back curiously as Pearlman raced toward the stairs like a little kid on his way to buy his first Popsicle. She was holding my jacket, two umbrellas, and a flashlight. She handed me the jacket and turned me around toward the hotel steps.

"We're going to the museum," she said, dangling a set of keys she'd borrowed from Kevin Tiemeyer.

"Now? In this weather?"

"Now, in this weather. And on the way, if you're nice, I'll tell you some interesting things I've uncovered concerning Mr. Percy Childs."

TWENTY-SEVEN

The downpour lightened as we walked beneath our umbrellas, but my shoes were still soaked through before we'd crossed the hotel parking lot and climbed the steps to the main street. As we proceeded south and the lightning flashed sufficiently bright we could make out the rows of headstones rising one above the other in the cemetery at the end of town, and above that the old, weathered house where Martha Frech had lived most of her life.

"Start talking," I said, "unless you'd rather listen to my teeth chatter."

"Ed Jones had a daughter." Templeton pointed the flashlight ahead of her along the wet pavement. "He never married the girl's mother. She stayed behind in Gulfport, Mississippi."

"I knew that. I read it in Pearlman's book."

"Just let me tell the story, will you?"

"Sorry."

"In his research, Richard never followed up on Ed Jones's family relations. He was too focused on Rebecca Fox and her family, along with the Hollywood elements. Jones's family was mentioned almost in passing. So I did some chasing of my own."

"Genealogical search?"

Templeton nodded. "The mother's name was Frederica, in honor of Frederick Douglass. They named their daughter Clarissa, after Jones's great-grandmother, a former slave. Clarissa grew up in Gulfport and eventually married a soldier stationed at the army base there. Gulfport's a fairly small town, and I was able to locate a childhood friend of Clarissa's. She told me Clarissa married the soldier in part because he was fluent in languages and due to be stationed overseas. She wanted to raise her children as far as possible from the country where her father had been lynched."

"If she and her mother knew how Ed Jones died, why didn't they claim the body?"

"Clarissa's mother was poor and decided to leave him buried here. And they weren't legally married, so claiming the body would have been difficult. All Clarissa knew as a child was that the KKK had lynched her father out west and no one had ever been charged or prosecuted for the crime."

"No wonder she wanted to put some distance between her kids and that kind of history."

Templeton stopped to face me. "The soldier Clarissa married was named Childs. They named their firstborn Percy, after her grandfather, a sharecropper."

"Percy Childs is Deep Freeze," I said. "Which makes him the grandson of Ed Jones."

Templeton nodded, grinning. "Raised comfortably on U.S. Army bases in Europe before transforming himself into Deep Freeze, the renegade rapper."

"Wow. Nice work, Templeton."

"You taught me well, Justice. Leave no stone unturned. That's what you always told me."

"It certainly explains why Deep Freeze wanted the role of Ed Jones so badly, even to the point of helping bankroll the production costs. But why do you think he hasn't made his lineage public by now? You'd think he'd want the whole world to know that his grandfather was the victim of a lynching by the KKK."

"If it did," Templeton pointed out, "everyone would also know that his gangsta image is a big fraud. The little rap empire he's built on that image might come tumbling down. He'd get some sympathy, but he'd also be held up to a lot of ridicule."

"Which brings us back around to Toni Pebbles, since she was apparently here to expose someone for their deep, dark secret."

We resumed our trek to the museum, following the beam from Templeton's flashlight. "I'm not sure the secret Deep Freeze has been hiding is grounds for murder," she said. "His link to Ed Jones was bound to come out at some point. He might have been waiting for the right time to break it, maybe when the movie comes out, for the extra promotional punch. But I'm not sure I see him committing murder to postpone the inevitable. Anyway, he's got an alibi, doesn't he? Didn't you get on Richard Pearlman's case about that?"

"I wanted him to give it more thought, to look beyond the obvious."

I don't think Templeton really heard me. She looked pensive, with her mind elsewhere. "I've been thinking a lot about Deep Freeze," she said, "since I discovered his connection to Ed Jones. It puts those ugly lyrics of his in a different perspective."

"Don't tell me you've suddenly become a Deep Freeze fan."

"I'm developing some empathy with the guy, Justice. His rage can't all be fake, manufactured just to make a buck. I don't like how he expresses himself, but I'm starting to understand him better. Maybe I always did understand him, and just didn't want to admit it, because his message is so repugnant. But there's a lot of truth in it, Justice. Maybe, in his own way, Deep Freeze has been more honest than I have."

"I doubt that your ancestors had it any easier than his did. Your skin is just as dark as his. You don't lose your skin color just because you have a wealthy father and drive a Maserati."

"That's just it. Despite his hostility, I feel a kinship with the guy. I can't help it."

We'd reached the little museum. Templeton pulled out her borrowed keys and unlocked the door. I flicked on a light switch, she shut off her flashlight, and we stepped once more into the past.

"So why'd you drag me here, anyway?"

"I wanted another look around," Templeton said. "I cut my first visit short to interview Kevin Tiemeyer, remember? And given what's been going on, I didn't want to come over here alone."

I followed her to the display on the Ed Jones lynching. I hadn't thought about it before, but the only photograph of Jones was the one of him hanging by the neck from a rafter of the Eternal Springs jail. No one connected to the museum, apparently, had bothered to find a picture taken of the man when he'd been alive, although Pearlman had managed to secure one for his book.

"The invisible man," Templeton said, in that way she had of sometimes reading my thoughts.

One section of the display was devoted to the history of lynching in California, a list that ended in 1956 with the hanging of Ed Jones for the alleged sexual assault and murder of Rebecca Fox, the state's last recorded lynching. Historians had also verified sixty-six others in the state, beginning with a Latino named Jose Antonio Ygarra in Mendocino County in 1875, for suspected murder; and just before Ed Jones, a black man, name unknown, in Siskiyou County in 1947, allegedly for cattle rustling. Two white men, John Holmes and Thomas Thurmond, had been strung up on suspicion of kidnapping and murder in San Jose in 1933. By then, lynching had become rare in California, with the great majority of hangings recorded in the nineteenth century for crimes as minor as theft; in a single lynching in 1901, a group of four "Indians" and "half-breeds" were strung up in Modoc County for theft and burglary. Most of the victims had been white or Latino—blacks were uncommon in California back then—with a sprinkling of Native Americans and Chinese. In a footnote, the report noted that this list included only *verified* lynchings; there were surely many more, including doomed men who'd been killed as they were hunted down or taken captive, and mass hangings of Chinese and other ethnic groups that had never been officially recorded. Another footnote put the total number of verified lynchings in the United States at 4,743; of these, 3,446 were African American, with the last recorded lynching taking place in 1968 in

Mississippi, a less populous state that nonetheless accounted for nearly 600 of the total. Only a handful of states, Alaska and a few in the East, had no recorded lynchings.

I mentioned to Templeton that my high school history lessons had never mentioned much about the lynching phenomenon in the United States, certainly not how widespread it had been, but I'm not sure she heard me. Her attention was riveted on the photo taken in 1956 in the Eternal Springs jail, as a single Ku Klux Klan member posed beside the dangling body of Ed Jones.

"Take a close look," Templeton said. "Notice anything interesting about the robe?"

I'd told Templeton about the KKK costume I'd discovered in the hotel attic when I'd gone looking for Audrey Williams. There was no way to tell, of course, if it was the same one pictured here. The photo was a grainy black-and-white, supposedly shot under coercion by Roderick Tiemeyer, the publisher of the *Hungry Valley Weekly,* whose hand might understandably have been shaky. I squinted my one good eye for a better look. Templeton pointed to the bottom hem of the robe, where I could just make out a thin black line running the width of it, suggesting another, darker garment underneath.

Then she directed me to a nearby photo of Enid Tiemeyer, standing tall in her long, black dress.

"From what I've read," I said, "the KKK didn't allow women to join."

"Maybe there was no KKK in Eternal Springs." Our eyes met the way they had so many times when we'd stumbled together on to something significant. "It was 1956," Templeton went on, "way out west. At that time, the KKK was out of commission or dormant just about everywhere, but especially out here, far from its southern roots."

"Enid came from Georgia in 1924," I said, picking up the thread, "where the Klan was thriving around that time. She could have brought this costume with her."

"Or it might have belonged to Roderick," Templeton suggested, "and she just borrowed it for the night."

"He's on the short side. She should have let it out."

"I don't think Enid was known for her fashion sense."

"No," I said, "but she ruled Eternal Springs with an iron fist, didn't she? I imagine a lot of people would have made false statements or looked the other way for her."

"Her brother was the town sheriff, who claimed he was overcome by a mob intent on hanging his prisoner. Her husband was the compliant publisher of the local newspaper, who took the photo and wrote up the story. Except for Ed Jones, it's possible they were the only three people involved."

"You're forgetting someone, Templeton."

She thought about it a moment and said, "Kevin Tiemeyer."

I nodded. We were cooking now, on all four burners. "Kevin claimed he saw Ed Jones coming out of Rebecca Fox's room that night—and a mob drag his father from the house and down to the jail, where he was forced to shoot this photo."

"It's all a lie—there was no mob, was there?"

"I suspect not," I said.

"But why would a family like the Tiemeyers go to so much trouble to frame Ed Jones for a sexual assault and murder in their hotel?"

"Good question." I moved to another display in the museum, one I'd glanced at before: A photo of Brandy Fox, taken on the set of a B movie in 1972, as she signed an autograph book for a fan, a stylish Mont Blanc pen poised in her left hand. Nearby was another shot, obviously cropped and blown up from a crime scene photo. This time, it was a knife, instead of a pen, clutched in her left hand, the edge of the blade turned outward, slick with blood; the caption mentioned that the photo came from the files of the *Hungry Valley Weekly*. I recalled that both Brandy and her mother had died from wounds on the left side of the neck; Brandy's had been a deep, clean slice, Rebecca's more shallow and messy. The photo from Brandy's autograph session told me that she'd been left-handed. The knife in the other photo was in her left hand, with the blade turned away from her. There was nothing incongruous about the two photos, or the facts they suggested: A left-handed woman had cut her throat on the left side, clutching the knife in her left hand, with the blade turned outward, which made perfect sense. From a forensic standpoint, everything matched up. That was the problem.

"What is it, Justice?" She tapped my bald spot. "What's going on in there?"

My mind was working fast, maybe too fast, so I tried to slow it down, tried to put what I was seeing here with the crime scene photo I'd seen in Richard Pearlman's book, showing Brandy Fox laying crumpled on the floor of Room 418. But I was having trouble envisioning what I needed to clearly, comprehensibly. It was like trying to solve a difficult math problem; just as you're almost there, you lose your focus for a split second, all the numbers collapse into a disjointed pile, and you have to start all over again.

"Justice?"

I raised a hand to quiet Templeton, afraid I'd lose the fragile grip on what I already had, afraid it would slip away from me and I'd never get it back.

"Not now," I said, moving toward the door. "Later, when I've got another piece or two in place. Right now, I need to speak with Richard Pearlman."

TWENTY-EIGHT

Templeton and I had just locked up and left for the hotel when I glanced back for another look at the Martha Frech place and noticed someone following us.

He was roughly a block behind, coming from the area of the cemetery, walking fast. No umbrella, collar up and head hunched down against the wet and cold. In the dark, and through the drizzle, I couldn't make out who it was.

I didn't want to alarm Templeton, so I simply suggested we get back to the hotel on the double, before we both caught a bad chill. We quickened our pace. So did the stranger behind us.

"Slow down, Justice. You'll do more harm to yourself getting all heated up than being out here an extra minute or two."

"Don't panic, and don't look back, but there's someone behind us." She started to peek. "I said don't look back!"

"If I'm about to be eliminated by a crazed killer, I prefer to know who it is."

"Forgive me if I laugh later, at your funeral. Anyway, it's impossible to tell in this weather. Just keep moving."

We took off at a good clip, Templeton taking my words to heart. The younger black woman with the long legs and flexible from regular yoga classes strode out ahead, quickly leaving behind the older white guy with the growing paunch. I watched her put some distance between us and tried to keep up, but it wasn't much use, especially in my waterlogged shoes. Within a minute Templeton was down the steps into the parking lot and out of sight.

I could hear footsteps behind me now, coming closer. I didn't like the look of the dark, expansive parking lot that lay ahead, with the vehicles belonging to the cast and crew scattered thinly about, without much cover for hiding. As I approached the steps I accelerated, determined to catch up with Templeton or get safely into the hotel, whichever came first.

Instead, I slipped on the wet steps and went down hard, rolling as I hit the asphalt to absorb the brunt of the fall. It wasn't as severe a tumble as I'd taken chasing Martha Frech down to the lake that afternoon, but I took a pounding just the same. I was down for a second or two and lost the grip on my umbrella, which the wind whisked away, leaving me without a weapon. I struggled painfully to my feet, but it was too late. Our pursuer was suddenly looming over me, blocking my escape. There didn't seem any way around him, so I pulled back a fist, ready to defend myself the best I could.

"You getting ready for combat, Benjamin?" I recognized the voice of Christopher Oakley, then the man himself as he stepped closer, grinning. "I have to warn you, I've done some boxing, though only in the gym."

I began brushing myself off from my fall and he asked me if I was hurt. I told him my pride was bruised, but that was about it. "You make a habit of chasing people in the dark, Christopher?"

"I saw you and Alexandra leave the hotel," he explained. "I wanted to talk, and I needed to get some fresh air, so I followed you until you got to the museum. You two seemed engrossed about something in there, so I decided to take a walk, catch you on my way back."

My guard was still up, figuratively speaking. "You like to walk in weather like this?"

"I'm a farmboy, remember? Where I come from, this is just humidity."

I glanced up; the rain was coming down steadily. "Sorry,

Christopher, but it's rain to me." He took off his slicker, stepped closer, and held it over the two of us. His tousled hair and stubbly face were wet, along with his Levi's jacket and jeans; I could smell him, a damp, musky, male scent, and it made me want to step even closer and bury my nose in him. "What was it you wanted to talk about, anyway?"

"You and me," he said. "Some things that have been on my mind."

"What kind of things?"

"Serious things."

He was about to continue when our faces were suddenly flooded with light, as the beam from Templeton's flashlight struck us full force. She approached with an upraised can of aerosol pepper spray in her other hand, sans umbrella.

"Justice? You okay?"

"Yeah, I'm fine. It's Christopher. We were just getting reacquainted."

She surveyed the space between us as we huddled beneath his slicker, which amounted to a few inches. "I can see that."

"Where did you disappear to?"

"I looked around as I reached the hotel but you weren't there. I came back to check, make sure you were okay."

"I took a tumble, but I'm back on my feet again."

"They're both on the ground, I hope." She smiled sweetly.

I glanced at the can of pepper spray in her hand. "Why didn't you pull that out before, when we needed it?"

"I forgot I had it with me. I've only started carrying it recently."

"You two consider me dangerous?" Oakley asked, grinning.

"Dangerously cute," Templeton said, and the three of us laughed, if a bit uneasily. Templeton slid her eyes toward me for a moment, like a warning to watch myself. Then she said coyly, "I'll leave you two alone. Don't get any colder staying out here." She hooked a thumb in my direction. "I don't want a sick puppy on my hands."

She turned and retraced her steps, back toward the hotel. I

noticed that she was taking her time and glancing back as she went. So did Oakley.

"She's very protective, isn't she?" Thunder rumbled and the rain came harder. "Maybe we should get inside, where it's warm and dry."

"And more private."

"That too."

"So we can have that talk you wanted."

"Exactly."

"My room?"

"That should work."

We started running together under his slicker, laughing, my heart lighter than it had been for a long time.

The power remained out, the generator on, and the lights dimmed; the hotel was a gloomy place, filled with shadows. Under other circumstances, it might have been considered atmospheric; the effect now was spooky and unnerving.

As we climbed the stairs in the southwest stairwell, Oakley put a hand on the small of my back, causing me to flinch. "You're sure you didn't get banged up when you took that fall?"

"Really, I'm fine. Nice of you to ask, though."

"I'm not such a bad guy," he deadpanned, "when you get to know me."

"I'd like to get to know you, Christopher. If that's something you're interested in."

He gave my head an affectionate rub, and we continued up. As we climbed in silence, I realized I'd have to tell him soon that I was HIV positive; I'd probably let things go too far already without letting him know. My admission might mean instant rejection, but that had to be Oakley's choice, not mine. To not tell him before things got sexual between us was not just indecent and unfair; under certain circumstances, nondisclosure could land you in court, even in jail. As we reached the third-floor landing, heading toward my door, the security guard posted there looked us over judiciously, acknowledged us, and cast his eyes elsewhere. I fumbled nervously with my key, sensing Oakley next to me, anticipating what might be ahead. Finally, I had the key in the old lock, was turning the tumblers, then the handle, and finally we were inside.

While I switched on a small table lamp near the bed, Oakley went into the bathroom and came back with a towel. I was standing near the window, in the modest lamplight, when he approached me and started toweling off my face. Gently, with that surprising familiarity and ease he'd demonstrated once before, when he'd caught me coming damp from the shower, wearing only a towel.

"I'd tell you you're all wet," he said, with just the hint of a smile, "but you might take it the wrong way."

"I'd say we're both all wet, Christopher." I took the other end of the towel and began patting his face as he patted mine; I could feel his rough beard catching on the cloth while his intoxicating aroma reached my nostrils again.

His eyes were clear and unerringly direct. "You're a fascinating man, Benjamin. You've had a remarkable life."

"A messy life," I said.

"Romance, tragedy, scandal, murder investigations, danger. It's quite a story."

"I'm not particularly wholesome or admirable."

"We all have our problems, our character defects. Personally, I find that kind of complexity attractive."

I took a chance, running my fingers through his curly hair, pushing it back off his face. He didn't resist. "It's a nice thing to say, Christopher."

"I can't wait to read that autobiography of yours."

"With any luck," I said, "it'll be in bookstores by this time next year."

He showed me his killer smile. "You're going to make me wait that long?"

I let my hand stray, resting lightly on the slope of his neck, imagining what it would be like to kiss him. It seemed a good time to tell him more about myself, the part about my health that might not be as attractive to him as some of my other flaws. "I suppose I could get an advanced copy to you, after it goes into galleys."

"What about a manuscript? Could I see that?"

"You mean now? The one I sent to my editor?"

"Sure. Why not?"

An unpleasant sensation took hold in the pit of my stomach, replacing the more welcome flutters I'd experienced moments ago. I touched his unshaven face, appreciating the contours and the texture, knowing it would probably be the last time. As much as I enjoyed it, I felt like I'd just stepped into another time and place, a colder space, with a completely different person, one I hadn't known half a minute ago.

I kept my eyes on his. "You're interested in the film rights to my story, aren't you?"

His eyes wavered, almost imperceptibly—very nearly the consummate actor, with perfect control, but not quite. "I have to admit, the thought's occurred to me. I'd at least like to read it, give it consideration."

"You're kind of young to play me, aren't you?"

"You were thirty-two when the Pulitzer scandal ended your newspaper career. Movies take years to develop, before shooting starts. I'd say I'm just the right age to grow into the project. Anyway, those kinds of adjustments can always be made in the script. It's a movie, after all, not a documentary."

"I believe that's Lois Aswell's line."

"Actually," he said, "she's the one who suggested your life story might be good for the screen."

"I'm queer, Christopher. That's central to who I am. You can't very well change that."

"I'd have no problem playing a gay man on film."

"You're sure about that?"

He didn't hesitate. "I want characters that are complex, roles that are challenging. They don't come along all that often. Everybody in Hollywood is looking for the next great book, the next great script, the next great character. I was hoping I might get a jump on the competition."

"That's why you're here with me now? That's what you wanted to talk about?"

"I thought we might become partners on the project, pursue it together."

"If you decided you wanted to move forward with it."

"Of course, I'd have to read it. Consult with my people. Nothing's guaranteed. There are all kinds of things to be considered."

"But you want the inside track."

"Like I said, it's a competitive business. If I wait, the book scouts in New York will have advance copies, sending their synopses to every major star and producer in Hollywood who might have an interest. I don't stand a chance if I work that way."

"So to get that inside edge you lead me on, making me fall in love with you a little, at least long enough to get first look."

Finally, he paused. "I haven't been dishonest with you, Benjamin."

"No?"

He laid a hand on my shoulder, gave it a gentle squeeze. "I like you. I want to be friends. I really do."

"How many friends does a guy like you have, Christopher? A lot, I'll bet. Hundreds, I imagine, filling your phone book back home."

"I'm sorry if you misinterpreted anything I've said."

"You had your hands on me, Christopher. I was naked. You could see how I was responding to you." I held up my fingers in a pinch. "I was this close to kissing you."

"When I was a masseur in New York, Benjamin, I saw plenty of erections. And it wasn't always my gay clients who had them. Erections don't bother me much."

"You said you hadn't been dishonest with me. So tell me something. Are you gay, Christopher? Can you be honest about that?"

His answer came so quickly I couldn't tell if it was spontaneous or just well-rehearsed. "I've never put much stock in labels or boundaries." His hand moved to my face, just for a moment.

"I'm truly sorry if I misled you. Or if you took things the wrong way." A gentle stroke on my cheek, and the hand was gone.

"You had me falling in love with you, Christopher. I think you know that. I think you knew it all along."

"I'm an actor, Benjamin, with a certain look and way about me. People make us the object of their fantasies. In a sense, we're trained to make people fall in love with us. It's what we do well."

He hadn't told me a single thing I hadn't known, only what I'd chosen to ignore out of my desperate desire for him. For a moment, I thought about the patterns so many of us repeat all our lives, over and over, even as they guarantee us unhappiness and hold us back from becoming someone stronger and better and more fully realized than we are. I didn't blame Christopher Oakley for how and where we'd ended up. I blamed myself.

There seemed nothing more to say to him, except maybe good-bye. Before I spoke, there was a knock at the door.

"I should get that," I said. "And you should probably go."

He didn't move, and I saw in him the single-mindedness, the perseverance and drive that someone in his line of work surely needs to get ahead and survive. "I'd still like to look at that manuscript of yours, if you're willing."

"I'll think about it."

I crossed to the door and he followed. Before I opened it he kissed me chastely on the forehead. "Either way," he said, "I wish you lots of success with it."

I pulled open the door. Richard Pearlman stood there, his knuckles poised to knock again. In his other hand he clutched a sheaf of computer printouts.

"Alexandra told me you were looking for me." He held up the clutch of papers. "I've got something I want to show you."

"Come in," I said. "Mr. Oakley was just leaving." I spoke to Oakley's back as he started down the hall. "Give my best to Heather."

He didn't respond, just kept walking, as Pearlman stepped inside.

Richard Pearlman spread his papers on the writing desk in my room. They were computer printouts from the Rebecca Fox archive material he'd scanned into a database while doing research for his book. He pointed to a clause in the insurance policy the producers of *The Ides of March* had purchased to protect them in the event production of the movie was delayed or shut down prematurely.

"This section specifically excludes malfeasance, moral turpitude, or suicide by any member of the cast or production team as one of the events covered," Pearlman said. He started reading it to me aloud but the legal jargon was so dense I stopped him and read it silently to myself.

"As I recall," I said, "Rebecca Fox was murdered only days before filming was to be completed, with a number of key scenes still to be shot."

"Fortunately for the producers," Pearlman said, "the crime of murder was not among those acts excluded, or they would have lost a bundle. It was quite a costly movie for those times."

"The movie was a total loss then, never released."

"Correct."

"The producers must have been horrified by the death of their star."

"Oh, yes. It was a terrible shock to everyone involved with the film."

"Had shooting been going well?"

"In what way, Benjamin?"

"Had there been any serious problems on the set? Were they behind schedule or over budget? Had the performances been up to snuff?"

"Nothing in my research suggested otherwise. Why do you ask?"

"It must have been quite an emotional ordeal for Rebecca Fox," I said, "making a movie that explored such a painful episode in her life, when she'd never really healed from it."

He looked at me curiously. "You're not suggesting the producers had their leading lady murdered for financial gain?"

"Not at all."

"What then?" He grabbed the papers, examining them as I had. "What is it you've discovered?" He fixed me with a pleading look. "What am I missing, damn it?"

"One other thing, Richard." I opened my copy of *A Murder in Eternal Springs* to the illustrations in the middle and found the crime scene photograph from the Brandy Fox suicide, showing the bloody knife clutched in her right hand. "Where did this photograph come from?"

"I got it from the Sheriff's Department, down in Hungry Valley. Why?"

"The Department gave you this photo?"

Pearlman shook his head. "I printed the photo from the original negative. The photos that existed weren't very sharp."

"Jack Hightower Jr. gave you permission to print from one of the crime scene negatives?"

Again, Pearlman shook his head. "Hightower and the public affairs office gave me the runaround. They didn't want to cooperate at all."

"Then how did you get the negative?"

He pursed his lips with concern. "This has to stay strictly between you and me."

"Okay."

"Sergeant Valenzuela contacted me privately. He heard I was writing the book. He got me the negative so I could make a print from it, as long as I didn't acknowledge him anywhere in the book or let anyone know how I got access to it."

"Valenzuela," I said.

"You sound surprised."

"I'd like to talk to him about this, if it's alright with you."

"He made me promise to keep it confidential. I shouldn't have talked to you about it in the first place."

"Maybe you could clear it with him after the fact, Richard. He doesn't need to know you already told me. He knows I'm curious about the Fox homicides. I don't think he'll mind if you talk to me."

"If you think it's important. But what does it all mean? Where are you going with this, Justice?"

The phone rang; I picked it up. It was Maurice, calling from West Hollywood. I covered the mouthpiece with my hand.

"You've done great work, Richard. I can't believe how fast you came up with what I needed. I'm very impressed."

"But I don't have a clue about what's going on or where you're headed."

"All in good time." He closed his eyes and groaned. "Really, Richard, I've got to take this call." I glanced hard at the door. He sighed with exasperation and slunk reluctantly toward it. Just before he stepped out, he glanced back plaintively, hoping for a tidbit. "You've been a great help," I assured him. "We'll talk later."

Maurice was chattering like an excited squirrel and I tried to slow him down. "Take your time, Maurice, and tell me what you found out."

I heard him take a deep breath. "Are you ready, Benjamin?"

"Ready, Maurice."

"For the whiff of scandal?"

"Whatever you have, Maurice. I'm primed."

"Fred and I got the lowdown on Club Ebony from a dear friend, Alejandro, who works in the fashion industry. He has a gorgeous black lover named Lester who works in one of the top Hollywood talent agencies. Wonderful man, has a law degree but wants to be an agent. Knows the film business inside and out. Alejandro and Lester met at one of those socials arranged for African-American men and their admirers. They've only been together a year but they're already talking about adopting a child. I've suggested they wait a bit longer just to be sure that—"

"Maurice—please, what did you learn about Club Ebony?"

He became a bit snippy. "Of course, you want just the facts, don't you? You don't need to hear about anything extraneous and insignificant, such as my good friends Alejandro and Lester and the wonderful relationship they share."

"Maybe another time, Maurice, when I'm not so pressed. We have a situation up here."

He cleared his throat, became more businesslike. "About Club Ebony then."

"Please, if you would."

"As you know, it's a private club for discreet and discriminating gentlemen of color, a very special clientele."

"Yes, I gathered that from the club's voice-mail message when I called."

"More special than you might realize, Benjamin."

"I'm listening, Maurice."

"Does the term 'on the down low' mean anything to you?"

Of course, it did. The phrase had been coined by African-American men who considered themselves heterosexual, and might even be married, but who secretly slept with other men on the side. Even though they were clearly attracted to men and enjoyed man-on-man sex, men on the down low were adamant about declaring themselves straight, going so far as to denigrate openly gay men and the gay subculture in general. One of the great dangers in their subterfuge and self-delusion was that many of them put the women they were involved with at risk of infection from sexually transmitted diseases, HIV and Hepatitis included. Countless white men operated similarly, of course, and had down through the ages. But denial and ignorance about homosexuality and HIV had run especially deep in the black community, where AIDS was having a devastating impact, on women as well as men. The down low trend was so serious it had spawned books, widespread news coverage, even discussions in black churches and on special episodes of the *Oprah Winfrey Show*.

"Maurice, are you telling me that Club Ebony caters exclusively to black men on the down low?"

"Precisely, Benjamin."

"Details, please."

"Fred and I obtained an address from Alejandro. We drove

over last night. The club's in a corner location in a strip mall, not at all impressive from the outside. We sat in Fred's pickup truck from eleven P.M. to midnight and never saw a soul go in. Or a soul brother, for that matter." He giggled at his little joke.

I glanced at my watch. "Maurice, please."

"Fred suggested we check around back, so that's what we did. Wouldn't you know it? Men were being dropped off in taxis and limousines, very fine-looking black gentlemen dressed and groomed impeccably. They hurried inside past the doorman, ducking their heads, obviously not wanting to be seen. Fred recognized a couple of professional athletes who arrived separately. Basketball and boxing, which I know nothing about, except that they look awfully nice in those colorful shorts."

"Maurice, you've done a first-rate job of detection."

"Fred was highly instrumental, Benjamin. We mustn't forget Fred."

"When I get home, I'm taking you both to dinner. Anywhere you want to go, my treat."

"Just seeing you back safely will be reward enough for us, dear boy. When will that be, by the way? We don't like you being up there a minute longer than you have to."

"Unfortunately, a storm's washed out the bridge. Templeton and I will be here at least through tonight. A lot depends on the weather."

"I want you to promise me you won't take any reckless chances, as you're prone to do. We want you back breathing and in one piece, young man."

"I'll do my best, Maurice. Thanks again. I've got to go."

I hung up, ran over some facts in my head, and decided it was time to clear up a few points with Kevin Tiemeyer, whether he wanted to or not.

TWENTY-NINE

It was half past eleven when I left my room for a chat with Kevin Tiemeyer. As I took the main stairwell down, thunder rumbled distantly like an old smoker's cough and lightning flickered against the windows, briefly fracturing the gloom. The storm had found its momentum again; I could hear it screaming its fury and pounding its fists against the hotel, reminding us to be grateful for the shelter we had, even if it meant being cooped up together with a killer among us.

As I neared the lobby floor, I sensed activity in the club room to my left, but the lounge was nearly empty; Tiemeyer was the only one around. He was back at his Steinway, lost in yet another rendition of *Rhapsody in Blue* like a man muttering a confession over and over, hoping someone might listen. I was finally paying attention.

"It's a beautiful composition, isn't it?" I'd come up to stand behind him, off his left shoulder, as he continued to play. The yellow roses in the tall vase had begun to pale; a few petals had drifted down to the polished black surface. When he looked up, I said, "You obviously have a fascination with it."

"I wrote my senior thesis on *Rhapsody in Blue* at music school," he said, without pausing in his performance. "George

Gershwin introduced it in 1924 with the Paul Whiteman Orchestra, drawing heavily on his knowledge of symphonic music and his appreciation of jazz." He laughed lightly as the melodies filled the air. "Had my mother known that it had its roots in Negro blues and jazz, she would have slammed this keyboard down on my fingers."

I circled around to face him, leaning on the piano. "Too impolite for Enid? Or was it the racial element that bothered her?"

"It's certainly one of the most popular compositions in American music," Tiemeyer said, ignoring my question. "Although I'm not sure it's the groundbreaking work some have made it out to be. There'd been hybrids of symphony and swing in earlier compositions, even by Gershwin himself. And he had help with *Rhapsody,* you know—a number of musicians and composers made suggestions that he incorporated into the piece." He played on for half a minute, as if listening more keenly. "As important a work as it is, it's far from perfect. Gershwin was a masterful musician and composer, but not in the jazz idiom. From that standpoint, the piece is rather sprawling and structurally weak."

"You seem to enjoy playing it, though. It's about all I've heard the past two days."

Tiemeyer smiled mildly. "It's a showcase for a pianist, particularly this solo arrangement. The melodies are exquisite—unforgettable."

"Rebecca Fox apparently thought so." His smile faded and his eyes returned to the keyboard. I suspected he'd been waiting for this moment, perhaps even wanting it to arrive, even as he dreaded it. "Wasn't it her favorite piece, Kevin?"

His eyes got that lost look again, while his fingers continued to caress the keys. I thought I heard a subtle change in the music, a surge of feeling. "Yes," he said. "She was quite fond of it." He glanced at the fading flowers. "Yellow roses too. Her favorite."

I listened to him play for a minute, letting his memories swell and ripen, before I pushed on. "If I'm not mistaken, you were seventeen when Rebecca Fox returned here to film *The Ides of March.*"

"Yes. I was a few months shy of my eighteenth birthday."

"She was considered one of Hollywood's most beautiful leading ladies, right up there with Ava Gardner and Rita Hayworth. You must have fallen head over heels in love with her." He said nothing, just continued to play, so I kept talking. "Living in this small town, so far from everything, under the roof of a strict and puritanical mother, you must have been inexperienced in matters of love. But you were a good-looking kid, on the brink of manhood. More importantly, you bore a striking resemblance to Brent Fox, the young husband who'd died so heroically fighting in the Second World War. Were you aware of how much you looked like him, Kevin?"

"Rebecca remarked on it once or twice."

"When the two of you were making love?" His eyes flickered in my direction but drifted quickly back to the keys. "She was heartsick and lonely," I speculated, "deep into the shooting of a movie based on the true story of her one great love. It triggered even deeper despair in her. In her troubled state she took you into her bed, in Room 418." Tiemeyer stumbled briefly, a missed note that he quickly covered, while I continued. "In your excitement and inexperience, you spilled your semen, before you could consummate the act. It was you who left that stain on her panties, not Ed Jones. Rebecca Fox was your first lover, wasn't she, Kevin? And you were her last. She was dead before the night was out."

The music stopped; his fingers remained on the keys. I followed Tiemeyer's eyes across the lobby and through the entrance to the club room, and the photo of the woman he'd been obsessed with for fifty years. The laughter and clinking of glasses from the club room became a lonely sound out here, where Tiemeyer remained riveted by the picture behind the bar, or perhaps the memories it held for him.

"Rebecca was very patient with me." His voice was subdued, his speech languid. "She reassured me, helped me regain my confidence, then drew me back into her spell, but not so rapturously that I lost control again. I'll never forget her smell, her softness, how warm she was. The way she kissed me with a gentle hunger, and touched me in ways and places I'd never imagined one could with another person." His Adam's apple bobbed, his eyes grew moist. "When she sensed that I was ready, she guided me inside her, that incomparable moment when you cross into another world, another time." He laughed, slightly embarrassed. "I was barely more than a boy, not quite a man. Yet I'd never felt so strong, so powerful, so sure of who I was at that moment. At the same time, I felt like I was melting inside her, losing myself forever." He sighed deeply, shaking his head as if still amazed. "Afterward, she held me in her arms and wept. Nothing in my life has ever equaled the time I spent with Rebecca that night."

"It must have been horrible for you," I said, "when not long after she ended her life."

He raised his eyes to stare unwaveringly at me, letting the seconds pass. From the club room, the raucous laughter of Scotty Campbell split the air. Then, trying hard to sound convincing, Tiemeyer said, "Rebecca Fox was murdered. Everyone knows that."

"Not quite everyone. You know better, don't you, Kevin?"

He looked away, resumed playing the *Rhapsody*.

"Why she committed suicide is anyone's guess," I said. "I don't imagine even you know, do you? Maybe she'd planned it all along, after a final fling with a boy who reminded her so much of her late husband. Maybe out of heightened misery, when she realized he was truly gone, and no one would ever take his place. Maybe out of guilt for having seduced a virginal boy in an attempt to assuage her pain and loneliness. Whatever the reason, she cut her throat with a knife she'd brought with her from Hollywood. Not long after, ten-year-old Martha Frech discovered the body. She saw that knife in Rebecca's hand, covered with her blood. Martha probably went straight to her mother, who informed yours—Enid, the dominant force in Eternal Springs.

"At first, Enid was aghast that such a famous actress had taken her life in the hotel. She was concerned what the scandal might do to business. But when she notified the producers that the star of their film was dead, she learned they weren't indemnified for suicide, possibly because the insurers were concerned about the emotional state of the leading lady. Together they conspired to make Rebecca's suicide look like a murder, so they could recoup the nearly three million dollars they'd spent on a production that would never be completed. They cut your parents in on the deal, at a time when they desperately needed cash to keep the hotel going. That's how they were able to remodel and refurbish this hotel the next year. In turn, your parents needed the cooperation of the housekeeper, Martha's unmarried and impoverished mother. Enid cut her in, which enabled Miss Frech to later build that house south of town. But it didn't stop there, did it, Kevin?"

Tiemeyer smiled bleakly, looking resigned to the truth. "No, Mr. Justice, there was a good deal more to it than that. As you've apparently surmised."

"To turn a suicide into murder, the film's producers and your parents needed a suspect. Ed Jones was ideal—a black man, a loner and a drifter, with a criminal record. They removed the knife from Rebecca's hand and disposed of it. Someone apparently discovered the semen on her undergarments and considered it providence."

"My mother never suspected I'd been in Rebecca's bed," Tiemeyer said. "She assumed it was someone from the cast or crew."

"So they had a crime scene and a murder suspect, even a motive, but they still needed something more. Witnesses—a person or persons compliant enough to provide just enough false testimony to implicate Ed Jones. And who is more compliant than a child who's utterly dependent on a domineering parent?"

Tiemeyer placed his elbows on the shelf above the keyboard, dropped his eyes, held his head in his hands.

When he didn't say anything, I picked up my story. "You and Martha Frech served nicely. Martha was to say that there'd been no knife in the room when she'd discovered the body. And you were to report that you saw Ed Jones coming out of Room 418 not long before that. Which you dutifully did."

He raised his head, looking stricken. "I didn't know they'd hang him. I swear, I had no foreknowledge of that."

"Would it have made a difference if you had?"

His voice was shaky, barely audible. "I'd like to think so."

"Go on, Kevin. I'd rather hear it from you."

He took a deep breath, staring at the portrait of Enid Tiemeyer above the mantelpiece. "My mother told me that it was our only chance to save the hotel, that we'd be out of our home and penniless if we didn't get the money the producers had promised us. I knew the hotel was struggling, and that my father's newspaper wasn't bringing in much money. My mother reminded me that God considers suicide a sin. She convinced me we'd be doing Rebecca a favor by removing the stigma of suicide from her legacy. Looking back, it's possible my mother suspected how I felt toward Rebecca, that I had a terrible crush on her. Enid was adept at spotting people's weaknesses and turning them to her advantage."

"And you went along with it."

He nodded miserably. "I was in shock from Rebecca's death. Emotionally, I was in bad shape. My mother—yes, I went along with it."

"And Martha Frech?"

"She resisted. She was a strong-willed child, much more than me. She didn't want to lie about the knife. My mother became angry with her. Martha got scared and ran down the stairs to get away. She fell as she neared the lobby and struck her head. After that, she was useless as a witness. My mother reported her own version of the conversation she'd had with Martha, tailored to her own needs."

"Are you sure Martha fell, Kevin?"

"What are you suggesting?"

"Are you sure your mother didn't push her?"

His eyes were swimming, back and forth. "Why would she do that?"

"Because Martha could tell the truth and ruin everything."

"My mother could be ruthless. I'm not naive about that. But she wasn't capable of killing a child."

"Only an innocent black man?"

"You don't know that."

"I know there's a white robe and hood in the attic upstairs, which Audrey Williams discovered buried among your mother's clothes. I know that only one person was photographed next to Ed Jones's body. If you look closely, you can see what appears to be the hem of a dark dress at the bottom of that white robe."

"That's all speculation, Mr. Justice." His chin trembled. "Nothing but conjecture."

I leaned forward, burned him with my eyes. "You didn't see a mob come up here and drag your father from the house that night, Kevin. Your mother coerced your father into going down to that jail with his camera, where she and her brother, Sheriff Jack Hightower, dragged Ed Jones from his cell and strung him up so there would never be an investigation or a trial. You may not have seen your mother murder Ed Jones. But you know in your heart that she did."

Seconds of silence passed before he spoke again. "I was seventeen, Mr. Justice. It was a different time. Children were more sheltered, less worldly. You have to understand, I'd never known anything but my mother's iron rule." He shuddered audibly. "She was a very formidable woman."

"But you weren't seventeen in 1981, were you, Kevin, when Brandy Fox was found dead in the same room as her mother?"

For a moment, it felt like the oxygen had been sucked out of the space between us, as if there was no room for anything but the truth that was about to be told. Kevin Tiemeyer sat perfectly still, bracing himself as he waited for my next words to fall on him like a sledgehammer. I decided to hold back, to let him come to me.

Finally, as the silence stretched out unbearably, he said, "No, by then I was no longer a boy, with a boy's excuses."

"You came back to this hotel after music school," I said, "settling into a routine here, playing your piano, living inside your head, with your memories of Rebecca Fox. From time to time, for company, you'd bed one of the female guests, almost reflexively, the way you did Nan Williams the other night. Is that what you did with Brandy Fox, Kevin, when she came here twenty-five years ago and checked into Room 418? Hopped in the sack with her for a quickie?"

"Brandy came here to commemorate her mother's death. She'd arranged it with us ahead of time. She had some reporters and photographers up. The idea was to generate some publicity that might be beneficial to her as an actress and help the hotel at the same time. We'd fallen on hard times again. My mother was quite concerned."

"You slept with Brandy?"

"I tried. I'm afraid I suffered a rare bout of impotence. I believe it had something to do with who Brandy was—Rebecca's daughter. Simply put, I couldn't perform. I apologized, dressed, and left her. A few hours later, her publicist found her dead. She'd cut her throat. Brandy was very dramatic. I think she saw suicide as a way to go out with some of the attention her mother had gotten, guaranteeing that her name would always be a part of Hollywood legend and lore. Needless to say, I felt horrible about what happened. I'd known she was emotionally fragile. I felt partly responsible, that perhaps by seducing her I'd triggered something in her that led her to take her own life."

"But she didn't end her own life, Kevin. Someone did that for her."

He looked genuinely stunned. "What are you saying?"

"She was murdered. Someone planted that knife in her hand. Only they placed it in the wrong hand, which caused problems."

I explained to him that Brandy Fox was left-handed. A photograph on display in the Haunted Springs Museum and Souvenir Shop, taken at an autograph session, confirmed that. Another museum photograph, cropped and blown up from a larger crime scene photo, shows the bloody knife clutched in her left hand.

"All of which makes sense," I said, "if she killed herself."

Tiemeyer studied me curiously. "Then what's the problem?"

"In the larger crime scene photograph published in *A Murder in Eternal Springs*, Brandy is clutching the knife in her *right* hand. The edge of the blade is turned outward, an extremely awkward way to cut one's throat on the left side, especially to make the kind of clean, deep slice that killed Brandy. Someone placed that knife in her right hand soon after she was murdered. Crime scene photos were taken. Too late, someone realized that Brandy was left-handed—that they'd placed the knife in the wrong hand, and the photos might give them away."

"But you said that in the museum, there's a photograph of the knife in her *left* hand."

"Where did you get that photo, Kevin?"

He hesitated. "From the files of my father's newspaper, after it folded and he died."

"To get that image, someone flipped the negative when they had the photo printed. By cropping out the rest of the body and isolating only the hand and forearm, it appears to be her left hand. Flipping the negative to reverse the direction of the subject is an old newspaper trick. It's often done with a head shot in profile, when the editor wants the subject looking into the page to draw the reader's eye to the text, instead of looking out toward the margin. It's something all of us learned studying layout in Journalism 101. I'm sure your father did it many times when he was publishing the *Hungry Valley Weekly*."

Tiemeyer was as pale as the withering roses on his piano. "But how do you know this?"

"The original negative was buried away, deep in the sheriff's evidence warehouse, where Jack Hightower Jr., the investigating officer, figured it would never be found. Or maybe he meant to destroy it, but forgot."

"If that's true, then—"

"Rebecca Fox committed suicide, and her daughter, Brandy, was murdered. Not the other way around."

"But why—?"

"Why don't you tell me, Kevin? Why would your mother go to so much trouble to make a suicide look like murder and a murder look like suicide?" He shook his head like a man trying to convince himself none of it was true, when he knew better. "It started with Rebecca," I said, "a chance for your mother to cut herself in on the insurance money and save her hotel and her social standing in a community that she ruled like a despot. Twenty-five years later, who knows? Maybe Brandy had caught on to the original scam, and had blackmail in mind. Maybe Enid resented your romantic interest in her. Maybe it was just for another shot of sensational publicity, at a time when the hotel was on the rocks again. Enid couldn't bear to lose this place, could she, Kevin? She couldn't stand to fail. She was an old woman by then, but she wasn't frail. She was still strong, especially when greed and fury were driving her."

His voice was small, pathetic. "I doubt that you can prove any of this."

"Someone can prove that you were in that bed with Rebecca Fox that night, once they get a sample of your DNA and match it to the semen on her panties. When they do, I imagine you'll become the prime suspect in her murder, since that's how her death is classified at this point."

"I loved that woman. I would never have hurt her."

"Then there's the matter of Brandy's death. The conflicting photographs suggest that someone placed a knife in the wrong hand. You've admitted you were in her bed that night. Perhaps you killed her in a rage, humiliated by your inability to get it up."

"Stop talking like that!" Tears glistened in his eyes. "I didn't hurt either of them. I'm not like that."

"You've lied before, Kevin. Your lie cost Ed Jones his life. It won't look good for you, will it? At the very least, they'll have you on accessory and obstruction charges."

He buried his face in his hands again. "Oh, God."

"Maybe it's not too late to turn all this around."

He looked up, wiping his eyes, trying to pull himself together. "What are you suggesting?"

"Atonement. You could clear Ed Jones's name once and for all, set the record straight on Brandy Fox. If you came forward on your own, I doubt that you'd see any jail time after all these years. I could speak to Valenzuela, set up a meeting for you. While you're at it, I'd also like you to have a chat with Alexandra Templeton."

"Air my family's dirty laundry in a major newspaper?"

"It might feel good, Kevin, confessing your sins publicly. I've found it quite therapeutic myself. The hardest part is accepting the fact that you're a vile creature, capable of all kinds of awful stuff. Once you do that, it's a breeze."

He shook his head mournfully. "I don't know—"

"It's all going to come out, anyway. Handle it right and you might actually come off looking like the good guy in all this."

"Therapeutic, you say?" I nodded. He smiled grimly. "After fifty years, I could use a decent night's sleep."

"Still, you've got a lot of blood on your hands, don't you?"

He raised them to study his long, nimble fingers, before resting them on the keyboard again. "I've got a lot of blood on my *mind,* Mr. Justice." Our eyes met and held, before his drifted again to the portrait of his mother. When he spoke, his voice was heavy with what sounded like shame. "Memory is like a wild beast. To live with it, you have to tame it, cage it, make it behave the way you want it to. Otherwise, it destroys you, eats you alive."

"But it's always there, Kevin, rattling the cage. Maybe it's time to let the beast out. Maybe it's time to let the beast run free."

His eyes stayed on the image of his mother awhile. Then he said, "I'll talk with Sergeant Valenzuela. And with your friend Miss Templeton. I'll tell them everything."

He faced his piano again and picked up *Rhapsody in Blue* where he'd left off. I went in search of Tony Valenzuela, wondering if this time he'd be honest with me.

THIRTY

The hour was edging toward midnight when I found Valenzuela in the club room, grilling Scotty Campbell in a corner booth, out of earshot of the other drinkers scattered around in nervous little clumps.

I stood at a respectful distance until he noticed me. He finished his business with Campbell, picked up his crutches, and hoisted himself in my direction.

I told him we needed to talk. He suggested the veranda, where he could grab a smoke. "I'm down to three a day," he said. "It's still a nasty habit."

We crossed the lobby to the interminable tinkling of *Rhapsody in Blue* but also a strange quietude beyond the sound of the piano that I couldn't quite figure out. Moments later, as we stepped outside, the reason for the background hush became clear. A number of crew members were standing out on the front walk, chatting excitedly and staring up as clouds parted to reveal patches of starry sky. The storm was over.

Valenzuela and I walked around to the east side of the hotel, for privacy and a view of Lake Enid, where a sliver of moon was reflected as the weather continued to break up. Tiemeyer had stacked and covered all the wicker furniture with plastic against the rain, so Valenzuela and I stayed on our feet.

"Nice to see the stars again," I said.

"For you maybe. Not for me." The detective took out a cigarette and held it without lighting it. "Come daybreak, I imagine we'll see a private chopper or two up here, whisking away certain people anxious to put Haunted Springs behind them."

"I hadn't thought of that."

"So what did you want to see me about, Justice? It wouldn't be about the crime scene photo of Brandy Fox, would it? The one in Richard Pearlman's book."

"Pearlman talked to you?"

"Called me after he met with you, said you knew where he got the photo."

"The original negative, you mean. With your help."

"Right, the negative."

"Want to tell me about that?"

His eyes slid away for a moment; he lit his cigarette and took a long drag before looking at me again, as if he was deciding how much to tell me, or how soon. Then he said, "I thought it might be useful, getting the real photo into a book, instead of the fake that's been in circulation the last twenty-five years."

"You've been interested in the deaths of Rebecca Fox and her daughter all along, haven't you, Sergeant? That's why you were so eager to gain my confidence when you first got here."

"There's some truth to that."

"You figured you could use me the way you used Pearlman, as another wedge to crack open a couple of old cases that involved Jack Hightower and his son."

"I was a twenty-six-year-old rookie in 1981 when the Brandy Fox thing went down. It never smelled right the way it was handled, not from the start. Jack Junior bidding for the case, his old man making sure he got it, just like he'd handled the Rebecca Fox investigation twenty-five years earlier. I asked some questions—I was a young hotshot back then—but I was warned to pull back, let it go."

"The Hightowers got away with it that easily?"

"Along with Tiemeyer, Hightower was about the biggest name in the Valley. The old man had risen to the top of the department as county sheriff. People figured Jack Junior had grabbed the Brandy Fox case for the publicity, since he had ambitions of his own."

"You suspect there was more to it than that. And you saw me as a way to get it all out in the open, after you gave Pearlman the chance but he dropped the ball."

"He's a nice man and I imagine he knows a lot about movies, but he doesn't have an eye for evidence or a feel for crime. He put the damn photo in his book and never saw what it meant, never followed up. It was right there in black and white. He missed it."

"You assumed I'd see it?"

"Before I got up here, over the phone, I grilled Tiemeyer for names of the most prominent guests. He included you, because you came with your friend Alexandra and because you come with a past. I didn't recognize your name at first, so I ran a background on you while I was driving up. The computer in the car spit out some of your history. I wanted you working with me, not against me."

"You played me like a Stradivarius, Sergeant."

"You don't take on someone like Jack Hightower Jr. by blundering straight ahead, out in the open. You sneak up on him sideways, working all your angles, getting your ducks lined up before you take a pop." He drew in more smoke, looking me in the eye. "You pissed because I played you?"

I shrugged. "We got to where we both wanted to go." I turned up my collar against the cold, shoved my hands deep in my pockets. "So where do we go from here?"

Valenzuela grinned. "I'll show you mine, if you'll show me yours."

"No more tricks?"

"No more time for that." He glanced up at the sky, where more stars could be seen, and fewer clouds. "Like I said before, choppers can come in safely now for the folks who can afford one. For the others, the Army Corps of Engineers will have a temporary bridge in place by tomorrow sundown. A lot of people in this hotel are going to skedaddle, which will only make my work more difficult."

"I take it no one came forward to cough up the information you've been after."

He shook his head, took a final drag on his cigarette, and dropped the butt into the water that filled an ashtray on the railing. "It looks like it's down to you and me, Justice. Why don't you go first?"

I started with things I'd seen in the hotel attic and the museum displays, moved on to the conversations I'd had with Richard Pearlman and Kevin Tiemeyer, sprinkled in a few other details I'd gleaned here and there and got the issues involving Rebecca Fox and Brandy Fox out of the way. Valenzuela was impressed with my powers of observation and said so; I didn't respond to that, because praise didn't interest me just then.

The death of Toni Pebbles did, so I went there next. I explained my strongest suspicions and related a few details that Templeton and I had come across that I thought cemented things together pretty nicely. I also mentioned the Club Ebony matchbook and the phone number I'd copied down in Room 418 the night Pebbles became a homicide, and what I'd learned about the club from Maurice. After that, Valenzuela filled me in on what he'd come up with, which duplicated a lot of mine. It turned out we'd been headed in the same direction and come to the same conclusions, which is encouraging when you're dealing with cold-blooded murder and running out of time.

Valenzuela glanced at his watch. "Zeke Zeidler's called a meeting of the cast and crew at midnight," he said. "Wants to go over his plans to get the movie back on track, so he can start making the necessary arrangements ASAP. Maybe you and I should be there."

"You plan to confront them as a group?"

He nodded. "Ideally, I'd like to have a confession, and I'd like to wrap it up tonight."

"The pressur-cooker approach."

"I haven't gotten what I wanted from them individually.

Maybe I can get it collectively." He winked. "You want to help turn up the heat?"

"If I won't be in the way."

He adjusted his crutches under his arms. "You haven't been so far."

THIRTY-ONE

As we stepped into the hotel, I saw Templeton off to my right at the far end of the front desk. Kevin Tiemeyer stood across the counter from her, on the business side. She had her tape recorder and notebook out and was scribbling furiously while they talked, so I figured he was unburdening himself the way he'd promised he would.

The meeting called by Zeke Zeidler was already under way in the lounge. Sergeant Valenzuela swung his stout body on his crutches to the carpet's edge, between the lounge and the piano, and stood listening, while I stood at his left shoulder.

Zeidler was on his feet, leaning on his cane, as he laid out what he hoped would be a new and acceptable shooting schedule, if he could get all the principals in the cast and crew on board. He seemed to have found a new sense of urgency and energy, as if this might be his last shot at salvaging a production that was close to falling apart and costing him a personal fortune. Most of the others were seated, including Richard Pearlman and Lois Aswell on a couch, with Karen Hori between them. Deep Freeze and Sweet Doctor Silk sat at a window table, slightly away from everyone else. Heather Sparks and Christopher Oakley stood together near the cold fireplace, although I noticed his arm was no longer around her and that her demeanor was on the frosty side. Scotty

Campbell was presumably still in the club room, banished from the proceedings, while a grieving Nan Williams was understandably absent.

As Valenzuela and I took our places on the fringe, Zeidler glanced over but otherwise didn't acknowledge us.

Oakley did. "This is a production meeting." His voice was sharp, no-nonsense. "No offense, gentlemen, but it only concerns those of us involved with the movie."

"I have a few things I wanted to go over," Valenzuela said, "now that you're all together for what may be the last time."

"I'm trying to avoid that outcome," Zeidler said. "Can't your questions wait?"

"Like you, Mr. Zeidler, I'm under serious time constraints." The detective smiled benignly. "I'm sure you're as anxious for me to wind up my work here as I am. A few questions, a few answers, and I won't bother you again."

"Make it quick," Aswell said tersely.

Zeidler frowned, then eased himself into an overstuffed chair, laying his cane across his legs. "You have the floor, Sergeant."

Valenzuela turned on his crutches, facing the group. "From everything I've heard, Toni Pebbles came here with the intention of 'outing' someone—exposing someone's shameful secret and potentially hurting their image and reputation."

"Oh, Christ, not this again," Oakley muttered.

Valenzuela ignored him. "I believe that's the reason someone put a knife through her heart before Audrey Williams mutilated the body in the manner that she did."

Lois Aswell sat forward on the couch. "You're certain that's what happened?"

"I am." Aswell sat back, looking grim. "One of you was concerned enough about being exposed," Valenzuela went on, "that you were willing to commit murder to prevent it."

Oakley cast his troubled eyes toward Hori and Aswell, who looked equally uneasy. Zeidler also frowned, his forehead furrowing below his bald pate. I realized that if a prominent cast member had committed murder, and was convicted of it, it would surely fall under the category of moral turpitude; the resulting shutdown in production might not be covered by the film's indemnity policy.

"My problem," Valenzuela said, "is that when I gave all of you the opportunity to be forthcoming, you withheld certain information that might have been helpful. If we'd gotten to the bottom of this sooner, it's possible that Audrey Williams might still be alive. Troubled, certainly, and facing some legal issues because of what she did to a corpse, but alive and breathing nonetheless."

There was a moment of guilty fidgeting, before Karen Hori, ever the loyal publicist, spoke up. "A number of people here are quite prominent, Sergeant. They're vulnerable to slurs and slanders, to the judgments of the public. They have a right to their privacy. I think all of us respect that. That may be why we haven't been as talkative as you'd like."

"Fine and dandy, Miss Hori—in most circumstances. But not when a murder investigation is under way. That's why I wanted to speak to you while you're all gathered in one place. Before this meeting breaks up, I'd like someone to step forward and tell me what they know."

Heather Sparks suddenly cried out, stepping away from Christopher Oakley. "I can't take this anymore!"

"Heather!" He reached for her but she pushed him off.

"I can't!" Her frantic eyes moved from Aswell to Hori to Zeidler, spilling tears. "I told you this wouldn't work. I warned you it would only complicate matters."

Oakley stood alone, arms outstretched, pleading. "Heather, please. Pull yourself together. You're worn out, that's all. This isn't the time to—"

She turned on him with a fury. "Don't you understand? I can't keep playing this game. It's over. I should have put a stop to it a long time ago." She ran her fingers through her long hair, which fell free, without the ponytail. "Christ, it never should have gotten started. Why did I let all of you talk me into it?"

"Don't say something you'll regret later," Oakley said.

Sparks shrieked at him. "I want it all to stop! All the lies, all the pretending." She wiped at her nose with the back of her hand,

and drew back her shoulders for some dignity. Her voice was calmer now. "We have to tell them, Christopher—the truth. I can't do this anymore." She tried to smile. "I'm sorry. It's over."

It sounded final and I could see all the hope go out of him. The looks on the others varied: Aswell, worried but sympathetic; Zeidler, stricken; Hori, badly on edge; Deep Freeze, enjoying himself; Sweet Doctor Silk, uncomprehending; Pearlman, confused. None of them said a word. Templeton and Tiemeyer had wandered over to stand on the other side of the piano, transfixed by the drama.

Heather Sparks faced Valenzuela squarely.

"I'm gay," she said. "I'm a lesbian. Okay? I'm the one with the terrible secret. But I swear to you, I didn't kill that woman. I had nothing to do with her death."

THIRTY-TWO

The silence that followed Heather Sparks's confession was whole, perfect; not even rainfall or the tinkling of a piano to disturb it.

The group in the lounge remained silent until Deep Freeze could no longer contain himself. "No shit," he said, looking Heather Sparks up and down. His laugh was close to a cackle. "A muff diver. What a damn waste."

"Shut your mouth," Oakley said.

"I always knew there was a reason the bitch didn't dig me."

Oakley took a step toward him, clenching a fist. "I'm warning you." Sweet Doctor Silk rose to meet him, putting his muscular bulk in the way, while Deep Freeze continued to sit and grin. Oakley glared in return, but wisely backed off. Sweet Doctor Silk sat down but kept an eye on him, like a well-trained watchdog.

Sparks stood in the center of the group. With a sweeping glance she took in the members of the production team who hadn't been in on the ruse, mostly crafts- and tradespeople who may have heard some scuttlebutt but had never really been in the loop.

"Please don't blame Christopher," Sparks said. "He was talked into it. He did it for me." She returned her attention to Valenzuela. "We'd gotten word that Toni Pebbles was coming here to expose someone, that she was planning to use whatever means necessary to get a confession. She has a reputation for being ruthless. My career's been going so well. I've worked hard to get where I am. I was afraid I'd lose it all if the truth came out. I want to be known as an actress, not 'that gay actress.' That's all I wanted. Just to have the same chance as anyone else, without the label."

"You could have come out on your own," I said. "Taken the wind out of Toni Pebbles's sails, maybe even turned it to your advantage. You had that choice."

When Sparks looked at me, her pain was palpable. "When you've lived a lie as long as I have, and built up so many lies to keep the big one propped up, the thought of finally being honest, admitting what a fraud you are, is terrifying. The longer you stay in the closet, the harder it is to come out."

"Men and women come out every day," I said, "without the financial resources and other means of support that you enjoy. And without using the media to perpetrate their fraud until they're ready to be honest."

"I know that, Mr. Justice." She spoke clear-eyed and without self-pity. "I'm not proud of how I've handled this."

"The engagement wasn't Heather's idea," Hori said. "Lois and I came up with it. We thought it might take some of the pressure off, that if Heather and Christopher were engaged, the editors would back off, despite what information Toni Pebbles might present them." Hori smiled ruefully. "It's worked for other stars, CEOs, politicians. We thought it might protect Heather. And protect our film at the same time."

"Heather was reluctant from the start," Aswell said. "But the prospect of an exposé by someone like Toni Pebbles seemed worse. I didn't want something like that to disrupt my movie, especially with its romantic scenes involving Christopher and Heather. I knew that if Heather was outed for being gay, that's all people would be talking about when my movie came out. Not the content, or the performances, or the entertainment value. Just a lot of idiotic gossip about whether Heather is attracted to women or men." Aswell shook her head in disgust. "In this country, we think we're so sophisticated, so advanced. Sometimes we seem like nothing more than a bunch of immature and spiteful children, sniggering about sex and body parts."

"I urged Heather to go along with it," Zeidler admitted. "I also pressured Christopher, who was kind enough to play along."

"Not exactly a bad move for his career," Deep Freeze said, sounding more playful than mean. "He got some nice publicity out of it. Millions of people know who he is today that never heard of him a few days ago."

"Not the kind of publicity I'd choose," Oakley said tersely.

"You never see a black couple in Hollywood get that kind of press," Deep Freeze went on. "I defy anyone in this room to tell me the name of Denzel's wife, or if Ice Cube's even married." He looked around, but no one spoke. "I didn't think so. Me and my wife been hitched twelve years, got four kids, no media big shot ever wanted to know about us."

He stood, buttoning his jacket; Sweet Doctor Silk rose a moment later, doing the same, almost like a mimic.

Deep Freeze said to Valenzuela, "You got what you were after. You found out who it was had something to hide. So if you'll excuse us, Silk and me is going to motor upstairs and pack our bags. We're going to be out of this place first thing tomorrow."

Templeton finally made her voice heard. "Back to the 'hood, Mr. Childs, to hang with your homeboys?" Her words stopped Deep Freeze in his tracks. "Or should I call you Percy?"

He tried for bravado, but it looked fake. "You got no reason to call me that, Miss Reporter Lady."

"Sure I do," Templeton said. "Percy Childs is the name your parents gave you, when you were born on an army base in Europe nearly forty years ago. The name you used when you enrolled at art school in Paris, before you decided to become Deep Freeze and cash in on the hip-hop craze."

He showed her a smile that was part snarl. "You got your facts wrong, lady."

"Toni Pebbles had a file in her room with your name on it," I said. "I saw it when I first went in, and now it's in Sergeant Valenzuela's possession, as evidence."

His eyes darted from Templeton to me. "That don't mean nothing, she got a file." He started nervously rubbing his fingers the way I'd seen him do when he'd first arrived, trying to work the pain and stiffness out of them.

Lois Aswell sat forward on the sofa. "What's all this about?"

"Before he was Deep Freeze," Templeton said, "masquerading as a street gangsta, he was Percy Childs, the well-bred, well-educated son of a career army officer and a successful businesswoman." Templeton paused before she dropped her bombshell. "Also the grandson of Ed Jones, the character he's playing in your film."

"What?"

Templeton turned on Deep Freeze again. "Right, Mr. Childs?"

"Stop calling me that, bitch."

"It's not something you want people to know about, is it?" Valenzuela asked. "That this tough homeboy image you have is just an act. That you've got about as much 'street cred' as Mickey Mouse."

"You all crazy," Deep Freeze said. "I don't have to listen to this shit."

He stepped from the lounge in the direction of the main stairwell, but Valenzuela moved in front of him, raising a crutch to block his path. From their various positions, the armed security guards descended or closed in, blocking all the exits on that side of the hotel.

Sweet Doctor Silk was staring at Deep Freeze like he was a Martian. "What they be sayin', Freeze? What they be talkin' about?"

Deep Freeze ignored him, addressing the group. "Maybe I did make up a few things about where I come from." He tried to wipe it away with a laugh that was high-pitched and nervous. "Maybe I did get me a persona, like a lot of entertainment people do. That's just show business, you fools. But I wouldn't kill nobody just to keep it quiet, especially a white bitch like this Pebbles chick that's in the public eye. You think I'm crazy, man? I don't need that kind of trouble. Yeah, my name's Percy Childs. So I got raised up in a decent family. So what? It don't bother me that people might find that out. I planned to make it public all along, when the time seemed right. You can't pin the bitch's murder on me on account of I changed my name and cut some rap music."

"Probably not," Valenzuela conceded.

"I'm glad we got that settled." Deep Freeze seemed to relax, as if he'd just skated free. "Now get out of my way, because you got no reason to keep me here."

I said to Valenzuela, "Maybe it's Sweet Doctor Silk you should be talking to, Sergeant. Maybe he's the one who's hiding a big secret."

Silk took a few steps in my direction, coiling with anger. "Say what?"

Valenzuela reached into a coat pocket, held up the evidence bag with the Club Ebony matchbook. "Remember this, Mr. Silk? The matchbook you gave Mr. Justice during the blackout?"

Silk patted his pants pockets reflexively. "So I gave him a matchbook. So what? The lights was out."

"It's a matchbook from Club Ebony," I said. "An exclusive club down in L.A., that caters to African-American men with certain tastes."

"What kind of 'tastes'?" Silk asked, pronouncing it like it was a sissy word.

"You should know," Valenzuela said. "You must have been there. Or you wouldn't have had this matchbook in your pocket, would you?"

Silk froze, except for his eyes, which slid toward Deep Freeze. Neither man said a word, though their eyes seemed to be speaking volumes to each other.

"It's a club for men on the down low," I said.

Silk's eyes came around to me, fast. "On the down low?" I nodded. "I ain't one of them," he said. "I ain't no faggot!"

"You had the matchbook, Mr. Silk," Valenzuela said. Silk went rigid again, except for those questioning eyes that landed back on Deep Freeze. "What other explanation could there be—except that you secretly sleep with men you meet at Club Ebony, while convincing yourself and the world that you're really straight."

"I told you, I ain't no faggot." Silk's furious eyes swept across us all; his big fists were balled up into clubs. "I know about brothers on the down low. I ain't like that."

"Then where did you get the matchbook?" Valenzuela asked.

"Keep your mouth shut," Deep Freeze said.

A mix of feelings played across the dark face of Sweet Doctor Silk, confusion among them. I also figured there was a good dose of fear in there, as the possibility of another long prison stretch wreaked havoc with his emotions.

Finally, without looking at Deep Freeze, he said, "I got it when I was cleaning out his pockets, like he has me to do before I hang up his clothes. He don't likes to put on clothes that's got stuff in the pockets. He's very particular about that."

"Don't talk to them," Deep Freeze said. "Don't play the fool."

"You the one played me for the fool, Freeze." Silk sounded both hurt and angry, a combination that can make a man want to tell the truth, no matter what the consequences. He turned back to Valenzuela. "I kept the matches because my lighter done gone dead. Freeze don't like to light his own cigars, not if I'm around. So I kept the motherfuckin' matches I got from his pocket. But I ain't on the down low."

"No," Valenzuela said. "I don't imagine you are."

"And I didn't kill that lady, neither!"

"Probably not," the detective conceded.

"One little matchbook don't mean crap," Deep Freeze said.

Valenzuela looked him in the eye. "Toni Pebbles had her tape recorder charged and set up with a fresh tape when she was murdered. Which means she was probably getting ready to do an interview. Did you call her and tell her you were ready to talk, Mr. Childs? Is that why she welcomed you into her room? Or did she call you?"

"I was never in that bitch's room. Not one time."

"It doesn't really matter," Valenzuela went on. "The point is, she was expecting you, and let you in. You stabbed her straight in the heart, made sure she was dead, and sneaked out the way you'd come in. Soon after, a troubled little girl climbed through the open window to cut a dead woman's throat, just to see what it was like. But you were the one who did the killing."

"But he has an alibi," Richard Pearlman said. "Everyone knows where he was when the murder took place."

"That's right," Hori agreed. "He could see Zeke and me from the piano, while we were talking in the dining room. He said so."

"By confirming your alibi," Valenzuela said, "he conveniently created one of his own."

"Everyone knows that a black man was playing the piano," I said. "A black man who generally resembles Deep Freeze and was dressed in his favorite getup, who passed for his boss with the lights dimmed, the way Mr. Tiemeyer keeps them in the evening."

"No one ever actually said they saw Deep Freeze at that piano," Valenzuela said, "clearly enough to be sure it was him. When he spoke up, confirming that Mr. Zeidler and Miss Hori were in the dining room, no one thought to question that he might have been somewhere else."

On the couch, Pearlman slapped his head for never seeing it, after I'd tried so hard to point him to it, hoping he'd figure it out on his own.

"Mr. Childs suffers from arthritis in his hands," Templeton put in, "severe enough that he had to give up a promising sculpting career as a young man. I doubt he plays the piano very well. Sweet Doctor Silk, on the other hand, is fluent with the blues, which was being played that night as Toni Pebbles was being murdered."

"Freeze put me up to it," Silk said, sounding desperate. "I didn't know he was going to stick that lady like he did. I just did what he told me, on account of he's the man that pays me and I gotta do what he says."

"Shut your fool mouth," Freeze said. "You think they won't put charges on you, you dumb nigger?"

"Tell us more," Valenzuela said to Silk, "and you might end up as a prosecution witness instead of a defendant. I imagine you could cut a decent deal for yourself."

"Freeze had me put on his clothes and play the piano. Told me to stay hunched over like, and keep my head low. When everybody run up to the woman's room, all screaming and shit, I slipped out and met Freeze in the parking lot, out behind that big rock, where it's dark. I give him his clothes, and he give me some kind of package."

"The knife," Valenzuela said.

"I didn't know what it was. It was addressed to hisself. He told me drop it in a mailbox when I get down at the casino. Told me if I did everything right and keep my mouth shut, he'll get me a recording contract on his label, so I can do my rap, tell my story and my messages just like him." Sweet Doctor Silk glanced around, his eyes softer, more imploring. "I been wanting that for a long time. To tell other folks what I feel like inside, and the trouble I seen, and how hard life can be for a black man in ways they don't even know about, that they can't understand. I want somebody to listen to me, that's all, the way they listen to Freeze. Freeze, he knowed that, and he promised me he'd get that for me, if I did what he ask."

"His word don't mean shit," Deep Freeze said. "He's done time. He killed a man. He's just a dumb nigger who's trying to cover his own ass."

"His story might make more sense when the DNA tests come back," Valenzuela said. "The forensics team combed every inch of that room, and every inch of the victim's clothes and body. There was quite a commotion up there when Toni Pebbles was fighting for her life. When we get a sample from you I suspect we'll find a match. All it takes is a hair, Mr. Childs."

"That don't mean nothing. Lots of people been in and out of that room, shooting scenes and shit."

"But not you, Mr. Childs. You arrived two days late, too late to shoot your scenes that were scheduled for Room 418. You shot those scenes in Room 318, Mr. Justice's room. You told us a moment ago that you'd never been in the Rebecca Fox Room."

Deep Freeze swallowed hard, his eyes all over the place. Suddenly, he turned and made for the big double doors. Scotty Campbell was there, flattened against them. He looked small and tough, the way bull terriers look small and tough against much bigger dogs, and sometimes tear them to shreds.

Freeze pulled up. When he turned back, Valenzuela was standing a few feet in front of him. The detective held a set of handcuffs in one hand and his gun in the other, as the security guards came up behind him. At that moment, I could see all the fight go out of Percy Childs. All the tough talk, the phony swagger, the exaggerated male posturing that had taken him to fame and fortune but had been his ruin in the end.

"The bitch was going to write that I'm a faggot." He glanced at us with eyes that were surprisingly plaintive, like his voice. "Okay, I'm on the down low. I get into it now and then with one of the brothers, maybe even a white dude if I get the itch. So what? That don't mean I'm gay." He laughed but it died quickly. "I'm married, I got kids. I dig ladies, man." Suddenly, his eyes flamed and his mouth became a snarl as his rage flared a final time. "Ain't nobody better call me a faggot, especially a white bitch who thinks she's more important than me."

Then the fire ebbed and sputtered out. Reality set in and Deep Freeze sagged, everything about him signaling resignation. He turned submissively with his hands behind his back. Valenzuela snapped on the cuffs and locked them with a key.

"Those aren't too tight, are they, Mr. Childs?"

The rapper shook his head. Valenzuela read him his Miranda rights, Deep Freeze acknowledged that he understood them, and the detective led him away. Templeton stepped over to my side to tell me what a good job I'd done, piecing things together. I told her she'd done a pretty good job herself, filling in a lot of holes.

"I guess I'd better call this one in," she said. "It's after midnight, but for a story like this, I imagine they'll replate the front page."

"How are you going to handle Heather Sparks's confession?"

"It's not pertinent to the story I'm filing. No reason I can think of to mention it. I cover news, not Hollywood gossip."

As Templeton made tracks for the stairs, on her way to break a story that half the world would be talking about by the end of the day, I felt a familiar pang. It was that reminder that I'd never write another newspaper piece of my own, because I'd thrown it all away at a bad time in my life—a time when I hadn't been strong enough to write honestly, because I hadn't been willing to face my own truth.

Zeke Zeidler sat in his chair, his head in his hands; he had to know that with all the facts that had just come out, and Deep Freeze headed for jail, he'd lost his movie, at least the version he'd been working on for the past couple of years. Lois Aswell, who surely understood the same, stood over him, looking shell-shocked as she stroked his bald head sympathetically. Richard Pearlman and Karen Hori sat on the couch, staring at the floor without a word. Pearlman looked vaguely excited about new possibilities; I suspected he was thinking about the next book he wanted to write, and how he might go about this one differently. Hori just looked stunned and bewildered, the neophyte whose first job as a film unit publicist had turned out to be the assignment from hell.

Aswell wandered over to talk. "I guess you know that you've destroyed our movie. Even if we can raise the money to reshoot, the script will have to be completely rewritten. And who knows what we'd do for a cast?"

"Look on the bright side," I said. "You've finally got an ending."

Scotty Campbell ventured by, looking up at Aswell. "I guess you saw what I did a minute ago," he said, "putting myself between Deep Freeze and the door."

"You were courageous, Scotty," she said. "Someone should give you a medal."

"How about a job on your next movie?"

"With your mouth, Scotty?" She smiled like a barracuda. "Not a chance."

Kevin Tiemeyer pulled out his piano bench, sat, and folded back the keyboard cover, looking lighter and less burdened than I'd ever seen him. "Any requests?"

"Anything but *Rhapsody in Blue,*" I said.

EPILOGUE

At dawn, the Lost Hills were awash in golden light as a gentle breeze chased away the last clouds hovering above Coyote Canyon.

Helicopters began circling overhead as camera teams shot coverage of the old hotel where Deep Freeze had been arrested for the murder of Toni Pebbles. Kevin Tiemeyer refused permission for the choppers to set down in his parking lot and heavy driftwood that had washed up on the beach prevented them from landing there. So we were spared an assault by the media that would surely come later, when the bridge was fixed and reporters invaded by way of Coyote Canyon Road, breathing new life into the Haunted Springs Hotel and its dark legend.

After breakfast, with Tiemeyer's permission, private helicopters began ferrying out selected guests. The first flight had been reserved for Nan Williams and the body of her daughter; for emotional support, Zeke Zeidler and Karen Hori accompanied Mrs. Williams on the trip. Martha Frech arrived on another chopper as it came in, her transport covered by contributions raised by Scotty Campbell, who'd passed the hat among the production crew. Kevin Tiemeyer met Martha as she climbed out; he explained to her what had happened, and that the lies they'd told as children at the behest of their parents had nothing to do with the latest death in Room 418. The voice that she'd heard swirling around the big rock was not that of Rebecca Fox, he assured her, but rather that of Ed Jones, whispering his forgiveness. In her childlike way she seemed to accept this explanation, and to find some relief in it. Tiemeyer asked if he might walk her home and she accepted. They ambled off together arm-in-arm like elderly sweethearts, toward her old house above the cemetery, which Tiemeyer had promised to renovate for her at his own expense.

Shortly after breakfast, without saying good-bye, Christopher Oakley boarded a chopper with Lois Aswell and Heather Sparks. From the window of my room, I watched it lift off and fly away down the canyon, knowing I'd probably never see or speak with him again. I harbored no resentment, realizing that he was a special breed of person who operated with his own set of rules in a world unlike any other. If there was anything I'd learned about Hollywood over the years, it was how readily its denizens expressed keen interest in something—be it a film project or a friendship—and how quickly they lost interest and moved on to the next one, without a second thought or a flicker of conscience.

By late afternoon, we got word that a temporary bridge had been installed across Rattlesnake River in place of the old one the storm had destroyed. Valenzuela's assisting officers finally arrived, and took Deep Freeze and Sweet Doctor Silk away in separate patrol cars. Valenzuela, whom Templeton had interviewed about the Rebecca Fox and Brandy Fox cases, thanked us both for our help, told us to drop by for coffee any time we found ourselves in Hungry Valley, and drove away singing a lusty version of *Cielito Lindo* in Spanish.

As Templeton and I loaded our luggage into her Maserati, she wasn't nearly as upbeat. In fact, she was so subdued that I asked if she was feeling okay.

"I've been thinking about the injustice of it," she said. "Percy Childs will surely be convicted for the death of Toni Pebbles, as well he should. But no one will ever face justice for the murder of Ed Jones. He's the forgotten man in all this, as if his life and death don't add up to much."

"He's not forgotten anymore," I said. "You've begun to rectify that, with your article this morning and other pieces you'll be writing in the future. Maybe even a book that amplifies his story, if you and Richard Pearlman decide to go ahead with one."

She closed the trunk, but stayed where she was, her eyes on mine. "They're linked, you know. Those three deaths in Room 418, all on the ides of March."

"How's that, Alex?"

"It's all connected—what happened deep in the past that caused Ed Jones to come to this town, impoverished and unwelcome. What was done to him fifty years ago in the Eternal Springs jail. The rage that still simmers inside his grandson today. The three women who died in that room over a fifty-year span." Templeton climbed behind the wheel of her fancy car, while I got in on the passenger side. "You can't separate each incident as if it's isolated," she went on, sounding like a writer thinking through her next project, "as if one has nothing to do with the other. Slavery, lynching, intolerance, ignorance, hatred, retribution, murder. They're all part of a chain that's still unbroken, that maintains its own violent momentum."

"Sounds like a good theme for a book," I said.

She smiled sadly. "I could write a hundred books, Benjamin. But what's the point? Some things never end."

"At least the lynching is behind us. We don't see that anymore."

"Don't we? Or does it just take different forms?" She switched on the ignition and we buckled up. "A black man named James Byrd Jr. dragged to death behind a car in Jasper County, Texas. A gay man named Matthew Shepard, beaten, tied to a fence post, and left to freeze to death in Laramie, Wyoming. A bunch of Jewish children at school in Los Angeles, run down by a car driven by a neo-Nazi. Are they really so different? Can we honestly separate them from all the rest? I'm not so sure."

As Templeton shifted from park to drive, about to pull out, Richard Pearlman came running from the hotel to bid us another good-bye. Templeton gave him a business card and promised to be in touch. He was waving in her rearview mirror as she pulled out of the parking lot and drove slowly south along the main street. As we passed the Haunted Springs Museum and Souvenir Shop, we could see Kevin Tiemeyer inside, getting ready to reopen and probably contemplating changes he'd have to make in some of the displays. As we approached the cemetery, Templeton pulled over and stopped, peering up the hill.

Martha Frech stood on her front steps with a broom in her hand. She'd put on a fresh dress, one with some color and pattern in it, brushed her hair, and fastened it back with a sky blue scarf. As she gazed out across the town and canyon toward the distant hills, she looked more grounded to me, more in touch with who and where she was. For all her problems, I thought, she possessed a clearer, saner vision than the people who'd surrounded her most of her life, unwilling to see what she'd seen, or let it bother them.

"I hope she finds some peace of mind now," Templeton said.

"Maybe you'll send her a copy of that book when you and Pearlman get it written, setting the record straight. I imagine she'd appreciate that."

Templeton seemed to like that idea; she leaned over and kissed me on the cheek. Then she pulled out and left Haunted Springs behind. I was glad to be going home, and realized I was taking back with me much more than I'd brought. Answers, yes, but also questions: Do we truly heal—as individuals, families, communities, nations—if we choose to remember selectively, to recall only that which is acceptable and comforting, to create lies in place of the truth? Would we be wiser to face our most painful memories and shameful deeds, and truly grieve, and possibly, by owning our past instead of denying it, finally exorcise it from our individual and collective souls? Is history nothing but a fable and memory nothing but an illusion, among all the other fables and illusions that we embrace with such desperate belief?

Perhaps there are no answers to these questions. Perhaps I'm foolish to bother myself about them at all. There are certainly people who would argue exactly that, whose lives are more exemplary than my own.

Still, I found myself pondering questions like these as Alexandra Templeton turned down Coyote Canyon Road, while the day grew warmer and the wind died to a hush, and the troubled surface of Lake Enid grew peaceful and still.